# If the Sunrise Forgets Tomorrow

An Outer Banks of North Carolina Novel

J. Willis Sanders

This is a work of fiction. Names, characters, organizations, places, events, and incidents are either products of the author's imagination or are used fictitiously. Any resemblance to actual persons, living or dead, or actual events is purely coincidental.

No part of this book may be reproduced, or stored in a retrieval system, or transmitted in any form or by any means, electronic, mechanical, photocopying, recording, or otherwise, without express written permission from the author, except for brief quotations in a book review.

Copyright © 2021 J. Willis Sanders

All rights reserved.

ISBN-13: 978-1-954763-07-4 (paperback)
ISBN-13: 978-1-954763-06-7 (ebook)

BUGGS ISLAND BOOKS

Printed in the United States of America

Cover design by MiblArt

## Amazon reviews of *If the Sunrise Forgets Tomorrow*

"What a captivating book. I read it in 2 sittings because we just couldn't put it down. Brought tears to my eyes!"

"To be honest, I wasn't certain I would enjoy this book. I've read other books at in the Outer Banks and a lot of them seem to be sloppily written and just capitalizing on the setting to prey on die-hard OBX readers. I was pleasantly surprised to find it very well written and descriptive. It was easy to visualize the island, the characters, and the story as it all unfolded."

"This book was captivating and it was difficult for me to put it down. If you like a touch of history and have a love for Ocracoke, this is a great book to read. It was very descriptive and made me feel like I was there. Virginia and Ruby are typical sisters who are loving each other one minute and the next they are disagreeing. I enjoyed the strength they displayed as they overcame many obstacles. A Great Read!"

Also By J. Willis Sanders

The Eliza Gray Series
*The Colors of Eliza Gray*
*The Colors of Denver Andrews*
*The Colors of Tess Gray*

The Outer Banks of North Carolina Series
*The Diary of Carlo Cipriani*
*If the Sunrise Forgets Tomorrow*
*Love, Jake*

Writing as J.D. James: the Reid Stone Series
*Reid Stone: Hard as Stone*

Readers: Please find the first chapter *of Love, Jake* after the book club questions in the back of this book.

## Author's Note

This is the second in a series of three novels that take place on the Outer Banks of North Carolina. Those who know this amazing place understand how it begs us to return every so often, like the tide tugs at our hearts and souls.

The first novel, *The Diary of Carlo Cipriani,* starts in 1521, and is a fictional account of how the wild Spanish Mustangs arrived north of Corolla. There's much more, of course, but why spoil a good story?

This novel, *If the Sunrise Forgets Tomorrow,* occurs in the early days of World War II, when German U-boats were sinking ships off America's eastern coast at will. It takes place on magical Ocracoke Island, where four British seamen were buried after a U-boat torpedoed their ship. Although serious, it contains two of my favorite characters: twin eighteen-year-old sisters who made me both laugh and cry, sometimes within paragraphs of each other.

*Love, Jake* takes place at Nags Head. It is decidedly contemporary, with a character who experiences problems that few were aware of in the distant past. It also contains romantic heat not found in the first two, described tastefully instead of graphically.

Each has a certain flavor. Each has a specific voice. Each should appeal to lovers of the area in different ways. And who knows? More books about this unique place may emerge from my imagination yet.
Please enjoy, J.W.S.

# If the Sunrise Forgets Tomorrow

## Chapter 1

## Discovery

*Ocracoke Island*
*May 14, 1942*

Creamy white, lit by waning starlight, the dunes lining the sandy path resembled the rounded backs of a pod of whales risen from the Atlantic. A gust of wind slammed into a crest. As if one of the whales had held its breath too long, it jetted a huge plume of sand from its blowhole.

Astride the Ocracoke pony, Virginia faced the path again. The cut from the last hurricane had to be nearby, but the shadowy dunes hid it well. She covered a yawn. Rising early to search the beach for wreckage from shipwrecks had been handed down from O'cockers for generations. Regardless, she preferred her warm bed at the moment, since the wind had a definite bite that chilled her cheeks.

Another gust sent sand flying over a dune's crest. As the cloud of white descended toward her, she caught the faint scent of some dead sea creature, likely a rotting fish. Even though a German U-boat had torpedoed a ship recently, and she'd come out here to search for wood for the cookstove and for repairs around the homeplace, those men had to be at the bottom of the ocean by now.

Toward the Cape Hatteras Lighthouse to the east, where its revolving finger of light pointed toward the horizon, the pink blush of a new day rinsed the darkness from the sky. Stars faded. Clusters by the billions. Glittering blooms of dusty yellows, hints of aquamarine, streaks of creamy white. Maybe with galaxies and people who knew better than to risk the insanity of war.

Virginia tugged the pony's reins, stopping him at the base of a dune. "All right, Jimmy. That cut's hiding and I don't feel like looking for it. Think you can haul this O'cocker gal up that pile of sand?" She heeled Jimmy's flanks and he lunged upward. Sliding on his bare back toward his rump, she gripped his heaving sides with her legs while leaning forward to keep from falling off. At the top of the dune, she jerked the reins, hardly believing the unexpected sight.

Another ship on fire?

From beneath the distant swells, crests white and whipping, not a ship but the bloodiest sunrise she'd ever seen. Thank Poseidon and Blackbeard and all the sea spirits that no one would ever find out how she'd mommucked the view so badly. Otherwise, they'd call her a silly dingbatter instead of a genuine O'cocker.

Along the wide beach, timed with the gusts, streaks of sand and sea grass swirled and stopped, swirled and stopped. Virginia compared the sight to several couples dancing a waltz, hesitating as they stepped on each other's toes.

Jimmy snorted and shifted restlessly. "Stop that foolishness," Virginia said, repositioning herself on his back. "I'll sandy up sure as forever if I roll down this dune."

She missed his saddle, sold for seeds for the garden, oats for himself, feed for the hens in the henhouse, and hooks and bait for fishing. Otherwise, there'd be no Jimmy nor eggs nor fish, and a person couldn't begin to survive on Ocracoke without those necessities.

Clumped and scattered along the dune, sea oat stalks, stripped of their flat seeds by the harsh winter's frequent nor'easters, whistled in the near gale. Virginia preferred them full and rustling in a soft summer breeze, because the sound reminded her of her and Ruby's midnight whispers as little girls in bed. The current gusts, full of bluster and bravado, were more like midnight giggles and talk of fancy dresses, fancier hairdos, and pinched cheeks for rouge. Little had she and Ruby known how those whispers, giggles, and talks were nothing more than young girl dreams of young girl things, or, as Virginia considered them now, childish notions drifting out with the tide.

A gust of wind snarled dark hair, which she fingered behind her ears. Better get her mind off things she couldn't change and enjoy this morning's glorious—yet unsettling—sunrise.

As if it *were* a ship burning on the horizon, the crimson ball shimmered within the salt mist that rose from the blue-green waves, which whispered and hissed as they neared the shore. Gurgling their growing disagreement, like two arguing fishermen, they ended their lives by curling and crashing and heaving themselves upon the sand, to roll over and over as the wave's foamy remains spread themselves along the slight rise to the beach, not unlike the yellowed lace on her and Ruby's tattered childhood nightgowns.

Virginia fingered the leather reins.

Yes indeed, young girl dreams of young girl things. A past caught in the maelstrom of a hurricane. The slimmest of hopes waiting to be spit out upon the sand. With the tragedy she and Ruby had faced concerning Papa—and now faced with Mama—where would the tide of life take them on Ocracoke?

She heeled Jimmy's flanks and steered him down the dune. Not a beam nor a plank in sight, just thick lines of tangled sea grass, sea grapes, and a dead fish or two, along with several ridged scallop shells, clam shells of all sizes, a gray oyster shell or three, and the multiple twists of a knobbed whelk, all reddening in the rising sun.

Jimmy's remaining winter coat warmed her hand as she rubbed his neck. Perched on him like this, Virginia pictured herself a huge, dark gull, come to pick the bones of the ship that had exploded a few nights ago.

Jimmy whinnied.

"Hush yer fuss, impatient pony. If I come out here any later, some other O'cocker will grab all the wood." She peered over the blue-green swells. "Not that there's a codfish's chance of anything to grab."

Another gust of wind scattered hair into her eyes. She swept it back, twisted it as if it were a ship's anchor line, and tucked it into the collar of Papa's old woolen jacket, which was so threadbare, the cold wind cut through the thin material at her elbows.

A sign of the times, the forgotten scarf for her hair signaled nerves on edge from the Germans sinking ships every other night or so, sending dull, thudding explosions echoing over the ocean. These events ruined concentration, upset villagers, and made people spend the day wondering when the next explosion might rock their homes to the point of cracking window panes.

The recent explosion, the first for May, had rumbled and roared in the night, rattling windows and making her jerk upright in bed. The full moon and thundering surf last evening had drawn the Atlantic almost to the dunes, but no wreckage littered the shore, at least none not partially buried by the sand.

Virginia snapped Jimmy's reins. He raised his head from sniffing a tangle of sea grass and the empty hulls of mole crab shells and trotted ahead, jarring her with his bouncy gait. Bouncy or not, she'd rather find wood first and go home for the wagon. Why get a sore behind on a wooden seat when she could experience the freedom of galloping Jimmy along the beach on the way home?

*If the Sunrise Forgets Tomorrow*

The ocean mist wet her lips with salt. A flock of sanderlings darted over the waves, searching for a place along the beach to probe the sand for their morning meal. Black eyes, brown wingtips, and pencil-thin beaks slashed within inches of the gray-green surface, dipping into troughs, rising above crests. O'cockers might complain about Ocracoke on occasion, but this sliver of sand and sandspurs certainly had its charms.

A stalk-eyed ghost crab, eight legs a beige blur, darted sideways toward its hole the size of a coffee cup. Jimmy snorted while high-stepping around the zigzaggy creature, which happened several more times along the beach. Laughing at his antics, Virginia again squeezed the pony's heaving sides with her legs. Land in the sand wrong, a rider could break something necessary for survival.

Jimmy jolted to a stop, and Virginia peered over his head. An object resembling a midnight-blue blanket, tangled with rope, protruded from the sand.

On the other side of the object, two herring gulls fluttered to a landing. Wings shuffling into place, one waddled forward, studied the object, and tilted its head to aim a yellow eye at Virginia. A gust of wind ruffled its downy breast feathers. It took another web-footed step and darted its orange beak out, plucked a ghost crab from near the object and took flight over the waves. The other gull followed, screeching for its share of the crab.

From beneath the object, another ghost crab scurried toward its hole, then another and another.

Whatever the object was, it drew gulls and ghost crabs, the scavengers of the beach. Only one way to find out why.

Virginia slid off Jimmy and rolled the sodden mess over, gasped and drew back as the supposed blanket unfurled.

The man—not a blanket—with curly brown hair and a full beard, was as white as any half-rotten sea creature she'd ever seen. Bloated like a pufferfish, his wrinkled skin had split from soaking in salt water. His wide-open eyes were the worst—a dull, dreary white, sunken back into their sockets.

He must be from the ship the other night, certainly not the fish she thought she had smelled.

She leaned over for a closer look. A ghost crab the size of a thumbnail, its pink tidbit of breakfast in one claw, scrabbled from a shriveled nostril.

Virginia gasped and covered her mouth, but not before a gust of wind struck the corpse, slinging sand and the sickly-sweet smell of human decay into her face. She spun away to heave … heave … heave until her empty stomach spewed a weak stream of sour bile from her throat.

Lips wiped clean on her sleeve, she studied the dark blue pants, coat, and the white, turtle-neck sweater, where sand clung to the cable-knit weave. No doubt about it, everything resembled a uniform.

She gripped Jimmy's mane, swung herself onto his back, and heeled his flanks. The Navy men building the base at Silver Lake Harbor needed to know about this.

Papa's body had never been found after he'd drowned during the ship rescue two years ago, so maybe that was why the body on the beach hadn't brought back the memory if his death. Still, the Lifesaving Station official coming to the house with the news had been harder than anything she, Ruby, and Mama had ever faced. Still again, Papa and Mama had raised her and Ruby to take hardship and twist it by the tail, and that's exactly how they preferred to live.

Then Mama got the influenza in December and had lapsed into a coma from a high fever. Between that and losing Papa, including the disappointment of childhood dreams never to be realized, life on Ocracoke had gotten even harder, and hardship was gaining the upper hand on the Starr family.

*If the Sunrise Forgets Tomorrow*

At the first Navy building—a small wood-sided structure yet to be painted—Virginia knocked on the door and returned to Jimmy's side. No hammers pounded the frameworks of the buildings behind this one. Too early for the dingbatters to rise yet.

A uniformed man stepped out. Dark hair peeked from beneath his cap. His nose bent a tad to one side. "Morning, miss. What's got you and your horse huffing and puffing so hard?"

"I found a body on the beach." Virginia took a breath. "About a half mile back."

Sunlight lit the man's face as he turned his head to the east. "Probably one of those men from that ship the other night."

"You don't know what ship?"

"I hardly know what day it is, so many ships have been sunk lately. We haven't received any radio reports with the name yet."

He entered the building and returned with another man. His sandy hair, cut short in a crew-cut, resembled the spines on a spiny starfish. Beady and black, his eyes roamed Virginia's body up and down. "Why ain't you the pretty young thing, livin' out here on this dreary strip of sand."

"Can it, Jerry," the first man said. "I've told you about flirting with the locals."

"C'mon, Charlie. Just 'cause you got a wife at home don't mean the rest of us guys cain't have some fun on this nothin' of an island."

Virginia didn't care for this Jerry person. He spoke with high-pitched twang that grated on her nerves, unlike Charlie's smooth baritone.

"Get one of the jeeps." Charlie tossed Jerry a set of keys. As he rounded the building's corner, Charlie faced Virginia again. "Ma'am, I apologize."

"No need," Virginia said. "I know the difference between a pony and a jackass when I see one."

"Jerry hee-haws a little too much for my tastes too."

Virginia swung onto Jimmy's back. Despite having a wife, Charlie was kind of cute. Better behave and get on home.

At the pony's small corral, he went to his stall and his oats. Needing a moment to catch her breath, Virginia sat on one of the limbs hanging low from the live oak trees surrounding Mama and Papa's—now her and Ruby's for all realistic purposes—property, which included the four-room frame house with peeling white paint and, through a thick grove of live oak trees on the other side of the house, a workshop where Papa had crafted their rowboat years ago.

Live oaks rarely grew taller than thirty feet; the twisted branches stretched out with the prevailing wind as if reaching for a throat to strangle. Papa built the house as a honeymoon present on the edge of the Pamlico Sound, on the backside of the island. He also built a henhouse and a pier, which stretched out into the dense marsh. Virginia kept two crab pots tied to the pilings and a fishing pole or two in his old rowboat. A short mast in the hole in the center seat allowed for sailing if need be. She only rowed to deeper water for spot or croakers. Flounder frequented water shallow enough to use Papa's flounder gig.

The front porch door, screened to keep the singing clouds of mosquitos out and to let air in during the sultry summers, squeaked open and slammed shut. Ruby placed her hands on her hips. "Did you find any wood?"

"If I had, *Rube*, wouldn't you have heard me leave in the wagon?"

"Not if I were tending to Mama in her bedroom, *Virgil.*"

"Breakfast ready?"

"I was out to fetch a few eggs."

"You haven't gotten the eggs yet?"

*If the Sunrise Forgets Tomorrow*

"Didn't I just say that? I think I just said that. Didn't I just say—"

"Fine, I'll help." Virginia and Ruby ducked and weaved between the low oak limbs to the gray and weathered chicken coop, where Papa had located it between Jimmy's corral and the lapping waters of the sound.

Inside the small, dark building, filled with the musty aroma of poop and dust, Virginia slipped her hand into the empty space beneath a warm feathered bottom. "Miss Prissy's lazy." She waggled a finger at the hen. "Keep it up, Prissy. I've got a taste for fried chicken."

"You're such a brute." Ruby took an egg from under a hen and placed it in the pocket of her red-checked apron. "These girls are my friends." She petted the next hen in line. "Isn't that right, Lucy?" The hen clucked. "See there, Virgil? Lucy agrees."

Virginia punched Ruby's arm. "I haven't done anything to warrant you calling me Virgil."

"You called me Rube first. I don't like Rube any better than you like Virgil, Virgil."

Virginia checked another hen. She had avoided the topic of finding the body because it might ruin Ruby's lighthearted personality for an hour or so. Between the long days on Ocracoke, along with Papa's death and Mama's sickness, humor was as rare as beef and laughter for her and Ruby.

"How about a truce?" she said, facing Ruby. "You fed Mama yet?"

"How could I do that without eggs? *Really,* Virgil, you must have sand in yer ears."

Virginia ignored the comment.

In the kitchen, she took the eggs from the jacket pocket and set them in a bowl on the cupboard. The cupboard sat beside a table with a white enameled wash basin; both sat beneath a

9

window facing the sound. Ruby preferred the view while washing dishes.

Virginia placed a blackened cast iron pan on the wood cookstove. The location, between her and Ruby's bedroom doors, warmed them on cool spring nights, colder fall days, and during the island's brutally cold winters.

She added bacon grease from last night's supper to the pan. Ruby stood at the window, elbows on the ledge, chin in her hands. "Daydreaming again, Rube? Scramble those eggs so I can eat breakfast before lunch."

Ruby spun around. Her blonde hair swirled a yellow cloud. "Do this, do that, that's all I ever hear around here. At least you get to work in the village and get wood while I'm taking care of Mama."

Virginia admired Ruby's blonde hair and blue eyes—the opposite of her dark hair and almost black eyes—but she didn't care for her naïve attitude concerning the facts of life.

"I can't have you working at the restaurant. Some Navy man would follow you home and I'd have to kill him."

"How do you know I wouldn't *want* him to follow me home?"

"You'd figure that out yourself, *if* you had any sense."

Ruby cracked eggs into a bowl and whipped them violently with a fork. "Oh, please. Like you and Even Evans never did that."

"Don't clatter that bowl so hard."

"Mind yer business."

"Mind Walter's name, it isn't Even." Virginia rattled a spatula from a drawer and pointed it at Ruby. "You'd do well to remember that and stop the insults. I'm all you have on this island except for Mama."

*If the Sunrise Forgets Tomorrow*

Ruby gave Virginia the eggs. "Do you know how sad that makes me? Not that I don't appreciate you—you know I do—but there's got to be more to life than this lonesome island."

"More to life?" Virginia eased the bubbling eggs around with the spatula. "At least life is life. That's more than I can say for some people, namely one I met on the beach this morning."

"Planning to scare me with some dark tale from one of Mr. Poe's books you like so well?"

"I'm trying to—"

"Was this person staked to the beach with a pendulum swinging over him until it sliced him in two?"

"The Navy man said the body was likely from the ship that exploded the other night."

"You ..." Ruby's pink complexion faded to runny-egg white. "You mean ...?"

"That's life. Or rather that's death, which would you like? A ghost crab crawled out of the man's nose with its breakfast when I rolled him over."

"That's— Why, that's terrible. How can you tease me like that?"

"It wasn't teasing when the stink made me heave. Hand me a plate before these eggs burn."

"You're ..." Ruby's chin quivered. "You're serious?"

Virginia took a plate from the cupboard. "You might want to read one of your romance novels after breakfast so your complexion turns pink again." She grabbed a dishcloth from near the basin and fanned her face. "Oh, dear Scarlett, will it be *Gone with the Wind* once more? Will you positively swoon while imagining Rhett carrying you up the stairs of Tara?"

Ruby snatched the dishcloth from Virginia and repeated the fanning. "Oh, dear sister, how will I *ever* find out if I don't leave this piece of sand stuck out here in the middle of nowhere?" She tossed the washcloth by the basin, her complexion normal again.

Virginia waved a hand toward the percolator. "Forget that and make coffee before it's rationed like I've been hearing."

She set the plate of steaming eggs on the table, then closed the front door to study the calendar hanging on the back. For a pastime, she'd been writing the names of ships sunk by U-boats: The *Empire Gem* off Diamond Shoals on January twenty-third. The *San Delfino* off Cape Hatteras on April tenth. The *Empire Thrush* on April fourteenth, again off Diamond Shoals. She needed to remember today's date, May 14, for when she found out the name of the ship from a few nights ago. Placing a fingertip there, she faced Ruby. "Ruby."

"Don't *Ruby* me. And don't schedule me any more housework."

Virginia pranced to Ruby and held out her arms. "Happy Birthday."

"What good is eighteen when there's no men to take us out because they've all gone to war?" She gave Virginia a quick hug. "I guess you'll do for a squeeze. Dang it to forever and back, I was hoping to be engaged by my eighteenth birthday."

Virginia pecked Ruby's cheek. "You'll even do for a kiss."

"Sure I will. You got no one to kiss 'cause Even—Walter I mean—is learning how to fly planes."

"Don't remind me. Time sure flies."

"He's been gone what? Six months give or take? I never thought he'd join the Air Corps before the Japanese attacked Pearl Harbor."

"I meant Papa being dead two years," Virginia said.

Ruby set the percolator on the stove. "And Mama's about to die too. What a twistygibbet world we live in."

Virginia took plates and cups from the cupboard, sat and spooned eggs into a plate. "You just make that word up?"

Ruby turned from the stove. "It's all just so sad, Ginny."

"Want to drown ourselves in the ocean?"

"I think about it sometimes. Then I remember what Mama said about Papa: 'We just have to do the best we can and keep him in our hearts.'"

Virginia couldn't agree more. She raised her plate. "Fetch me a leftover biscuit, Rube. I'll tend Mama after breakfast so you can have some time to yourself."

## Chapter 2

## Mama

Breakfast done, Virginia mixed milk from the icebox with the leftover eggs. The clatter of spoons and forks in the white enameled basin stopped, and Ruby glanced over her shoulder. "That's a horrid story you told me about the body. You should read something besides Mr. E. A. Poe."

"It's the truth, Scarlett," Virginia said, pointing a fork at her.

Ruby huffed a hard breath. "How do I know that when you went right into joking about my romance novels? Good Lord above, I've often wondered when a body might drift ashore." Dishes rattled again. "Was he British? You said they're patrolling for U-boats."

"I didn't care to dig him out of the sand for evidence."

"Was he cute? What color hair did he have?"

Virginia pointed the fork again. "Are your hormones so ripe you'll consider the looks of a man whose skin is about to peel like a crab molts its shell?"

Ruby snatched her apron off. "I said it before and I'll say it again, you're such a brute."

"Which is what it takes to survive on this island of ours." Virginia took the eggs to the door. "This 'brute' is going to feed and change Mama."

"I'll be at the pier with a book."

Virginia took the eggs to the nightstand by Mama's bed. She lay straight as a dock piling, hands crossed over the quilt-covered chest that rose and fell with the same slow, steady pace since Doc Wills had said she was in a coma. Once a medium sized woman, she now resembled men imprisoned on both sides of the Civil War. Skin like fish skin, dried in the sun over curling ribs, stretched over high cheekbones.

History, as well as Poe's reads, fascinated Virginia, including the few books about the Civil War on the shelf in her room. She varied her selection, but books were almost as scarce as young men and wood on Ocracoke.

Not ready to begin the feeding, she stepped to the window that faced the narrow lane leading to the house. Little more than a path, the sandy track barely fit the wagon. The live oak limbs, ignored after Papa had died, scraped the wheels with nearly two-years growth. She needed to cut them back soon, a difficult task compared to scrounging wood from the beach.

When Papa was alive and earning decent money, Virginia considered college and returning to Ocracoke to teach. Now, with the long days and longer nights because of her dwindling family, including the red glow of ships burning on the eastern horizon, when the low rumble of explosions echoed from the ocean, she'd rather live on the mainland. She and Walter had discussed living there before he left, and he agreed how this island was a hard place to live. If she could take Ruby to the civilized life of motor cars and running water and a nice dress now and then instead of Papa's faded blue denim pants and worn work shirts that fit better than Mama's plain cotton shifts, she might bloom with enough confidence to realize how life held more promise than being with a man. Still, no place came any prettier than Ocracoke.

Virginia left the window and those thoughts—possibilities more than anything—aside. The war might take every hope away, like when Papa had drowned.

She sat in the creaking ladder-back chair by the bed and gently opened Mama's eyes. Feeding Mama with her eyes closed made Virginia cry, and she'd cried enough to float a three-masted schooner in the last two years. She scooped a small bit of egg and milk with a spoon. "Morning, Mama. Ready for breakfast?"

The blue eyes, unfocused and unseeing, stared at nothing. Crow's feet etched each corner, white where they once were tan. Her laugh, loud and boisterous, could spread like wildfire in the marshes from a lightning strike. She couldn't even smile now.

Virginia eased the spoon into the closed lips and worked the teeth open. The white-yellow liquid seeped in. The throat swallowed. Virginia swallowed also, like when someone yawned after another person yawned. The last spoonful went down. A rank aroma rose from beneath the blanket.

How much longer could she, Ruby, and Mama go on like this? Were they meant to live out their lives in this Poe-ish manner until they all died? To be swallowed up amongst the marsh? Amongst the live oaks? The spoon filled with runny white and yellow the pendulum that kept them more dead than alive?

Virginia took the bowl to the kitchen, gathered old sheets torn into rags and a bowl of water and a bar of soap. It struck her as improper how neither she nor Ruby had mentioned dressing Mama in a nightgown, although they'd have to pull it up to clean her if they had. They did keep several layers of rags beneath her skeletal hips and bottom and washed them after every mess.

Virginia's cheeks still warmed when she bathed Mama, because the self-sufficient woman always liked to do for herself. She'd be embarrassed to no end if she knew the burden she'd become.

Virginia took the bowl of smelly rags to the kitchen, dumped the water outside and set the bowl and rags beside the basin.

She poured water from the pail on the counter into the basin. Scrubbing the smelly rags, she looked out the window at the brightening day.

Book in hand, wearing one of Papa's old tweed suit jackets, Ruby sat on the pier, feet hanging off the edge. A red-winged blackbird lit on a cattail and called its shrill, warbling warning: *kree-kreeeee, kree-kreeeee*. The cattail swayed and bobbed with the bird's weight. Ruby faced the bird. It flew away, red and black wings shimmering in the sun.

The whine of a vehicle engine came from the path. Virginia wiped her hands on the apron she'd donned while washing the rags and hurried to the screen door. Charlie pulled up in a jeep and tipped his hat. "Hope you don't mind me stopping by."

"I would have your jackass friend." Virginia went outside, easing the door closed so it wouldn't slam.

Running from the pier, Ruby stopped at the porch. "I finally get to meet someone." She took a breath. "I'm Ruby Starr. And you are?"

Charlie faced Virginia. "I mentioned you to Mr. Austin at the restaurant. He told me where you live and how you have a twin sister. "I hope you don't mind me saying, but y'all don't look one bit alike."

"Fiddlesticks," Ruby said. "There's times I hardly believe we're twins myself."

"Why's that, ma'am?"

"Are all you Navy men this hardheaded? I tell you my name is Ruby and you insult me by calling me ma'am. Ginny, are all Navy men this hardheaded?"

"Ginny?" Charlie asked, turning his attention toward Virginia. "Mr. Austin said your name was—"

"That's what Ruby calls me when she's feeling pert. When she's neutral, which is never, it's Virginia."

"Or Virgil," Ruby said.

"Care to explain that one?" Charlie said, still facing Virginia.

"That's what she calls me when she's feeling pert, like that smart aleck man of yours earlier."

"Who's that?" Ruby said.

"Mind yer business." Virginia faced Charlie. "What can we do for you, Charlie? Do you have a Navy title you'd prefer?"

Ruby looked him up and down. "He looks like an admiral. Are you an admiral? I bet he's an admiral."

"Charlie's fine. I—"

"Charles is more romantic," Ruby said.

"Please ignore my sister," Virginia said. "What brings you here?"

"The Coast Guard found another body this morning. Seems they're Brits from the armed trawler *Bedfordshire*."

"Will the Navy send them back to their families in England for burial?"

"Not sure. They can't stand much travel."

"That's awful sad," Ruby said. "I'd rather be buried where I was born."

"Pardon me for saying so, ma'am. They might melt if we wait much longer."

Ruby's mouth fell open. "Did you tell him to say that, Virgil? He's a brute—a brute exactly like you are."

"He just got here. How could I—"

"I'm going back to the pier."

The woven seat of one of the two rickety chairs on the porch creaked when Virginia sat. "Rest your bones, Charlie. I rarely speak to a dingbatter."

"Not the first time I've been called that since I got here. Do all you Ocrakokers wish the Navy would leave?"

"We say O'cocker. No doubt you've heard more of our brogue. For the most part, Ruby and I keep to ourselves and haven't picked up those old English pronunciations. Reading a lot helps too."

"To repeat the question properly," Charlie said, taking a seat, "do you O'cockers think the Navy shouldn't be here?"

"I doubt we can claim that idiosyncrasy for our own. People in small towns everywhere are likely wary of strangers. Where are you from?"

"You're right about that claim." Charlie crossed his legs. "Small towns can be positively tribal."

"I never thought to call it that."

"I read too. I'm from Charlottesville, in the Blue Ridge Mountains of Virginia."

"Is that where your wife is? Jerry said you were married."

"I tell the men that so they don't drag me out to hunt for girls. Do you have a special someone? Maybe a fellow in the service?"

Virginia hesitated. She and Walter had spoken of a future together, but he hadn't proposed. She cared for him, but she sometimes wondered if she might care for someone else who might happen along, such as someone who shared more things in common with her like her love for books of a certain type.

"There's a fellow. We're mostly acquaintances."

"Too bad your village doesn't have a movie house we could visit."

"You must not have seen it yet. I'm sure you've noticed we don't have much of anything, really. We've a hardscrabble life, living off the water and the land."

"What about entertainment? All work and no play ..."

"I prefer a sunrise walk on the beach and a sunset over the Pamlico to any movie ever made." Virginia pointed toward the pier, where Ruby lay with the book over her face. "We have the perfect spot for sunsets."

"Have you ever *seen* a movie, Miss Starr?"

"Have you ever *read* a book, Mr. Dingbatter?"

"Do comic books count?"

"You've *got* to be kidding."

Charlie's grin faded. "I read Edgar Allen Poe now and then. My little sister says his work is horrid."

Ruby hadn't said Poe's work was horrid, but saying the story of the body on the beach was horrid was almost the same thing.

"Ruby says that too."

"You read Poe?"

"I'm simply flirting so you'll allow me to prove how a sunset over the sound is a much better diversion than a movie." Desire sent a tingle along Virginia's lips. How could she be so brazen?

"Then don't be surprised if—" Charlie uncrossed his legs. "No, I'd rather you know I was coming so you don't shoot me for a stranger, especially at night."

"I do keep a shotgun handy."

Charlie leaned forward to rest his elbows on his knees. "Is tonight okay?"

"I have to work at the restaurant," Virginia said, wishing she didn't. "Did Mr. Austin tell you I work there?"

"I had breakfast there when all the hubbub concerning the bodies had calmed down. Naturally, I asked about you."

"What's 'natural' about it?"

"I have a thing for dark."

"As in?"

"Eyes. Hair. A smile I imagined you might have. My imagination is extremely satisfied."

"You're quite the flirt, Charlie."

"I generally keep to myself unless piqued. Consider me piqued."

"I don't think you're using that word correctly, Mr. Comic Books. Piqued means annoyed."

"Like I've annoyed Miss Ruby."

"She's easily piqued."

"What night will you be home?"

"For?"

"Our movie, the sunset."

"Would you consider a moonrise around nine tonight, when I get back? Ruby's in bed by then."

"Your parents too?"

"No. I'll tell you why later."

"Nine it is." Charlie stood. "I might bring a surprise to enjoy with our moonlight."

"A surprise means you're *piquing* me by not *telling* me." Virginia stood also. "I'm using it correctly too."

"What are you two brutes peeking at?" Quiet as a marsh rabbit hopping across the sandy path, Ruby had snuck to the end of the porch.

Charlie stopped at the bottom of the steps. "Ask Virginia, Miss Ruby, I've got to go."

"You need to stop that 'Miss' business. I'm Ruby, plain and simple."

"I seriously doubt there's anything simple about you." Charlie tipped his hat. 'Good day, ladies." He turned the jeep and drove up the path, dodging the twisted oak limbs.

Ruby faced Virginia. "Why's your face so flushed? There's no sun under the porch to— I recognize that look. You had it when Walter kissed you on the cheek goodbye."

"I was just enjoying the conversation."

"And I wouldn't? I want to go where people are. I could work at the restaurant, same as you. I could ride Jimmy to the beach and look for firewood. I'd take the wagon too. Riding all the way back here for it is silly."

Virginia opened the screened door. "I might take you up on that."

"When?"

"We'll see, *Rube*. We'll see."

## Chapter 3

## Surprises

Virginia rode the bicycle—one that Papa had surprised her and Ruby with on their sixteenth birthday—from beneath the shed adjoining Jimmy's stall. She stopped at the house for a flashlight, a luxury on which she'd spent part of her meager waitress earnings. The path coming home at night resembled a dark tunnel from the live oak limbs stretching overhead, barring any hint of illumination from either the moon or stars. She had considered using one of their kerosene lanterns, but the flashlight was easier to use. Also, tied to the basket, it beamed its light to the ground without shining upward, where it might attract patrolling U-boats. Most everyone in the village—some still burned their lights with electricity supplied by a small power grid that didn't reach out here—expected the government to issue blackout orders. It hadn't so far, so the short lighthouse's beam still reached across the Atlantic.

She found Ruby on her bed reading. "See you later, Rube."

Ruby rolled over. "There she goes again—Miss Virgil Starr—off to feed the masses of Ocracoke Village."

"Yammer all you want. One day I'll let you give tending the public a try. It's not as easy as you think it is."

"How hard can it be?" Ruby hopped from the bed with the book in her hand as if it were a serving tray. "Here's yer flounder, Mr. So-and-so." She fluttered her eyelashes. "I'd appreciate a nice tip if you've a mind to." She threw the book on the bed. "Do you wink at the men and smile at the ladies? If the man is cute like Charlie, do you wiggle your hips when you walk away?" Ruby walked across the wood floor, swinging her hips like a woman on the prowl.

Virginia couldn't decide whether to laugh or jerk Ruby's hair. "You'll see. One day I'll—"

Ruby whirled around. "You won't do a slippery eel thing but keep me stuck in this shack until I'm ready for the grave."

"That might happen sooner than later if you keep complaining. As you well know, my job keeps us in flour, milk, sugar, and ice for the ice box. How'd you like doing without those things? Don't forget the occasional new book and kerosene for the lanterns."

"Wanna bet Charlie visits you at the restaurant? You flirted more with him than you ever did Even Evans."

Virginia clenched her teeth. Ruby must've been listening at the porch last night for more than just a minute or two. "Why, you sneaky little ..."

"That's right," Ruby said, waggling a finger at Virginia. "I was standing by the corner of the house long enough to hear all your carrying on. You better hope Even doesn't show up when you and Charlie are out on the dock moonlighting tonight."

"Charlie's just a nice person I have things in common with." At the bedroom door, Virginia turned. "Don't you dare spy on me tonight. I'll make sure you stay here until you *are* ready for the grave if you do."

"Whatever, dear Ginny. Just make sure you bring us any leftover food like you sometimes forget to do."

Virginia mounted the bike, made much easier with denim pants than a dress. Male customers, Navy men mostly, sometimes asked about her legs. Good thing she and Ruby couldn't afford dresses.

By the time she emerged from the path onto the road, hard packed by the Coast Guard vehicles traveling the length of the

*If the Sunrise Forgets Tomorrow*

island on the lookout for U-boats, her legs ached from peddling in the soft sand. The half-mile ride to the village done, she leaned the bicycle against the rear of the restaurant and entered to wave at the round-bellied, dark-mustached Mr. Austin, who wore a stained red apron. "Looks like a quiet night," she said. "No jeeps out front."

"Early yet," Austin said. "Better fill them napkin dispensers so them ill-mannered dingbatters don't wipe thar hands on my tablecloths."

Virginia found the name the O'cockers gave outsiders amusing. 'Dingbatters', for the most part—because of how they complained about sand, wind, and how the salt air rusted metal almost immediately—fit them perfectly. She took a box of napkins from a cabinet.

In the outer room, ten tables covered with white and red-checked tablecloths waited for customers. As she stuffed the last holder with napkins, the front door creaked open on rusty hinges.

"Look who's hard at work," Charlie said, glancing around. "We can share my supper if nobody else is hungry." He sat by a window in the front corner. "Got us a cozy spot picked out too."

Virginia took a handwritten menu from a stack at the order window and gave it to Charlie. "You wouldn't think it was so cozy if you knew what happened under that table last weekend."

Charlie peeked under the table. "Do I get three guesses?"

"That's where old man Hildebrandt threw up after finishing off a jar of his spirits."

"My CO said alcohol wasn't sold on Ocracoke."

"What's a CO?"

"Commanding officer."

"He doesn't know his grits from his griddle. Old man Hildebrandt makes spirits in his barn."

"Plenty of old boys tucked in the hollows back home in the mountains do the same thing."

Virginia glanced through the order window at Austin, busy stirring sliced potatoes and onions in a huge cast iron pan. She sat beside Charlie. "Does that mean you're a sipper, a drinker, or a drunkard? I can abide the first, the second so-so. You come home late at night one time too many, I'll get my shotgun after you."

"I'm a sipper, not the strong stuff. You?"

"Who cares for throwing your guts up like that body on the beach almost made me do?" Virginia asked, admiring Charlie's deep brown eyes.

"I didn't care for the site myself," he said. "Their funeral's tomorrow. A local family offered part of their plot in the cemetery. Mighty Christian of them."

"What time?"

"Around ten, you coming?"

"I'd like to." Virginia checked on Austin again. Steam rose from the pan. She faced Charlie once more. "Why did you ask me about drinking?"

"I'd rather it be a surprise for later."

"Being mysterious on purpose. I'm not sure how I feel about that."

Charlie sniffed the air. "According to the smell coming from the kitchen, I'm not sure how I feel about supper."

"That's right, this is the first time I've seen you here."

"I've been a time or two."

"Did Agnes—she works on my off nights—sit in your lap? She does that with handsome men when she's trying to get a better than average tip."

"Thank you for the compliment, Miss Starr." Charlie tapped her hand on the table. "The last person to call me handsome was my grandma."

"Call me Ginny if you'd like."

"If you don't mind, I prefer Virginia."

Virginia stood. "We're having potatoes and onions and onions and potatoes tonight. That comes with a side of both."

Charlie pointed at the menu. "What about meat loaf and mashed potatoes and biscuits?"

Virginia snatched the menu away. "Pile your potatoes in a loaf shape and cover it with ketchup. There's your meatloaf."

"But—"

"Not much in the way of beef around here—milk cows don't count. I think it's Mr. Austin's way of aggravating the dingbatters."

"There's that word again. No fish?"

"The few fishermen who're left didn't have much luck today. Maybe the fish don't care for the smell of oil from the sunken ships in their waters."

"Oysters?"

"No."

"Clams?"

"Mr. Austin has bad knees. Money's tight, so he can't afford shellfish too often." Virginia plucked an imaginary pencil from behind her ear and wrote on an imaginary pad. "One order of potatoes and onions coming up. Do you want ketchup for your pretend meatloaf?"

"Plain's fine."

"To drink?"

Charlie glanced at the menu. "Is the lemonade lemonade? Do I have to add mustard and pretend?"

"Made it myself before I left last night. Used fresh mustard too."

"I'm sure." Charlie gave Virginia the menu.

In the kitchen, Mr. Austin spooned a serving on a plate and gave it Virginia. "You know that fella? I seen 'im in a time or two." Austin's "I," including in "time," sounded like "Oi," how most O'cockers pronounced it.

"I met him this morning." Virginia didn't like gossip. No need to mention the body she'd found either. "He seems nice enough."

Austin's mustache twitched. "Nice enough before they serve a plate of heartache. I thought you was seein' that Evans boy?"

"I *see* lots of people. I'm *seeing* you right now. Let me feed our one customer, I doubt we'll *see* any more."

She placed the plate on the table. Charlie sniffed the steam. "Looks good. I especially like how brown it is."

"That's from the whale blubber. Mr. Austin renders it into cooking grease."

Charlie forked a mouthful, chewed and swallowed. "Might I have a glass of mustardade to wash my whale blubber down?"

Virginia returned with two glasses and sat. "I happen to think my mustardade is perfect." She sipped. "Don't you?"

Charlie sipped. "On par with the whale blubber." He set the glass on the table. "How's your manners for watching moonrises? My mother warned me about fast women on these remote islands."

"I can only go fast on my bike or Jimmy. He's my horse."

"Is he from the local herd? I noticed he's on the short and sturdy side. His coat is thicker than on the horses back home too." Charlie swallowed more potatoes. "You say you ride a bicycle?"

"That's what I ride here. Jimmy, so I'm told, is a descendent of the Spanish Mustangs." Virginia sipped lemonade. "What do you do out here?"

*If the Sunrise Forgets Tomorrow*

"Jerry and I run security while they build the base. We make sure the guys don't bother pretty locals like you and Ruby, stuff like that." He glanced at his watch. "What time's our moonrise?"

"Around eight. That's when it rose last night."

"I might go early. Should I tell Ruby? I'd hate to get shot."

"Park farther up the path and she shouldn't hear you. Ignore her if she comes out, she'll leave soon enough."

Charlie stood and dropped a few dollars on the table. "Are you worth a tip?"

Virginia snatched the bills up and waved them toward Charlie. "More than you can afford."

He gave her a few more dollars. "For the whale blubber. See you in a bit."

He turned toward the door. Virginia took his empty plate and left for the kitchen. The door squeaked open, and a voice said, "'Scuse me, sir," and Charlie said, "Certainly."

Virginia whirled around. In uniform, Walter dropped a duffle bag. "Hey there, O'cocker gal. Where's my hug?"

## Chapter 4

## Erich

*On the outskirts of Bremen, Germany*
*April 26, 1942*

The spicy aroma from the evergreen branches above Erich rode the breeze. He loved the fragrance, similar to Thea's cologne. Stomach full from her picnic lunch of bratwurst, kartoffelknödeln, and for dessert, apfelpfannkuchen, he dropped to the blanket and lay his head in her lap.

"Ah, Mr. Fischer," she said, running her fingers through his hair, "did you eat too much?" She patted his tight stomach. "Or are you hoping for some romance for a second desert?"

Erich slipped his fingers into her blonde curls and pulled her to him for a kiss. "Does that answer your question, my darling Thea?"

"You're such a sweet boy. Sweeter than the apples in my *apfelpfannkuchen.*"

Erich sat up. "I wish you'd make up your mind. Last night you called me a handsome man instead of a sweet boy." He bumped her shoulder with his. "Several times, if I remember correctly."

"What would you have me do on my honeymoon night? Not make my husband think he's the best I've ever had?"

Erich grinned at her teasing. "The *only* you've ever had, I should hope. Have you forgotten telling me that not long after we met, or are you simply being dishonest?" He grabbed her hand and tugged at the wedding ring he'd slipped onto her finger yesterday afternoon. "If so, I can always take this back to the store. After all, the country is in dire need of brass for artillery shells."

Thea snatched her hand away. "If it's truly brass—not gold as the jeweler said—maybe I should let you. I'll find a man who knows I'm worth the genuine article while you're on patrol."

Erich kissed her again. "No worries, my darling, not a single one."

Thea grew quiet, completely unlike her. Her head dropped. Erich lifted her chin. "Of all your expressions, I know this one too well. The war worries you, yes?"

"The war I can handle, losing you I cannot. Does it bother you to fight the British when your stepmother is a citizen?"

"I'd rather not fight at all. Hitler is ... I can't think of a word to describe him. Still, I must do my part to protect our people. Try not to worry. I'll be hidden beneath the waves where no ship can see my *unterseeboot,* or U-boat, as the British are calling it."

Thea lay on the blanket. "Let me hold you." Snuggling his shoulder, she fingered a button on his shirt. "Tell me you love me and nothing will happen to us."

"*Ich liebe dich,* Thea. More than I can say."

"In English? I love the way it sounds."

"I love you, Thea."

She rolled on top of him. "I believe we have the forest to ourselves, my sweet husband."

Erich unbuttoned her blouse to reveal the white lace of her brassiere. "I think you're quite right, my darling."

---

Dressed again, Erich cuddled Thea in the curve of his arm.

Stories from returning seamen contradicted his lie about the safety of a U-boat. Whether with depth charges or bombs dropped from airplanes, each shook their vessels as if a bone gripped within the jaws of his German Shepherd, Gertrude. Those seamen had lived to tell the tale, but many had not. The British were taking the war more seriously on the open seas, and now that the Americans had been forced into the fight by the Japanese bombing of Pearl Harbor, their military strength would soon come to bear. He'd told Thea another lie, or rather, he'd kept information from her, which was how his patrol on the long-range XI U-boat would extend to the east coast of America, designated Operation *Paukenschlag*.

He'd also deflected her question concerning his British stepmother, who thankfully had no family in Britain. She loved the country of her birth, but she understood Erich's efforts in protecting Germany. She also treasured education and made sure he had learned to speak, read, and write English as he grew up, in addition to German. At the age of thirteen, when the family, including his older brother, Ernst, had spent a weekend in London, he practiced English by ordering their meals. Not a single waiter or waitress questioned his accent or word usage, but many a young waitress commented on his curly blond hair and blue eyes, embarrassing him to no end.

Thea caressed his cheek. "You're very quiet, my sweet boy."

Thea called him that because he looked much younger than his twenty-one years. He took it as a compliment, but he would've liked to at least look his age.

"I'm only enjoying your arms around me and the aroma of the trees," he said.

Thea sat up and opened her purse. "I have something for you." She took out several envelopes tied with a red ribbon. "I've written you a letter for each week of your two-month patrol."

*If the Sunrise Forgets Tomorrow*

Erich took the bundle. "The first one is numbered?"

"They're in order, of course."

"Thank you, sweetheart. They'll keep me dreaming of you."

"I wrote them in English, so you'll know all those lessons you taught me weren't wasted. I only wish I could speak it as well as you."

She handed him a picture he had taken on their first date, when they spent a day at the ocean. She wore her hair pinned up on one side, a white skirt that fell to her knees, and a snug red blouse that accented her bosom. Her radiant smile nearly took his breath when he snapped the photo. He took the offered picture. "I'll make sure none of the men see this. They might try to push me overboard during my watch if they do."

"Excellent idea."

"You'd have them push me over?"

Thea poked his arm. "I mean you not showing them the picture, silly boy, not them pushing you overboard. If one of those American women got her hands on you, you might not return to me."

Astonished that Thea knew about his coming patrol, Erich managed to keep his mouth from falling open. "How did you know we're going to America?"

"I heard talk at the market when I bought the bratwurst. Actually, I'm happy you're going there, far away from the British who so enjoy harassing our vessels." She paused, head dropping for a second or two before facing him again. "Will you forgive me if I don't see you off tomorrow? All that gray metal floating on the water slick with oil at the docks makes me as melancholy as I've ever been."

"I understand, my darling. We'll simply make tonight so utterly special that it lasts until I return."

## Chapter 5

## Moonrise

Walter held out his arms for the hug. Virginia dropped the plate, which shattered at her feet.

"Don't be breakin' my good dishes out there, Ginny!" Mr. Austin yelled. "They make my taters taste better!"

Walter knelt to pick up pieces of plate. "Looks like I mommucked things up."

Virginia knelt to help him. "You didn't write you were coming."

"I wanted to surprise you." He duckwalked to another piece.

Hands filled with shattered plate, Virginia stood and bit her lip. If Walter saw the two glasses on the table, how would she explain it?

Walter offered plate shards. Virginia gathered the corners of the apron with one hand. The pieces clattered in.

"Any lemonade left?" he said. "I got a ride at the Marine base in Havelock on one of them bugeye boats. It's a long way and I'm parched." He started toward the table and Virginia grabbed his arm.

"How about washing up in back first? I'll bring you a bite of Mr. Austin's potatoes and onions you like so well."

"I ate before I left." Walter took his duffle to the table with the two glasses. "That fella that left here a minute ago must've been mighty thirsty to need two glasses."

"Mr. Austin cooks potatoes and onions too salty sometimes."

*If the Sunrise Forgets Tomorrow*

"He coulda used the same glass." Walter looked her in the eye, his own eyes narrowing. "Were you sittin' with that Navy man, Ginny?"

Virginia whirled and went to a trash can in the corner, where she rattled the shards into it. Walter pointed at a glass. "Don't ignore me. If you were sittin' with that swabby, I deserve to know why."

Virginia stomped to him, cheeks heating. "We're not married nor engaged," she said, waggling her finger in his face. "That means you don't *deserve* a thing."

Walter worked his jaw as if he were chewing an oyster shell. "It's not like the Ginny I know to lose her temper so easy."

"Well, it's been a long day and I'm tired. You know how it is living here, trying to make ends meet." Virginia sat. "I'm sorry for snapping at you. I was asking that man about the ship a U-boat sank recently. You do know how the Nazi's are right off Ocracoke and Hatteras, don't you?"

"I know all that. I'm sorry for accusing you of anything." Walter sat. "I'm shipping out to England day after tomorrow." He reached into his pants pocket to pull out a black velvet box and opened it to reveal an engagement ring. Virginia swallowed as he gave her the box. "I never officially asked," he said, a slight smile brightening his expression. "But will you be my wife?"

Virginia almost cringed at the word "my." It was as if she were property, to be bought and sold simply because a man offered her a ring.

"No, Walter."

"My Ginny, always the kidder. Wonder if Mr. Fulcher is still awake for the ceremony?"

"You're right," Virginia said, "you never officially asked. It also bothers me how you act as if the last thing in the world you need to do before going overseas is to get married so you can take from me what I would only give *if* we were married."

Walter's smile fell. "It's not like that at all, Ginny. I never said the words, but being away from you made me realize how much I love you. All I want is to come back from the war and give you everything you ever wanted in life."

The sadness in Walter's brown eyes kept Virginia from blurting out how being away from him had made her independent and not so wanting of a husband.

"I'm sorry," she said, "but our time apart made me see how I depended on you too much. Wouldn't you rather have a wife who doesn't cling to a man for everything?"

"Well, I suppose that makes sense. This war should be over in no time anyway." He returned the velvet box to his pocket and took a book from the duffle bag. "I saw this in a store in Norfolk."

Virginia accepted the copy of Edgar Allen Poe's works already on her shelf. She'd shown it to Walter one summer night last year. "That's very thoughtful." She yawned. "I'm *very* tired. If Mr. Austin lets me, I'm going straight home to bed. I assume you'll see your mama and daddy."

"I was hoping I could walk you home. Could I see you tomorrow? I'd like to say hello to Ruby and—" Walter shook his head. "I'm sorry, Ginny, I forgot all about your mama."

"She's still in a coma. I doubt she'll hang on much longer."

Walter stood. "I'll get home to my folks and pay my respects to your mama tomorrow."

"Come around ten. She's usually fed and cleaned by then."

Mr. Austin agreed to let Virginia leave early, offering her the leftover potatoes and onions. Thanking him, she spooned the sticky mass into a bowl, double-bagged it with brown paper bags, and placed it in the basket on her bicycle. Flashlight on, she pedaled home.

*If the Sunrise Forgets Tomorrow*

In the narrow path, the light cast eerie shadows of the live oak limbs, grasping out as if to snatch her from the bicycle. Would the path scare Ruby if she pedaled home after working at the restaurant? Since she wanted to trade chores, she might find out. With her romantic attitude concerning almost everything, Ruby was too naïve for her own good, and ever since the Navy men had arrived, Virginia feared one of their sorrier sorts might take advantage of her twin.

Live oak branches brushed her jacket, claws reaching from the dark. A marsh rabbit, with short, stubby ears and a tail to match, hopped in front of her and darted back into the brush.

Like the rabbit, Walter had appeared in the restaurant, expecting her to jump at the chance to marry him. She might've agreed before he left, but that had changed. Still, since Walter had understood her refusal, she shouldn't discount him so quickly. After all, regardless of forgetting she had the same book, he had remembered her love for Poe's writing.

The flashlight reflected the red tail lights on Charlie's jeep. At the house, no lamps glowed, meaning Ruby was asleep. Virginia left the food and the book on the porch, returned the bike to the shed adjoining Jimmy's stall, and took the flashlight for the walk to the pier. Her worn flats thudded softly on the gray boards, curled with time and salt air. Charlie turned around. "You walk mighty soft, Miss Starr."

"All the better to sneak up on Navy rogues like yourself, Mr.—" Virginia stopped. "I'd like to know your last name before I sit with you."

"It's Smithson, Miss Starr."

Virginia sat beside him at the end of the pier and offered her hand. "Nice to meet you, Mr. Smithson." She peeked around him at a paper bag. "Is that your surprise?"

Charlie took a bottle and two glasses from the bag. "Care for some wine?"

"Some gentleman you are. Planning on getting me tipsy and taking advantage of me."

Charlie popped the cork from the bottle. "It's sweet wine, not very strong. My dad makes it. We have a glass on special occasions. Easter, Christmas, New Year's." Charlie half-filled a glass. "Besides, I don't believe anyone would take advantage of Miss Virginia Starr unless she allowed it."

She sniffed the wine. "Smells like grape juice, with a small nip at the end."

Charlie filled his glass and sipped. "Not bad. I'll write Dad and tell him he did a good job with this batch."

Virginia sipped her first taste of alcohol. The nip tingled her tongue.

"So, Miss Starr, is it fair to say this is one Navy man you don't mind being on Ocracoke?"

"It's too early to tell. I see you're wearing your pistol on your belt. You didn't have it earlier."

"Never can tell when a German might swim ashore." Charlie sipped wine. "You handled finding that body this morning a lot better than I would've expected."

"Because I'm a woman?"

"Not especially. In training, I saw men crying to go home. Does the war bother you much?"

"Like most villagers, I try to ignore it. Then, like with that body, it's forced upon us. It makes me wonder how Hitler can get his people—more importantly, his military—to do his will with such disregard for human life."

"Maybe some of them are just as evil as he is."

"Probably, but less than more."

"Even in the German military?"

"It's about the person, not the uniform. If good people didn't let evil leaders take power, the world would be a lot more peaceful."

*If the Sunrise Forgets Tomorrow*

"What would you do if you came face to face with a German soldier or sailor?" Charlie gulped his glass empty and set it on the pier by the bottle.

"If he tried to hurt me or mine," Virginia said, meaning it, "I'd blow his head off with my shotgun—same as an American."

"Let's change the subject," Charlie said, starlight gleaming on his grin. "Does this lonesome island of yours ever make you feel like moving inland?"

"This morning it did."

"Because of the body?"

"That's part of it. When Jimmy and me topped the dune, there was something about the sunrise that spooked me. It was as red as I've ever seen. No clouds hung low to make it like that either. It was like it was trying to make up its mind whether or not to rise on this sad world of ours in the middle of this terrible war."

Charlie nodded. "Kind of like if the sunrise forgets tomorrow, because we don't deserve it if we can't get along any better than we do."

"Something like that."

Virginia regretted her melancholy. Here she was, with a nice man on her pier, and all she could talk about was sadness. The overwhelming urge to lay her head on Charlie's shoulder hit her like when her only aunt, Aunt Selma from Manteo, Papa's sister, had visited a week after his memorial. All Ruby did was cry and cry, retreating to her room when the tears came. Aunt Selma did her best to comfort Virginia, who laid her head on her shoulder time and time again.

"Charlie?"

"Yeah?"

"Our movie's playing."

"I love it when the moon is huge and orange. You can see the dark spots."

"Papa said that's mold on the cheese."

"Ready to tell me about your parents?"

"Papa worked at the lifesaving station. He drowned a couple of years ago during a rescue. His body was never recovered." Virginia lowered her head for a second. "Mama's been in a coma since December. A high fever from the influenza did that. She can manage food if it's liquid enough. Life was tough enough before Papa died but now it's sticky. It's like walking through a sandspur thicket barefooted. You never know when the next step might take you down."

"I'm sorry to hear that, Virginia. Young ladies like you and Ruby shouldn't have to deal with sadness like that."

"It's harder on Ruby. She takes care of Mama mostly, since I work and gather firewood. She wants to trade chores and work at the restaurant."

"And?"

"You saw how she is, pretty as a flower in the morning. I'm afraid she'll latch onto the first man who comes along, no matter how sorry he is. That's a sure way to a broken heart, or worse."

"Like" —Charlie patted his stomach— "with a baby?"

"Exactly." Virginia let the silence bloom between them. The night was too beautiful to allow her worries to take away the moment. "Charlie?"

"Yeah?"

"Can I lay my head on your shoulder?"

Charlie slipped his arm around her. "I wouldn't mind that one bit, Virginia."

A breeze rustled the marsh grass. The row boat bumped against the pier once, twice, and stopped as the breeze settled, leaving the slight hint of salt in the air. Briny and ancient, as if

Poseidon had stirred the Pamlico with his trident, the aroma faded as the breeze softened further.

"I didn't think you'd mind, Charlie." Virginia snuggled into his warmth. "I didn't think you'd mind at all."

## Chapter 6

## Departure

Erich slapped the jangling alarm clock before it woke Thea. She slid her warm hand to his chest. "Please don't go. I'll make it worthwhile, my sweet boy."

"I wish I could stay, my darling. You know I do."

He swung his feet off the bed and stood. She grabbed his underwear and pulled him back down. "Leave these for a keepsake. I'm sure they have many fine memories in them."

"Your wish is my desire, even for my stained underwear."

Showered and dressed, Erich returned to the bedside to caress Thea's soft curls. "I'll be heading out, my love." He kissed her cheek, wet with tears. "Thea, what's—?"

She wrapped her arms around his neck and wept. He simply held her, trying to let her know with his embrace that all would be well. Her shoulders stopped heaving, and she pulled away. "Aren't I a mess, sobbing like a schoolgirl who's lost her first love. You will be careful, won't you, my sweet boy? I don't know what I'd do if I lost you."

"It's going to be fine, Thea, just fine. We'll likely see nothing more than a whale, or a dolphin popping up to say, *"Hallo, junge sirs, mögen deine reisen sicher sein und die meerjungfrauen sind viele."*

Thea poked his ribs. "Saying hello is fine, but some of those old U-boat captains are hardly young. As far as mermaids, keep your hands to yourself."

Erich kissed her a final time and left the hotel room. Thea's letters were safely in his duffle, her photo secure in his shirt pocket. That day on the beach, she had placed the camera on a boulder, set the timer, and ran back to his side for another picture. That photo now sat on her dresser at her home in the center of Bremen, where her parents lived on one street and where his lived behind them.

His footsteps echoed hollowly in the dark city, lit only by starlight because of the blackout. Cold chilled his neck, so he buttoned his coat collar to ward off the chill. His breath puffed from his nostrils in twin jets. In the harbor, a ship sounded its horn, almost like an oversized cow injured in one of the bombings outside of town. The Royal Air Force assaulted the country weekly now, dropping incendiaries and high explosives that either burned cities to the ground or blew them out of existence.

To the left of the U-boat pens, the blackened hulk of a small cruiser—destroyed by a bombing run by the RAF six weeks ago—rose jaggedly from the water. He stopped to thumb his lighter for a cigarette.

"Careful, Erich. Don't want a bomber lighting that for you." A shadowy figure with a rifle emerged from behind a thick pier piling.

Erich put the lighter and cigarette away. "Guarding things well, Otto?"

"Napping actually. As long as those damn bombers don't appear, there's nothing to guard *against.*"

"Don't let the old man catch you asleep. He'll feed you to the fishes once we're out to sea."

Otto set the rifle on his shoulder. "I'd rather be out to sea than where the British bastards drop bombs. Has your family left for the country yet? Thea and her family too?"

"They're trying to locate housing. Thank God the targets so far have been in the shipyards."

"We're not in the shipyards. "Otto nodded toward the cruiser. "A lucky hit?"

"Not for the men on board. Has everyone arrived?"

"There's a few stragglers. Better go ahead."

The U-boat rested in the water like a half-submerged sea serpent made of gray scales. In his perch in the conning tower, the old man himself, Captain Schubert, faced him. "Better get aboard Fischer. We're getting under way when the rest arrive."

Erich jumped to the deck, climbed into the tower, and eased down the narrow ladder into the bowels of the U-boat. He gave the downed periscope's shining oily exterior a rub, his station until the captain took over to track a ship and fire torpedoes.

Standing by the lights that monitored the various electrical systems, Hans, the seaman who slept above him, laughed. "Did you stroke Thea's thighs like that on your honeymoon night?"

"A gentleman never talks about such things. Did you and Greta have a nice weekend?"

"We did—several times."

"Talking about Greta like that, now we know who the gentleman is around here." Erich started away but stopped. "Do you have any extra waterproof document bags? Thea gave me a photo I'd like to keep out of the humidity."

Hans glanced around. "Don't tell anyone, they'll want one too. I used one for a picture of Greta. Look under my bunk, there's three left."

"Perhaps you're a gentleman after all, or at least a man who knows what love means."

"Keep that to yourself also. I have my reputation to uphold."

Erich made his way through the snug confines of the U-boat, past valves, controls, and levers of all shapes and sizes. Men at their stations studied various gauges in the dim light. Except

*If the Sunrise Forgets Tomorrow*

for a small crew that piloted the sub out if air raid sirens announced incoming bombers, the vessel was vacant over the weekend. Regardless, body odor and the musty stench of stale, humid air permeated every crack and crevice.

In his quarters, Erich took a document bag from beneath Hans' bunk and inserted Thea's photo. Adding the packet of letters, he made sure Thea's smiling face shone on top, sealed the bag and placed it beneath his pillow.

Outside the door, voices echoed as if from the inside of a steel drum. Two men entered the small, oval doorway. Werner, with short blond hair and a crooked nose from when he boxed in basic training, came in first. "Ah, Fischer, I see you made it."

Behind him, dark-haired and bearded, Uwe laughed. "Of course he made it. Otherwise his Thea might have broken his back for him. Isn't that right, Fischer?"

"Perhaps, but I would die a happy man."

Werner untied his duffel. "I wonder if we'll get close enough to the *Amerikaner's* coastline to see their *frauen* frolicking in the waves?"

Uwe punched Werner's arm. "I've heard their women work hard in their factories. One might aim a gun your way if she saw you."

"No doubt," Erich said, "if she looks at *your* ugly faces." He rubbed a finger across his chin. "As for myself, she might fall in love with me."

"She'll diaper you," Uwe said. "Didn't your parent's have to give permission for you to join the *Kriegsmarine?* With your boyish looks, you can't be more than fifteen."

"Perhaps my face looks fifteen." Erich patted his crotch. "But I'm plenty of man where it counts."

Werner snorted laughter. "All newlyweds say that. Then, when the husbands are off fighting, the wives tell the next man the same thing. Then the next, then the next, then—"

Erich faked a punch at Werner, who slapped the fist away. "I know, I know," he said. "You're in love and don't care to hear all that. Believe me, I hope the best for you and Thea. I also hope we can get out of this war alive."

"I hope we *all* can get out of it alive," Uwe said. "Our loved ones too. The damned RAF keeps sending more and more bombers. Our families might be in worse peril than us."

Gritting his teeth, Erich turned away from Uwe and Werner to lift his pillow and peek at Thea's photo, illuminated by the dim, yellow lights. That day at the beach had been magical. Perhaps she and their families could get out of the city soon, away from any and all potential danger.

## Chapter 7

## Thea

In the hotel room, Thea hugged Erich's pillow, which held the faint, sweet aroma of his aftershave tonic. Sobs wracked her body until her throat ached and his pillow was soaked.

Before they were married, anytime he brought up how their families were attempting to get out of the city but couldn't because there was no place to go, she had answered with silence. Now, with him gone, the emptiness of the bed filled her with foreboding. Barely six weeks ago, when they told her parents they'd set a wedding date, the previous RAF bombing at the shipyards cracked and barked and shook the house to rain plaster dust. Everyone in the center of the house—with all the doors closed and curtains drawn due to the blackout, plus candles flickering due to the lack of electricity—looked around, eyes white and rolling, obviously wondering if the next massive explosion would shatter them all. When the air raid sirens, the anti-aircraft fire, and the faint droning of the departing bombers finally faded, Erich rubbed her tension-filled shoulders. "There, there, my darling, I told you we have nothing to worry about." Later, when they were alone and he told her goodnight, she glared at him. "Nothing to worry about? Then why, when we're alone, do you constantly ask if we've found a place to stay yet?" He shrugged his shoulders. "One can never be too safe, yes?"

Her answer had been a quick kiss and a renewed promise to ride into the countryside on her bicycle to ask farmers if they might have a spare building where their families could seek shelter if the bombing grew in intensity, as well as in frequency. The farmers always answered the same, with slow shakes of their heads followed by, *"Es tut mir leid, aber ich halte das, was ich für die Familie frei habe, voraussichtlich bald an."* On one such trip, she bit her tongue so hard that it bled, wanting to ask why, if they were holding the building for expected family, they weren't there now?

In the bathroom, she placed a hand on her stomach. Although she and Erich had never discussed children, they also had never discussed how to avoid pregnancy either. With their almost continuous lovemaking since the honeymoon, could she be pregnant now? She smiled, then frowned. Have a baby in the middle of a war? She smiled again. A child would be a small piece of Erich to cherish, including news for when he returned home.

Outside the hotel, she placed her small bag of clothes onto the rack on the rear of her bicycle and wound through the rows of two-story brick buildings, both shops and residences. A light haze of fog shifted and swirled in the shrubbery. A boy riding a bicycle, with a pack on his back from which he pulled a bundled newspaper, threw the morning edition into a building's alcove. A dog barked somewhere. Another answered. Yet another. She passed a house where an old man, gray-whiskered and wearing white pajamas with narrow blue vertical stripes, smoked a cigarette on the stoop. At another, a middle-aged man wearing a dark suit and a hat kissed a woman goodbye, likely heading to a job that supported the war effort, like Erich's father did at a local warehouse.

At the next street, instead of turning right toward her parent's house, she continued toward Erich's parent's house. Living with their backyards joined had led to their meeting. Many nights they had snuck out and sat beneath the stars in a swing to discuss their future.

Half a block later, she leaned the bike against the black wrought iron fence at Erich's parent's home. Erich's mother, blonde hair in a bun and wearing a lavender housecoat, opened the door at the third knock. "Why, Thea, what a surprise. Come in, come in."

Irna kissed Thea's cheek. "Did Erich leave already? I was hoping to say goodbye."

"You know Erich, keeping his mind on the business of protecting us."

"Was your parting ..." Irna's cheeks reddened. "Is *satisfying* a good word? Perhaps I'll be a grandmother in nine months, yes?"

Thea sniffed. "Where did you manage to find coffee with the rationing?"

"Let's have a cup." Irna led Thea down a hall lined with pictures of the family throughout the years, including Erich's brother, Ernst, killed on the battleship *Bismark* when it sank last May.

At a table by a window overlooking the backyard, where grass was greening from the warming weather, Irna pulled out a chair. "Sit, sit." She fetched two cups and a coffee pot from the stove and sat also. "Have you been home yet?" She filled Thea's cup.

"I thought I'd say hello." Thea sipped coffee. "Mmm, I've missed this."

"Alfred got a small bag through a connection at the warehouse."

Thea nodded. "I've missed many of those small luxuries we take for granted since the war started. It seems the smaller, like a cup of coffee, the more significant." She sipped again. "There's been no bombing since last month. Should we continue the search for a place in the country?"

Irna was looking out the window. Perhaps she was seeing Erich and Ernst as boys, running around the yard barefoot in the cool, green grass. Her eyes dropped to the cup. "So much sorrow has come to us. I pray Erich comes home to you." She raised her head. "Alfred wavers concerning a place in the country, but he continues to carefully inquire at work. What does your mother say?"

"She wavers almost constantly."

"And you?"

"My fears tell me we should leave. I believe this war will last longer and be more brutal than anything we can imagine."

"Why think that?" Irna said, eyes widening.

Thea hated to state the obvious, but she must. "The American's have joined the war. As bad as it is for the British to bomb us, imagine how it will be when the military might of America comes to bear."

"I've considered that also." Irna sipped coffee. "Are you going home now? I was thinking about getting dressed and taking a drive to the country. Maybe there's a farm we've overlooked."

"I haven't seen my mother since the wedding."

"No news from your father?"

"He sends letters now and then. Money, of course."

"As you know, being a major in the SS comes with responsibilities."

Thea said nothing. She and her father were squarely split on the war. When she had told him so on his last visit, he had claimed her love for Erich had blinded her to the necessities of the country. He had avoided the wedding as if she were marrying a Jew, damn him. People were people, and all people deserved a life.

"Forgive me," Irna said. "I can see my mentioning him has upset you."

*If the Sunrise Forgets Tomorrow*

"*He* doesn't upset me. It's his damned loyalty to that egomaniac Hitler. I wish the RAF would drop a bomb down his throat and see how he likes it." Thea slammed a palm on the table. "He cares nothing for his— No, I don't consider myself one of *his* people. We die by the score while he hides in Berlin, the coward."

"Albert and I feel the same. You know how Erich feels."

"Mother does also, which makes it difficult to understand my own father. Perhaps if I die in the next RAF strike, he will gain the perspective necessary to understand the depths of his depravity."

"Thea, don't say such a thing." Irna placed her hand on Thea's. "Erich would be heartbroken."

"I'm sorry I'm ruining our visit." Thea ignored the steaming coffee's delicious aroma. She needed to get home and say hello to her mother and possibly return later to take that drive with Irna to search for shelter. If not, her father may soon get the perspective he so badly needed.

## Chapter 8

## Ruby

Ruby giggled while dressing in faded denim pants and one of Papa's yellowed button-up shirts. She had put the lamp out last night and had snuck out to the edge of the marsh grass by the pier to eavesdrop on Ginny and Charlie.

It amazed her how her twin had rested her head on his shoulder, something she'd never done with Walter.

Ruby brushed her hair a time or two and nodded in the mirror, satisfied. She'd have to press the issue of working at the restaurant soon. If these Navy men could make a girl forget the few local fellows who hadn't left for the war so easily, she might find one who interested her.

She opened Ginny's door a crack. The sunlight through the window illuminated silky dark hair flowing over her sister's face. Ruby would never admit it to Ginny, but she preferred dark over light. Dark eyes, lashes, eyebrows. Her own blonde brows were so fair, she could hardly see them in the mirror. It was as if she were a ghost or a ghoul, or a ghastly being in one of Poe's horrid tales. Regardless, she loved her twin more than she'd dare let on. To be alone in life without her would be a tragedy she couldn't bear.

She eased the door open and dived onto Ginny, digging her fingers into her sides. "Wake up, you sleepy seagull! You were supposed to be roosting last night instead of snuggling up to Charlie to all hours."

*If the Sunrise Forgets Tomorrow*

Eyes blinking, Ginny grabbed Ruby's hands. "What would you know about it, Miss Hermit Crab? You were supposed to be snug in your shell." She sat up and fingered hair from her eyes. "You snuck out and listened, didn't you?"

Ruby jumped from the bed and pranced in a circle on tip toe. "Me, little old me? Miss Scarlett from Tara eavesdrop on little old you?" She fanned her face. "Why lands sake, Chile', how dare you suggest such a thing? If'n I didn't know no better, I'd say you was a damned yankee, come to steal my virginity."

Ginny smiled hugely. "You have absolutely no sense whatsoever." She glanced at the ancient windup alarm clock on the nightstand. "What time is it? I forgot to wind that thing, and I intend to go to the funeral for those British sailors."

"Charlie will be there too, of course." Ruby sat on the cedar chest at the foot of the bed. "I'm the only one doing all the work around here. That means it's the same time it always is when I wake up at seven."

"Then you won't mind getting our breakfast ready while I bathe, Miss Early Riser."

"Would it make any difference if I did mind?" Ruby left to check on Mama.

At the bedside, she touched the frail woman's forehead. Still warm. Still alive. Still another day to feed. Still another day to clean the foul-smelling mess from beneath the hips not suited to be on a skeleton. She took less and less eggs and milk these days, as if she were preparing to leave. Ruby closed the door, sat, and held the bone-thin hand.

"I'm sorry for having such thoughts, Mama, please forgive me." Ruby tilted the sunken-cheeked face her way and gently lifted the paper-thin eyelids. "Do you forgive me? Please do, I couldn't bear it if you didn't."

The blue eyes stared at nothing. The mouth murmured not a word nor a whisper. Drool seeped from a corner of the chapped lips, to stream a slow, wet line down the chin. Wiping the spit away with one of the torn squares of sheet she washed daily, Ruby dredged up a sigh from so deep, it could've risen from the depths of the Atlantic.

She certainly didn't desire it, but Mama would die soon. What then for her and Ginny? Remain on this spit of sand and sandspurs, marsh grass and sea oats, stunted oaks and stunted spirits of those who chose this place as home? Ruby folded her hands in her lap. That wasn't fair. Ocracoke held a wildness about it that matched her own heart, her own innate desperation to make all she could out of as little as possible. To see the fullness of a new day's sunrise over the Atlantic on one side of her existence, followed by the sunset over the Pamlico Sound at the start of twilight, drew her like bees to blooms. Even the ever-present taste of salt in the air, the hurricanes that sometimes overwashed the island, and the nor'easters that battered the dunes for days on end, resembled the heartbeat of a living thing. Maybe that's what brought people here, and maybe that's why those few stayed to have their last remains buried in the sands of the village cemetery.

The door creaked behind her. "How's she doing?" Ginny asked.

"Same as yesterday. The day before. The day before. She'll stay the same until she draws her last breath." Ruby stood. "I better see if my girls have any eggs ready."

In the kitchen, Ginny placed a bag from the ice box on the table. "If you'd like, we can heat Mr. Austin's leftover potatoes and onions to have with our eggs."

"Would you mind …"

In the middle of opening the bag, Ginny stopped. "What?"

"I was about to ask if those spuds were all we could have." Ruby's chin trembled. "But I forgot about Mama." She dropped into a chair at the table. "How could I do that, Ginny? It's like I wished she were dead and buried."

Ginny pulled a chair close and slipped an arm around Ruby's shoulders. "You don't wish that. No doubt she's a burden we didn't choose, and a duty. We'll care for her until God takes her like he took Papa."

"As good as they were to us when they were alive, it's the least we can do." Ruby leaned close to Ginny and sniffed. "Don't you smell as fresh as the morning? Did you use extra soap to wash the smell of onions from under your arms for Charlie?"

"He stopped by for supper at the restaurant last night." Ginny skootched the chair over. "Walter stopped by too."

Ruby couldn't stop her mouth from falling open. "Oh, my stars and starfish. Don't tell me he saw you and Charlie in a passionate embrace over a plate of spuds 'n onions?"

"Not at all, he—"

"What's wrong? You look like you did that time a ghost crab crawled up your cut off denims while you were lying on the beach."

"The funeral's at ten," Ginny said. "Durned if I didn't tell Walter to visit at ten."

"The salt air's pickled yer brain, Virgil."

"I'll leave early and let you deal with him. How's that for an idea?"

"I'll get him to sit with Mama and go with you to the funeral. How's *that* for an idea?"

"He might if I ask. Would it be evil to take advantage of him like that?"

"Depends on your definition of evil, *Virgil.*"

"Well, *Rube,* I hate to use him poorly."

"Uh-huh, like letting him think you were his girl. Then, as soon as you meet a handsome fellow in the name of Charlie, you invite him to watch the moon rise and who knows what else."

"Good point, sounds exactly like something you'd do. I'd help with the eggs but I don't care to smell like chicken poo. Off with you, Rube."

## Chapter 9

## Fights and a Funeral

After breakfast, Virginia fed and cleaned Mama while Ruby finished the dishes. Virginia told Ruby to bathe in case Walter agreed to watch Mama so they could attend the funeral.

Ruby washed at the basin and dressed in her room. Virginia crossed her arms when Ruby came out. "Very nice, Scarlett. I especially like the pink ribbon around your ponytail. You look like an innocent young waif."

"I wish we could afford dresses." Ruby rubbed at a set-in stain on the yellowed shirt. "Even if it were only one, we could take turns wearing it."

"Oh, please," Virginia said. "We might be twins but not in the bust. Your bosom would pop the buttons of any dress that fit me. How'd you get so lucky?"

"Who says I'm lucky? Remember when Tom Parker used to sit beside me in church before Papa died? He never looked me in the eye."

A vehicle horn beeped outside. "Who in the world could that be?" Virginia said.

Ruby skipped to the window. "Were you expecting Charlie?"

Charlie climbed the steps. Virginia opened the door. "Did I miss something, Mr. Smithson?"

Charlie entered. Ruby eyed him up and down. "Smithson? You don't look like a Smithson? How could you be a Smithson?"

"You'll have to take that up with my parents, Ruby." Charlie faced Virginia. "I thought you might like a chauffeur to the funeral rather than riding your bike." He glanced out the door. "I passed a man in uniform walking down your drive. I think I saw him last night when I was leaving the restaurant."

Virginia peeked out the door past Charlie. He had to mean Walter. "He's a friend who's visiting. I forgot about the funeral when I told him to stop by."

"If you'd rather not go ..."

Shoes clomped up the steps, across the porch, and Walter barged in toward Charlie. "You damn fool, didn't you see me in the path? If I hadn't jumped out of the way, you'd—"

"I can't help it if that road's narrow, Air Corps. You're not in the sky, where you have all the room in the world to maneuver."

Walter poked Charlie's chest. "An excuse of a Navy man by that excuse of a uniform. You think that path is the ocean for you to drive wherever you please. Ginny, what's this excuse for a man doing here? Did you lie to me last night? Is somethin' going on twixt you two? I won't abide a lyin' woman. By God in Heaven, I'll—"

"Whoa there, Air Corps, don't be using the Lord's name in vain around these two fine ladies."

"Was I talking to you, Swabby?" Walter eyed Virginia. "Was I talking to him? Did it look like I was talking to him?" Walter rolled up his sleeves. "By God, I'll take him outside and—"

Virginia grabbed Walter's arm. "You'll do no such thing, Charlie's a guest in my home. When you mentioned coming by last night, I forgot about attending the funeral for the two

*If the Sunrise Forgets Tomorrow*

British men that washed ashore from the *Bedfordshire*. He's offering me a ride, is that a crime?"

"Why do you care about two Brits being planted in our cemetery?"

"She found one of them is why," Ruby said.

Virginia pulled Walter's arm. "Come outside, I've a favor to ask."

Walter eyed Charlie. "Okay, but he stays in here."

"Which is why I asked *you*, Mr. Hammerhead Shark." Virginia led Walter to the end of the porch. "I'm sorry for the mix-up."

"I don't mind that near as much as I mind that swabby comin' 'round my girl. You're a beautiful woman, Ginny, don't you know that? He's bound to try and get you in a situation that ought to be for a husband alone and—" Walter scuffed his shoe against the porch's boards. "Well, you know what I mean."

Virginia knew *exactly* what Walter meant. He expected the same thing from her last night, using a ring as a tool to pry her legs open. "Don't you give me credit for knowing how a man's mind works? I'm flattered you think I'm beautiful. But I'm aware—*well* aware—of how beauty tends to make a man's brain turn to mush while something else turns to rock."

Walter's cheeks reddened. "You ought not talk about such things, Ginny."

"Why? Because you're guilty of the same thing?" She fluttered a hand to clear the air. "Will you stay with Mama while Ruby and me attend the funeral?"

"Some dadburned favor that is, leavin' me so you can gallivant with that dingbatter."

"Ruby needs to get out of the house. Please? It'd mean the world to me if you did."

"It's not right, Ginny, not right at all. I've gotta leave early tomorrow and I've hardly seen you."

"I'll come back right after. You can stay for supper if you like."

"Do you promise?"

"I surely do." Virginia kissed his cheek. "Let me show you Mama." Virginia went in to Charlie. "Walter's being so nice as to watch Mama so Ruby can go with us to the funeral. You two get in the jeep. I'll be right out after I show him what to do."

"Show him what?" Ruby said. "He doesn't need to—"

"Mama likes to have her hand held. You know important that is." Virginia tilted her head toward the door. Ruby, rolling her eyes, followed Charlie outside.

"What's wrong with Ruby?" Walter said. "She's strung tighter than old man Sanders' banjo."

"Don't pay her any mind." Virginia led Walter to the ladderback chair. "All you have to do is sit here and hold Mama's hand."

Walter sat. "I'm awful sorry about this, Ginny. Is she in pain?"

"Doc Wills says no."

"That's a blessing. Me and your mama will get along fine."

Virginia climbed into the jeep behind Ruby. Charlie looked over his shoulder. "You sure calmed that fellow down." He cranked the jeep.

"Ginny's got a silver tongue," Ruby said. "She can talk an oyster plumb out of its shell. Ain't that right, Ginny?"

"*Isn't* that right. Don't forget your raising."

"Well, *isn't* that right, Miss Particular?"

"If that were the case, Rube, I'd never get an argument out of you about anything."

Ruby stuck her tongue out. "That's because you can't be right all the time, Miss High Britches."

At the cemetery, tucked within the stunted live oaks, Ruby crossed her arms. "I'm staying right here. If I go up there in

Papa's denims and yellowed shirt, all those rich-dressed folks will look at me like a starfish is stuck to my forehead."

Charlie offered his arm. "How dare you think such a thing, Ruby. You and Virginia are the prettiest pearls around." He offered his other arm to Virginia.

"He's right, Ruby. Get your behind out of that jeep and allow this fine gentleman to escort us."

Ruby's blue eyes darted from Virginia to Charlie. She hopped out and took his other arm. "Aren't you the lucky man, Mr. Smithson, handling us two fine ladies at the same time?"

"Don't give him any ideas," Virginia said. "It'd be his dream to climb into bed between us."

"Good Lord above," Charlie said. "You two would make a prostitute blush nine shades of red."

"Like you're doing now?" Ruby said.

"Darn tootin'. Let's get over to the graveside and try to be serious. These men died in the service of our country."

"Are they burying them in sink boxes?" Virginia whispered. "Like are used for hunting ducks?"

"We couldn't spare the lumber to make coffins."

They neared the pile of sand on this side of the two graves. Two men—one of the them Jerry—finished spreading British flags over the sink boxes. He came over. "Daggone, Charlie, why're you hoggin' these gorgeous gals to yourself? He offered Ruby his arm. "You can't trust this fella, ma'am, he's got a wife at home."

"I've been trying to tell my sister he's a rogue." Ruby took the arm. "But she's as hardheaded as the day is long. For myself, I'm as free as the wind off the ocean."

As Jerry led Ruby to the graveside, Virginia leaned close to Charlie's ear. "I can see the day coming when I'll need my shotgun for your friend."

"Please explain to Ruby how I'm not married," Charlie said, his tone solemn. "I'd hate for her to think badly of me."

"Let's hush and get around this sand so I can keep an eye on her."

Five men in dark suits and a couple of ladies in black dresses stood in a semi-circle around the make-do coffins. The morning sun warmed Virginia's forehead as well as theirs, judging by the perspiration running down the men's temples. The women fanned themselves while the men cleared their throats.

Amasa Fulcher, lay leader of Ocracoke's Methodist church, wearing his black suit and stiff, white collar, stood at the head of the graves. "By now we all know the tragedy that befell these men who came from so far away to protect our shores. The soul to my right was Sub-Lieutenant Thomas Cunningham, just promoted posthumously to Lieutenant. The soul to his left was Stanley Craig, telegraph operator. The Royal Navy thanks our village for tending its dead. I also thank the Williams family for offering this plot." He nodded to a couple nearby, who nodded back. "I could go on and on about the war and its impact on our world, but there's no need. Many of us on our fair island have sons fighting in lands far away and daughters who are nurses. We never know the day nor the minute nor the hour when we'll be taken from this earth, but those young men and women surely know their time may come much sooner, exactly like these two brave souls surely knew, God rest their souls."

Mr. Fulcher said a final prayer, and the crowd went their separate ways. Jerry stepped over with Ruby. "A mighty touchin' service, Charlie."

"I need to get these ladies home." Charlie's cheeks were red, a likely sign of his disgust with Jerry's antics concerning Ruby.

Virginia tugged her arm. "Come along, we've—"

Ruby jerked her arm away. "Jerry's buying me lunch at the restaurant. You *did* promise to let me work there soon."

*If the Sunrise Forgets Tomorrow*

"It was nice of him to offer, but—"

"You and Charlie go ahead so you can see Walter. Jerry will give me a ride home."

"I'd rather you come now." Virginia started to waggle a finger in Ruby's face, but slid a stray lock of hair behind her own ear instead. "Must I ask again?"

"The longer we fuss, the longer it'll take me to get there."

Virginia wanted to shoot Jerry here and now. His beady eyes and sneering grin would take her sister down the wrong path, sure as the devil took Eve. "Fine, be home in an hour."

"And if I'm not?"

Ruby needed a slap, but they'd end up tearing at each other's hair like when they were children. Still, to show such disrespect in private, when it could be laughed off, was one thing, but doing so among others was inexcusable. Virginia faced Charlie. "Please take Jerry aside while I have a word with my sister."

Charlie took a step toward the twisted live oaks. "You heard the lady, Jerry, let's—"

"I know what I heard, dadburnit. I'll bring her back safe and sound."

"I'm your superior officer, Ensign. Do I have to make that an order?"

"No need to get your back up, *Lieutenant*."

The men stepped out of earshot. Virginia snatched Ruby toward her. "How dare you act like a spoiled child out here among people. I can handle you here like I can handle you at home."

Ruby slapped Virginia's hand from her arm. "The time's long gone when you can turn me over your knee like you did when we were in braids, Virgil Starr. You might be taller but I'm stouter."

"In your damn bosom is all. What'll you do, smother me with 'em?"

Ruby's tight lips pressed tighter. Her rosy cheeks expanded like she was trying to blow up a balloon. *"Ha!* that's a fine idea!"

Virginia couldn't help but giggle. "At least I'd have smothered laughing."

"Even so, what's wrong with—"

"Jerry's got the look of a womanizer about him."

"How do you know? If I knew how you know, I'd know. Doesn't that make sense?"

Virginia held in a grin. "Barely."

"Then what—"

"He makes me feel like a fish somebody's scaling. I don't know why you can't see it."

"Maybe I've been cooped up in the house so long, I don't know one man from another." She glanced toward the men. "Who're you to tell me what to do? Flirting with a married man."

"That's one of the things I'm talking about. Charlie tells the men he's married so they won't drag him out looking for women. I think that's a fine trait."

"How do you know he's not lying?"

"I like his eyes. When I look in a man's eyes and feel comforted, I think he's a decent man."

"I suppose Walter makes you feel comforted too."

"We'll talk about that some other time, I need to get home."

*"You* need to get home? Does that mean I can stay? I'll be back in an hour, like you asked."

"And no longer. I'll load rock salt in one barrel of Papa's old double barrel for you and buckshot in the other for Jerry if you're a minute late." Virginia waved Charlie over. Ruby skipped to Jerry's side, and they left for the village. Virginia took Charlie by the arm. "Please take me home so I can tend to Walter."

Charlie drove with his eyes ahead, which Virginia admired even more. He wasn't one to meddle in her affairs concerning Walter and Ruby, while that beady-eyed Jerry would sneak around like a rat looking for the least bit of insignificant nothing to gnaw on.

Halfway into the shadowed path, she placed her hand on Charlie's arm. "Can you stop here?" The jeep's brakes squeaked to a halt. "I owe you an explanation about Walter."

"Not really." Charlie's eyes lowered for a second. "I trust what you told me about him. Still, it's obvious he thinks more of you than you do of him, or you wouldn't have asked me to watch the moon with you on the pier."

"He asked me to marry him after you left the restaurant. There was a time I might've considered it, but ..."

"Really?" Charlie turned toward her, twisting in his seat. "Don't tell me I've had that effect on you in just a few days?"

"I think it's the sense of independence I've gained from being able to take care of myself and Mama and Ruby, without help from anyone."

"I like that in a woman, Virginia, I like it a lot. I never cared to involve myself with women who act like a fragile flower in their frilly dresses and plastered-on makeup and floofy hairdos. You're as natural a woman as I've ever met." Charlie glanced around him. "You remind me of this island ... the gnarled trees, the dunes, the sea oats. It's as wild an area as I've ever seen, and it makes me believe you have that wildness born into you, like the salt mist coming off the waves when the sun first rises over the ocean."

Charlie's poetic words confirmed Virginia's opinion of him. Falling in love would be the easiest thing in the world, especially if she kissed him right now. She blinked away the impulse. Too soon, *much* too soon.

"My goodness," he said. "Mr. A. E. Poe could write a novel on the depths of whatever's going on behind those beautiful black eyes of yours, Miss Starr."

Warmth engulfed Virginia in places never engulfed before — a burning heat that made her want to mount him like an Ocracoke pony mounts his mare. "My goodness, Charlie, you almost had me entranced with your fine words."

"Like that's a bad thing."

"It's not a bad thing, you roguish man. As far as Walter, I'll walk from here. He's heading to war soon, and I'd rather he leave with thoughts to see him through instead of thoughts to make him sad."

"I can do that, Miss Starr. You certainly are a pearl."

"Sure I am, hidden beneath the nasty, gray muck of what an oyster looks like."

"I happen to love oysters."

Virginia climbed from the jeep. "Maybe I'll fetch us some for dinner one night."

The whine of the jeep backing up the path echoed amongst the live oaks. Virginia waited until Charlie reached the main road before leaving for home. She'd met a poet on Ocracoke, the last thing in the whole wide world she'd ever expected. Not really. The last thing she'd expected was to meet a man — any man — who made her want to strip off his clothes and ride him bareback like she rode Jimmy. Talk about *freedom*.

What else might happen on this island?

## Chapter 10

## Loss

On the dresser, the picture of Thea and Erich at the beach drew her attention like her lips to his. She left the bed and the book she'd been reading to take the picture within her hands for what may well be the hundredth time. Had it really been two weeks since the wedding? She missed him with an ache that refused to be subdued, and longed to hold her sweet boy and love him as if the sun might not rise tomorrow.

The aroma of the coffee Irna had given her lured her to the kitchen, where Mother stood over a bubbling percolator. "Wasn't it sweet of Irna to share the coffee?" Thea said.

Mother glanced over her shoulder at Thea. "I knew this delicious aroma would tease you out of your mood over Erich."

"Are there any eggs?"

"Not today. The war is ... I can't put into words how tired I am of it."

Thea went to the window overlooking the backyard. A gust of wind shuddered the wooden swing, hanging from a maple limb. Erich had first kissed her there, had proposed there as well.

Mother placed a gentle hand on Thea's shoulder. "I'm sure you miss him terribly."

"He didn't seem worried about us finding a place to hide from the bombing." Thea turned. "I could see right through him regardless." On the wall beside her, the phone rang. She placed the handset to her ear. "Hello?"

"Thea, this is Irna. Alfred called from work. A farmer offered us a barn in the forest."

"Are you certain? It's been so quiet."

"That's why he's concerned. He thinks the British will renew the bombings after this layoff. We're leaving tonight."

"We can't possibly pack everything so soon."

"We'll move what we need in stages."

"How far?"

"About forty-five minutes outside the city. Talk to Anna and let me know what you decide. We're leaving at twelve, when everyone should be asleep."

Thea cradled the phone. Pouring coffee, Mother glanced her way. "Has Alfred found a place?"

"A barn outside the city. They're leaving tonight, do you think we should join them?"

"Your father has virtually abandoned us to his SS ideals. Yes, we should join them."

They ate breakfast quickly, packed two suitcases with food and two with clothes, and waited to abandon their home.

※

An hour before midnight, Thea went to the swing. Similar to Erich's lips, a gentle breeze, warm and sensual, caressed her cheek. The aroma of grass, damp from a brief shower, rode the night air surrounding her.

How had the world gone so insane that good people had to scurry from their homes in the middle of the night like vermin? No, they weren't the vermin, the damned Nazis were the vermin. Then how could so many Germans believe the propaganda churned out by Hitler and his cohorts on the radio,

*If the Sunrise Forgets Tomorrow*

all lies told about the Jews to blame them for anything and everything for political purposes? How completely and utterly despicable the Nazis were.

She raised her eyes to the sky, where the stars, twinkling and silent, offered no answers to her many questions.

Memories of her and Erich sifted through her mind like wet sand through a child's fingers.

Clumps of occasional arguments as teenagers discussing goals and dreams. Making up with kisses that threatened their vow to wait until marriage. The first time they made love on their honeymoon night. The day of the picnic, evergreen needles in his blond hair and lipstick on his chest. His soft moans. Her biting her lower lip to stop a moan of pleasure from echoing within the forest.

Could she be pregnant? Erich, with his gentle ways and sweet demeanor, would make a wonderful father.

She leaned back in the swing and closed her eyes. "I miss you so much, my sweet boy. May God grant you safe passage to America and back. God, please grant our families passage to the safety of the forest as well."

Someone shook her shoulder. "What?"

"It's time to go," Mother whispered. "I know how important your memories are, so I allowed you a final hour with Erich." She gestured to two suitcases beside her, where two more waited. "We'll cut through the backyard instead of using the street. No one should see us."

Passing from their backyard to Erich's," Thea pushed the wrought iron gate open with her hip. "Look at what Hitler has reduced us to—running around like animals, ignoring our friends and neighbors."

"I know, darling, I know."

They met Alfred and Irna at their back door. "I'm happy you've decided to join us," Alfred said. "Erich would be happy that you'll be safe and sound until he returns."

"Are you leaving Gertrude?" Thea said.

"She's fast asleep. I'll bring her tomorrow."

Alfred placed the suitcases in the trunk of his car and climbed in. Irna looked through the side glass. "God help me, I have the feeling we'll never return home again."

"Nonsense." Alfred cranked the car.

Less than a block from the house, Thea grasped Alfred's shoulder. "Please stop. I forgot the photo of Erich and myself on my dresser."

Mother patted her arm. "You can get that later."

Alfred slowed the car. "I understand, Thea. Go ahead, I'll get out for a smoke."

"We'll all get out," Irna said. "My nerves are jangled and I need some air."

A chill clung to the night, replacing the earlier warmth. Thea shivered despite her coat. Her shoes clicked on the road with an ominous, hollow sound, until Gertrude's deep-throated bark made her stop.

An almost insignificant something niggled at the edge of her hearing. Where had she heard that sound?

It grew louder, the buzz of bumblebees flitting around Mother's flow—

*Bombers!*

Air raid sirens blared at the southern end of the city, then spread north. Thea whirled to face the car.

Two explosions bracketed the street beyond it, twin roses blooming into gigantic fireballs.

Incendiary bombs.

"Thea, ru—!"

Mother's blue overcoat transformed into a figure bathed in fire that dropped to the road. Thea whirled to run, but two more explosions buffeted her body. Heat licked her skin. Her coat flared into yellows, reds, and oranges. The acrid aroma of her own hair burning assaulted her nostrils. The very air around her roared with the power of what must be hell itself.

Superheated air filled her lungs. Flames scorched her eyes. Blinded, she fell to the road and tried to drag herself through the melted asphalt. The sound of her own flesh crackling grew to a crescendo. Her hands collapsed, fingers burning to stubs.

*Dear God, save my sweet—*

## Chapter 11

## Tanker

Taking his turn at watch in the conning tower, Erich raised his binoculars.

"You don't need those," Captain Schubert said. "I can see the lights in that house without them."

"Their blackout discipline could use some work, sir." Erich lowered the binoculars. "The charts say that island is Hatteras, off the east coast of a state called North Carolina."

"Exactly right. Our intelligence reports say these people are calling this stretch of water 'torpedo junction.'" Schubert chuckled, low and raspy. "I don't have to tell you why, do I? Perhaps we'll have a go at a ship soon. I'd like to add at least one to the list of our fellow boats."

Erich looked overhead. "It certainly is a clear night. I believe I can see every star. If I didn't know any better, I'd say I was at home."

"A least here they don't have to worry with having their cities fire bombed into ash and rubble." Schubert turned from the rail to face Erich. "You're from Bremen, correct? Your bunkmate mentioned you were a newlywed also. Can't recall his name."

"Hans, sir. Honestly, I don't even know his last name yet."

Schubert scanned the ocean once more. "I'll have him join you. Wake me if a target shows itself."

Hans climbed from below. "Wake up, Erich. The honeymoon's over."

"Maybe when we're old and gray and Thea no longer pounces on me when we're picnicking in the forest outside of town."

"Was that before or after the wedding?"

"After."

"Lucky dog. My brother said romance is the first thing to go after a man says 'I do.'" Hans glanced around. "Looks like a quiet nigh—" He pointed. "Look there."

Erich raised the binoculars. "I don't see ... smoke, I see smoke. Call the Captain, it looks like a tanker."

Hans stuck his head down the hatch. "Pass the word to the Captain. We've spotted a tanker."

Schubert climbed up almost immediately. "What have you got, Fischer?"

"Hans spotted him, sir." Erich handed the captain the binoculars and pointed. "You can see the smoke rising in front of the stars."

Schubert raised the binoculars. "Look at that, without a single escort in sight. We won't even have to dive, we'll run in close before we fire to save our fish for the next target." He gave Erich the binoculars. "Keep an eye on him, Fischer. I'm going below to inform the crew instead of sounding battle stations. I don't want to take a chance on alerting our friend."

"Sir," Hans said, "should I wake the watch officer?"

"Let him sleep, I'll handle this myself."

Erich raised the binoculars to study the tanker. Adrenaline seared his blood. The entire trip here had been quiet, and his first hunt stirred him.

"With our ranks so thin," Hans said, "it's a shame we don't have enough crew to keep a full watch. We'll all be at the bottom of the sea at this rate."

"Keep a sharp eye," Erich whispered. "We don't want an escort to sneak in and ruin our fun."

Hans poked Erich's side. "Listen to you, the pacifist. After all that talk about how the war should've never started, you sound as bad as the old man."

The captain emerged from the hatch. "Two fish are in the tubes in case we miss. "We're going to close in to 350 meters before firing. I want to see the bastards burn."

"That's barely enough time to arm the torpedoes," Hans said."

The diesel engines thrummed. The sub vibrated beneath Erich's feet. The hint of black smoke leaving the exhaust thickened. Water white with foam washed over the bow.

"Closing," Erich said. "400 meters."

"Look at that fat fish for the taking." Captain Schubert's voice growled with anticipation.

"I see men on the deck," Erich said. "They seem completely oblivious to— Sir, they're manning a deck gun!"

Schubert knelt to the hatch. "Fire both and dive as soon as we're clear!" The vessel shuddered twice as the torpedoes left their tubes.

Erich secured the hatch and focused on his watch while the captain did the same, "Anytime now … anytime now …"

Twin explosions resonated; the Captain pumped his fist. "Got him, and with both fish. Move in, navigator. I want a close look. Raise periscope."

Shimmering with oil, the periscope slid upward. The captain peered into the eyepiece, turned the periscope one way and then the other, and stopped. "There she is, a tanker all right. Looks like the pits of hell over there." He stepped away. "Take a look, Fischer."

Erich took the captain's position. Burning oil coated the water. The men, having little choice, jumped into the flames.

One man rose in the middle of the inferno, hair alight, arms flailing, and sank below the watery firestorm. Erich swallowed and stepped away. "Hans?"

Hans peered into the eyepiece. "Good God, what a way to die. I almost feel sorry for the poor devils."

"Hell of a thing to say." Schubert folded the periscope's handles up. "Imagine your loved ones burning from incendiaries falling on their homes. That oil was likely headed to a refinery for plane fuel, so that's one less bomb dropping on their doorsteps. Navigator, surface and set course southwest. I want to get a look at that other island I saw on the charts. Ocracoke, I believe. Quite the quaint name, eh?"

## Chapter 12

## A Goodbye and a Jeep Ride

Sitting on the pier with Walter, Virginia jumped to her feet. "Good Lord above, one of those damned U-boats has sunk another of our ships. That explosion sounded like thunder during a hurricane."

Walter stood also. "Don't say that, Ginny."

"Don't say what, damn? You don't like it when I say damn? I can tell you don't like it when I say" —she poked his chest— "damn. You think because I cuss now and then, it makes me less a lady?"

"Damn it, Ginny, I— Looka there, you got me doin' it."

"Look yonder," Virginia said, pointing. "See that orange glow in the east? Looks like it's beyond Hatteras. With all that fire, I bet they sunk a tanker."

"Bastards," Walter said. "I'll be glad when I get in the air and bomb those sons' a bitches."

Virginia snorted laughter. "Listen to you, Mr. High 'n Mighty, cussing like a sailor."

"I'm a man, I can do as I damn well please, damn it."

"Remember this, Mr. Evans—men started this damn war, not women." Virginia took his arm. "Now walk this cussing lady to her door."

At the porch, Walter kissed her cheek. "Try not to miss me too much while I'm gone." He patted his pants pocket. "This here ring's ready for your finger."

Virginia crossed her arms. "Really, Walter, a peck on the cheek is all I get?"

"Well, I don't want to make you think all I want you for is … you know."

"Sex?" Virginia placed her hand on his chest. "Go ahead and say it, it won't bite."

"Your lamps are still lit and Ruby might hear."

"How about this?" Virginia turned her ear toward him. "You can whisper it to me."

"Uh … uh …"

"You're so silly. Don't you know that's the sound you'll make when—perhaps—maybe—we have sex?"

"You're making this awful hard on me, Ginny."

"Should I grab it and check?"

Walter jumped back. "You wouldn't." The light from the window reflected in his wide-open eyes.

Virginia held in a giggle. "You better find an experienced British gal—maybe even a *fraulein*—and learn how to please a woman before you come back. Women have needs too, not just men." She grabbed his shirt and pulled him close. "And this is a start." She kissed him full on the lips, hard and firm, and stopped to see his reaction.

Walter touched his mouth. "Is it supposed to hurt like that?"

"How do I know? I've never been kissed." She held out her arms. "Now give me a proper hug goodbye." He hugged her, and she whispered in his ear, "You be safe, okay? You mean an awful lot to me."

He released her to smile hugely. "You're the bee's knees, Ginny Starr, you know that?"

"And you're the honey in the pot, Walter Evans. See you soon."

Walter's form faded up the dark path. Virginia went inside. Ruby lay across her bed, reading. "Jerry bought this book for me. Wasn't that nice of him?"

"It's probably a down payment on something he thinks he can get sooner than later."

"Sex? I heard you trying to get poor Walter to say that word. I bet he turned a hundred shades of red."

"'Poor Walter?' When have you ever referred to Walter as 'poor Walter?'"

"It isn't right for you to give him hope when you're enamored with Charlie."

Virginia sat on the bed. "Did you learn a fifty-cent word like 'enamored' from that book, or did Jerry offer fifty-cents for it? Let's hope it's worth more than that."

"More than ..." Ruby's blonde eyebrows twisted into a bowknot. "Why you dirty-minded thing, talking about my privates as if they were for sale on the auction block. I'd have you know, I'd not be bought for less than a dollar."

"You better be joking, Rube, because Jerry likely thinks all your good for is a roll in Jimmy's hay."

"He'll be sorely disappointed."

"Meaning?"

"He reminds me of a rat. Then he'll smile and be him again."

"You seeing him again?"

"He's coming by the restaurant tomorrow night. You did promise to let me work and take Jimmy out to find wood. Tomorrow morning's as good a time as any, since that ship exploded."

"It sounded like it was east of Hatteras. I doubt anything will float here. Even if it does, it'll take longer than one night."

"A promise is a promise." Ruby opened the book, blue eyes peeking over a page. "And you promised."

*If the Sunrise Forgets Tomorrow*

In the kitchen, Virginia drank a few swallows of lukewarm water from the dipper in the bucket by the basin. She'd have to keep her promise and trade chores with Ruby. The work would do her good, as would getting out and meeting people she hadn't seen since December. That Jerry, though, maybe he'd figure out it was a waste of time to chase Ruby and find some other woman to annoy, like one who might shoot his sorry self.

She creaked into the ladder-back chair by Mama's bed. "What do you think, Mama? Is Ruby headed for ruin with that awful man?"

Barely a bulge beneath the sheets, the chest raised, lowered, and raised as it had since she'd lost consciousness: steady and unrelenting, like the tide.

"You sure are a fighter, Mama, I'll give you that. Living out here in the middle of less than nothing must've given you that trait." Virginia chanced a grin. "That and raising two hellions like Ruby and me. It's a wonder we didn't drown in either the surf or the sound, get trampled by those wild ponies when we caught Jimmy, or fall from the lighthouse that time we snuck in behind the keeper and climbed to the top."

The stringy throat muscles worked with a swallow.

"It's hard, isn't it, Mama? Ruby and me will be fine if you want to be with Papa."

Virginia held the skeleton-thin fingers to her cheek. Over the years, time and time again, Mama had comforted her twins this way. Whether at birthdays, when flour for a cake couldn't be afforded because Papa hadn't caught any fish for the market, or at Christmas, when the stockings tacked to the wall over the wood stove held only an apple and the rare banana, she'd caress her and Ruby's cheeks, telling her "darling pair" not to worry. As long as they have each other, they have everything they need.

Virginia lay her head on the bed and placed the cool hand to her cheek. "It's true as forever, Mama. Except for each other, Ruby and me are almost out of family."

She jerked upright. A chill had passed over her. More than a few elderly O'cocker men described such a chill as a warning that a loved one would soon die. That was obvious with Mama, so why the chill? Was death stalking someone she cared about as much as Mama? The only person she cared about as much as Mama was Ruby.

Virginia returned her head to the cool sheets. She couldn't bear the thought of being alone on this island with no one to tease, aggravate, and enjoy the simple pleasure of scrambled eggs, while the sun rose over the twisted live oaks. She might as well be dead herself if Ruby passed from illness or accident.

She pinched her arm. Idiocy, pure idiocy. Ruby was young and spry and full of vinegar, which would keep her rattling around on Ocracoke to a ripe old age. Why the warning then? If not her twin, who?

Shaking her head, Virginia went to the kitchen. No light shone beneath Ruby's door. She was likely dreaming of finding the perfect man. Virginia brushed her teeth at the basin and stepped out on the porch.

Jimmy softly knickered. She fetched the flashlight and walked to his stall. At the gate he nuzzled her hand with velvety soft lips. "What's on your mind, ornery pony?" A scratch on his forehead. Wiggling ears. "Look at you, as long as you're fed and watered and taken for a trot now and then, you're as happy as an oyster in its bed."

Jimmy snorted.

"Don't think so, huh? Are there any special mares you miss from the herd?"

Huge brown eyes peered into hers. Long eyelashes fluttered.

"I can't read all that, Jimmy. I suppose it's not likely since I helped Papa geld you." One more scratch on his forehead.

Charlie's deep brown eyes had almost made her lose control that day on the path. Walter had been right about her kiss—hard and firm probably wasn't the way to do it. How much experience did Charlie have giving kisses and being kissed? She snapped her fingers. He said he loved oysters, and she knew exactly where to find them.

Flashlight tied to the bicycle basket, she hopped on. She might be able to catch Charlie before he went to bed. With no marsh rabbits to dodge, she pedaled hard through the soft sand, legs burning. Yellow light spilled from a window in the building where Charlie worked. Footsteps clomped following a knock. The squeaking door opened to reveal Jerry's black rat eyes.

"Well, well, well, if'n it ain't Ruby's sister. What can I do you for?"

"Is Charlie here?"

"He's patrollin' fer hooligans." Jerry hitched his pants. "Maybe I can help you out with whatever you might need."

Virginia bit her lower lip. Keep calm for Ruby's sake, but this trash would have a palm print upside his sneering face if he made the wrong move. She climbed onto the bike. "I'll look for him."

Jerry grabbed the handlebars. "Tell me somethin', I'll let you go. Why's Charlie takin' such an interest in you when he's married? The man grins like a mule eatin' briars whenever your name pops up."

"I hardly think what Charlie does is any of your affair, Mr. …"

Jerry offered his hand. "Artknot's the name, pretty little miss. I never thought to find two such beauties as you and Ruby on this oversized anthill."

Virginia ignored the hand. "Your compliments are wasted on me, Mr. Artknot. I see who and what you are behind those black eyes of yours."

"Miss Ruby don't seem to mind my eyes. Why, I bet I get a kiss the next time I see her."

"Where are you from?" Virginia squeezed the handlebars when she'd rather squeeze Artknot's scrawny neck.

"I hail from Richmond, Virginia. Finest city in the world. Culture out the wazoo."

"Does your culture tell you what a gelding is?"

"Is that some type of sea shell you sand folk dig a blob of goo out of and fry like old man Austin does? I'll be glad when our commissary opens. That wannabe cook of yours done gave me the runs twice this week."

"Thank you for sharing that, I'll make sure Ruby hears it first hand from me. A gelding's a horse that's been castrated." Virginia waited for a reaction to the word and its obvious intent but got a blank stare instead. "'Castrated' flew under your radar too, did it?"

Jerry crossed his arms. "Bein' a smart aleck ain't earnin' you no points."

"Let me educate you, Artknot. A gelding is an animal—usually a horse—that's been relieved of his family jewels." She held up two fingers and snipped them together as if they were a pair of scissors. "Get my meaning?"

"What of it?" Jerry hitched his pants again.

"It's this, Artknot—if you harm my sister in any way—my definition of harm, not yours—I'll fetch the scissors I snipped my pony's jewels off with and do the same to you. That's 'what of it.'"

Jerry took a step back. "To have a sister sweet as pie, you sure come off as a salty witch. I bet it's from breathin' all this salt air that rusts everything in sight."

*If the Sunrise Forgets Tomorrow*

Virginia curled her finger around an imaginary trigger. Good thing he'd said "witch," or buckshot would fly this night. "Ruby's all I have in this world. I'll not lose her to the likes of some man who'd as soon ruin her as look at her."

"You call it 'ruin,' I call it a romp you'd never forget. You been givin' Charlie a romp now and then? Come see old Jerry if'n he ain't gettin' the job done."

Despite teasing Walter about cursing, Virginia didn't care for it, but this was the perfect time to curse to make a point to this sorry excuse of a man. "I'd sooner eat horse shit, Artknot. I'll cut your damn balls off and bait my crab pots with 'em if you harm my sister."

"The day some woman does that to me is the day—"

A vehicle engine whined. Headlights rounded the corner. Charlie pulled the jeep to a stop and climbed out. "I thought that was you, Virginia. You're out mighty late."

Virginia cut her eyes toward Artknot. "I take my trash out late on occasion."

"I guess you heard the explosion earlier. Radio reports said a U-boat has torpedoed a tanker. I'd like to ride to the beach and see if the flames are visible. Want to come?"

"If you don't mind loading my bike into the back of your jeep."

She hopped off. As Charlie climbed from behind the wheel, Artknot hefted the bicycle into the jeep and stepped away to tip his hat. "Glad to be of service, Miss Starr. Be careful how you and Charlie fan any flames." The aroma of alcohol rode his breath.

Charlie cranked the engine. "Better snap that seatbelt. Last time I was out on the beach at night, a few ruts surprised me."

Within minutes they'd driven over a low dune to the beach. About halfway along the island, Charlie killed the engine. "Mind if we enjoy the stars, Miss Starr?

"You have something in mind, Mr. Smithson? That tanker's likely slipped beneath the waves by now."

Charlie glanced away, then faced her. "Am I that easy to read?"

"You're a man, not that you're all alike."

"I'm mysterious now, am I? I thought that trait belonged solely to the fairer sex?"

"I like straightforward myself. Take where we are for instance ... it's almost as romantic as when we parked beneath the live oak limbs over the path to my house. That give you any hints?"

A sly smile teased Charlie's lips, barely visible in the moon light. "Have you ever been kissed, Miss Starr? Maybe by your friend Walter?"

"I kissed him goodbye, jealous?"

"Look where I am and who I'm with. Did you enjoy that kiss?"

"My experience in such matters is extremely limited. How about you?"

"I dated a gal through high school. Asked her to marry me and she turned me down flat."

"Gracious me, you're that bad a kisser?"

Charlie slid close and cupped her cheek in his palm. "She was quite fickle. Married a fool with big lips."

Charlie's warm hand on Virginia's cheek sent even warmer sensations coursing through her body. They concentrated where feelings such as those she'd experienced on the path had concentrated, deep within her belly, but lower.

"I've never been properly kissed, Charlie. Are you an adept teacher?"

"Not with that gal. She tried to suck my toenails out by my tonsils. I doubt a kiss is supposed to be like that."

*If the Sunrise Forgets Tomorrow*

Virginia eased closer, until Charlie's breath warmed her mouth. "Just how are we supposed to know what a proper kiss is like, Mr. Smithson?"

He rubbed the tip of her nose with his, kissed her barely, feather-light and deliciously wet. Then, in stages of growing pressure and heat, he kissed her firmer, until their lips joined together as if they were made for each other.

Virginia pulled away. She wasn't ready for all the responsibilities that came with a sexual relationship, including babies. She fanned her face. "Oh, my, Charlie, I'd hate to find out what real sex is like. I might behave like a harlot."

He slid back over in his seat. "You're a smart gal, Virginia. I doubt I've ever wanted a woman more. I feel like a stallion my dad once had. When he was in one of those moods, he'd trot around his corral with everything hanging out like he was the grandest thing in the world."

"Despite such an interesting stallion, Mr. Smithson, I was out on my bike to ask you over for an oyster dinner tomorrow. I can fetch them after Ruby comes in from searching for wood in the morning."

"What a shame. I'm leaving in the morning for the Marine air base at Havelock. They're helping the Navy with security training for when more men arrive here, plus training in medical aid."

"How long will you be gone? The oysters can be your welcome back dinner."

"I'm not sure exactly. Shouldn't be more than a week."

"Well phooey on a flounder, Charlie, I'll miss you."

"I've not heard that one? As a dingbatter, will I learn more 'Ocracokisms' the longer I stay on your fair island?"

"Depends on how long you care to stay. I guess you intend to leave when the war's over."

Charlie raised his eyes to the stars for a moment. "How long have we known each other?"

"A few days, why?"

"And we're kissing already."

"Just one, want more?"

"Have you ever heard of anyone having serious feelings for another person after only a few days?"

"Old man Sanders—he used to play the banjo for the Saturday night dance when Ruby and me were girls—told Papa how he fell in love with the banjo the first time he heard one. Is it something like that?" Virginia placed a hand over her mouth to hide a grin.

Charlie pulled her hand down. "I see those mischievous eyes of yours, Miss Starr. You know what I mean."

"Surely you're not trying to tell me you're in love with this salty witch already."

"Is that something else Ruby calls you when she's pert?"

"Your buddy Jerry called me that when I turned down his less than gentlemanly advances."

"He was probably joking around. I think he does that because he's having a hard time dealing with the war."

"By chasing women?"

"I think he's trying to keep his mind occupied. Don't mention it, but he lost a brother at Pearl Harbor. His sister's fiancé died there too. Both were stationed on the *Arizona*."

"That gives him no right to—"

"He and his brother—he was younger—were extremely close. He almost had a breakdown when he heard the news. Imagine how'd you'd react if something happened to Ruby, or how Ruby would react if something happened to you. I trained in how stress affects people. It can make them do things you think they'd never do."

*If the Sunrise Forgets Tomorrow*

"As long as he treats Ruby decently, there's little I can say. Ready to take me home?"

"You forget what I said about having serious feelings?"

"Planning on buying a banjo while you're in Havelock?"

"I might get more honesty out of it."

"What is it you want me to be honest about?"

"Can I kiss you again? I'll tell you after." Charlie raised his palm toward her cheek, but she pushed it away.

"No, sir. Maybe when you drop me off at my door. Come on, out with it."

"What kind of feelings do you have for me other than sexual attraction? Don't deny it either, that kiss was perfect."

Virginia glanced at the stars, dredged up a huge sigh, and faced him. "I have a hard time thinking of the future. With this war and all—death at our very doorstep—who knows what will land on our shores next?"

"What if there was no war?"

"You mean marriage. I've got to learn to trust you beyond simply saying so. You might turn your back on me in a heartbeat if it came between me and a friend of yours."

"That's the silliest thing I ever heard, Virginia. Love is all the trust you need."

"Men do crazy things, Charlie. Look at this damn war, started by a fool like Hitler. Look at all his own people dying in the bombing of his country because he wants to be the king of the entire world, with us dancing around like puppets on a string at his every beck and call."

"You need to get your mind off that mess and get it back on me. Do you think we could be a match? If not, while I'm in Havelock, I'll give my old gal a call and see if she's tired of kissing old big lips what's-his-name yet."

"You must not like having toenails."

"That doesn't answer—"

"All right, doggone it, I'll admit it's possible to get serious about someone after so short a time." Virginia shoved his arm. "Satisfied?"

Charlie cranked the jeep. "Only after I get that kiss you promised me."

## Chapter 13

## The Insanity of Loss

Captain Schubert yelled below for the navigator to make an all stop. Erich raised the binoculars. "I see headlights, sir. I think it's a jeep driving along the beach."

"Huh. Even their military vehicles don't practice blackout protocol."

"A few bombs in the middle of the night would darken them up a bit, like in Bremen."

"They even have their lighthouse working," Schubert said. "Too bad it doesn't do much in the way of helping us spot ships. Is your wife from Bremen also?"

"Our parent's backyards border each other."

"You're lucky no bombs have fallen in the city. The British have certainly kept busy elsewhere. It's been almost two months since the RAF came anywhere near. Maybe they'll leave it alone for the duration of the war."

Schubert yawned. "I'll let the old girl submerge a couple of hours so we can get some rest. We'll surface at oh-four-hundred to be ready when the eastern sky begins to lighten at oh-six-hundred. Then, lookouts such as yourself can have time to let your eyes acclimate to the dark and have a better chance at spotting a ship's silhouette against the horizon."

"Yes, sir. We learned that in training."

"You'll forgive an old seaman for reminding you of the obvious."

"A reminder from experience is nothing to forgive, sir."

Schubert descended the ladder. Erich secured the hatch. The radio officer rose from his station, papers in hand. "Sir, we just received a message." His eyes darted toward Erich. "Two messages."

"Anything out of the ordinary?"

"The RAF hit Bremen last night. Along the shipyards again and ..."

"Go on."

The radio man handed Schubert a folded piece of paper. "I think it best you read this one, sir."

The captain unfolded the paper beneath a nearby light. His eyes tracked sentences. His temples pulsed. "Let's step into my quarters, Fischer."

"Sir, what ...?"

"I understand your father-in-law is an officer in the SS."

"He is, but—"

"No arguments." Schubert picked his way through the tight doorways, turning sideways when another crewmember passed. He flipped on a light, closed the door behind Erich, pulled a chair from the small desk. "Have a seat, Fischer. Drink?" He took a bottle of brown liquid and a shot glass from a desk drawer.

Erich remained standing. "Sir, has something happened to my father-in-law?"

Schubert filled the shot glass, downed it in one gulp, slammed the glass on his desk. "This damnable war." He slid a holster from his belt, which held a Luger 9mm pistol, and tossed it on his bunk.

Erich assumed his father-in-law must be dead or wounded. Since he and Thea weren't on the best of terms, it wouldn't bother him greatly if the man ceased to exist. "Just tell me, sir. I understand we sometimes lose family in war."

"Sure you won't have that drink?" Erich shook his head. Schubert unfolded the paper. "This is directly from your father-in-law. Do you want me to read it?"

"Whatever you think best."

Schubert filled the glass again. "Consider it an order."

Erich gulped the bitter, slightly caramel-flavored liquor. He winced as it burned his throat, to settle like fire in his stomach.

Schubert raised the paper.

*Dear Erich,*

*I realize you're aware of how Thea and I disagreed on the war, which included my zeal in prosecuting it by becoming an officer in the SS. However, that doesn't keep me from my duty of informing you of our loss.*

Erich's hands shook. He collapsed to the chair.

"As much as I hate it, Fischer, I need to finish."

*Last evening, RAF bombers dropped incendiaries in the center of the city. I knew of Thea and her mother's and of your parent's intent to find shelter in the country. I only wish I had helped them do so long before now. They were found in the road near your father's car. The suitcases in the trunk we're burned. Some held food, so apparently they were—"*

Erich heard no more. His stomach convulsed, threatening to heave the liquor from his belly. His vision faded in and out. He'd lost his darling Thea, the woman he loved more than life itself. All their dreams of a home and of children were lost. He jumped from the chair. If only he could run to the hatch and dive into the sea to wash the pain from his tortured mind. The captain's Luger—grab it and put a bullet through his brain to silence her screams he could imagine, which must've been the same as that man burning in the oil from the tanker.

"I'm sorry, Fischer. Losing everyone you love in one terrible moment is more than a man might bear. There's a bit more you should hear."

*Please know how sorry I am for not being more of a father to Thea, but also to you. I kept my feelings close, perhaps too close. More than anything I dreamt of bouncing my grandchildren on my knee one day.*

*In closing, I can't say where our journeys might end. Regardless of where, I wish you well. Thank you for giving Thea so much happiness in the short time you knew her.*

Schubert slipped the paper into Erich's limp fingers. "You have my sincerest condolences. Consider yourself off duty for twenty-four hours."

On legs weak and trembling, grasping at various pipes and valves—cold as the sea around him—Erich half-stumbled through the dimly lit passages toward his quarters. Each time a crewman passed, his stare bore into Erich's with pity. Word made the rounds all too quickly in these cramped vessels.

Inside the oval door to his quarters, relief that Hans, Werner, and Uwe were at their posts swept over Erich. He didn't care to cry in front of his bunkmates—his fragile psyche couldn't take it—nor could it take his imaginings of Thea, her mother, or his parents, screaming torches alight in the streets of Bremen.

He took the document bag from under his pillow. Thea's glorious smile met his filling eyes. How could he live without seeing that smile again? Without hearing her voice calling him "sweet boy?" Without feeling the warmth of her lips or the rise and fall of her body in rhythm with his as they made love?

The obvious answer was he couldn't. Schubert kept the Luger with him constantly. The rifles used for boarding ships were locked in storage. Pills? Locked away also. A knife to the throat? The crew ate canned facsimiles of meat, so their knives were dull. Beat his head against the metal skin of the boat? He'd pass out before dying.

Erich took Thea's letters from the document bag. He'd read two so far, and they mirrored her words—short and filled with her undying love. The second one mentioned how happy she was that they'd first kissed on the swing in her backyard: a reminder of the tentative touch of their inexperienced lips probing one another's with delightful experimentation.

Now, at the end of their love, he chose the eighth and final letter. Perfume rose from the envelope. She would scent behind her ears with the sweet aroma, drawing him there like a huge, yellow butterfly to a golden cornflower in his mother's garden. He loved to tease those perfect ears with gentle kisses, before moving to the sensitive areas along her neck and shoulders. He loved her small gasps of pleasure. He loved when she could no longer stand the tentative touch of his lips and pulled his mouth to hers in a hunger that had often surprised him. He loved—

A tear fell to the cream-colored paper. It spread like a thunderhead in a clear summer sky along the coast back home, where they had taken the pictures. Read this last letter and wait until the boat surfaced to end himself. He must be with her again. No other option existed.

*To my dear, sweet boy,*

*As I write this final letter, I realize you'll be back before I know it. No doubt you've performed your duty admirably while looking incredibly handsome in your uniform.*
*I write these letters while you're asleep. I watch your chest rise and fall, your lips purse and relax, and I'm overcome with how much it means to me to have had you walk to my backyard that day when we were eleven and offer to push me on my swing. Sometimes I believe I sense a slight cringe when I call you sweet boy, but you'll always be that blue-eyed boy with the mop of blond curls who smiled and peeked at me to ask, "Higher, Thea? How high would you like to go?"*
*My God, how I love you. You've taken me to heights I never knew existed, from passions heated embrace to quiet times, my hand in yours while we strolled the beach on the day we took the pictures.*

*Though I often recall those times with affection, I wonder, too much I'm sure, what this war might bring. You'll likely be safe beneath the seas, but I'm not so certain of my fate. It seems every farmer within a radius of twenty kilometers of Bremen has no shelter for his countrymen and women, only shelter for his cows and horses.*

*We've never spoken of this, but if one of us doesn't survive the insanity engulfing the world, the other must go on, if for no other reason than to show those around us, arrogant as that might sound, that a love such as ours exists so our kindred humanity may understand that true caring for each other, regardless of differences, is what can end such trying times.*

*I have to laugh. I'm not so naïve to believe that ideal when others are attempting to kill us. That's Hitler's fault, damn his soul to hell, not the good people of Germany's fault, nor the world's fault.*

*Will you live for me if the worst happens? Will you do your best to survive a world gone mad? Please try, if for no other reason than to carry me within your heart always.*

*Your love has no boundaries, my sweetheart. If you return to discover I'm no longer among the living, find someone with whom you may share that love. Life is too long to live it in sadness and remorse, pining away the endless nights with tears and mourning, is it not? I imagine your pursing lips as you read this, as well as hear your voice. "You want me to do what, Thea, my darling? How could you ever desire that I lie with another woman?"*

*The answer is simple, my sweet boy. You'd want the same for me if it were the other way around.*

*Oh, I can see those lips twisting. To the end of time you'd deny standing the thought of me in the arms of another. Then you'd think about it, concentrating with your brow furrowed until those wrinkles smoothed and you took my hand. "You're right, my darling," you'd say. "How could I ever wish a lifetime of sadness upon you if I were unable to return?"*

*There we have it. I've wanted to tell you that since you joined the Kriegsmarine, but I knew you'd ignore me. The written word allows us to meander over the meaning, without argument or derision, so read this as often as you need my assurance that I'll always love you, no matter what.*
*May you always treasure my hugs, kisses, and warm embraces, now and forever, as I will treasure yours.*

*With all my love, my sweet boy,*
*Thea*

Wiping tears, Erich placed the letter in the document bag and sealed it. The emotion he'd been fighting released with gulping sobs and shaking shoulders. To keep any man walking by the door from hearing him, he climbed into his bunk and buried his face into his pillow, bit a mouthful of the foul material, tasted his own sweat while muffling his cries.

Time passed in bitter, retching sobs. He rolled over and rubbed his eyes. How could he sleep with Thea gone? It must be tonight, before he surrendered to slee—

Thea had implored him to make the attempt to live. He could do that, at least.

Gathering the scattered envelopes, he returned them to the bag, facing Thea's smile outward. One last kiss to the cold material. One last look at the smile he loved so dear. He stuffed the bag inside his sweater, shoved the sweater into his pants, tightened his belt to hold it in. To keep from falling asleep, he stayed upright on the bunk. Within a span of seconds, he wavered like a drunkard walking the late-night streets of Bremen. How to stay awake until—

A note—he needed to write a note. He did so, folded it into a narrow sliver and, to tie it to the conning tower rail, removed a shoelace. Shoes were only necessary until he reached the conning tower. After that. ...

The note and lace in his pants pocket, he sat up straight again, then wavered as before. He slapped himself awake. His plan would fail if—

Hans climbed through the doorway. "You awake, Erich?"

"Somewhat."

"I don't have the words to tell you how sorry I am."

Erich flicked a tear away with his fingertips. "I may get out of the bowels of this dank grave of a vessel and breathe the fresh air on my next watch. Will you wake me?"

"You know I will." Han's clicked the light switch, bathing them in blessed darkness. The mattress sagged over Erich's head.

The boat shuddered with the gentle murmur of the electric engines. The voices of the men working nearby echoed softly, like ghosts whispering dread secrets from their graves.

⋆

"Erich, it's time."

Erich blinked to loosen the stickiness of dried tears from his eyelids. "I'm awake." He swallowed, throat aching with pain from his crying. "But I'd rather be dead."

"I know, my friend."

Erich sat up. "I see Uwe and Werner are asleep."

"They came in about thirty minutes ago. Are you hungry? Coffee?"

"Not at all."

Hans left the compartment. Erich followed.

At the periscope, the watch officer faced him. "The captain's asleep. Says you can skip watch."

"I'd rather not, sir."

*If the Sunrise Forgets Tomorrow*

Erich swung the hatch open. The salt air assaulted his nose with its dense, humid aroma. He placed his hands on the cold, damp rail. Still calm, the waves lapped against the side of the hull with shimmers of white froth that disappeared with the easy rise and fall of the U-boat. In the east, a thin line of ruddy red foretold of the coming day.

A day without Thea. A day without parents. If God's mercy managed to find him, a day he'd join them.

The island the captain had called Ocracoke still sat in the west, a distant white strand. Hans kept watch toward the east. Erich tied the note to the rail and cursed.

"What's wrong?" Hans said.

"I forgot my binoculars—they need cleaning too. I was thinking about Thea and feel too faint to climb down."

"What are bunkmates for?"

Erich placed his hand on Han's shoulder. "You're a good friend, Hans. Thank you for everything."

Hans dropped below the opening. Erich clambered onto the lower deck. His coat would drink water and sink him like a drunk drinks whiskey and sinks into a gutter. He threw it in, kicked his shoes behind it, dove into the waves. The cold took his breath. Surfacing to get a bearing, he swam toward the island that looked to be about a third of a kilometer away. As a teenager, he'd used the front crawl stroke in school competitions. Never this far and not with pants and a sweater pulling him down. Sunrise behind him, island to his front, no one in the tower should see him. With any hope, his aching arms and legs would soon tire, leaving him to be with Thea.

✯

Hans gave the eyepieces a quick wipe and climbed the ladder. "Feeling better, Erich?" He glanced around the conning tower perimeter, climbed to the lower deck for a quick scan of its surface, and rushed back up the ladder to yell down the hatch.

But didn't.

Tied to the rail, a piece of paper fluttered in the breeze. He clicked his flashlight and read.

*Hans,*
*No doubt you know why I've chosen to end my life. Tell the captain and crew I wish them well. May you all have loved ones at home when you return.*
*Erich*

Hans gave the waves a scan with the flashlight. A single shoe floated, probably holding air in the toe, and nothing more.

## Chapter 14

## Footprints

Pinkish orange beyond the twisted live oaks, the sun hinted of the coming day. Seated on the hard wagon seat—no jacket because of the warm morning—Ruby snapped the reins. "Get on up there, Jimbo pony. This working girl's gonna fetch us a treasure of firewood."

Bits of chain along the sides of the wagon rattled as she passed the house. No light shone from the windows.

"Better have some eggs scrambled when I get back, Virgil. You expect it of me and I expect it of you."

At the end of the path, where it entered the main road of packed sand that led from the village, she turned left. Jimmy trotted along until she steered him through a cut in the dune to the beach, somewhat difficult to find because of the shadowed slopes.

Humid wind off the Atlantic caressed her face. She might complain about living on this strip of desolate sand, but she never grew tired of the ocean's intimate touch. The foaming surf, gentle this morning, whispered along the shore. Gulls dived for their breakfast, squawking their dissatisfaction when one snatched another's minnow-sized morsel. A line of pelicans skimmed the water, barely flapping within an inch of the glassy surface. They wheeled upward and folded their wings, to dive like gray-feathered javelins through the gulls, which sent them into a squabbling and squawking tornado of ruffled white. The pelicans pierced the blue-green water with hardly a splash, surfaced with skin-basket beaks to gulp, and slowly heaved themselves skyward again, wide wings sweeping, glimmering droplets of sea water dripping.

Jimmy neared a flock of sanderlings, and Ruby pulled the reins. "Whoa, Jimbo. I love watching these critters."

With pencil-thin backward-kneed legs, the sanderlings—not much larger than a robin but taller and stouter, with white and brown feathers instead of dark and orange—scurried away from the waves and then raced back after them, probing the wet sand as if they were woodpeckers searching for whatever meal their narrow beaks might find. Ruby shaded her eyes from the brightening rays of the sun as it rose above the horizon. God had certainly created a glorious beginning for her first day of work.

A marsh fly lit on Jimmy's ear. He shook his head, rattling his bit and bridle. The sanderlings flurried down the beach to find peace in another section of shimmering sand.

Ruby snapped the leads. "Ornery pony, you ruined my show."

She spotted and loaded four pieces of driftwood—no pieces of ship blasted by German U-boats, thank goodness—and wiped sweat from her forehead. "This is hard work, Jimbo."

The waves died on the sand with foam and hiss. Sand flea shells, clumps of sea grass, and a dead jellyfish washed beneath Jimmy's hooves. Ruby jerked the reins. "What in the world?"

A set of shoeless footprints led from the wet sand but not to it, as if some idiot had taken a morning swim further down the beach and came out here. She shaded her eyes. The footprints continued to the dune. O'cocker or dingbatter, whoever left these footprints had no sense whatsoever.

*If the Sunrise Forgets Tomorrow*

Crouched behind a cluster of sea oats, Erich waited for the girl with the long blonde hair to pass. In a way, though he couldn't define it, she resembled Thea. Perhaps it was how she held her shoulders. Perhaps it was the set of her chin. No, nothing so readily identifiable, but beauty definitely found itself in this attractive young woman.

His swim had tired him, but not as much as he believed it would. Once he settled into the familiar swimming stroke, the muscle memory returned, and he paced himself until his bare feet touched sand, heart pounding within his chest as if it were one of the submarine's diesel engines at attack speed.

The girl continued along the beach, loaded more wood, wheeled the horse around, and returned his way. The chains on the wagon rattled by, and Erich crept dune to dune. With any luck she'd lead him to a hiding place.

The wagon rolled through an opening between the dunes and followed a road of some sort. He ran behind it, ducking between short, twisted trees, low branches similar to a scarecrow's outstretched arms. The rattling turned into a path between the trees. Keeping to the woods, Erich dodged the low limbs while trying not to step on whatever hazards this place might hide. Up ahead, not far from another body of water, the gray boards of a building caught his eye. Scrub brush, wiry looking stuff, grew around it. A vine snaked along one wall, spread into dried, blackened veins. Cracked windows. A partially open door.

He waited beside the building's corner. The jangle stopped just beyond another building, barely visible through a thick grove of those trees with their wildly reaching limbs. The girl's lithe form, wearing faded blue pants and an off-white shirt, went to a building, possibly her home.

This building's squeaking hinges, thick with rust, relented. The interior resembled a workshop of some kind. Wood planes, saws, and two mallets—one small, one large—hung on the wall to the right, over a workbench coated with dust. On the left wall, above a spiderwebbed window that faced the girl's home, four pegs held two oars that might propel a rowboat. Below the window, furled loosely, what must be a sail hung on two more pegs. Rags lay in a pile in a corner. In the other corner, a wooden box held a saw, an assortment of files, more planes, and a large and small square. A chest that resembled a pirate chest of old sat by the workbench, as if someone had used it for a seat.

Erich shoved the door closed. The chest held rusted nails and cans of varnish. The building must be a workshop for boats of some type. He loaded the chest with the tools from the wooden box and hefted it to block the door. Regardless of the building's unused state, someone might visit. If so, the chest may delay them enough to allow him to climb from another window that faced the body of water, where he could slip into the marsh, unnoticed.

Leg and arm muscles quivering from the exhausting swim, and from following the girl, Erich dropped into the rags in the corner, the only place for a decent rest. The rags smelled faintly of varnish, but he was too heartsick to care.

What future did he have here, with the enemy? Only time would tell.

*If the Sunrise Forgets Tomorrow*

## Chapter 15

## Warning Song

At the cookstove, Virginia opened the oven door and braved the heat to touch the rising biscuits. The wagon rattled to a stop at the front porch. She opened the door for Ruby. "Have any luck, Working Girl?"

Ruby hopped down. "Watch it. You know as well as I do how that term might be used otherwise."

"Such a grouch this fine morning." Virginia placed a plate of scrambled eggs on the table. "Biscuits are browning in the oven. Milk okay?"

"That's what I call service." Ruby sat. "Mr. Austin taught you something after all."

"Do I have to remind you how I don't get any eggs until I help gather the darn things?"

"What a whiny waitress." Ruby poked the eggs. "I could bounce these off your forehead." She forked eggs and pretended to fling them at Virginia, who set a plate of steaming biscuits and two glasses of milk on the table.

"You act like that at the restaurant tonight, you won't last the evening with Mr. Austin."

"When can I get a lesson in waitressing?"

"Such a short memory for such a pert sister." Virginia sat. "When you danced around your room with your book for a tray, you said there was nothing to it."

"I was vexing you." Ruby swallowed milk. "Don't you know by now when I'm vexing you? I'd think you know by now when I'm vex—"

"Hush and eat your eggs before they get cold from all your tongue flapping." Virginia handed her a napkin from the stack Mr. Austin included when he gave them food. "I might change my mind about the restaurant. That Jerry will come calling and I don't want him around you."

Ruby's cheeks puffed for the inevitable comeback. Virginia stood. "Don't say a word. I already ate and I'm going to feed Mama. What are you going to do after you unload— Did you find any wood? You didn't say when I asked."

"I found a treasure of wood. The wind's coming from the east and the flies are after Jimmy. I'll give him a rub with some of those rags Papa used to varnish the rowboat. Maybe the smell will keep them away."

Virginia took a spoon from a drawer and mixed milk and eggs. She splashed a bit on her shirt and cursed under her breath. With Charlie away—Walter too, even with his idiosyncrasies—the lively feeling she'd enjoyed had vanished like cattail fluff in a hard gale.

Ruby placed the empty dish and glass by the basin. "Much obliged, gal." She popped Virginia's bottom. "You'd have earned a tip had you leaned over and showed me yer boobs."

Virginia rubbed her stinging behind. "As we've discussed, Scarlett, I don't have enough to show." She dropped the spoon into the basin. "Don't you dare try that at the restaurant. One of those lonely sailors—maybe even that Jerry—might follow you home."

"Phooey on you. We'd have a kitchen full of handsome fellows if I had my way."

"Fellows I'd have to shoot, I'm sure." Virginia took the bowl of eggs and milk to Mama's bedside.

*If the Sunrise Forgets Tomorrow*

Ruby scowled at the gnarled logs of driftwood in the back of the wagon. Loading it had made her underarms sticky enough to sour a buzzard off a carcass.

At the shed, she unhitched Jimmy and led him to the cool shade of the live oaks in his corral. Ginny liked to unload and cut wood right away. Not today, Miss Bossy Pants. Jimmy deserved relief from the flies.

Leaning and ducking, Ruby watched for sandspurs on the way to Papa's workshop. Those pea-sized balls of hooked stickers could even pierce a leg through denim. As a girl she'd managed to imbed two in the sole of her bare foot, and the infection had taken a week to clear. A song came to mind, one Mama used to sing about how wives sometimes lost their men to the sea, and she sang:

*When the nor'easters wail, and the hurricanes blow,*
*When our brave men sail out to the sea,*
*When our hearts are all broke, and our tears are all shed,*
*We'll pray for their souls, we'll pray for their souls,*
*We'll pray for their souls, on old Ocracoke.*

She hummed the song as she jerked the door, then stopped when it wouldn't budge. Either she or Virginia should've kept the rusty hinges oiled. She jerked again, mumbling, "Papa and his double swinging door. It usually opens easier out than in." She grabbed the knob once more, placed her foot on the frame, and pulled until her elbows threatened to pop from their sockets. The door flew open and her behind thumped to the sand. She rolled over, stood to brush sand from her rear, turned around and goggled.

In the doorway, a young man with impossibly blue eyes and curly blonde hair offered his hand. "Good morning. I'm Erich."

## Chapter 16

## Merman

Erich woke from his nap in the rags. It took a moment to get his bearings as to where he lay: Not in his bunk beneath Hans. Not in his bed at his parent's home. Not with Thea, silky hair across his chest. He took the bag of letters from inside his sweater. Safe and dry, Thea smiled at him still.

In bare feet, he tentatively stepped around the interior of the building, dimly lit by what sun shone through the dirty, cracked windows. Dust motes floated in the yellow shaft of light. The musty smell of mold and decay permeated the dank air.

Partially covered with warped boards, an ancient chest of drawers sat against a wall beside the workbench. He moved the boards and opened a drawer to check for anything of use during his stay. Finding nothing, he cursed beneath his breath in German, then smacked his forehead because of it. Better start speaking English in case someone surprised him.

At the door, he slid the chest over, pulled the door in, and peeked outside. The sun hadn't risen much farther than when he'd fallen asleep.

Opening the chest of drawers again, he found more tools and rags. A metal container with a spout and a screw-on cap sat between the chest of drawers and the workbench. Cap off, he sniffed kerosene. No use without matches and a lantern. Those would allow light if he hung some of the rags over the windows to keep a passerby from noticing. Also, hunger would force him to search the marsh grass for some creature or other, but only if cooked properly.

What about drinking water? The girl and her home might have a well. He scrounged around the room again and found a small tin cup beneath the rags, which must've protected it from the ever-present salt air and subsequent rust.

Another glance around revealed a raincoat, dust-covered yellow, stuffed beneath the workbench. Worthless, as was almost everything else.

Lying in the rags again, he huffed a deep sigh. Wait until night to search for something to eat raw and get water from the well.

Clutching the bag of letters to his chest, he closed his eyes. Would Thea be pleased with what he'd done, abandoning his country, his home, his fami—

No, he had no family—his father, mother, and brother were dead—and so was his darling Thea.

He had his life, though, as she had wished. How long might he have that life, at least a free life? In a meeting aboard the sub, a day before arriving off this coast, Captain Schubert said the Americans were building a Naval base on this island. How long before they found him? How long might he last in a prisoner of war camp? With no information or experience about such things, he surrendered any attempt at an answer and rose to peer out a window. The charts described this expanse of calm water opposite the ocean as the Pamlico Sound. It likely held crabs or clams, maybe a fish or two he might catch with his bare hands.

What then? Live here like a hermit until he rotted from the inside out from disease, or from the outside in from the elements? With his language skills, as well as his writing skills, could he pass himself as an American claiming to be washed ashore from a fishing boat on the sound? Not likely—he spoke with too much of a British-German accent. Pass himself off as a British sailor washed ashore from a torpedoed ship? Not likely either—the first person he attempted to fool with that lie would take him straight to the Navy, who would investigate and debunk his claim.

What then?

He kissed Thea's smile, closed his eyes.

Perhaps she'd send an answer on a prayer from Heaven.

Perhaps.

Sleep took him with a dream of a girl singing a song about the sea. Her voice, light and high and full of youth, sounded so genuine, she might be right outside.

He jumped from the rags.

She *was* outside, now humming. The doorknob turned. No time to climb out the window. The door opened a crack and stopped. She was pulling the door instead of pushing. It must open both ways—how could he be so stupid? She pulled again and the door flew open. Losing her grip on the knob, she fell and rolled over to get up, facing the other way, then brushed sand from her behind. How to handle the situation? Mother always said to treat a lady with kindness and respect, and everything would work out.

The girl turned to enter the building, and he offered his hand. "Good morning, I'm Erich."

She jumped back. "Why ... why ..."

Erich lowered his hand. "I hope you don't mind me using your building for a short while."

"Using it for what exactly?" The girl looked him up and down. "Those footprints ... did you come out of the surf and walk to the dunes?" She waved the question away. "Turn around."

"Might I ask why?"

"I want to see your tail."

"My what?"

"Don't make me ask again. My sister says that's one of the things that makes me pert." She twirled a finger. "Please? I'll say please. Please?"

Erich turned until he faced the girl again.

Frowning, she placed her hands on her hips. "Well phooey and fiddlesticks, I'm disappointed. Still, I expect to be disappointed a time or two more in my young life."

Erich tilted his head to one side. Despite mother's admonition to be kind, joking sometimes helped when meeting someone for the first time. "Do I get to look at yours now?"

The girl twisted her lips to one side. "I'm not the one who came from the ocean like a merman. I was looking to see if you had a tail. My mama told me about merfolk when I was a girl."

"I've heard those stories." Erich offered his hand again. "May we meet properly?"

"How do I know you aren't after my virtue? Better yet, how do you know I'm not after yours? You're just a boy—an extremely pretty boy. Do you even shave yet?"

"Shake my hand and tell me your name, and I'll tell you."

"You've not done it right. Add your last name, Erich, we'll see."

Erich paused. Why not be honest about his name. After all, Fischer fit this island perfectly. "Fischer, Erich Fischer."

The girl pumped his hand once. "Ruby Starr's my name, Mr. Fischer." She pointed. "My sister and me live in that excuse for a house through that thick grove of live oaks. Her name's Virginia. When I'm feeling kindly toward her, I call her Ginny. When she acts a fool—meaning when she tries to tell me what to do—I call her Virgil."

"Thank you. I'll try to remember not to, as you say, 'act a fool.' If I did, though, what might you call me?"

Ruby placed a fingertip to her chin. "I'd have to think on it. I doubt you'd upset me enough to call you anything bad. I already said it once but it's worth saying again—Mr. Fischer, you're as pretty as a newborn Ocracoke colt."

"Erich, please. May I call you Ruby?"

"You might if we can sit. Then, since you're not a merman, and then, since you seem to speak with a touch of the O'cocker brogue, you can tell me how you came to our island."

## Chapter 17

## Apology

In the kitchen, Virginia dumped the leftover eggs in the trash and slammed the lid. Mama had eaten only one mouthful, and that by prying her clamped teeth open with the spoon. It was as if she wanted to die. Virginia closed her eyes to calm herself. She still had to scrub the same foul-smelling mess from the bed.

The skeletal bottom clean again, she washed the soiled pieces of sheet. A jeep's downshifted transmission whined from the path, followed by the squeal of brakes. Might Charlie have returned already? At the screen door, she latched the hook as Jerry Artknot climbed from the jeep.

"Ruby's not here, Artknot." Virginia pulled the wooden door aside to verify the shotgun in the corner. One wrong move, she'd blow a hole in him big enough for a whale to swim through.

Artknot removed his cap and clutched it to his chest. "I took a chance comin' out here. Should've waited until I saw you 'round town, I s'pose."

"Meaning?"

"It's awful hard to apologize while lookin' through that screen, Miss Starr. I'll stay right here by the jeep if you'll come out on the porch. B'lieve me, ma'am, I'm no threat, no threat at tall."

"Just a minute." Virginia hurried to the drawer and slipped a butcher knife in the back of her denims. On the porch she leaned against the post by the steps, hand on the knife handle. "What is it?"

"I'm sorry about what I said when you came looking for Charlie. I brought a few bottles of bourbon with me and ... well, I don't normally talk like that to women."

"I've seen drunk and you weren't drunk. I did smell it on you."

"I won't so drunk I'd stumble or slur. I was drunk enough to not hold my tongue. I get mad, Miss Starr. Mad enough to need somethin' to cut the edge."

Virginia supposed Artknot meant how he got mad because of losing his brother, and his sister losing her fiancé. Made sense—men got mad for less—which led to alcoholism. Few men were honest about their weaknesses, but the drinking might be a problem.

"Drinking or not, Artknot, you said more than your share of vile words to me that night. How do I know I can trust you not to say them again? Or—more vital—to not drink around Ruby? I might consider letting her be in the same room with you at the restaurant, or ride with you in the jeep in broad daylight. Only if she came home when I say, though." She released the knife handle. "I don't know if she mentioned our mama's illness, but Ruby's all I have. I'll not let just anyone take her from me."

"Seems ..." Artknot blinked, sniffled, and rubbed at the corner of one eye. "Seems we have that in common."

Was the man crying? Virginia waited. He cleared his throat.

"I lost two people to this damn war already. I mean, we're hardly in it, and my brother and the boy my sister was gonna marry both die on the same ship in Pearl Harbor. It's been hard on my folks too, me bein' their last boy. What I want is to kill Germans, damn 'em all to hell. They started this war and they need to pay for it with their own blood."

Artknot's nostrils flared as he spoke, hands shaking at his sides. No wonder he'd turned to alcohol, as he said, to 'cut the edge' off his anger.

"I'm sorry for your loss," Virginia said. "I'd feel the same in your place, but I still don't want alcohol around Ruby."

"I appreciate you hearin' me out." Artknot's thin lips attempted a thinner smile. "I understand why Ruby means so much to you. She's as sassy a gal as I've ever met. Makes me smile with all her cuttin' up."

"Ignore that pert tongue of hers. She'll use it on you like a butcher knife if she's a mind to."

"No worries, ma'am." In the jeep, Artknot looked over his shoulder. "Better turn around, huh?"

"Afraid so. Don't let one of those live oak limbs take your head off." Virginia shook her head as the jeep whined into the path. Artknot apologizing. Imagine that.

In Mama's bedroom, she creaked into the ladderback chair. "How about that, Mama? Surprises still happen on this salt and sand ridden island." The usual ashen pallor had changed to light pink. Virginia touched the forehead. Normally cool, it warmed Virginia's palm. "Look at you, perking up and getting color in your cheeks. I'll fetch Ruby so she can see."

On the porch, she aimed her cupped hands toward the corral. "Ru-by!" She turned toward Papa's workshop. "Ru-by!" Nothing but the ever-present rustle of the breeze through the live oak leaves and the *lap-lap-lap* of the sound against the pier pilings answered her.

Virginia weaved through the live oaks, dodging and ducking branches on her way to the workshop. What in the world was that girl up to now?

## Chapter 18

## Introductions

Erich waited as Ruby took the tattered raincoat from beneath the workbench and pulled out a couple of rickety stools.

"Rest yer fanny," she said, patting one. "I'm thinking this story might take a while."

He sat, raised the stool to slide away a bit, and she slid closer. "No, sir, I want to watch those blue eyes up close. I can always tell if a man's lying by his eyes."

"I may resemble a boy, but you can't be much more than a girl. Young girls might tell a tale now and then too."

"Twistygibbet. Why be bored to death by someone who tells the truth all the time?" Erich started to answer, but she patted his hand to stop him. "Forget all that and tell me your story. Does it include a special someone from home, wherever that might be?"

Erich's answer caught in his throat as if it were a fishhook. He'd been so consumed with planning his survival on this island, as well as evading capture by the Navy, the pain of losing Thea had temporarily left him. Tears stung his eyes. No matter how many times he swallowed, he couldn't fight the agony of losing the love of his life. He covered his face, hiding his sobs, and Ruby slid an arm around his shoulders. "Why, you poor, sweet boy. I suppose you're missing that special someone I mentioned so callously. Go ahead and have a cry if need be."

A few shuddering sobs later, Erich wiped his face and nose on the sleeve of his sweater. "I apologize for letting myself go like that."

Ruby slid closer. Impossibly long lashes. Eyes bluer than any sky he'd ever seen. Flecks of gold around the center that matched the hair curling around her cheeks. "I wish—" He cleared his throat. "I wish missing someone was all it is. I'm from Britain. I lost my wife and family in a bombing."

Ruby pulled her arm away. "That's— Oh, my God, that's so terrible. Why are you here? Did the Germans sink your ship? They sunk— No, you couldn't have washed all the way here from Hatteras. I doubt British sailors manned that tanker either."

"I wasn't on that—" Erich bit off the comment. To say "I wasn't on that tanker" would give a familiarity between it and him that would create more questions than he could answer. "I was on patrol boat. We were heading toward a ship that sent an SOS. I don't know what kind."

Ruby pursed her lips into a perfect red bow. "You're not explaining much. Can you do better? *Explain* better? How exactly—and why—are you here?"

"I'd just heard about my wife and family before we left port. My captain said I could stay behind, but— Well, I thought going out might take my mind off everything. I'm here, so that might tell you what happened."

The red bow twisted to one side. "I don't—" The bow formed an O. "You were trying to drown yourself?"

"I had nothing to live for."

"That's so sad. Don't you think your wife would want you to go on, like you'd want her to go on if you died instead?"

"That's why I'm here. Before I jumped from the ship, I read her last letter. She said if either one of us died, the other should live on." Erich sighed. "Or at least make the attempt. My

*If the Sunrise Forgets Tomorrow*

attempt brought me to your island. Your Navy has a base here. Do I have to tell you what would happen if they returned me to my ship as a deserter?"

"You weren't deserting, you were—" Ruby closed her eyes and gave her head a quick shake. "Sometimes I'm slow. I suppose jumping off a perfectly good ship would be questioned."

"Especially since I swam here. The strange thing is, had I committed suicide, I'd have been forgiven, in an ironic sort of way. Instead, I made it here when they think I drowned."

"So, you'd like to hide in my papa's workshop. How long?"

"As long as you'll have me." Erich smiled the slightest of smiles. Ruby's manner—as well as her innocent, childlike curiosity—grew on a person. Even to the point of unintended sexual innuendo. "As long as you'll *allow* me, I should say. Does your family ever come out here?"

"Papa would if he were still alive. Mama's in a coma from the influenza, so the doctor says."

"I'm surprised you have a doctor on this tiny island."

"We don't."

"But you said—"

"He's not a real doctor. Rumor has it he was going to school for it when his wife died. Rumor also has it that he took to drink and came here to sober up. He liked Ocracoke so much, he stayed."

"Will your sister come over?"

"Ginny won't come unless she's feeling lonesome for Papa. That happened a lot right after he died. Not for a good while now. Maybe a year or more."

"You have two sisters?"

"I told you, Virginia's Ginny and Ginny's Virginia. They're one in the same unless we're fussing." Ruby stood. "Are you hungry or thirsty? I'd bring something, but Ginny keeps an eye on me worse than Papa and Mama ever did." She stepped to the door. "I'm not sure when I'll—"

"Ru-by!"

Erich jumped from the stool. "Don't forget our secret."

"I won't. Ginny's a stickler for proper, and you being here would make her get our shotgun out."

⭐

Ruby peeked out the door. Through the tangle of twisted live oak limbs, Ginny's dark hair appeared. "Oh, applesauce, I better scoot. See you later, pretty merman." She closed the door and rushed through the oaks, hitting her head on a low branch as she neared Ginny, who had walked partway and now waited with her hands on her hips.

"Where's the rags? That's what you went for."

Ruby rubbed her smarting forehead. "See what you made me do? Yelling and making me forget the rags and bumping my poor head too? What're you caterwauling about?"

"It's Mama. Her complexion's pinker than normal."

Ginny turned to leave. Ruby grabbed her arm. "Ginny, we need to talk."

"Don't you want to see Mama?"

Ruby sat on a particularly low limb and patted the rough bark beside her. "Sit."

"For what? I—"

"For one, the fact that I rarely speak with you about serious subjects."

Ginny plopped to the limb, shaking Ruby. "I suppose you're right. Surviving day to day takes up so much of our time, along with taking care of Mama. What's on your mind?"

"Mama, of course. Mostly you believing she's going to come back to us. That's not going to happen. You clinging to that

*If the Sunrise Forgets Tomorrow*

hope is going to let you down worse than when Papa drowned."

Anger flashed in Ginny's dark eyes, which softened. "Leave it to Miss Scarlett to remind me of the stark realities of life and death on Ocracoke."

Ruby slipped her arm around her sister's shoulders. "That's me, the burden of truth. I like to think I keep things lively between us instead."

"You have a tendency for overstatement on occasion." A low chuckle raised Ginny's shoulders. "That wasn't one of them. I'd still like you to see Mama. I was wondering too, if you'd like to try your hand at the restaurant tonight? I'll ride to the village and sort it out with Mr. Austin right now."

Ruby hesitated. She wanted to take Erich whatever food she could scrounge and spend more time with him. She could do that if Ginny went to the village, but her time with him would be limited if she worked tonight. Another question popped into her mind. "Why the change of heart about me working?"

"I suppose you didn't hear the jeep. Your Mr. Artknot paid me a visit."

"I don't know any Artknot. What a peculiar name, sounds like 'ought not.'" Ruby giggled. "That's a good name for you. All I hear around here is what I 'ought not' do."

Ginny elbowed Ruby's ribs. "Hush up your cackling. Jerry's last name is Artknot."

"What'd he want?"

"Got sand in yer ears? I told you, he paid *me* a visit."

"Why? It's me he likes. Besides, Charlie likes you."

"Last night, when you were asleep, I rode my bike to the village to invite Charlie to supper. He was leaving early today to train for the week in Havelock. I—"

"What's that got to do with Jerry?"

"Stop interrupting, I'm trying to tell you."

"You drag things out too much. Did I ever tell you how you drag things out too much? You drag things out too—"

"Shut yer yap. Charlie wasn't there. Artknot came out and we had words. I smelled liquor on his breath, so maybe that's why. Anyway, he came to apologize."

"You're not throwing a fit. Did you accept?"

"Possibly he's not the bad sort I thought he was. Not completely. A man who drinks enough to make untoward comments to a woman is a man to be wary of."

"I suppose you're right. A drunkard might do anything, like show up unannounced to do who knows what."

"I told him you could see him during the day. A man's likely to drink at night, when folks can't see his weakness."

Ruby stood. "Maybe I can change his ways."

"He'll be leaving when the war's done. Besides, a man who needs changing isn't worth the salt it takes to season his beans."

"Charlie will leave too. That particular grain of sand cross your mind?"

"I'm not worried about that. What will be will be."

"But it's all right to use that as an argument against Jerry. My sister, the hypocrite."

"I know me, that's all. And I know you too. You'll let your emotions take you places that might get you in trouble." Ginny patted her stomach. "Know what I mean?"

Ruby stood from the limb. "I ought to piss in your eggs, calling me a whore." Ruby whirled to start toward the house but whirled back around. "After eighteen years together, don't you know me better than that? I wouldn't do that with a man unless I loved him."

"I wouldn't do that with a man unless I married him. Quite the difference."

"Quite the difference such as what? How wet yer drawers get because he made a bunch of promises at the altar that he might break anyway?"

"The vows are right when the man is right. It's a commitment, plain and simple. That doesn't let the woman off the hook either. Doesn't that make sense rather than spreading your legs because of compliments and trinkets? Love has to be more than that—damned if I'll give myself over to less."

Ginny, always the intelligent and thoughtful Ginny. What woman wouldn't want what Ginny described? "Believe it or not, I understand." Ruby shoved her twin's shoulder. "I'm tired of fussing. Let's look at Mama and see why you're so excited."

At the bedside, Ruby sat while Ginny touched the pink forehead. "She's warming up." She touched her own forehead. "Feels close to mine."

Ruby nodded. "Her cheeks are nice and pink, like when Papa teased her about how pretty she was in those threadbare cotton shifts. I always liked how they laughed *with* each other instead of *at* each other. No matter how hard times were, they always managed to fill this rough old house with love."

Ginny touched the bony fingers. "Those memories are what gives me my attitude about men and marriage. It doesn't take much of a man to wet a woman's drawers—make him rise in his pants either—but it takes a lot from both the man and the woman to make a lifetime of happiness. I just wish they could've had that lifetime instead of a piece of one."

Ruby slid a stray lock of hair behind Mama's ear. "I'm happy she's looking rosy. Sad to say, it won't change her outcome." She stood. "Isn't that right?"

"Yes, Miss Reality." Ginny shook her head. "I can't believe I called you, of all people, that. Are you getting the rags for Jimmy or not?"

"That pony needs pity." In the kitchen, Ruby took a biscuit from the icebox and added eggs from another bowl.

"Didn't you get enough breakfast?" Ginny said, eyeing her.

"Would I be getting this biscuit if I did?" Ruby closed the icebox door. "What will Mr. Austin have on the menu tonight? I'd like to know what's on *our* menu."

"Anything from seafood to pork to potatoes. If someone's old cow gets past her milking prime, he sometimes butchers it for a share."

"When did he ever have pork or beef? I don't remember that."

"Where do you think our bacon comes from?"

"I'm wanting a pork chop or three. Maybe a slice of ham. Whatever he'll offer I'll take." Ruby licked her lips. "A steak would be scrumptious."

"He offered pork liver one night. I didn't think you'd stomach that."

"With gravy? With enough gravy I could eat the oink."

Ginny laughed. "I suppose we *both* could eat the oink. Maybe you'll get lucky tonight. Go on, take care of Jimmy before the flies eat his whinny."

At the workshop, Ruby knocked. "I hope mermen like egg biscuits."

Erich pulled the door open, the rusty hinges much quieter. "This one does." He took a bite.

Ruby studied the hinges. "How'd they get so quiet?"

"I found a squirt can of oil behind the varnish cans on the workbench. Thank you for the food. My stomach couldn't have been emptier."

"I'm sorry I didn't bring water. Ginny might have gotten suspicious and— Ugh, I could have sneaked a cup for water at the well."

## If the Sunrise Forgets Tomorrow

Erich swallowed another bite. "I found a can I can use. I'll get water after she's asleep."

"You'll need some light out here." Ruby knelt for a lantern, hidden beneath the workbench. She tipped several of the tin cans on the workbench until a box of matches fell out. "I thought Papa kept some matches out here for his pipe." She set both on the workbench. "Be careful with the lantern. Ginny's as sharp-eyed as any gull ever hatched."

"I'll wait until late. The well is where?"

Ruby eyed him again. "That's funny, most people say 'where's the well.' It's left of the house. We used to have a cistern, but Papa got tired of hurricanes flooding it with salt water. Took five years to save the money to get the well drilled."

"Perhaps I'll see you through your window when I go for water."

"I'm working at a restaurant in the village later. I hope to bring some food home. Is there anything you don't like to eat?"

"Anything is fine."

"Maybe I can sneak out when I get back, when Ginny's asleep. If not, wait a while after the lights go out to get the water."

"Is she a light sleeper?"

"Just be as quiet as you can. I'd hate for her to get our shotgun after you."

"I'd hate that too." Erich finished the biscuit. "I'm sure you have things to do."

Ruby started to gather the rags but picked up a bag instead. "I don't remember this being here." Inside the material, clear like a window, a woman in a picture smiled back. "Is this your Thea?" She gave Erich the bag.

"She gave me that before I left."

"She's beautiful. Are those envelopes her letters?"

"One for each week of my patrol length. Eight in all."

"I'm sorry you lost everyone you love." Ruby grabbed a handful of rags. "Maybe you'll find someone else to love." Erich's blue eyes blinked, likely in an attempt to understand the meaning of her simple statement, but she'd withheld what she'd wanted to say, that perhaps the someone he might find to love could be on this very island.

## Chapter 19

## Realizations of a Working Girl

Done with rubbing Jimmy with the rags that smelled somewhat sweetly of old varnish, Ruby spent the rest of the day with various chores. Regardless of the task, whether raising Mama's spindly limbs while Ginny changed the bedding, sewing tomato, potato, or summer squash seeds in their meager garden spot, or sweeping the sand that seemed to birth itself constantly from the wide plank floors on the porch, she glanced through the live oaks at Papa's workshop whenever the opportunity arose.

Erich's presence drew her. His blue eyes drew her. His slight smile drew her. His blond curls drew her. More vital—more genuine rather—than those physical qualities, his kind manner drew her, including the pain he'd exhibited while weeping over his dead wife. A man who sincerely loved—a man who considered ending himself because of losing the love of his life—might be worthy of devotion.

Jerry hadn't been that man from the moment Ruby had met him, and neither had any of the boys she'd gone to school or Sunday school with. Feelings ran contrary to survival for most O'cockers. Nature, the environment, hurricanes, nor'easters—they all conspired against love. In romance novels, love took nature by the tail and twisted it. In romance novels, love won, even over death. All these instances meant love's depths, trials, and triumphs might be for the taking whenever Ruby envisioned Erich's blue eyes.

In the early afternoon, while Ginny read one of her Poe novels at the end of the pier, Ruby made a bundle of a pair of Papa's denim pants, one of his work shirts, several pair of his underwear that she and Ginny refused to wear, and socks, all for Erich after she worked at the restaurant. The sandy sweater sagged around his waist. The pants, salt stained and sandy, must chafe terribly. She didn't want him going out at night for water without shoes either—sandspurs hurt like hades. She hid the bundle and a pair of Papa's scuffed leather shoes under her bed.

With her hair pinned back at her temples, she washed at the basin, dressed in her best pants, shirt, and shoes, and sat at Mama's bedside until time to leave for the restaurant. The pink complexion bordered on flushed. Ruby palmed Mama's forehead. A fever? Maybe she was too warm beneath both a light blanket and a sheet. Ruby pulled the blanket back. Beneath the sheet, the toes curled and uncurled. The fingernails scraped the bed. She gently lifted the paper-thin eyelids.

"Are you trying to tell me something, Mama?"

Not a blink. Not a nod. Ruby lowered the eyelids. "It's all right to go, Mama. Papa will tease you by raising your dress to look at your legs. You'll smile and slap his hand away like you always did. At night you'll make love. You never knew I could hear you talking after, telling each other how you both wanted the world for Ginny and me. I'm certain you meant happiness—the world's not much without happiness." Ruby rubbed the bony hand. "It's possible I might have found happiness. Would you believe in a merman, of all things? He's capable of deep love, and I wonder if he might love me like he did his Thea one day. I won't rush it, that runs some people away. I'll try to comfort him if I can slip out to Papa's workshop in the night and visit. His name is Erich. I believe you and Papa would like him. Ginny too, if things ever square so she can meet—"

The screen door squeaked. "Ruby, you ready to—" Ginny stuck her head in the bedroom. "How's she doing?"

"Pinker. What that means, I have no idea. Warmer too, I believe. Might that mean she has an infection?"

"We'll see how she is in the morning." Ginny touched the forehead. "I might ride to the village and ask Doc Wills to come."

"Do you want me to stay home and not go to the restaurant? Between reading and supper, you didn't leave to ask Mr. Austin about me working there."

"He knows you. Besides, all he wants is someone to serve the customers and help clean up at closing. Truth be told, I think he cooks too much so he can give us the leftovers. Go on ahead."

"That's awful nice of him." Ruby left for the kitchen, and Ginny followed.

She took the flashlight and the length of leather boot lace from a drawer. "Don't forget to tie this to the basket of your bike for the ride along our path. Some nights I'd swear something was about to reach out and grab me."

On the way to the shed for the bike, Ruby fought the urge to look through the trees at the workshop in case Ginny was watching. She tied the flashlight to the basket and rode up the path, weaving in and out of those grabby live oak limbs.

Near the village, she glimpsed the top of the lighthouse. Completed in 1823, the stubby structure, white as a ghost within the trees, had offered its light to sailors for almost as long as any other lighthouse on the east coast, so Papa had said.

At the restaurant, Mr. Austin turned when she entered the back. "Why Ruby Starr, I haven't seen you in a seahorse's age. Is Ginny sick?"

"I'd like to try waitressing. Ginny said I could."

Plucking a chicken, Austin dropped a handful of feathers in a trash can. "Think you can handle them Navy dingbatters? I don't get many. Still, with the likes of your sweet face lightin' up my dinin' room, they might ask you out on a date or five."

At a knife rack hanging from a wall, Ruby took one out and thumbed the edge. "This will do for those frisky dingbatters." She slipped the knife inside her pants, at the hollow of her back.

"You put that back," Austin said, pointing at the rack. "If your tongue's as sharp as Ginny's, you'll cut 'em worse with that."

Ruby did as he asked. "Us Starrs are known for sharp tongues, but we do keep a knife handy when the need arises." She took an apron from a hanger beside the knife rack and held it to her chest. "Is this for me?"

Austin's moustache twitched upward. "I think me an' you is gonna get along like onions an' taters. Menus in the window, holler when you get an order. Do you know how to make lemonade? You can do that while I get this old hen plucked and fried. She's been wobblin' 'round a day or two and finally capsized this mornin'. I don't suppose she'll make any of them dingbatters sick."

"As long as they throw her up outside. Where's the makings for the lemonade?"

Austin waved a feathered finger toward a refrigerator. "Lemons and ice in there, water from the spigot. Ginny squeezed them lemons twice already. They probably got some juice left yet."

Ruby opened the refrigerator. "I'd love to have one of these instead of an icebox. It'd save hitching Jimmy to lug ice home in the wagon."

"Yup, no power down your way."

"We couldn't afford it if it was."

Austin plopped the plucked bird in the sink. Feathers drifted to the floor from his fingers. "I hated how your Papa drowned, fine man that he was. It's hard enough scroungin' a livin' off the

*If the Sunrise Forgets Tomorrow*

bones of this sandy isle with a full family, let alone with only you two gals makin' do the best you can. How's your mama gettin' along?"

"The same. Ginny and me appreciate what you do for us."

"Why, young gal, if you're talking 'bout me having leftovers and Ginny takin' 'em home, I can't help it if them dingbatters don't know good cookin' when they taste it." At the sink, Austin rinsed his feathery hands. "Go on 'n get that lemonade ready so's them Navy boys have somethin' to wash this tough old bird down."

Ruby made lemonade while Austin sliced the chicken into pieces quicker than Papa could bone a flounder. The front door didn't budge. No jeep engines whined. The peck of hammers gradually stopped as construction workers building the Navy barracks ended their day. She licked her lips at the aroma of fried chicken sizzling in hot grease. Wobbly or not, a few pieces of that bird would be finer than fine at home. Austin plopped several potatoes in water to boil. Mashed and buttered, salt and peppered, what a treat to go along with the chicken.

Austin placed the steaming chicken and potatoes in platters and removed his apron. "Care to sample that bird? Looks like no one's hungry."

"Unless you plan to take it all home, I'll let Ginny get the first bite."

"Go ahead if you want. I was only pullin' your leg about that hen wobblin'. She run me ragged chasin' her 'round the coop."

The brown crust tempted Ruby to choose a drumstick. "Goodness gracious me, this is going to be a treat beyond all—"

The dining room door squawked like an injured gull, and in strutted Jerry. Ruby dropped the drumstick to the platter. "We got a live one, Mr. Austin."

"I seen that fella 'round. Care to slip that knife in yer pants again? I don't much like his beady eyes."

"I can handle this dingbatter." Ruby stepped to the order window. "Hey there, sailor. How's yer appetite?"

Jerry strode to the window. "Look at you all aproned up. Is that fried chicken I smell?"

"Boiled potatoes on the side, lemonade to flush it all down."

"Bring me out a plate then, sweet thang. I'll be at the table by the window."

Ruby plated the chicken, potatoes, and poured lemonade. "I'll grab that drumstick, Mr. Austin. That dingbatter needs company."

"Keep an eye on his hands. One of the other girls said he pinched her worse 'n a blue crab."

"He'll get pinched back if he does." Ruby added a drumstick and sat at Jerry's table. "Here you go." She snatched the drumstick. "Mind if I join you? All the other customers won't mind."

"Damned loud bunch too." Jerry salt and peppered his food, sliced a potato, and took a bite. "Not bad," he said, still chewing.

Ruby grabbed a slice. "It's hard to mommuck a potato with butter."

"Danged if you island folk cain't come up with some of the tongue-twistin'est words I ever heard." Jerry drank lemonade. "How about I butter you up by asking you to the matinee at the movie house?"

Ruby swallowed potato. "What kind of movie is a matinee? My favorite stars are Vivien Leigh and Clark Gable. I'll go if they're in it."

"I was hopin' for a shoot 'em up."

"With this war, I'd think you had enough shooting."

"I meant a western."

*If the Sunrise Forgets Tomorrow*

"There's a western by the name of matinee? That's a strange name for a—"

"You ever seen a movie?" About to take a bite of chicken, Jerry stopped. "A matinee is a movie that plays in the afternoon."

"What day?"

"Every day but Sunday, I expect."

"Sounds like you haven't seen a movie either."

"Seen my share. Not here, but— Wait a minute, how do you know who was in *Gone with the Wind* if you haven't seen the movie?" He dropped the chicken to the plate. "Might as well give up on this bird until I get you straightened out."

"I read the book and read about the movie in the paper. As far as straightening me out, you can forget that."

Jerry picked up the chicken. "I'm beginning to think you're right." He took a bite, chewed, and pulled something from his mouth. "Looks like that old fool in back is tryin' to feed us Navy fellers feathers."

"Watch yer mouth. Mr. Austin's good to Ginny and me."

"Would you eat feathers? I don't plan to eat feathers. Feathers in your gut's libel to do things they ought not do." Ruby covered her mouth and giggled at Artknot's and 'ought not's' similarity. Artknot clattered a fork to the plate. "What's so dadburned funny?"

Ruby lowered her hand. "Nothing. Not a thing. Want to trade yer feathers for more potatoes?"

Artknot picked up the fork. "Let's meet at the movie house tomorrow around— That's right, I don't know what time the matinee starts. I'll check and pick you up."

"How will I know when to be ready?"

"All you ever wear is faded denims and a ragged shirt."

Ruby jumped from the chair, which tipped over backwards and slammed to the floor. "I just lost all interest in a movie. *And* you."

She spun toward the back, and Artknot said, "What's got your drawers in a female knot?"

Ruby spun back around, fighting tears. Damned if she'd let him make her cry. "I can't help that my papa's dead and my mama's dying." She paused to get her quivering chin under control. "I can't help being poor either, damn you. Ginny and me do the best we can with what we have." She started to the kitchen, stopped, and whirled again. "You *are* a rat! A *beady-eyed* rat!"

She burst into the kitchen. Austin bellowed laughter while slapping his leg. "Little gal, you told that dingbatter off fer sure. He's redder than a blue crab been boiled." The front door slammed. "Got the message, he did. Want to stick that knife in yer pants for the ride home in case he tries any more foolishness?"

"I might take you up on that." Ruby retrieved Jerry's plate and glass and set both by the chicken platter. "That fool's libel to appear when I least expect it, damn his soul."

"Now, now, young miss, don't be damning that man's soul to hell. He might have good reason for his bluster."

"He has a poor way of showing it if he does. Do you think anyone else will come? I'd like a little light for my ride ho—"

The door squawked. Ruby grabbed the knife. "I'll whack his rat tail off is what I'll—"

"Hello in back. What's for supper?"

"That's Doc Wills." Austin stepped to the window. "Evenin', Doc. Fried hen and boiled taters is what we got. Can Ruby dish you a plate?"

The ends of Doc Wills gray handlebar mustache drooped. "The missus fixed that for lunch." He peered over his black-rimmed cheaters. "Ruby you say? Bless my salty soul, if it isn't Miss Ruby Starr. How're you and Virginia getting along over on the sound side these days?"

The doctor shuffled to the window. Ruby joined Mr. Austin, who leaned against the shelf at the window's bottom. "'Course it's Ruby, Doc, you blind? She's prettier than a sunset over the Pamlico. Got her mama's look about her, I'd say."

Doc Will's mustache drooped again. "My word, I didn't think to ask about your mama."

"I'm glad you stopped by. She pinked up, but she's warmer than usual. I'm afraid she might have a fever. Can you come see her in the morning?"

"About nine all right?"

"That's fine."

"Let me get home and see if I have leftover chicken for supper."

Door locked, Mr. Austin returned to take a large paper bag from a shelf. "Let's pack up that chicken and taters so you can surprise Ginny with tomorrow night's supper. Just make sure you keep an eye out fer that Navy dingbatter. I'm 'fraid you done made an enemy outta him."

## Chapter 20

## Prophesy

With the bag of food in the bicycle basket, Ruby pedaled home. No Artknot in sight, thank goodness. She fingered the knife handle sticking out the back of her denims. She'd hate to have to cut a man tonight.

Toward Hatteras, dusk drew a quilt of blackness from the eastern horizon toward the west, leaving nothing more than a sliver of blue, with a thin red line marking the sunset. The Hatteras light lit suddenly, to reach its beam out to sea.

At the turn to the darkening path, she stopped. No whine of a jeep engine. No headlights. Since she'd left the restaurant early, maybe she could take Erich his bundle of clothes and a bite for supper. She pedaled into the path. Not unless Ginny was asleep.

The oak limbs enclosed overhead and around her, casting misshapen shadows that twisted and turned on the sandy path. An owl cried *who-who-o-o*, then flew in front of her so close that the wind from its wings brushed her face. A chill crawled ghost crab claws up Ruby's spine. Rarely did anything frighten her, but something about those reaching limb-claws tugged at her guts. Up ahead through the trees, yellow lamplight in the window calmed her nerves somewhat. She hadn't realized it, but she'd pedaled so hard that runnels of sweat slipped from her underarms and ran down her sides.

*If the Sunrise Forgets Tomorrow*

How silly to be worried about a beady-eyed rat like Artknot. If he jumped from the shadows, she'd stick him with the knife as quick as she could say twistygib—

Artknot leapt from behind a tree and grabbed the handlebars. "Gotcha!"

Holding in a scream, Ruby hopped off the bike and grabbed a handful of air where the knife should be. "Good lands, Jerry. If you wanted another piece of chicken that bad, all you had to do was ask."

He leaned the bike beside a tree. "You made me mad back there, Ruby gal, mad as all get out. I sat in the jeep and waited. Next thing I know, I seen your side of the story. I'm sorry 'bout what I said. Whatever you wear to the movies is fine with me." His teeth shined in the dimming light. "Wear nothing at all if you want. I bet you got a fine, womanly body 'neath them tight denims and ragged shirt."

"Yer manners are slipping, that's not something to say to a lady." She stepped to the bike. "You understand my side, meaning you understand how a woman needs time to get over a fuss." She mounted the bicycle. Artknot barred her way.

"How're you planning on getting over your fuss?" He took a few steps behind her to pick the knife up from the sand. "By stickin' this in me?"

"There's hooligans about." She held out her hand. "Might I have it back?"

He slapped the handle in her palm. "Between you and your sister, I don't know which witch is meaner."

Ruby pedaled toward the lamplight, heart pounding in her ears while even more sweat streamed from her underarms. Artknot's loud voice thudded into her back. "Remember our date. I ain't forgettin' it an' I don't expect you to neither."

At the porch, Ruby dropped to the steps. Tell Ginny or not? Not. She'd grab Papa's double barrel and chase Artknot down for certain. He didn't seem all that mad now, but when he had mentioned seeing her naked, his eyes had roamed her body as if he were a man studying a tender morsel of something to take a bite out of. Teenage boys gave her similar looks in high school, when her body began blooming, but Artknot's beady-eyed glare made her want to shed her skin like a snake.

Taking a deep breath, she took the bag and knife from the bicycle basket, climbed the porch steps, and peeked around the corner at the workshop. Her poor, sweet boy must be starving and stinking in his filthy clothes.

She reached for the doorknob and stopped. How might it be to wash his back, soap his hair, and even clean the curlicues of his ears? A warmth never quite known surged far below her navel—a warmth that startled her, coming so soon after the run in with Artknot. She needed to get her head on straight before she ended up like when Ginny patted her stomach. Feelings more than physical were required before anyone did any washing of Mr. Merman, with his blue-eyed, blond-haired self.

Ginny opened the door. "Thought I heard you clunking across the porch. No customers at the restaurant? How about Jerry, he show up?"

Ruby set the bag on the counter, blocked Ginny's view of the drawer, and dropped the knife in. "I've got fried chicken and boiled potatoes. Mr. Austin sure is nice."

"What about Jerry?"

"He stopped by, Doc Wills too. He'll check Mama in the morning."

"I'm glad you told him. She feels warmer to me."

"Is she restless? She was restless earlier. Did I tell you she was restless?"

"How so?"

"She curled her toes and scratched the sheets with her fingernails."

*If the Sunrise Forgets Tomorrow*

"She moaned a bit. I've never known her to do that."

Ruby's chest expanded with a slow breath. "I hate to say it, but I think she's getting ready to tell us goodbye."

Ginny's dark eyes narrowed. "Then don't say it."

Ruby went to the bedroom, placed her hand on the thin one. "It's okay, Mama. We'll be fine if you go."

Ginny shoved Ruby's shoulder. "Don't be telling her that."

"What should she do, Virgil? Stay here forever so you can mourn her while she's more dead than alive in this funeral-home of a house? How many times do—"

A weak, raspy groan came from behind Ruby. "Don't fight, girls. Come sit with me while I sew this hole in your papa's pants."

Ruby's knees sagged. "Mama? Are you ... are you really...?"

Ginny brushed by her to the bed. The frail hands held a fold of sheet while the other, thumb and forefinger together, shoved at the fabric as if pushing a needle through it. Ginny dropped to the chair, sobbing. "I can't ... I can't believe it. You've come back to us, Mama."

The hands stopped sewing. "My goodness, I never left my girls. Come give me a kiss." Kisses done, she swallowed. "I sure am parched. Could I get a taste of that sweet well water of ours?"

Ruby ran to the kitchen for a dipper of water. "Right from the pail, Mama." Ginny held Mama's head up. The Adams apple rose and fell. The sunken cheeks puffed in and out. The lips smiled.

"Mmm, that's good. Not as good as what your papa had."

"What do you mean?" Ginny said.

"Don't talk until I get back." Ruby ran to the kitchen and plopped the dipper in pail. "What do you mean, Mama? Where did Papa have water like ours?"

"I'm ... I'm not sure. Was a nice place. Lots of singing there."

"Were there clouds? Did the singing people play harps? Did you see—"

"Hush," Ginny said. "Let Mama tell us already."

"I was just asking questions. Why won't you ever let me ask questions?"

Mama chuckled, low and soft in her throat. "That's why I woke from my nap, to tell you two to get along."

"We do." Ginny said. "For the most part. As you know, Ruby's head can be harder than an oyster shell when she's a mind to."

"Aw, we fuss like sisters is all," Ruby said. "You know we love each other, Mama. Always have, always will."

The pink cheeks faded to dull white. The eyes, which sparkled bright and blue, dimmed. "Listen, girls, I've something to tell you." Ruby and Ginny leaned closer. "That's right, come on in, my voice is giving out on me. I don't like to talk about bad. There's enough bad in the world with that fool in Germany making people fight for no good reason. All you need to do is love each other and watch out for each other. You do that and everything will be fine as sunrise."

Ruby straightened. "That's awful vague, Mama. Isn't that awful vague, Ginny? Tell us more, Mama. Why are you being so—"

Mama chuckled, weak and raspy instead of low and smooth. "Always the precocious child, exactly like me when I was a young'un." She patted Ginny's hand. "And you, my dark one, like your papa. All black-eyed and handsome. You met a beau yet? For a while I thought Walter might be the one until. ... Never mind that, I've a feeling you're hiding a secret."

"I don't know what you mean, Mama"

"No matter, you will." She patted Ruby's hand. "And you, all full of light and blonde, exactly like me. I've a feeling you're hiding a secret too."

Ruby tilted her head to one side. "Why say a thing like that, Mama?"

"Something a little bird whispered in my ear while I was napping." She coughed, cleared her throat, coughed again. "My, that's painful." She raised her arms, skeleton-thin fingers grasping. "Time for a hug. I'm tired as forever and need my rest."

Ginny fell within one wavering arm and Ruby within the other. "My goodness, girls, your papa and me are so proud of you ... both strong and ready to ride the tide of life like we raised you to be. Stand up now, so I can get one last look at you."

Ginny jerked upright. *"No,* Mama, don't say it, please don't say it."

"Say what, dear heart?" She chuckled softly. "Land sake, don't I deserve my rest after raising the likes of you two?"

Huge, warm tears rolled down Ruby's cheeks. "We'll miss you, Mama. Always. You and Papa raised us fine. We'll watch out for each other like you told us." She slipped her arm around Ginny's shoulders. "Ain't that right, Ginny?"

Ginny's chin quivered.

The body in the bed seemed to shrink beneath the sheet. The chest raised and lowered, then settled into the barest hint of breathing. The thin, pale lips smiled. "I love you so much, my girls. Take care of one another. Take care of those beaus of yours too." The paper-thin eyelids closed.

Ginny dropped to the chair, sobbing. "She's gone, Ruby. My Lord above, we don't ... we don't have anyone now."

"We have each other, remember? Besides, she's still breathing, likely hanging on to torment you a bit longer. Do you have any idea what she meant about those so-called 'beaus' we're supposed to have?"

Ginny raised her head and wiped her face. "Listen to you, sounding like you've got a pier piling for a spine. Where'd that come from?"

"I suppose it's Mama's hinting that we have the makings of serious relationships in our future. That and how she said her and Papa raised us, to be strong and ready to ride the tide of life."

Ginny stood. "I'll make coffee. I want to be with her when she passes."

"You think that's what she's fixing to do?"

"Didn't you hear everything she said?"

"I meant anytime soon."

"She's made her peace. I'd be surprised if she lasts until Doc Wills gets here."

In the kitchen, Ruby took two pieces of chicken from the bag and plated them, along with a few potatoes. "We can have a snack with our coffee."

Ginny stood beside the percolator. Ruby sat at the table, trying and failing to keep her fingertips from rolling on the wood. No food or bathing for Erich until Ginny left the house. At least he can get water from the well later if he's quiet.

Ruby stopped rolling her fingertips. She'd never witnessed a genuine miracle, and it certainly seemed a miracle that Mama woke from a coma, if—as she'd suggested—only to speak to them before leaving for good. Who had Mama meant when she mentioned her and Ginny having two beaus? For herself, surely not Jerry. That only left Erich, which was fine. And since Walter didn't flush Ginny's cheeks like Charlie did, Charlie was likely the other beau.

She glanced at Ginny, who was eyeing the percolator as if a starfish clung to the glass bubble on top.

What might Erich be up to? Whatever it was, he best be careful about it out in the dark. One wrong step, he'd be laid up in Papa's shop without coming to the well for water.

## Chapter 22

## Violinists and Sandspurs

Erich licked his chapped lips. No water for two days. Nothing to eat but an egg biscuit. He longed for a gallon of water to wash the dust of the workshop away. Not to mention filling his empty stomach.

The setting sun's orange glow in the window faded to purple-pink. He filled the lantern with kerosene, covered the windows with the largest rags, and struck a match to light the wick. Smoky flame licked upward until he adjusted the height of the wick to get a clean but orange flicker. Lantern on the work bench, he stepped outside. The barest of glows shone along the edges of the window. He added enough rags to hide the glow.

Outside again, the quilt of darkness gradually covered the island. Crickets chirped in the oak grove. The waters of the sound washed a soothing rhythm along the marsh-lined shore. The cooling night air tasted of time, of watery life. Spare yet soul-settling in its complicated simplicity, Ocracoke must challenge two young women in their teens, who only had each other, including what few friends this desolate island offered.

A single star blistered into view. Another. Then another. The moon rose in the east, silhouetting the clawed oak limbs, a perfect half-circle supplying enough light to ease along the shore. The tide, on its way out, licked along the tall grass but withdrew in places. Glistening black mud reflected the moonlight. Erich breathed in the briny aroma. Time to find something to eat.

When his eyes adjusted to the darkness, he stepped to the water's edge and stopped. At least a dozen crabs scuttled about, crabs unlike any he'd ever seen. These crusty fellows waved one huge claw at him in miniature defiance, almost as if it were a violin ready to be tucked beneath their chins. Regardless of their musical whimsy, their flesh might make a decent meal.

He went to the workshop for the tin can to chase the crabs, but each time he neared one, it darted sideways. The last attempt ended with him slipping on his bare feet in the gooey mud and falling on his backside. With the sand from his swim chafing his groin, and now a stinky, slimy coat of mud on his rear, feet, and hands, a bath or a wash or *something* must be placed on the agenda.

He started to close the workshop door but stopped. Was that Ruby's voice at the house? A flickering glow shone in one of the windows. Ruby wouldn't visit with her sister awake. Best to wait until they went to bed before locating the well.

Feet, backside, and hands wiped of the mud as well as possible, Erich settled down in the rags to cherish Thea's smile. What might she say about his predicament? *You idiot, haven't I told you about making silly choices? That time you talked me into swimming in the ocean at night naked, only to have a constable come running to catch us, is one such time.*

A slight smile forced Erich's twinge of melancholy into retreat.

She'd complained bitterly when they grabbed their clothes and ran, but she complained no more when they hid in a thicket of evergreens while the constable searched the waves. Behind her, as she tried to slow her heaving breaths, Erich traced the curve of her buttocks with his fingertips. She smacked his hand away at first, but when he touched her again, she pulled his hand around to her navel, circled his finger there once, twice, then slid it down slowly, moaning as she pushed him lower.

That was his Thea, making the best out of bad. In her final letter, she'd admonished him to do as much with his life as she would hers if one of them perished in the war. Now he must do so.

He closed his eyes to wait. Closed his eyes to make sense of tragedy. Closed his eyes to make sense of so much loss of love. Not only of Thea but of his mother and father. What loss existed for those on this tiny island because of Germany and its *unterseeboots?* Might families have lost loved ones because of torpedoes fired from other boats, or possibly his own?

The men from the tanker—those who flared in tongues of orange and red as the burning oil consumed them—surely they possessed families similar to his and Thea's. Why did the good people of Germany stand aside while Hitler led the entire world to slaughter?

Erich swallowed the dust of the building, of pain, of loss. Any answer he might claim escaped any logic he might claim. Again, for his situation, the best he could offer was to do as Thea desired.

Survive and—if life permitted—love.

He rose from the rags and started toward the window to pull the makeshift curtain aside to check the light in Ruby's home.

His vision blurred.

Dehydration.

The wall caught him at the window's edge. The dim glow still shone through the oaks. He'd gone without water far too long. To wait longer meant crawling to the well.

Easing along through the moonlit path to Ruby's home, he leaned under and stepped over limbs hanging inches from the ground. Leaves stuck and crunched in the mud still clinging to his feet. Briars penetrated his pants and pierced his legs.

He paused where the path opened at a small garden at the rear of the house. Voices murmured inside. The aroma of coffee drifted from a window ajar. Did Ruby say the well was on the other end of the house?

He crouch-stepped sideways in the edge of the woods. Moonlight shone on the metallic handle of a well pump. Clenching his teeth, he dreaded the screech of rusty joint against rusty joint when he raised the handle. Nothing came but cold, crisp water. He washed his hands and drank can after can, the cold chilling his throat and stomach, and filled the can to take back to the workshop.

Again, he worked his way through the gauntlet of limb and thorn. If Ruby used a path, he must've missed it, hidden amongst the twisted shadows of the trees. Within several steps of clearing the thicket, he hissed when something bore into the sole of his right foot. He tried to extract whatever pained him, almost upsetting the can when he lost his balance.

In the lamplight, he sat on a stool and tugged at the ball of thorns, covered in what resembled miniature fishhooks. The wound ached as if pierced by a newly forged nail, still red and glowing. The ball hardly budged. He gripped it with a rag and gritted his teeth, managed to snatch it from his foot and threw both ball and rag beneath the workbench. A tentative touch revealed the tips of several spines protruding from his skin, like bones left in a fish fillet.

Using water from the can, he wet another rag to clean the remaining mud from the stickers. With half the can wetting his lips and tongue, he stopped drinking and set it on the work bench. Why risk the woody, thorny, fish-hooky maze for more water and attempt to return unscathed on his aching foot?

A silent prayer of thanks to God and Thea on its way to Heaven, he curled into the rags. With any luck at all, as well as compassion from his keeper, Ruby, perhaps tomorrow would be better than today.

## Chapter 23

## Deaths

In the ladderback chair beside Mama's bed, where Virginia had slept in fits and starts, she raised her head from the sheet and rubbed her aching neck.

On the other side of the bed, Ruby blinked like a turtle extending its head from the sound. "Is she still with us?"

Virginia placed her hand on the chest. "Still rising and falling like the tide. Feel like breakfast?"

"Well, flip me a flounder," Ruby said, stretching her arms over her head. "We'll have chicken for supper and eggs for breakfast. What would we do without chickens?" She stood. "I'll fetch the—"

"I'll fetch the eggs so I can move around." Virginia stood also. "My back and neck are stiff."

"Don't you think mine are too?" Ruby ran to the kitchen. Virginia followed.

"Look at you, acting like you're ready to swim to Hatteras. I'm getting the darn eggs and that's final. Dump those old coffee grounds and make a fresh pot." She started for the door but stopped. "What time did you say Doc Wills is coming?"

"Nine, why?"

"I'll give him until 9:30. Then I'll— Why are you looking at the ceiling?"

"Seems I recall him saying eight. Maybe you should go now."

"I'll give him till 8:30."

In the chicken coop, Virginia searched the warm feathered bottoms for eggs. She never expected Mama to wake, a surprise filled with both melancholy and amusement, including talk of prospective beaus. Ruby had also surprised Virginia with how she'd handled the moment: steady and stoic and practical. As far as the beaus, Walter and Charlie might be two. Ruby, on the other hand, certainly had none. Not if Jerry was her only choice.

Placing an egg in the apron pocket, Virginia paused. Hadn't Mama said something about Walter being her beau, then hesitating as if something had changed her mind? Strange, all of it, in so many ways.

The sun, now high enough to bathe the trees in orange, nearly blinded her. She stopped walking toward the house and shaded her eyes. A curtain hanging in the window of the workshop? Hard to tell through the thicket of gnarled limbs. Possibly it was one of Ruby's silly housekeeping ideas.

In the kitchen, she placed the eggs in a bowl. "I'm going for water. The ladies dirtied the eggs more than usual."

"I'll get it." Ruby slammed the stove door shut and grabbed the pail. "I want to rinse to wake up."

"Suit yourself." Virginia measured coffee—the chore she'd told Ruby to do—into the percolator's strainer basket. She then chopped two potatoes and added those and a dollop of bacon grease in the pan to brown. The aroma of sizzling potatoes soon spread around the kitchen. She glanced at an old cuckoo clock hanging over the stove. That sister of hers could spend the longest time with a quickest chore, including a simple pail of water. Virginia stuck her head out the door. Ruby hopped onto the porch.

"I'm here."

"Why're your hands dirty? All you were doing is washing your face and fetching water. Your face isn't even wet."

"I, uh ... I fell coming back because I knew you'd fuss at me for taking too long. Then I had to get more water."

"Go back and wash your hands." Virginia took the pail. "You're a mess."

In the kitchen again, with the eggs rinsed, stirred, and about to be poured in a pan, Virginia clucked her tongue. What *was* that girl doing?

Ruby creaked the door open. "What's taking so long with that coffee, Virgil? Doggone, you're slow."

"That's your job, Rube. I needed water for the percolator too." Virginia pointed at the pan. "I've been toiling over potatoes and I'm about to cook the darn eggs, all while you were galivanting around outside."

"About time you did something around here. I'll get the percolator percolating. I'll even feed Mama after we eat."

Breakfast passed silently. Ruby took her empty plate and cup to the basin. "Fine eggs and browns, Chef Ginny."

Virginia set her dishes in the basin also. "I'll wash these while you feed Mama."

Ruby mixed the egg-milk mixture beside Virginia, went to the bedroom for a minute or so, and returned. "I think she really means to leave us. She won't eat a spoonful."

"You have to work her mouth open. Did you work her mouth open?"

"Only for about four months now, Miss Forget-every-friggin'-thing-I've-been-doing-around-here-since-December." Ruby offered the bowl. "You try."

Virginia did, but Mama's teeth wouldn't budge. "She's being stubborn like someone I know. Maybe she's really decided to leave us." She checked the time on the clock on the dresser across the room. "Why's that say 8:30 when the cuckoo clock says 7:45? It's ticking, it should be right."

Ruby left for the kitchen. "Mr. Cuckoo's on vacation."

"I don't have time for nonsense."

"We must not have wound it lately."

Virginia gave Ruby the bowl. "I'm going for Doc Wills."

※

Ruby took an old paper bag from the cupboard, threw in two pieces of chicken, several potatoes, grabbed the bundle of clothes in her bedroom, and ran to the workshop.

"It's me, Merman, you hungry?" A groan came from inside. Ruby opened the door. Erich lay in the rags, mud on his feet. "I thought you made that mess at the well. You need to be more careful if—"

Erich groaned again. "I couldn't see very well in the dark." He sat up slowly. "I think I have a fever. I stepped on some kind of ball with thorns on it. My foot is aching worse than any toothache I ever had."

Ruby knelt and palmed his forehead. "You're definitely warm. Did you have a hard time getting that ball out of your foot? I bet it was a sandspur. Those things are—"

"Is that food I smell in the bag? I might try it later."

"Aren't you starved? I couldn't come out last—" Ruby sat on one of the stools. "I'll go ahead and tell you about the situation Ginny and I are in. Our papa died a while back and our mama is in a coma from the influenza she got in December. Ginny's gone for the doctor, not that he can see you. I'll say I've got a headache and ask for aspirin. He feels kindly toward Ginny and me. Maybe I can get a whole bottle and sneak out. I'll fill an old milk bottle with water right now. No need in trying to do too much at one time with how Ginny watches me."

"Can you bring tweezers for the thorns in my foot?"

"I surely will."

*If the Sunrise Forgets Tomorrow*

At the well, instead of filling one milk bottle, Ruby filled two. She ran inside to throw soap, a wash cloth, a towel, and tweezers in another bag. Back in the workshop, she knelt at Erich's feet. "Scoot my way and lift your foot so I don't get your bed wet. I'll put a few rags here too. Don't want to wet the floor."

He raised his foot. "What do you call those crabs that run around in the mud at the edge of the water? They have one big claw like a violin."

Ruby wet his foot. "Fiddler crabs, why?"

"That's what I tried to catch for dinner. As you can see by my muddy self, I wasn't successful."

"Not much meat on those critters." She soaped the foot, scrubbed it despite Erich's wincing, and rinsed it. "One more and we're done."

He raised his other foot. "I appreciate everything, Ruby. You're a rare young lady to take care of a stranger like this."

Drying his foot, she ran a fingernail along the sole. He jerked his foot back and she giggled. "Ticklish, are you?" She rinsed the wash cloth and towel and spread them on a stool to dry. "I'll leave these here in case you'd like to wash places I shouldn't." She patted the bundle of clothes on the workbench. "You're about the same size as Papa, shoes too. That way you can avoid sandspurs. As far as being strangers, washing your feet put a stop to that."

"Excellent point. Please don't forget the thorns."

Ruby took the tweezers from the bag, dropped cross-legged to the floor, and rested the injured foot in her lap. Moments later, with the offending sandspur hooks teased free, she lowered the foot. "There you go. You'll be dancing in no time."

Erich wiggled his toes. "Thank you. Whatever you brought in the bag smells a bit more interesting now."

"I forgot a knife and fork." Ruby gave him the bag. "I guess you can eat fried chicken and boiled potatoes with your fingers."

Erich pulled out a drumstick and took a bite. "Mmm," he said, chewing. "I've not had fried chicken before."

"How do you cook chicken in England?"

"Roasted, usually." He tried a potato. "I'm used to boiled potatoes."

"Your fever doesn't seem to be affecting your appetite." She handed him the second bottle of water. "This should last in case I don't get back soon. It'll please Ginny to no end, but I'll tell her I'd rather care for Mama than fetch wood or work in the restaurant."

"I don't wish to take you away from your mother."

"I won't be away long. That way I can feed and water you every day."

Erich's blue eyes brightened. "I thought I was a merman, but I sound more like your fine pony." He laughed, low and sultry, like a hot breeze off the ocean in mid-summer, which sent that same surge of warmth below Ruby's navel as she'd experienced earlier. She placed her palm to his cheek. "My, you're a pretty boy. I could listen to you laugh all day long."

"You'd soon tire of me." He tucked a strand of her hair behind her ear. "You're not pretty at all, Ruby. You're a beauty who just strolled out of a fairy tale."

She tapped his nose. "Maybe if I had a fancy gown to wear. It's been so long since I wore a dress, I'd be self-conscious of my gangly legs." She stood and twirled around. "Aren't they too long? My behind feels too big in Papa's denims too."

"I'll not comment on the obvious attributes of an extremely attractive young lady," Erich said, his cheeks coloring.

*If the Sunrise Forgets Tomorrow*

Ruby sat again. "My goodness, Mr. Merman, I like the way you talk. I read a lot, and I know every one of those fifty-cent words. They mean you'd like to bed me sure and proper."

"Pardon me, I didn't say that."

"Like mermen don't have needs too. Listen to me yammering, I need to get back before Ginny does. I'll bring that aspirin when I can."

Erich offered his hand. "Might I offer a token of affection for everything you've done?"

Ruby eyed his hand. "Such as?"

"Give me your hand and you'll see." Ruby did as he asked, and he kissed her knuckles. "That's how a gentleman says farewell to a lady who's as kind as you."

"Really?" Ruby held in a grin. "What do I get if I bring back a side of beef?"

Erich chuckled, low and sultry as before. "Let's not go there, or I'll not seem so much a gentleman."

"Gentleman or not, Mr. Merman, you're a pearl in my eyes. See you when I can see you."

Ruby rounded the corner of the house as Virginia rolled to a stop on the bike. "I saw those make-do curtains in Papa's workshop. You hiding something in there?"

"Keep it up with the questions. I'll move out there for privacy. Did you find—"

Doc Wills old Ford station wagon, red with rust around the fenders, sputtered from the path. He climbed out, bag in hand. "Driving through that dark tunnel gives me the spooks. With all the ghost stories some of the elder O'Cockers tell, I wouldn't be surprised if one or two haunts that place."

Climbing the porch steps, he yawned. "Lord above, I'm tired."

"Why's that?" Ginny held the door open.

In the kitchen, the doctor stopped mid-stride. "Doggone, Ginny, I didn't think to tell you." He pulled out a chair. "You might want to sit."

"I've been sitting all night. Please tell me whatever it is you want—"

"Then *I'll* sit." He dropped to the chair. "I don't know how to say this, so I'll simply say it. I was over to Walter Evans' folks' house most of the night, tending his mother. She—"

"Don't tell me she's got the influenza?"

"Not at all, but this has about killed her. The news came late yesterday that a U-boat sunk Walter's ship."

Ginny's knees buckled. Ruby jerked a chair from the table. "Sit yer fanny down before you fall down."

"I can't believe— I just talked—" Ginny's throat worked with a hard swallow. "I just talked to him the other day." She dropped to the chair. "There's no chance he survived?"

"Two explosions broke the ship apart, so the Navy told Sam. The men they rescued were badly burned."

"How're his folks doing?" Ginny said, fingering a tear from one eye.

"Sam's weathering it." Doc Wills pushed his black rimmed cheaters up his nose. "You know men, they act all brave and such about the war." His eyes cut away for a split second. "Mary Anne's a different story."

"Do you think they'd like a visit from Ginny?" Ruby said.

"I'm not sure about ..." The doctor cleared his throat. "Here I am, words stuck in my craw like a ball of sandspurs. I had to sedate Mary Anne. She's more upset than sad."

"That's understandable," Ginny said. "She's lost her son because of the Germans."

"That's part of it, but ..." The doctor rubbed his bulb of a nose while scrunching his eyes. "I hate to be the bearer of more bad news, Ginny, but she's upset because Walter proposed and you didn't accept. She stomped around and gathered pictures of him from shelves. Then she put them back. Every other step or so she'd mutter something about how you could've given him the happiness of being his wife before he died and didn't. I'd wait to visit if I were you."

Ginny's lips parted, closed, parted again. "Will there be a funeral?"

Ruby rubbed her shoulders. "There's no body, Ginny."

"I'm sorry about him dying," Ginny said. "How can she think I should've married him just like that?"

"She's hurting, is all." Ruby faced the doctor. "You say Mr. Evans is taking it decently?"

"As well as he can. Out on their porch, when I was about to leave, he said it'd be harder to watch Walter die from some illness rather than knowing he died while being where he loved."

"On a ship?" Ruby said.

"Sam said he was on what the Navy called a 'baby flat top.'"

"A what?"

"It's a small aircraft carrier. He was with the planes he loved to fly."

"At least he had that," Ginny said. "I never gave much thought to him flying a plane. It had to be an amazing thing to do."

The doctor stood. "Walter was a lot smarter than he let on. Had to be to fly combat aircraft. You two ready for me to visit your mama?"

Ruby started toward the bedroom door but stopped. "Did Ginny tell you about Mama waking up last night?"

The doctor faced Ginny. "You didn't mention that."

"I was in a hurry to get back. She woke up and talked to us. Drank water too. It was like she was saying goodbye."

"I wouldn't be surprised. The bond between family is strong. Maybe she came back to comfort you before she leaves." He went to the bed. Ginny and Ruby stood beside him. He touched the still hand and glanced their way. "Didn't I see you both outside when I got here?"

"I was taking care of something," Ruby said.

"I just got here," Ginny said.

The doctor slowly nodded. "Well, I think your mama decided to spare you girls the pain of seeing her pass away."

Ruby slipped her hand into Ginny's. "You mean…?"

"Afraid so. Her hand is as cold as a nor'easter's bite." He touched her wrist with his fingertips. "No pulse either."

"Good Lord above," Ginny said. "I don't think I really thought she'd die. I knew she was deathly sick, but …"

"It's nothing I haven't seen before," the doctor said. "No one wants to believe they're going to lose their loved one."

"She's with Papa now," Ruby said, grasping the frail hand. "She's all young and beautiful. All flowing blonde hair and bright blue eyes that sparkle when Papa teases her about her pretty legs."

"They were a pair all right," Ginny said. "Now the hard part."

"What?" Ruby said.

"You mean a service," the doctor said.

"Exactly." Ginny faced the doctor. "How much does a decent burial cost? As you know, that issue never came up with Papa. We can't spend much. Hardly anything, really."

"Let's step in the kitchen and give your Mama some quiet. Do you want me to pull the sheet over her?"

Ruby darted into the kitchen. "Now you can. No matter how happy I am that Mama and Papa are together again, I can't take seeing that."

*If the Sunrise Forgets Tomorrow*

"Me either." Ginny left for the kitchen, closing the door behind her.

A moment passed. The doctor came out and closed the door. "Please accept my condolences. Your mama and papa were two of the finest people I've known in all my years on Ocracoke. I'd have to check my records, but I think you two might have been my first delivery. You were first, Virginia, with a head full of dark hair. Then Ruby, with a head full of blonde fuzz. Ruby, you wailed and complained like nothing I'd never seen nor heard."

Virginia raised a single eyebrow at Ruby. "Makes sense, Rube."

"Why *wouldn't* I complain, Virgil? You shoved me over so you could come out first."

The doctor chuckled gruffly. "I'm glad this isn't upsetting you girls. It's early yet, though." He turned at the door. "I'll see what I can work out for your mama's service. You know how it is on Ocracoke, when things get tough, like with hurricanes or shipwrecks, we help each other."

"Mama and Papa always taught us to take care of ourselves," Ginny said. "I don't mind help but not charity. I'd feel better if I worked the debt off somehow."

"Me too," Ruby said.

"We don't have an undertaker," the doctor said. "Hardly any wood for a decent coffin. Just need to hire some men to dig the grave."

Ruby placed a palm to her head. "All this is giving me a headache. Do you have any aspirin?"

"Where's that pier piling for a spine you had last night?" Ginny said. "Doc Wills is trying to be practical, is all." She faced the doctor. "Mama wouldn't like a coffin. The few funerals we went to, she said she'd rather be planted natural than in a box. In fact, I've an idea she might like."

The doctor took a bottle of aspirin from his bag and gave it to Ruby. "Haven't even opened it yet. Far as the coffin, makes it simpler without. Pardon me for saying, but we need to settle her no later than tomorrow. I'll spread the word and check on a plot in the village cemetery."

"I appreciate that," Ginny said. "Let me know the cost."

"Do you have an idea what time you'd like to have the service? I can tell folks when I'm passing the word."

"What's good for folks who might like to come midweek?" Ruby said. "You know, when they're working?"

"If it were me," the doctor said, "I'd pick late afternoon. That'll give people time to finish their chores or work and get home to clean up. Most of the men need to get the fish smell off their hands too. How's four sound?"

"All right with me," Ginny said.

Doc Wills clomped down the porch steps. Ruby faced Virginia. "What kind of idea do you have about Mama?"

"You never listen. I said it was something she'd like."

"You expect me to catch every teeny bit of every twistygibbet thing you say? You can kiss my durn fanny, Virgil Starr."

"I suppose I deserve that. Then again, maybe not. Our nipping at each other is part of our affection, or it's part of how we deal with living on this island. Can we put it to an end for now?"

"I can do that" —Ruby poked Ginny's ribs— "for now. What's your idea about Mama?"

"It involves getting the sail for the rowboat from Papa's workshop. Be right back."

## Chapter 24

## Comfort and Caring

Erich swallowed water to wash the last of the salty chicken down. Time to clean up and change into the clothes Ruby had so thoughtfully brought.

He peeled the sandy sweater, shirt, underwear, and pants off, then rinsed and scrubbed his chaffed neck, partially ridding himself of the sour odor from his underarms and soothing the inside of his stinging thighs. Thank goodness Ruby had washed away the mud embedded in the soles of his feet. In clean clothes, including fresh socks and a pair of scuffed leather shoes, the day looked brighter. He gingerly placed weight on his aching foot. Not too bad.

He jumped at loud voices coming from the direction of Ruby's home. A vehicle with its sputtering engine had arrived after she'd left him, and its sputter had just faded away. Could Ruby and her sister be arguing about whatever news the driver had brought? He moved a rag aside and peeked out the window.

Both sisters were at the corner of the house, hands waving.

"What's wrong with me getting it?" Virginia said.

Ruby grabbed her arm. "Get back inside and leave it to me."

Virginia jerked her arm free. "Why can't I get the dadburned sail? You never answered me about those ragged curtains either."

"Keep up your caterwauling," Ruby said. "I'll move in there and leave you all alone. What's your idea for Mama with that sail?"

"I thought it'd be fitting to bury her in it. That's how they used to bury men at sea."

"Weren't you going to dress her first?"

"Do I look like I just washed in with the tide? I was, in one of her dresses."

"Fine. Get everything together while I get the sail. I don't see a problem with that. Do you see a problem with that? Tell me if you see a problem with that."

"O-o-o-h, why do I even try?" Virginia huffed around the corner of the house. Ruby ran toward the workshop.

Erich opened the door. "I overheard you and your sister. I assume your mother …"

"Likely while I was out here."

"I apologize for taking you away from her."

Ruby closed the door. "Ginny was in town getting the doctor. Mama passed while we were both gone. I think she did that to spare us the pain of watching her leave." Ruby's blue eyes filled. "She's with Papa now. That's what matters, but …" She fingered tears, wiped them on her denims. "Could you hold me? I don't … I don't care to stain the memory of your wife with my crying. I just … I just …"

Erich took the trembling young woman into his arms. "Thea would chastise me if I didn't comfort a precious young lady who just lost her mother."

Even though Ruby sobbed, her warmth, along with the aroma of wind in her hair, brought back memories of how the unique presence of a beautiful and sensual young woman could feel in his arms. Would Thea forgive him this transgression? Since she wanted him to live—and since life meant loving—she would.

*If the Sunrise Forgets Tomorrow*

He rubbed slow circles on Ruby's back. "I'll hold you as long as you need, love. Get your cry out if need be."

She pulled away. "Is that something you told Thea?"

"What did I …"

"You called me 'love.'"

"I told Thea that when the bombers came." He kissed Ruby's forehead. "I won't lie to you, Ruby, I'm drawn to you in ways I think improper after losing Thea so soon. That's the rational part of me. Forgive me, but the other part—the part that misses the physical closeness she and I shared as husband and wife—would like to strip you naked and kiss you from head to toe. Though that part is considered lust, a part of me would like to discover if we might become more than that." He kissed her forehead again. "Does that make sense?"

"More than you ever know. Still, I don't care to rush into it by taking each other like I've seen Ocracoke ponies do." The corners of her lips quirked upward with a partial grin. "Well, I doubt I'd simply stand there like the mare does." She stepped away. "You've made my day, pretty boy. I'd love to taste those lips, goodness knows I would. I better get that sail and scoot before Ginny—"

"Ru-by! Git yer fanny up here right this minute!"

Ruby giggled. "Right on time, bellowing like always." She grabbed the furled sail from the pegs. "Don't you look spiffy in Papa's clothes?" She tousled Erich's hair before he could answer. "I'd bring a comb but your curls make you such a pretty boy. See you later, sweet merman. One day I'll taste those salty lips without stopping to worry about what might happen."

Erich closed the door. She'd been correct concerning their kissing—stopping at her lips might well be impossible.

However.

He took a seat on the stool. Relationships—solid relationships—took time. His parent's long marriage, including how they treated each other as equals, proved that.

But what he recalled most about them was how they laughed together. Whether in the morning during breakfast on the weekends, at lunch when they avoided the discussion of the war, or in the evening after dinner, they always managed to find the time to share a chaste kiss, a knowing look, and when the opportunity presented itself, a hand-in-hand twilight walk around the neighborhood, laughing like children at play.

Envisioning those moments with Ruby, Erich's loins quickened. He'd seen a stallion take a mare once: repeated thrust after repeated thrust, rippling muscle and struggling sinew, the equine urgency to continue its lineage.

Ruby deserved tender kisses and gentle touches. He'd start by— No, to think of the possibilities conjured up scenes of her willing body beneath him, skin glowing in lamplight, red bow of her lips parting, small moans as her hips writhed against him, that final cry of release.

Erich stomped his injured foot. Burning pain cleared the vision of Ruby's sensual body from his mind.

A woman who cared for a complete stranger as she did for him—even washing and drying his feet—deserved no less than love before lust.

But as an enemy on foreign soil, how long could he hide in this building? Without a stove, it would be frigid beyond measure in the winter. Even if a stove existed, the smoke would signal curiosity. He'd have to entrust himself to the precious— he grinned—and precocious Ruby. With her imagination, quick mind, and eager attitude, she may discover a solution.

Erich knelt on the rags and took Thea's final words from the document bag to read. Returning everything to the bag, he stopped at the letter from her father. Keeping it was a risk.

Better burn it when he got the chance. For now he'd hide it beneath the rags.

He lay down for a nap. His nose had gotten so used to the varnish smell, he hardly noticed.

Supporting Ruby at her mother's service was impossible. Still, he'd be there in spirit.

Rolling over, he closed his eyes. Since the ritual of wrapping a seaman in a sail for burial at sea filled many a novel's pages, perhaps that's what the sisters planned to do with the sail Ruby had taken from the wall, but on land?

Interesting.

What might the sisters have in mind, and what would each contribute in her own unique way?

## Chapter 25

## Decorations

Waiting for Ruby on the porch, Virginia unclenched her teeth. "Don't drag that dadburned sail like that."

"Keep your finger out of my biscuit dough. I'll brush it off."

In the bedroom, Virginia showed Ruby a dress. "This is the best cotton shift Mama had. You want her wedding ring?"

"I think it proper to leave it." Ruby touched the gold band. "What about her necklaces?"

"I didn't think of that." Virginia opened the cigar box, where Mama kept a few letters, old bills, and three necklaces Papa had given her. She raised one. "I always liked this sand dollar." She set it on the dresser and took out another. "This starfish is nice."

Ruby dug around in the box and held up the last necklace. "I always liked this one. The two big and two little seahorses remind me of a family. I think she'd enjoy this one the most."

"I'd like us to keep the starfish and sand dollar," Virginia said, touching one of the slender gold chains. "Do you have a choice?"

"You keep the starfish."

"Why's that?"

"I always liked the ring of your name." Ruby waved her hand in the air and bowed. "Miss Virginia Starr, dark and handsome, intriguing and worldly. May her reign over the salt and sand and sandspurs be long."

Virginia giggled. "You have no sense whatsoever." She rubbed Ruby's shoulder. "What would I do without you?"

Ruby shrugged. "Cry and wail and moan, no doubt." She turned around. "Kindly place that sand dollar around my neck, Miss Starr. I'll do the same for you with that starfish."

"Not without the same introduction." Virginia waved and bowed. "Miss Ruby Starr, light and lovely, romantic and dreamer. May her reign over the wind and waves and sound be long."

Ruby pranced in a circle, one hand out as if carrying a parasol, the other as if holding an imaginary fan, fanning herself. "Oh, it's *so* wonderful to be held in such high esteem amongst the commoners on dear Ocracoke." She bowed. "Thank you so very, very much."

Virginia laughed out loud. "What would people think of us acting a fool in here, with Mama lying dead?"

"People? Who gives a flying flip what people think? Do you give a flying flip what people think? I don't give a—"

"You've made that quite clear and I agree—what matters is what Mama thinks."

"Exactly right." Ruby touched the thin foot beneath the sheet. "Her and Papa are probably looking down at us, fit to bust."

"I surely don't doubt it. Let's get Mama dressed."

They worked the cotton shift onto the wasted body, circled the thin chain around the wasted neck, nestled the golden seahorse family in the hollow of the throat, and brushed the thinning hair. "Mama's hair once looked like yours," Virginia said, returning the brush to the nightstand.

Ruby slid a strand of hair behind the ghostly white ear. "I'll always remember her before the influenza and before Papa passed. That was their happiest time." She slipped an arm around Virginia's shoulders. "Ours too."

Virginia patted the hand on her shoulder. "We're due a bit of happiness, don't you think?"

"Maybe you can have that with Charlie. Did you catch what Mama said about Walter, that she thought he might be the one? Then she said 'until,' like she knew Walter might not be the one anymore."

"Ruby ..."

"What?"

"I just thought ..."

"Better close yer yap before a fly buzzes down yer throat."

"Do you think she saw Walter in Heaven?"

"Oh, that. I already knew that."

"Uh-huh. What about the part about you meeting someone?"

"Danged if she meant that rat-eyed Jerry."

"Surely not. Don't tell me you've got a beau hidden in Papa's workshop?"

"I— No, of course not. How do you come up with such wild ideas? Is it too much Poe?"

"I'm teasing. Let's brush the sand off the sail and get it inside."

Sail free of sand and unfurled, Virginia said, "Go to the other side and ease her over while I work the sail under. I can pick her up while you pull it the rest of the way."

Ruby did so. "She's light as a cattail stalk."

"Tarnation," Virginia said. "We need the thread and the awl to sew it."

Ruby took off, blonde hair flying, shoes pattering across the porch.

Virginia overlapped the sail's edges, taking care to leave the pale but serene face uncovered. Her lack of emotion, likely due to her and Ruby's firm belief that Mama was already in Heaven, laughing with Papa, surprised her.

She sat on the side of the bed to wait for Ruby. Although she joked about her sister's infatuation with the workshop, every time she ran there for a quick chore, she stayed entirely too long.

Virginia fingered the seahorse necklace at Mama's throat, gold like the wedding band.

Mr. Charlie Smithson.

She missed him, missed his laugh, missed his way of comforting her that night on the pier while they watched the moon. She touched her lips. Two tempting kisses, she missed those also. Might they have a future together? She liked to believe so.

As far as Walter, she had cared for him too. Then again, he'd revealed a somewhat childish nature at times. He might've been a better match for Ruby, had he lived. Walter in Heaven, more happiness than he could handle. Guilt strangled Virginia's heart like salt water strangled two little girls during their first swimming lesson in the shallow waters of the sound. The guilt from Mary Anne Evans' harsh words needed to sail off into the sunset.

The screen door slammed. "You had a good idea with the sail." Ruby took a breath. "I have a good idea myself."

Virginia took one of the cattail stalks from the bundle in Ruby's arms and rubbed the dark brown head to release the white fuzz underneath. "You want to decorate Mama with these?"

Ruby gave Virginia the cattails, revealing another surprise in her arms. "With this marsh grass too. We can put everything on the sail and tie it with what's left of that roll of blue ribbon that Mama tied her ponytail with."

"Good idea. Fetch some bluebells in that patch of sun between the henhouse and the sound. They'll be pretty mixed in."

Ruby took off again, screen door slamming behind her. "What a mess that girl is, Mama. I don't know what I'll do if some man comes along and takes her away from me."

Ruby rushed in moments later, clutching two handfuls of the deep blue blooms. They resembled clusters of bells hanging from the stems. "Lay the cattails and marsh grass on, Ginny. I'll spread the bluebells on her chest like a jacket."

"With all your running around to gather these things, did you forget the awl and thread?"

"There you go, poking my biscuit dough again." Ruby took the items from her pocket. "Two awls so I can help."

Virginia sat in the chair on one side of the bed. "Have a seat and sew, idea girl."

Several stitches later, Ruby hummed a familiar tune. Virginia looked up from her stitches. "Is that the song Mama sang when she worked around the house?"

"Until Papa left us, it is. Did you realize she stopped singing after that?"

"I suppose I didn't. I don't recall the words, are they sad?"

"They're about Ocracoke and how our men leave us. Sad isn't the word for it."

"Can you sing? I'd like to hear it."

Ruby looked up from a stitch. "Can't do it, Ginny, not a word. I'd bawl sure as forever."

The stitches reached the top buttons on the plain, white shift. Virginia set the awl aside. "Do you want to leave while I cover her face?"

"You left when Doc Wills covered her face too, Virgil."

"I can steel myself long enough to do this one last thing for her."

"Then I stay too." Ruby leaned over to kiss the pale forehead. "I love you, Mama. Ginny and me will watch over each other like you said. You keep Papa straight up there in Heaven. Don't let him raise any of the angel's dresses and make comments about their legs."

Virginia kissed the cold forehead. "I love you too, Mama. Ruby and me aggravate the oyster out of each other, but that doesn't mean we don't love one another. Tell Papa we miss him. Like Ruby said, we'll watch over each other. I wouldn't have it any other way."

They fingered tears. Virginia enfolded the ghostly face in the sail. They finished sewing, alternating between wiping more tears and sniffling. "She'll like a last wagon ride to the cemetery," Virginia said.

"Like when she and Papa took sunset rides on the beach," Ruby said. "We can add the cattails and the rest before we leave tomorrow afternoon."

"I'm ready for a bite of lunch." Virginia left for the icebox.

Ruby brushed by and took the bag of chicken and potatoes to the table. "I ate some last night."

Virginia opened the bag. "Some? There's only a couple of scrawny wings and a few potatoes left."

"Can't I get hungry without you fussing about it?"

"You do whatever you want whether I fuss or not." Virginia sat. "Mind if I have the rest?"

Ruby sat too. "Do you miss Charlie yet?"

"What if I do?"

"I'm sure you know I'm not pleased about Mama."

"Go ahead, spit it out."

"We're free to marry now. I think you like Charlie more than you let on."

"I'd rather not leave you."

"Now, Virgil, I expect to move in with you if you marry. You have to do the same with me too."

"What do you think our prospective husbands might say about that?" Virginia took a chicken wing from the bag.

"You're teasing, right?" Ruby took a potato from the bag.
"How so?"

"With the likes of you and me in a household, how would they get a say in the matter?"

About to swallow a bite of chicken, Virginia spit the mess in her palm and laughed. "That's the truth if you ever told it. Leave off the funny-isms before I choke. I'd like to live long enough to get married. You would too."

Finished with the food, Virginia stretched. "Sitting in a chair all night didn't do my sleep any good. I'm taking a nap, you?"

"I'll take the thread and awls back to Papa's workshop first."

※

Ruby drummed her fingers on the table. Wait until Ginny snores, then visit Mr. Salty-lips himself, the merman.

Did she appear too childish to Erich? She didn't intend to, nor to anyone else. Life, especially life on Ocracoke—short, sweet, and oftentimes bitter—should be relished instead of taken entirely too seriously every minute of the day or night. If she and Erich somehow managed to marry, longshot though it may be, she refused to settle for less than light hearts, laughter, and more love than he could handle, like Mama and Papa's marriage. Erich better enjoy reading too, or they'd have a problem. Reading—even romance novels—opened the mind to more than the daily drudgery of living.

Regardless of all those remote possibilities, as remote as Ocracoke itself, he couldn't live in the workshop forever. They needed a plan that could have him accepted as a normal part of village life without drawing suspicion.

Ruby stepped to Ginny's door. A slight snore, similar to the purr of an old tomcat they once had, seeped through the wood.

She opened the workshop door. "It's just me."

"Hello, just me." Erich cupped her cheek with his palm. "I hope it didn't upset you to prepare your mother. It's brave of you and Virginia to care for her like that."

Ruby placed her hand on his. She could stand here forever, with his tender touch and his eyes filled with concern. "Thank you for saying that. Dingbatters don't know how hard life on Ocracoke can be."

"Dingbatters?"

"People not from here. Did you know we're over twenty miles from the mainland? When hurricanes hit, the entire island can be washed over. We're lucky that Papa spotted how this property sets a bit higher than most of the island, or we'd flood every time. He still built the floor so we can take it up to keep the house from floating away."

Erich took his hand from her cheek. "When do hurricanes come?"

"Anywhere from June to November. September's worse."

"How cold are the winters?"

"Exactly. You can't stay here forever and I don't expect you to."

"You're quite the intuitive and intelligent young woman, Ruby. I've tortured my brain for an answer to our predicament and can't think of a single one."

"I've thought about it until my head hurt." They sat on the stools. "I ran out here because I have aspirin. How are you feeling?" She touched his forehead. "You're still a bit warm."

Erich sat on a stool and took the offered bottle. "I'll take two after you leave. What time is the service?"

"Tomorrow at four. I'll make extra scrambled eggs." Ruby sat on the other stool. "You can go to the house and eat while we're gone."

"You can't feed me constantly. We've got to think of something."

Ruby ran a finger along his chin. "Nothing but peach fuzz. People will think you're too young to enlist in the military. Your accent is another thing altogether."

"I have much to overcome."

"Too bad you can't disguise that proper talk. Oh, I didn't tell you. Ginny's interested in one of the Navy men. His name's Charlie and he's fine as fish hair. He might even understand your situation." Ruby snorted laughter. "Unless you're German. Imagine that? Me hiding a German in Papa's workshop."

"What does this Charlie do?"

"Ginny said something about security. There's another fellow working with him named Jerry—they both carry pistols. Jerry would arrest a deserter like you. He'd put lead in you on sight if you were a German too. He's got a mean streak and beady eyes, like a durned rat. You don't want to talk around him if you can help it. Huh, I was joking about me hiding a German out here, but I bet Jerry would shoot me too if I were."

"We shall make sure to stay away from this Jerry fellow then. As far as my problem, I'll continue to think about it." Erich stood. "You should get back. Oh, how is it that you're here without your sister knowing it?"

"She's napping." Ruby stood. "What's the chance I could get a hug that will last me through the service tomorrow?"

"Honestly, I'm afraid to. Thea and I weren't married long. When I hold you it's like I'm holding her. We had an amazing honeymoon. The memories linger still."

"It's appealing to be with a man who's honest." Ruby held out her hand. "I'll settle for a kiss on my knuckles."

Erich's chest rose and fell, like a billowing sail on a four-masted schooner that Ruby once saw sailing off the beach. She pulled her hand away. "Do you trust me?"

"How could I not?" Erich said, his eyes blinking. "You practically saved my life."

She stepped close enough to feel his breath upon her eyelids. "You're barely taller than me, my elegant merman. I'd cherish a kiss. My first one too."

"Ruby, I ... I'm not sure I can control myself."

"What if I kiss you?"

"My hands would roam on their own."

"Put them in your pockets."

"You trust me that much? I could pull them right out and—"

"Why not? You said you trusted me."

He shoved his hands into his pockets. "Now what?"

She ran her fingers through his hair. "All that sand, you need a bath." She sniffed his shirt. "Goodness, my pretty boy, you smell pretty sour, even after washing with the soap I brought you." She stepped closer. "Let's play doctor, say ah."

"I can't say 'ah' when you make me grin."

"No matter, your breath's as rank as a buzzard's butt."

"How many buzzard butts have you sniffed?"

Ruby poked his chest. "You need a bath and your teeth need a brush. No kisses for you."

Erich pulled his hands from his pockets. "That's quite a bit of hygiene to expect from a man with no access to hot water or a toothbrush. How do you and Virginia bathe?"

"We heat water on the wood stove and fill a big washtub. We wash our clothes in it too."

"We can't do all that in here."

"Washing in the sound's out because of the mud. Too bad I can't make Ginny take a trip." Ruby kissed Erich's cheek. "Bye for now, stinky boy."

## Chapter 26

## Funeral

Virginia woke to darkness.

Although the curtain in her window hinted at a bloody sunrise, fitting because of the war and because of Walter's death, she rolled over to snuggle the warm quilt and to consider the coming day.

Outside, live oak limbs scratched against the house, foretelling a breezy service. Wind beat rain any day. Rain resembled tears, tears she couldn't take.

How many people might show up for Mama? As helpful as O'cockers were to each other, families still kept to themselves. On weekends, though, they might talk about recent events while shopping at the two general stores in the village, or picking up mail at whatever store currently housed the post office.

She should've given Charlie their address—a letter from him would brighten her melancholy. Today was ... where had the time gone? Some O'cockers claimed to enjoy living here because time stood still. That was fine, but too often—when death stalked happiness as if it were Poseidon with his trident, ready to stab those wicked prongs into the heart of joy—time weighted the soul instead of lifting it, while humble living with a loved one usually did the opposite

She flung the covers off to allow the cool air to nip at her drowsiness. What did she need to stir, to live, to take in the salty breath of life like before, when Papa and Mama brought so much happiness to hearth and home?

The answer made her smile.

To start, a hearth and home and a man who loved her like Papa loved Mama. Children one day, certainly that. Still, the idea of teaching appealed to her, especially literature. Since Charlie liked Poe, surely he understood the importance of higher education before children.

Virginia hopped out of bed. Honor Mama. Wait for Charlie to return. Let this terrible war run its course and see what the tides of life held in store for the Starr sisters.

The aroma of bacon teased her into tying her shoes faster. In the kitchen, Ruby looked up from a pan where several strips sizzled. "Howdy, Miss Lazybones. Can you percolate the percolator while I finish the bacon? The girls were generous this morning. I'll scramble eggs in a minute."

Virginia filled the coffee pot with water from the dipper. "What's got you feeling so pert this morning? Pert in a good way."

"Can't I feel pert?"

"How will you feel during the service?"

"How will *you* feel during the service?" Ruby turned a strip of bacon.

"Will you forget that doggone bacon and answer me?"

"I'll be fine." Ruby looked over her shoulder and frowned. "Unless somebody sings."

"Doc Wills said he'd tell folks, meaning Mr. Fulcher will be there to preach. Where there's people and a funeral and preaching, there's singing." Virginia spooned coffee grounds into the strainer basket.

Ruby tapped her chin with a fingertip. "I'm sure we went to a funeral that didn't have singing. Why should we have singing?"

"Out of respect for those who might be there, allow them that. Besides, you don't have to sing." Virginia placed the percolator on the stove. "Have you thought how things will be different around here? It would've horrified Mama to think she was keeping you cooped up in the house for months and months. Now you can get out and ramble."

Ruby plated the bacon and cracked eggs to a count of eight.

Virginia peeked into the bowl. "Why so many?" She set the bacon on the table. "You plan on feeding that man you're hiding in the workshop with all this bacon and eggs?"

"I pity the man who marries you." Ruby clattered a fork against the bowl as she whipped the eggs "Questions, questions, questions—all I hear is questions."

"I didn't mean—"

"Then don't." Ruby pointed at the cupboard. "There's a plate of hot biscuits under that dishtowel. Try to butter them without backtalk."

"Biscuits too? Tarnation, Chef Ruby, maybe we should open a restaurant?"

"Mr. Austin's too nice to give him competition." Stirring the eggs in the cast iron pan, Ruby looked over her shoulder. "I'm sorry for being snappy. I've got a lot on my mind."

"Thank you for cooking this wonderful breakfast. Other than fried or boiled, I wonder what other ways there are to cook eggs?"

"All I know is we need to eat and dress and finish getting Mama ready. Can you plate everything and pour the coffee?"

Virginia did as Ruby asked. "How's our firewood holding up?"

"That load I brought will last a while. Some of the pieces were hard to lug into the wagon." She poured a pile of scrambled eggs in a bowl and sat at the table to spoon a serving on her plate. "You ever think about hiring a strong hand around here? He could cut wood and help in the garden. He could even trim back those limbs out of the path to the road you're waiting forever to do. They'd burn as good as driftwood after they dried, or ship wreckage off the beach."

"Sounds like you've already got a prospective husband hidden away in Papa's workshop." Virginia spooned eggs. "One who might handle all that work."

"Stop saying that. I just thought a hand around here would come in handy."

"What we need to do is get *handy* with this food so we can get ready."

"Why the hurry? We don't need to be at the graveyard until a little before four."

"I'm just in a mood, I suppose."

Breakfast done and dishes washed, they donned work clothes, fed and watered Jimmy and the hens, tended the garden, and sawed wood. Ruby didn't mention lunch when the sun hung overhead, so Virginia didn't either. They continued sawing wood, until Ruby went inside for a drink of water. Virginia followed, glancing at the cuckoo clock. "Three on the dot. Better wash the stink off and get ready."

They did so at the basin. Dressed in their best denims, somewhat yellowed shirts, and scuffed shoes, they decorated Mama as planned, tying the cattails, marsh grass, and bluebells on her chest in a colorful display of life on Ocracoke.

Ruby crossed her arms. "She needs something else. Doesn't she need something else? I think she needs something else."

"How about something from the beach?" Virginia straightened a cattail. "She loved collecting shells."

Ruby opened a dresser drawer. "I think … here it is." She held up a small mason jar filled with several curlicued shells, a few clam shells, and a handful of tiny shells resembling baby clam shells. "These'll do fine. We'll scatter them over her after—" Ruby's chin trembled.

"You don't have to say it." Virginia rubbed Ruby's back. "We'll wait until the men lower her. Go ahead and harness Jimmy and get some fresh air."

The screened door slammed behind Ruby. Virginia sat in the ladderback chair. "You'd be proud of how your girls are holding strong, Mama. We'll watch out for each other like you said." She kissed the forehead beneath the sail. "Whoever gets to see you and Papa first will tell you how we tackled life. I love you."

Virginia leaned back into the creaking chair. Too bad Charlie wasn't here, to offer a strong arm around her and Ruby's shoulders. A sister's bond as intimate as theirs could use a sensitive and caring man like Charlie at a time like this.

Smooth a fold in the sail. Tuck a stray lock of blonde hair inside a loose stitch.

"You'll watch over us, won't you, Mama? Like with Papa, and now you, there's no telling what might take either Ruby or me from Ocracoke."

Oak limbs scraped and clattered against the house.

"I hope that's not a bad sign, Mama. It's straight out of a Poe novel."

The chains on the wagon rattled toward the house. Ruby came in with the starfish and sand dollar necklaces they had taken off while washing. Each raised their hair while the other fastened each necklace.

At the head of the bed, Virginia slipped her arms beneath the sail. Ruby did the same at the foot of the bed. They lifted and eased through the bedroom door, into the kitchen and outside, where they gently placed the featherlight bundle in the wagon. Virginia climbed into the seat. Ruby went inside and came back out with the shells. She stopped at the end of the wagon. "It's not right, Ginny. Not right at all."

"You want to sit with her?"

Ruby jumped in, feet hanging off the wagon.

Virginia steered Jimmy in and out of the oak limbs. One scraped the full length of the wagon regardless. She watched it to make sure it wouldn't snag Ruby. It pulled free at the end of the wagon to shake and shudder, like a crooked finger accusing one of those damn Germans of sinking ships off their shores.

To the left of the road to the village, the line of dunes muffled the surf. Still, the occasional watery thud managed to remind a passerby of how the Atlantic birthed the ebb and flow of the tides, waves, and endless wriggling, swimming, flying, floating, diving, dying cycle of life.

Sea oat stalks—trios, couples, and more—some bent like old women, some broken like old men—huddled in windswept swirls to whisper of youthful pasts when they once strolled the sands, warmed by the sun.

At one low dune, Virginia craned her neck. What was that out on the frothing blue-green water? Up ahead, where the last hurricane had cut the crest off a dune, she reined Jimmy to a stop. "Look yonder, Ruby. I haven't seen one of those grand old ships since we were five or so." She shaded her eyes. "Looks like a three master."

Ruby stood on tiptoe "Four at least. Look how the sun brightens those sails. Reminds of the time we had snow. The dunes looked just like that, all white and glistening."

"I like how the bow cuts through the water. The blue-green rolls up and turns frothy-white as it curls back into the ocean." Virginia shaded her eyes. "I can't see any of the crew."

"It's a ways out." Ruby sat. "We best get along."

Virginia steered Jimmy into the cemetery, grateful for the sight. A huge group of people waited near the far end, where a particularly large live oak stretched into the sky. On this side of the group beside Mr. Fulcher, Doc Wills waved her over.

The chains stopped rattling. Ruby hopped from the wagon. "Goodness gracious me, I had no idea so many folks would come."

Doc Wills, Mr. Fulcher, Mr. Austin, and—Virginia couldn't believe it—Walter's father, Sam Evans, came over.

"Morning, ladies," Doc Wills said. "We thought you might like us to ease your Mama down first. No need to see such a thing."

The men gathered at the end of the wagon, and Mr. Fulcher said, "My Lord. You girls have honored your Mama something special with all these wild things from our fair island."

"I like the sail too," Mr. Austin said. "It's right proper fer a maid of Ocracoke to be comforted in such a way." The crusty cook fingered a tear from one eye. "Your papa would be proud."

Virginia rubbed Austin's back. "Please don't cry. Ruby and me are on edge as it is."

He sniffled. "I'm sorry, Ginny. I s'pose I'm gettin' tenderhearted as the years blow by."

Virginia looped her arm through Ruby's. "Let's give Jimmy a rub. I can't bear to watch them carry Mama to—" She choked back a sob. Ruby led her to Jimmy.

Virginia rubbed the pony's neck. He knickered softly. "You know what's going on, don't you, ornery pony. You always loved it when Mama fed you carrots or the rare lump of sugar."

Ruby rubbed Jimmy too. "Remember that time he got loose and pooped at the front steps?"

In spite of the tears stinging Virginia's eyes, she smiled. "I sure do. Mama found out when she went to gather eggs."

"By stepping in it. Jimmy got no sugar for a month."

Doc Wills returned. "We're ready, ladies."

*If the Sunrise Forgets Tomorrow*

Arm in arm, Virginia and Ruby entered the crowd, who split and allowed them to stand at the head of the grave. The thin, sail-wrapped form, nearly covered with the mix of cattails and marsh grass, lay in the sandy hole. Tied in shoelace knots, four lengths of blue ribbon secured the vivid vest of blue bell blossoms. Virginia twisted the brass lid from the mason jar and poured half the shells in one hand. She poured the remaining shells in Ruby's hand. The white and pink curlicues struck the uncovered section of sail, thudding like huge raindrops from a summer storm.

Virginia nodded to Mr. Fulcher. He opened the Bible.

A gust of wind clattered the oak limbs. Sand hissed into the grave, followed by rattling leaves. A single lock of blonde hair escaped a stitch, to flutter with the dying gust. Ruby gasped and covered her mouth. Virginia held her breath to keep her heaving chest from exploding.

Mr. Fulcher closed the Bible.

"Friends, the good book says dust to dust. Here on Ocracoke, it's sand to sand. It's fitting to live where life resembles an hourglass … some grains fall before the rest. We can't explain it, nor does God want it explained. Love is like that too. We can't explain God's love. We can't explain His Son's love. Most times we can't explain the love we have for this spit of sand we call home."

He paused to glance around at the crowd. Several heads nodded.

"But we see and feel glimpses of why we love our home in the sun, when that great orange ball rises over the waves to touch our face with warmth. We experience the same when it sets over the Pamlico, all yellow to orange to deep shimmering red, glorious like the Almighty meant it to be. It touches us then too, but with the calm hand of comfort." He took a short step backward. "Let us sing a verse of Amazing Grace."

Muzel Bryant, one of Ocracoke's few black residents, stepped from the crowd. "That's a fine tune, Mr. Fulcher, but we all know one a bit more fitting."

"Lead us then, Muzie. I couldn't agree more."

Muzel cleared her throat. Her fortyish years had left not a line nor a wrinkle.

> *When the nor'easters wail, and the hurricanes blow,*
> *When our brave men sail out to the sea,*
> *When our hearts are all broke, and our tears are all shed,*
> *We'll pray for their souls, we'll pray for their souls,*
> *We'll pray for their souls, on old Ocracoke.*

Muzel's rich voice, syrupy and sweet, drew the crowd in after the first words. Baritones and tenors, gruff and thin, quavering and smooth, filled the air. Wives leaned against husbands. Husbands placed arms around wives. Children clutched pants legs, dresses, and skirts.

Ruby's arm, still within Virginia's arm, trembled. Sobs hitched in her throat, but her arm stilled as Muzel took a breath. Virginia gave up the struggle as well. Time to send Mama off properly, despite hot tears streaming.

> *Brave on, we'll brave on,*
> *For our sons and our daughters, you see,*
> *Until life is near done, and our sails are sewed on,*
> *We'll settle our bones, we'll settle our bones,*
> *We'll settle our bones, in old Ocracoke.*

Muzel nodded toward Virginia and Ruby. Several women, white handkerchiefs fluttering, wiped tears. Men's noses honked. Mr. Fulcher bowed his head.

"Dear Father in Heaven, please comfort our sisters as only you can. Remind them how they'll see their mama and papa again one fine day. And Lord, when the sun rises with all its glory, let it show Virginia and Ruby how there will always be a tomorrow, through Your blessings of hope, friendship, and love. Amen."

Offering condolences, Mr. Fulcher shook Virginia and Ruby's hands. Several villagers, including Doc Wills and Mr. Austin, did also. Mr. Austin said to take whatever time off from the restaurant they needed. Virginia led Ruby to the wagon, where Sam Evan's walked over. "Much as hate to ask, Ruby, would you mind if I spoke to Virginia alone?"

Ruby's eyes darted to Virginia and back to Mr. Evans. "We know Mrs. Evans is upset with Ginny. That's no call to chastise her about—"

"He's not likely to do that," Virginia said. "He came to the service, didn't he? He helped with Mama too."

"You want me to go? I'll go if you want me to go. Just say the word and I'll—"

"Hold Jimmy's reins in case the wind makes him restless."

Mr. Evans opened his mouth to speak, but a woman's voice came from behind him, her words taken with a gust of wind. Virginia cringed as Mrs. Evans strode up. The last thing anyone needed today was a knock-down-drag-out, no-holds-barred, hair-pulling-face-slapping fight.

Ruby jumped off the wagon. "Hold on, Mrs. Evans, you can't—"

"Please accept my condolences, Ruby. Virginia, I'm so sorry I didn't make the service. I—" Mrs. Evans' lips tightened. "I'm so ashamed. I've been on my knees since Sam left coming here. I was mad at you for not marrying Walter, but not anymore. A mother should be thankful instead of selfish." She touched Virginia's arm. "And I'm thankful for the happiness you brought him regardless. Please forgive me. And come up to the house when you feel like company. Ruby, you too. You coming, Sam?"

"In a minute."

"I'll wait at the post office."

Mrs. Evans passed the grave. Mr. Evans reached into his pocket. "Walter wanted me to give you this ... you know, in case he didn't come back." He opened his hand, which held the velvet box that Walter had offered Virginia at the restaurant.

"I can't— Please don't make me take that."

"He told me how you talked about teaching. This won't pay for college, but it's a start." He offered the box. "It's his final wish."

Virginia took the box. How could she not?

"Obliged, Ginny. Like the missus said, I appreciate the time you spent with Walter. He said you and Ruby were the most interestin' girls on all of Ocracoke."

"Well, durn," Ruby said. "After all the teasing I gave him, turns out he liked it."

"He sure did. He told us about your run-ins, and we'd almost bust laughin'. Well, I better see what Mary Anne's up to. She's probably got some woman hemmed up at the post office, trying to figure out another way to cook eggs."

"Common problem, isn't it?" Virginia said. "Most of us have hen houses and live off eggs when the fishing and crabbing is slow."

"Sure do. See you ladies around the village."

Virginia climbed in the wagon beside Ruby. At the grave, two men took shovels from the pile of sand. She snapped the reins. "Get us out of here, Jimmy. Ruby and me have had enough dreariness today to last the rest of our lives."

The wagon jangled past the place in the dunes where Virginia had stopped to see the ship. She pressed her lips into a tight line. She had treated Walter terribly, having him watch Mama while she and Ruby went to the funeral for the two Brits. Not only that, she'd given him the hope of marriage when all she wanted was Charlie. Now, his ring in her pocket poked her with even more guilt. Like everyone on Ocracoke, Mr. and Mrs. Evans could use the money by selling it on the mainland. Still, for Walter to remember how she wanted to further her education had proved his heart was in the right place, which made the guilt even worse. Jimmy flinched when she snapped the reins against his back. "Giddyap with your poky darn self. I want to get home today, not tomorrow."

Ruby popped her knee. "Don't mistreat Jimmy because you're in a mood."

"I'm not in a—"

"Tell that to someone who hasn't been at your side for eighteen years. You feel guilty because Walter left you that ring."

"I don't know what you're talking about."

"Hear that, Jimmy? All of a sudden Miss Know-it-all doesn't know what I'm talking about." A vehicle horn beeped behind them. Ruby whirled around. "Look who showed up early from his trip." She nudged Virginia's knee with hers. "Charlie the sweet talker will have you over your mood in no time."

## Chapter 27

## Invitation

Virginia jerked Jimmy's reins, stopping him nearly in his tracks. Finally, Charlie was here. Maybe he'd send her foul mood packing like a hurricane's gusts sent a flock of gulls winging sideways over the whitecapped waves in September.

He parked beside the wagon, climbed out, and removed his hat. "Jerry told me about your mother. I apologize for not being at the service."

"A hug will do." Virginia jumped from the wagon. "It's not like you were here to know about it."

Charlie took her in his arms, and she whispered in his ear, "I missed you, Mr. Dingbatter."

"I missed you too." He kissed her cheek. "I still wish I'd been here for you and Ruby."

Ruby climbed down from the wagon and poked her cheek up at Charlie. "Enough with all this sadness. Don't I get a kiss on the jaw too?"

He did so, laughing after. "Too bad a man can't marry two lively ladies in North Carolina instead of one. There'd never be a dull—"

"Dull my behind," Ruby said. "We'd kill you on the honeymoon night sure as marsh rabbits make baby marsh rabbits. Ain't that right, Ginny?"

"*Isn't* that right."

"That's what I said."

*If the Sunrise Forgets Tomorrow*

Virginia let the gaffe go. "I'd just as soon be an old maid than to share." She grabbed Charlie's arm and pulled him close. "Find your own fellow, Charlie's mine."

"I like the sound of that," Charlie said.

"Why are you back on Wednesday?" Virginia said. "I thought you'd be gone a week?"

"You haven't heard? The Coast Guard found two bodies in the surf yesterday. They were wearing the same clothes as those men from the *Bedfordshire*."

"Couldn't Jerry have handled it?" Virginia said.

"The instructor came down with appendicitis. Classes were cancelled until Monday." He slipped his hand around Virginia's waist. "I had an ulterior motive as well."

"I'm glad," Ruby said. "Ginny's mood is better already."

Charlie glanced back toward the village, looked toward his feet, and cleared his voice.

"Look at him all nervous," Ruby said. "He's going to propose right here and now. That's why he came—"

Virginia shoved Ruby's shoulder. "With what he'd gain for a sister-in-law, I doubt it."

"I'd never be bored, that's for sure." Charlie took his hand from around Virginia's waist. "I do want to ask you something." He faced Ruby. "Ruby, my dearest love, what's the chance you could take Jimmy home so this dark twin of yours and I can have a minute?"

"Drop a hint why don't you?" Climbing into the wagon, Ruby giggled. "Don't keep her out too late. I don't want to come looking with Papa's old double barrel." She clucked her tongue, and Jimmy headed down the road.

Charlie got in the jeep. "Care for a ride on the beach, ma'am?"

They climbed over a small dune to bounce over wide ruts on the beach, likely left by Coast Guard vehicles. Few O'cockers owned cars or trucks, and wagon wheels created narrow tracks in the sand that didn't bump. Nearing the surf, Charlie accelerated the jeep toward a flock of gulls sitting on a slight rise, where the waves ended their rolling, crashing life to feather into a foam-laced finale. The gulls lifted on the wind, wheeling and crying their discontent as they flew out over the blue-green swells.

Charlie parked facing the ocean. "I shouldn't harass them like that but I love watching them fly. I love the Blue Ridge—I love the way the haze hanging over the forested peaks gives them that color." He faced Virginia, then the ocean again. "I've come to love this place too. There are times when the mountains make me feel closed off to the rest of the world. It's different here, and I like it. Here you can see as far as the eye allows." He took in a deep breath. "You can smell the life of the ocean in the salt." He took Virginia's hand. "I'm not sure I can leave when the war's over."

Not only Charlie's words, but his low, calm baritone, including his profile with his slightly crooked nose, and the wonder in his brown eyes of a boy seeing the ocean for the first time, affected Virginia unexpectedly. She didn't want to have sex with the man. With no commitment, sex could be tawdry. With commitment, she'd love nothing less than to spread one of Mama's handsewn quilts on the beach under a full moon and love Charlie until the sun rose. Time would tell their story. Presently, she'd better adopt a patient attitude. Kisses she could handle; anything more she could not.

"Do you read poetry along with Poe? That was beautiful."

He slipped his fingers into her hair behind her ear, brought his palm to her cheek. "Not only do I admire your beauty, I admire your resolve with everything you've dealt with. Most women would crumple at the prospect of living here at such a young age, having lost their parents."

"Ocracoke ages O'cockers ... that's a fact of life O'cockers can't deny. Are you saying you're willing to take on that aging?"

Charlie took his hand from her cheek. "There's a difference in aging and maturing. You're the most mature young woman I've ever met." He tapped her nose. "Please tell me you're at least eighteen. I didn't think about that when I kissed you those two times. Also, when I said I had something to ask you, I wouldn't dream of asking it if you're under eighteen."

"Are you saying you'd kiss a fair O'cocker maiden without batting an eye and wait until after to ask if she's fifteen?"

"What? You're only—"

"Look at you, all red-cheeked." Virginia grabbed his face and pulled him to her. "Care to try again and see how old you think I am?" The kiss lasted far longer than Virginia intended. Heat not only rose in her cheeks, it rose deep within the innermost reaches of her womanhood. She ended the kiss. "Fifteen or not, Mr. Smithson?"

"With my limited experience—only with that one gal who preferred Mr. Big Lips—I'd say you're at least old enough for me to ask my question, right?"

"Yes, I'm eighteen. What's your question?"

"You just lost your mother. I don't want to be rude."

"Let me decide that."

"Like I said, I'm going back to Havelock Monday. Well, I'll go back Sunday for class on Monday morning. And since I have a lonely hotel room ..."

Virginia crossed her arms. "That, Mr. Smithson, is not going to happen."

"The room has a fold-up cot in the closet." He shoved her knee. "I get to find out if you snore before our relationship progresses."

"I thought you'd be on the base."

"I don't care to be around a bunch of loudmouthed men. My classes are four hours in the morning—then I'm all yours. There's a steak place in town with a dance floor. I'm sure you'd like a change from seafood."

"No doubt about that. As far as dancing, I'd look a site in Papa's denims and old shirts."

"There's ladies' shops in town for a dress." Charlie winked. "Besides, I need to see your legs before I propose."

Virginia faced the blue-green Atlantic. Spending time with Charlie to discover if love might wind its way into their hearts—what a lovely idea. She never danced, but Mama and Papa had slow danced to a tune on the radio in the kitchen a time or two. The radio broke last November, right after Mama bought new batteries, and right before she got sick. The luxury of a new ones couldn't be afforded—neither could a dress for dancing—but the idea of Charlie admiring her legs warmed her womanhood exactly like their kiss. Young girl dreams of young girl things—kisses and dresses, what next?

"Mighty deep in thought, Miss Starr."

"Does Havelock have a jewelry shop?"

"Whoa now, little mare, let's not—"

"Oh, hush." She took velvet box from her pants pocket. "I wasn't sure if I was going to tell you this but—"

"You ... you ... you ..."

"*Ha!* Your manly lips are puckering like a fish out of water. I'm surprised at you, Charlie. Just when I think you're special, your brain goes jellyfish on me. Here's an example of not having a jellyfish brain. You were about to ask if I'd already bought a ring for you to propose with. No, no, no and no."

"So ...?"

Virginia told the story of Walter's attempted proposal, including how he died and everything about his parents, ending with his father making her take the ring. Charlie, who'd leaned toward her to take it all in, slumped into the seat. "Seems like he was more than an 'acquaintance.' Regardless, I'm sorry about what happened to him. At every turn, this war takes people both near and far. Are you saying you want to sell the ring?"

"How else will I afford a dress so we can dance?"

"I would've bought it. I'm doing all right monetarily."

"I like to do for myself when I can. Papa and Mama expected no less of Ruby and me, and that's how we try to live."

Charlie's head turned as he watched a line of pelicans dip into the trough of a wave. In perfect feathered coordination, the lead pelican flapped wide wings once, twice, and as it completed its third flap, rising it above the crest, the next pelican in line began its three flaps, followed by the entire line, which skimmed the curling wave.

He cranked the jeep. "So, Miss Starr, how will you break the news to Ruby?"

"Let's hope she doesn't want to come along. How long will we stay?"

"The week." Charlie steered them toward the dunes. "Can we ask her now?"

"Don't tell her we're staying in the same room. She'll try to shuck me like an oyster if she gets wind of our plan."

"What'll you tell her?"

"That I'm selling the ring to afford a room."

"She'll still think you're going to stay with me. How about I drop you off and see if anything else is known about those men washing ashore? I can imagine the look she'll give me if I'm there when you tell her."

Having taken Jimmy to the corral to feed and water him, Ruby went to the kitchen to see if Erich had eaten. She nodded in approval. Not a biscuit bit, a bacon crumble, nor a scrambled egg curd on the table—the man cleaned better than a woman. His polite self had even left half the eggs and bacon in the icebox.

She started to run to the workshop.

And stopped.

The outline of Mama's narrow body remained in the bed, pillow sunken with the shape of her head. Since December, Mama's presence—worthy of private talks with her—had filled the room. Ruby dropped into the ladderback chair.

"Mama, with your talk of Ginny and me having beaus, did you mean me having Erich?" Ruby glanced around. "Can you hear me, Mama? I'd sure like a sign if—" On the dresser, one of Papa's tobacco pipes fell from the stand. "Papa, are you with Mama and that's your way of answering? My merman is as sweet as morning dew on a strawberry fresh from our patch, so an answer it is."

She ran to the workshop. Erich opened the door before she knocked. "You're here, which means your sister isn't. I hope the service wasn't too much of an ordeal for you."

She closed the door. "I cried during the singing but that's no matter. A lot of people came, more than I thought. How was breakfast?"

"Delicious. I'll make you an omelet if I ever get the chance."

"A what?"

"It's hard to explain. I'd rather make it and see how you like it."

"I have no idea how that might happen. Have you thought of a way to get out of here?"

"Some. I've never been in a predicament like this."

"It's the Poseidon of all puzzlers."

"That's an excellent analogy, Poseidon being the Greek god of the sea. Will your sister return soon?"

"She's talking with Charlie. He'll bring her along directly."

"You should get back before—"

The jeep's engine puttered in the path.

"Durn Virgil's timing. We've got to fix this mess we're in."

"Ru-by!"

Ruby ran from the workshop. Walking from the direction of Jimmy's corral, Ginny met her at the front porch. "Back at the workshop again? When are you going to tell me what—"

"What kept you so long with Charlie? Are you using Walter's ring for the engagement?"

"I need to ask you something."

"Charlie couldn't stay?"

"He had to run back to the village. Let's get inside, I'm hungry." In the kitchen, Ginny took the plate with the eggs and bacon from the icebox and set it on the table. "What happened to all the leftovers?"

"What happened to your eyesight? They're right there."

"You must have eaten more than I thought. Have a seat while I pick them over."

"When's the wedding? Do I get to be the maid of honor?"

Ginny swallowed eggs. "You'll be the first to know when that happens."

"What's the big question? I'm certain it has something to do with Charlie."

"He wants me to go to Havelock with him."

"Stand up and pat your stomach."

"Why?"

"Because that's what you did when you told me about letting my emotions make me do things I shouldn't."

"Part of the reason I'm going is to sell the ring Mr. Evans gave me." Ginny picked up a piece of bacon. "I'll rent my own room with the money from that."

"What's the other reason?"

"Do I need one?"

Ruby tilted her head to one side. "What about Charlie?"

"What about him?"

"Will he stay on the base or in the same hotel?"

"He'll have his own room."

"Like that'll keep you two from doing what oysters do while they're in bed."

"The other reason is I want to buy a dress." Ginny pointed a strip of bacon at Ruby. "Wouldn't you like a dress?"

Ruby cupped her breasts. "How will you know my size?"

"What's your brassiere tag say?"

"The ink's long gone and I don't remember."

Ginny opened her fingers like claws. "Cantaloupes?"

"Uh, no. Try smaller cantaloupes."

"I'll figure it out."

Ruby paused. She needed to say something to keep Ginny guessing. "Why can't I go if you're getting your own room?"

Ginny closed her eyes and pinched the bridge of her nose. "I cannot get a moments rest with you about anything." She opened her eyes. "Can't we go another time?"

"When are you leaving?"

"Charlie's classes start again Monday but he's leaving Sunday. He'll be back in a few minutes to make plans."

"Think you can wait until Sunday?"

"You act like I'm a mare in heat."

"I didn't say that. Did I say that? I'm sure I didn't—"

"Hush."

Ruby stood. "Done with your plate?" Ginny nodded, and Ruby returned it to the icebox. Time for another comment to keep her guessing. "Go on, have your fun and leave me all alone. I'll probably die and you'll see how it is without me."

"Spare me the drama, Scarlett."

Charlie's jeep engine puttered from the path. Ginny left for the porch. Ruby went to the screen door. The jeep brakes squeaked to a stop and Charlie hopped out. "Looks like we'll head to Havelock in the morning instead of Sunday. The base radioed that they replaced the instructor until the other one returns. It takes four hours to get there, so they're allowing tomorrow for the guys from the other bases to get back."

Ruby twirled around. Yes! Complete privacy with Erich for however long Ginny might be away.

Ginny and Charlie came in. Ruby poked him in the side. "You realize I'll blow your head off with our shotgun if you do my sister wrong."

About to enter her bedroom, Ginny turned around. "As I would any man who did you wrong."

"Where are you going?"

"To pack some clothes."

"Ain't you the itchy-bottomed mare?"

Ginny slammed the door. Charlie kissed Ruby's cheek. "I could take you instead."

"You're not my type."

"I thought you liked teasing?"

"How long will you keep Ginny in Havelock?"

"We'll be back Tuesday. Afraid we might come back early and surprise you and Jerry?"

Ginny's door opened. "Come here a minute, Ruby." She closed the door behind them. "I have your brassiere size. One of yours got mixed with my clothes last time we washed."

"Get me a dress I'd like, not a dress *you'd* like." Ruby started for the door. Ginny grabbed her arm.

"Turn around and give me a hug."

Ruby relished her sister's warm embrace. When had they last hugged like this? Or at all? Ginny took a step away, tears filling her eyes. "I doubt you'll believe I'll miss you."

"You act like I'm about to die, like I said."

"It's ... well, ever since Papa died, and especially since Mama's been sick, we haven't had the time to just be sisters."

"You'll be back in no time." Ruby kissed Ginny's cheek. "Don't have too much fun with Mr. Smithson. He likely couldn't handle *too* much fun."

Charlie knocked on the bedroom door. "I need to get back. I'll pick you up around seven."

Ruby went to her room and looked out the window at the workshop. "Guess who gets to have a bath in the morning, Mr. Merman?"

## Chapter 28

## A Bath and Buckshot

The next morning, as the jeep with Ruby's sister and the Navy man puttered toward the main road, Erich opened the door for Ruby. Regardless of where they were going, the spritely young woman would bound through the oak grove any minute. He longed to hold her again, to feel her body conforming to his, even if only to comfort her from the death of her mother.

She ran through the grove, blonde hair streaming as she dodged and ducked limbs. Her youth and innocence took his breath away—took his resolve to not take her when the first chance arose. Love must come first. *Had* to come first.

Breathless and sensual, pink-cheeked and smiling, lovely as a sunrise, she stopped at the door. "Guess who's having a bath, Mr. Merman?"

"I saw your sister and the man leave. What's happening that you think we have enough time for me to take a bath?"

"They're going to Havelock, on the mainland."

"How long? We don't want surprises."

"Charlie said they'll be back Tuesday. Counting today that's six whole days."

"Should we give them some time? They might return for some reason."

"I like how you're a thinker. Ginny's eyes sparkled like nothing I'd ever seen when she left. I doubt she'd come back even *if* she forgot something. I even acted like I wanted to go to fool her."

In the kitchen, Ruby took the plate of eggs and bacon from the icebox and set it on the table. "Ginny ate part yesterday but there's some left. She was too excited to worry about breakfast this morning."

"Might I have a cup of coffee? I thought I smelled some one day."

"I'll have to stoke the stove to heat it."

"Don't let me put you out."

Ruby giggled. "Says the man I've been hiding in Papa's workshop. Wood's stacked on the porch."

Erich started toward the door but stopped. Ruby was leaning over to prod the embers of the fire. Her shapely behind filled snug, blue denims. Waves of blonde hair fell about her shoulders. Temptations past temptation, especially with her sister gone a week. How should they handle it? "Ruby?"

She continued prodding. "What?"

"Nothing." He gathered wood in his arms. Love first, then lust. He opened the door. The whine of an engine similar to the one that had left earlier came from the path.

Ruby whirled. "Oh, shoot, drop the wood by the stove and get under my bed" —she pointed to a door— "in there." She slammed the door.

The dust beneath the bed tickled Erich's nose. About to sneeze, he pinched his nostrils and breathed through his mouth until the urge left.

Footsteps clomped up the steps and across the porch. "Hello there, Ruby gal. That sly dog Charlie told me 'bout his trip with your sister. Thought I'd drop by and see if you need tendin' to while she's gone."

Erich clenched his fists.

"I just buried my Mama not two hours ago. Damned if you're already making passes."

"I'm sorry 'bout your mama. I just thought—"

"I'd give you as much chance at thinking as I would one of Jimmy's turds."

Stifling a laugh, Erich clamped his hand over his mouth. "Them ain't kind words, Ruby gal. Ain't kind at all."

"You think they're meant to be kind? I'm fine as horsehair without any help from the likes of you."

Something clunked, like wooden door hitting a wall.

"And as you can see, if any riff-raff comes along, I'll set their asses on fire with buckshot. Get on out of here and don't come back."

"Ruby, you got no call to—"

*Boom!*

The engine cranked. The whine accelerated up the path. Erich crawled from under the bed. Ruby, with a smoking shotgun in her hand, came in laughing. "You should've seen his face when I popped that shot over his head. He—" She bent over, holding her stomach with one hand. "Ow, my belly aches. That's the funniest thing I've seen in years."

Erich took the shotgun. "We better reload this in case he comes back."

"Shells are in the drawer in the kitchen next to the cupboard. Why aren't you laughing? Don't you think it was funny?"

She followed him into the kitchen, where he reloaded the shotgun. "Were you keeping this behind the door? It sounded like it."

"That's right."

He placed the shotgun behind the door, then sat at the table and laughed until his own stomach ached. "You are, without a doubt, one of the most interesting women I've ever met. Not only are you attractive to a fault, you're kind and caring and willing to take on any adversity that comes along. Do you have any idea how that makes me feel about you?"

"I'm sure I do." Ruby leaned over and shook her behind. "Didn't think I knew you were looking, did you?"

Erich laughed again. Ruby sat and they finished their cold eggs, bacon, and biscuits, along with coffee. Hunger sated, he stood. "Is there something I can do while you're washing dishes? I'm tired of sitting in that workshop."

"Don't you want to know who that was?"

"I remember you telling me about a man who worked with Charlie. You had nothing good to say about him."

"Name's Jerry Artknot. Let's hope that's the last we see of his sorry self. As far as something to do, it's time for your bath. The washtub is under the porch. The bucket we use to fill it is inside it. You can rinse the tub out and bring it in. Bring a bucket of water after that and I'll start it heating."

Erich poured bucket after bucket into the tub. When his arms ached to the point of feeling as if they were about to fall off, the tub, filled about half full of hot water, steamed.

Ruby placed a towel, a wash cloth, and a bar of soap on the table. "Let's see those scales, Mr. Merman."

"You want to watch?"

"Only until I see if you have a tail or not."

"Tell me you're joking."

Ruby shoved his shoulder. "Had you going, didn't I?"

"Why do I think you'd have watched regardless?"

"Wouldn't you like to watch me take a bath?"

"Women's bodies are far more sensual than a man's."

"Says you, silly, say it again."

"Say what?"

"Sensual. I like how it makes your lips pucker."

Erich threw the towel at her. "Out."

"But—"

"Now. Must I say please?"

Ruby tossed him the towel and picked up the bucket. "I'll check the crab pots for supper."

Erich peeked out the screened door. On the way to the pier, Ruby waved. He undressed and eased into the hot water, moaning as the heat settled into his leg muscles, sore from carrying the water up and down the porch steps. Sitting around the workshop was his physical undoing. Surely the sisters had work that needed attention, giving him the activity he craved.

He washed his hair and rinsed it with a bowl Ruby left. Next came his chest, arms, and below his waist, in which the only available option—an extremely revealing option at that—was to stand. He rinsed and set the bowl aside to reach for the towel. A tap came at the screen door from a peering Ruby. He wrapped the towel about his waist. "You, young lady, lack courtesy."

She came inside. "What I have is my fair share of curiosity. You looked as proud as a stallion chasing a mare."

"Thank you for making my point."

Ruby leaned against the cupboard. "I've done no such thing. Like I asked earlier, wouldn't you watch me take a bath? Or rather, wouldn't you peek in the door like I did?"

"I'd hope to be a gentleman."

"Gentleman my fanny." Ruby's fingertips raised to the top button of her shirt. "Here's a test ... I'll unbutton one at a time until you close your eyes. That'll tell me whether you're a gentleman or a rogue." She unbuttoned the first button, revealing the edge of a white brassiere and a portion of cleavage.

Erich licked his lips. "Stop that."

"Your eyes are still open." Another button. More cleavage.

Erich's mouth watered. "Ruby, please ... "

Another button. All bra. More cleavage. "One more and I'll have to take my bra off altogether."

Erich snapped his eyes shut. "A temptress is what you are."

"And you love it, don't you?"

"Please go in your room so I can dress."

"Take your time, pretty boy." Ruby's voice passed him. "I'll fetch you some clean clothes." Her footsteps padded by. Drawers slid open and closed. Her footsteps returned, stopping from the direction of the table. "The clothes are on the table. I'm going in my room now."

Out of the washtub at last, Erich leaned over to dry his feet.

"Quite the view, Mr. Merman."

Erich whirled the towel around his waist.

Standing in the doorway, Ruby winked. "You didn't tell me to close the door."

Erich marched to the door, slammed it shut, and smiled. The next few days were sure to be interesting.

Likely *too* interesting.

## Chapter 29

## Breenda

The bugeye boat—Virginia had no idea why they were called that, and Charlie didn't know either—docked at the Marine air base near Havelock. They carried their suitcases to a phone booth, where he called for a cab.

A plane roared off from the field, banked over the Neuse River, and turned out to sea. Walter would've loved doing that. Now he rested at the bottom of the Atlantic, while his ring rested in Virginia's pocket.

Charlie slipped his arm around her shoulders. "Something on your mind?"

"I was thinking how Walter would like to be in that plane."

"Excuse my language, but it's a damn shame we have to be in this war at all. Like with the U-boats sinking ships right off Ocracoke and most of the east coast, we never know when death will hit close to home."

"Can we not talk about the war while we're here?"

"Good idea." Charlie's eyes left her. "Here comes the cab."

In the back seat, he leaned toward the driver. "Slocum Creek Bed and Breakfast, please."

Virginia shoved his knee. "What happened to the hotel?"

"I stayed in one the first time."

"I meant now."

"Your island spoiled me—I want a view of the water. Mrs. Taylor—she owns the place—is a great cook."

"How many rooms? I might want one for myself."

Charlie's twitching lips fought a grin. "I have the nicest one. It has a huge canopy bed and a balcony that overlooks the water. There's a table where we can eat on the balcony too."

Virginia shoved his knee again. "For a sunrise breakfast, I'm sure. I hope you'll be comfortable on the sofa."

"What sofa?"

"Then the floor."

"Wanna bet we sleep together before we leave?"

"Will you hush?" Virginia nodded toward the cabby, his eyes visible in the rear-view mirror.

Charlie leaned near her ear. "I only meant sleeping. Think we can control ourselves?"

Virginia grabbed his head and placed her lips next to his ear. "The best way to avoid *your* lack of control is to sleep on the darn floor."

Charlie pulled away and offered his hand. "Scared to make that bet?"

"What do I get if I win?"

"I can't think of anything I wouldn't give you."

Virginia pumped his hand twice. "You're on, sailor."

The cab slowed, took a right toward an ancient white-painted two-story house, and stopped in the circle drive in front of the double doors. Ivy climbed a trellis at one end of the porch, where a double wooden swing swayed in the gentle breeze. A huge oak, not the stunted and twisted live oaks on Ocracoke, reached into the sky, limbs filled with budding leaves. A hammock hung from the lowest limb. In the back yard, slightly crooked like a snake, a pier extended into the wide creek. A black pelican, its beak down as if it were praying, was perched on the last piling on the right.

Charlie opened the cab door. "Like it?"

"It's gorgeous." Virginia climbed out behind him, small suitcase in hand. She sniffed the delightful aroma of something baking. "Is that homemade bread I smell? Mama used to bake bread on Thanksgiving and Christmas instead of biscuits. I never did learn her recipe."

"It's probably croissant."

"Mrs. Taylor's aunt lives here too?"

Chuckling, Charlie paid the cabby, who drove away. "Sort of sounds like 'aunt,' doesn't it?"

"What sounds like aunt?"

"Croissant. It's a crusty, flaky French roll that melts in your mouth."

"Mrs. Taylor's French?"

"I'll let her be a surprise."

"You're full of them, like making bets about us sleeping together. I think we should modify that bet."

"Afraid you'll lose already?"

"It's not interesting enough. Let's make it so the first person who suggests sleeping together loses. That should keep you in line."

"You're forgetting what I said about not having anything I wouldn't give you. That means I win either way."

"What do you want if you win?"

"It depends."

"On?"

"We'll see. What do you want if *you* win?"

Strolling toward the house, Virginia glanced at Charlie beside her. "You never know what I might want, Mr. Smithson."

They reached the top of the steps. The double doors opened, and a shapely, middle-aged black woman—with shoulder-length hair and wearing a flowing dress with a floral pattern—stepped out on the porch in high heels. "*Bonjour,* Charlie, *bonjour*. I see you've managed to bring your lovely young lady for a stay." Mrs. Taylor pronounced Charlie Char-*lee*.

"*Bonjour* to you, Mrs. Taylor. Yes indeed, I talked her into visiting."

"She's as lovely as you said. Your room is clean. Fresh linens on the bed too. Would you like lunch on the balcony? I've croissant hot from the oven, as well as *borgiounion de boeuf*."

"Sounds great. Do you have a nice red to go with it?"

"I do, I do. You must call me by my name, though. It's not like I haven't asked."

"Okay, Brenda, how's that?"

"I must maintain a bit of my French heritage, no? How many times must I tell you? *Breenda*, remember?"

"*Breeeeenda* it is," Charlie said, grinning broadly."

"You are so silly. Please introduce me to your fair Ocracoke maiden. My, she's striking, she could be a model in France." Breenda offered her hand. "If I must wait on Char-*lee*, I shall wait until sunset. "It's so nice to meet you, my dear."

Virginia released her hand. "You have a gorgeous place here."

"It is very peaceful, no? *Oui*, I like it very, very much. My father left it to me."

"Is he from France?"

"My *mère* is from France, my *père* is from Havelock. Do you wish me to tell you the story or let Char-*lee* tell you? What am I saying? Let me prepare your lunch. Char-*lee* can tell you while you eat. Char-*lee*, show Virgeenia your room. Such a lovely name, *oui*?"

"Absolutely." Charlie took Virginia's hand. "Come on upstairs, Virgeeeeenia."

In the room, exactly as Charlie had described, Virginia set her suitcase on the canopy bed and left for the balcony.

Startled, the pelican abandoned the pier. The water, black and glassy, reflected its wide wings.

Virginia placed her hands on the wrought iron rail, thick with black paint. "What a view."

"Definitely."

Virginia faced Charlie. "You are so sweet."

"I meant the pelican."

"Mr. Smithson, this week is going to test my willpower."

"Meaning?"

She faced the river again. "I like pelicans too. I'll have to wait until another one comes along before I answer you."

Charlie's footsteps came closer. He slipped her arms around her waist and pulled her against him. "I think we both know we weren't talking about pelicans."

Charlie's breath warmed Virginia's cheek. "You *are* a rogue, as delightful a rogue as I've ever met."

"How many rogues have you met on Ocracoke?"

"Only one like you."

Charlie nuzzled her neck. "Virginia?"

"Hmm?"

"I'm dying."

Virginia took his hands from her waist and kissed the palms. "I've never felt this—this wanton. I'd love your hands all over my naked body. Head to toe and everywhere between." She writhed against him. He wouldn't argue. Obviously. Turn around and kiss him? No, because she wasn't ready for what would certainly happen after. "Charlie, I—"

*Knock-knock.* "Char-*lee?* Virg*ee*nia? Shall I set your tray outside?"

Virginia hurried to the door. "Talk about timing."

Charlie opened the door. "We'll take it from here."

Breenda's eyes darted from one to the other. "I hope I didn't disturb you."

"Virginia just commented on your impeccable timing." Thanks for everything, smells great."

Breenda hummed as she went down the stairs, then sang: "Don't sit under the apple tree, with anyone else but me."

Charlie took the tray to the balcony and placed two china bowls of what resembled thick beef stew—it smelled better than any beef stew Virginia had ever smelled—on the small circular table, also black-painted wrought iron, along with a plate of rolls shaped liked curlicued sea shells. He sat and screwed a corkscrew into the wine bottle's cork. "The wine we had on your pier that night was sweet compared to this. It goes great with the *borgiounion de boeuf.*" The cork popped. Charlie poured glasses half full. "Have a sip."

Virginia took a tentative taste. "It's not as sweet but I like it. It's ... rich is the best way I can describe it."

Charlie clinked his glass to hers. "Thank you from the bottom of my heart for coming here with me."

Virginia picked up her fork. "Why do I have the feeling you've been here before now?"

"Because of how I'm familiar with Breenda?"

"And your familiarity with the wine."

"Some of the guys I trained with mentioned her cooking. Give it a taste." Charlie forked a piece of browned beef with gravy to his mouth. Virginia did the same.

The succulent meat, flavored slightly with what must be red wine, could not have been tastier. "I'll ask Breenda for the recipe, this is heavenly." Virginia sipped wine. "What's the rest of her story?"

"Her mother traveled with her family to North Carolina back in the late 1800's. Her mother's father hunted ducks and geese."

"That's a big business late in the year. I think there's a hunt club in Corolla, near Virginia."

"Breenda mentioned him going to the Currituck Shooting Club."

"Sounds right. My aunt in Manteo talked about it when she was down after Papa died. How did Breenda's mother and father meet?"

"When the family stopped for a week in Havelock, she saw him at a garden stand. According to her, it was on after that."

"You mean it was on until her family went back to France because Breenda's father was black."

"Sounds like a book, doesn't it?"

"Your food's getting cold."

Virginia took a bite. "I can eat and listen at the same time."

Charlie sipped wine. "That's exactly what happened, except they didn't count on Breenda's father following them back to France. By the time he got there, it was obvious he and Breenda's mother had been *together* in America." Charlie patted his stomach. "If you know what I mean."

Virginia nodded. "Shotgun time."

"You got it. Rather than face their neighbors with an unwed pregnant daughter, the family allowed them to marry. He worked in the family winery for a while."

"Breenda said her father left her this place. How did they get here from France?"

"He built this house so he and his family could stay a week or so during the summers. The farm stand was just up the road. Like I said, this place never lets you go once you see it. Still, it's nothing like Ocracoke."

"That's quite a story." Virginia took another bite and washed it down with wine. "You called Breenda Mrs. Taylor. I assume she married?"

"She met her husband during one of those summers. He died a few years ago."

"Any children?"

"A son who's head chef in a creole restaurant in New Orleans and a daughter who married a doctor in France. She got so interested in the medical field after marrying him, she became a nurse."

"Sounds like Breenda has done well for herself—this place and two fine children."

Charlie sipped wine. "Plan to have any?"

"Children?"

"No, seahorses." Charlie stuck his tongue out. "Yes, children."

"If I meet the right man, not some Navy rogue who lies to a perfectly honorable woman about a hotel room."

Charlie took another bite of beef and sip of wine. "I'd like kids. I'd teach my son how to surf fish and my daughter how to drive a jeep on the beach."

"Sounds suspiciously like you've picked out your wife and home, Mr. Smithson. What do you plan to do after the war?"

"I'd rather talk about you, Mis Starr. I doubt a woman who reads Poe intends to stay on Ocracoke Island the rest of her life."

"I've thought about teaching, but an education takes money I don't have and more money than I can get from selling that ring." Virginia paused. Her first Poe story had given her a girlish thought. What might Charlie think of it? "I thought about owning my own book store once. You know, since I like to read. That takes money too, unfortunately."

Charlie placed his elbows on the table and steepled his fingers. "Don't give up on your dreams. I just found mine, and I plan to hang on for everything I'm worth."

In the middle of a sip of wine, Virginia coughed. She wiped her lips with a napkin and smacked his hand. "The wine has affected your brain, you roguish man."

"I doubt it's affected my heart."

Virginia finished the last bite of beef and sipped the last taste of wine. "All your sweet talk's not getting you in bed with me." She took a roll. "We forgot the cro— What did you call these?"

"Croissant." Charlie took one from the plate and tore it in half. "This is the best part." He slid the croissant through gravy and took a bite."

Virginia repeated his performance with the crusty bread and meaty gravy. "Sopping, something I know about."

"Got that right," Charlie said, sopping more gravy. "I wonder what Ruby's up to?"

"She's probably reading one of her romance novels. There's no telling with that child."

## Chapter 30

## Secrets

Ruby stamped her foot on the kitchen floor. "You need one and you know it."

Erich hesitated. "How do I know you'll do a good job?"

"I did Papa's, he never complained."

"I suppose …"

"Will you please sit so I can cover you with this sheet and trim your hair? I love your curls, but you're starting to look like a girl."

Erich dropped to the chair. "At least you don't want me to undress."

"You liked me looking at all your pretty boy parts and you know it. Hold your chin up so I can get this sheet on you."

Erich did as she asked. "Did you catch any crabs? You never said."

"A bucketful. I'll boil them and save what meat we don't eat." Ruby snipped the scissors twice. "Ready to get whacked?"

"Do I have a choice?"

*Snip-snip.* "Not a one." Ruby trimmed the blond curls in the back and sides, making sure to not snip an ear. She circled to work on the curls above Erich's forehead, straddling his knees to tease him with her cleavage. "It's looking good, don't you think?"

"You're incorrigible."

"What I am is done." Ruby sat in his lap. "Time for that kiss I've been waiting for." She started to kiss him but stopped. "Brush your teeth, Mr. Coffee Breath. No, first tell me what that fifty-cent word means."

"Incorrigible means you're unable of being reformed."

"As with my teasing? Do you really, deep down in your heart of hearts, want me to *reform* my teasing?"

Erich nuzzled her neck. "Not at all. That's one of the things about you that make you so loveable."

Ruby hopped from his lap. "Good answer. Teeth. Now."

"No, ma'am."

"Why in the name of Poseidon not?"

"While I enjoy spontaneity, I enjoy romance also. I want to court you."

"How so?"

"A romantic dinner on your pier for one. What are we having with the crabs?"

"I could make biscuits."

"Do you have any vegetables ready in your garden?"

"Maybe some young carrots."

"I'd like to make a fresh salad, but it's too early for tomatoes."

"We have some canned. Green beans. Onions. Things like that."

Erich stood. "Dandelion greens would be a start. Add a few tomatoes and carrots and a bit of vinegar, we'd have a fine salad."

Ruby followed him to the porch. "Listen to you, Mr. Fancy Pants Chef."

"I like to cook. If that makes me all that, so be it."

"I'm teasing, is all. I think it's very sweet of you to cook for me."

At the bottom of the steps, Erich faced her. "You know I must keep you guessing. Can you get me a bowl? As far as the crabs, you handle them, all right?"

Ruby saluted. "Yes, sir, Mr. Merman sir." She unbuttoned a shirt button." Care for a side of boob to go with that?"

Erich covered his eyes. "Completely incorrigible."

With a dishtowel, Ruby lifted the lid off the steaming pot, revealing blue crabs transformed to red, fragrant with briny aroma. On the porch, she looked for Erich. Not seeing him, she looked around the house and did the same at the other end of the porch. He wasn't there either. She shaded her eyes from the bright sun reflecting off the sound. Erich sat at the end of the pier. The bowl she gave him to collect items for the salad sat beside him, including the bag with Thea's picture and letters.

At the pier, she stopped before her shoes clomped on the boards. Erich sniffled and wiped his nose as he softly cried. Tears immediately stung Ruby's eyes. She could only imagine why he sobbed—from the pain, heartache, and sheer helplessness at losing his wife and family, let alone being in a country he had yet to call home.

One final sob left him. She joined him, slipping her arm into his. "I wish I could make it better. I'd even transform myself into Thea if I could."

Erich slipped his arm around her waist. "You'd have me crying again if you did that."

"Oh, poo, you're just being sweet."

"Not at all. I care for you because of the unique person you are."

"Are you sure? I think it really bothered you when I peeked through the window at your naked self. Your voice reminded me of Papa's whenever I misbehaved, all stern and gruff."

"Which I imagine was quite often."

"Enough about me. Not that I'm rushing you—Heaven knows I wouldn't do that—but is Thea's memory keeping you from kissing me?"

"The exact opposite, dear one. We knew each other since we were children. Our backyards joined. The first time I kissed her was on a swing hanging from a maple there. I proposed to her there too."

"I'm sure all those memories made your love much more than everyday average love."

"Yes." Erich kissed her forehead, holding his warm lips there longer than usual. "Part of my tears were because of missing her. The other part ... that part is difficult to speak of."

"Secrets between you and Thea are sacred. I don't need to know."

"It's likely my all too fertile imagination is thinking things better left unthought. All I can imagine is how she might've been pregnant when ..." Erich's chin fell to his chest.

Ruby snuggled her head into the hollow of his shoulder and neck.

The soft breeze, scented with sunlight, bumped the rowboat into the pier, *clunk, clunk, clunking* hollowly. The marsh grass added its note of nature, whispering and rustling near-silent secrets of the Pamlico—secrets more ancient than the stout lighthouse rising like a squat ghost with its single glaring eye to warn ship after ship of the hazards off the slender strip of sand known as Ocracoke.

Ruby liked secrets. Still, the secret she carried—that Erich carried—needed to be told.

"I can't tell you anything that will make you feel better about losing Thea." She raised from his shoulder to look into his eyes. "But I can tell you this, because you need to know what I'm about to say doesn't make any difference in how I feel about you. I know me, I act like a child at times. That's because I see life as something to light a fire under, not something to smolder like a barely burning ember."

"Very eloquently said, but what are you attempting to say?"

"People might not know it—Ginny especially—but despite my childish ways, I'm a thinker like you are. That means I've thought about how you're a German and how it doesn't bother me one bit."

Ruby expected Erich to either jump and run or deny it. Instead, he softly smiled. "I'm happy you know. My story is the same, except I was on a U-boat. I'm happier still how none of that matters to you." He kissed her forehead. "I'm sure most Americans would feel quite differently. Might I ask why you don't?"

"The most important reason is your love for Thea. How can I call a man my enemy when he shows who he is in the tears he cries for his lost wife?"

Ruby folded her hands in her lap. "Another is a lesson I learned from Papa. A hobo once came over on a tug boat from Hatteras. He had a beard halfway down his chest and wore a ragged pair of bib overalls. His shoes weren't much more than soles and laces. I was out on the porch when he came strolling down the path, whistling some strange song. I ran inside quick as a minute to get Papa. The hobo said he'd just arrived from Hatteras and wondered if Papa had any work he could do for a meal. Papa asked the hobo if he minded turning over our garden spot with a pitchfork. That's before we got Jimmy and a plow."

"Did the hobo tell you what he was whistling?"

"Caught that didn't you? He whistled it all afternoon while he turned over the garden spot. He took a break now and then and I'd pump him a glass of water."

"Where was your mother and sister while all this was going on?"

"They were in the village getting the mail. They came back while the hobo was working. Papa took Mama inside and told her what was going on. Ginny stayed in. Her eyes got big as fifty-cent pieces when she saw the hobo. Anyway, Mama cooked fried chicken and mashed potatoes with gravy and biscuits. When the sun started slipping into the sound—Papa always told to me listen for the hiss—he told the hobo he'd worked long enough. Told him to take a seat on the porch and he'd be right out with his supper."

Erich licked his lips. "I'm sure he enjoyed it."

"I watched him eat every bite. When he sopped the last drop of gravy, I asked him what the song was he was whistling. He said it was called *Whistle While You Work*. Said it helped the day go by if you did your job with a happy heart instead of a sour one. After he left, Papa sat by me on the porch steps and asked what I thought of the hobo. I told him I thought it'd be an interesting life to wander around meeting new people wherever I went. I also told him I thought it'd be a sad life too, with no family or place to call home."

"What was the lesson he told you?"

"He said he asked me what I thought of the hobo because of how he was dressed. When I didn't say anything about it, he said he was glad I didn't judge him based on his outside. That things sometime happen for people to be in the position they're in, like things not their fault. Of course, you can't go around letting hoodlums steal and kill, or like Hitler, start wars. I'm sure you know that already."

"Your fathers's philosophy on life matches mine perfectly. Since it's his, it's yours too. You're a constant surprise, dear one."

"Is that your pet name for me now? You called me that while ago."

"Does it please you?"

"It's better than incorrigible."

"Since you admitted to being curious, I admit to being curious also. How did you know I'm German? And how long?"

"It's been teasing me for a while. I only knew for sure when you just told me."

"Aren't you something, leading me on like that?"

"Ginny always says if she gives me a thread, I'll unravel the whole blanket."

"How did you unravel my mystery?"

"You said you were a British seaman and jumped ship. A British seaman's crew would radio the nearest Navy folks to be on the lookout for the body. The Navy's building a base here, so that's Ocracoke. That means Charlie would've told Ginny and Ginny would've told me."

"All that never crossed my mind, my extremely intelligent and beautiful mermaid. Have you given my dilemma any thought? I'd rather return to the workshop as a guest instead of to hide."

"Not enough to amount to much. You?"

"About the same."

Ruby stood. "Let's not worry about it and get supper ready. I'm looking forward to your cooking."

Erich gave Ruby the bowl filled with dandelion greens and carrots from the garden. He collected the document bag, and she took his hand and led him back to the house.

Inside, the crab's briny aroma made his mouth water. "On the pier I saw one of your crabs beneath my feet. It was a beautiful, iridescent blue. We have brown crabs in …"

Ruby tapped his head with a carrot. "Go ahead, the secret's out, you had brown crabs in Germany. Where did you live?"

"In Bremen. I hated lying to you."

"I'd have done the same."

"Everything else was the truth."

"Everything except the U-boat you jumped from."

"We call them an *unterseeboot.*" Erich winced. "Talking about what I did in the war makes me feel as if I'm still the enemy. Also, whenever we get my problem worked out with me being around people, I might inadvertently speak German, which cannot happen."

At the basin, Ruby paused from washing the greens and carrots. "I agree. Too many people around here have lost family in the war." She whirled around. "I … well, I hate to ask, but …"

"You want to know if we sank a ship nearby."

"Please tell me you didn't sink—" She pulled a chair from the table and collapsed into it. "No, thank goodness. Walter's ship sank after you got here."

"We sank a tanker. The only reason I fought was to protect my country, like your men fight to protect theirs. I despise Hitler for starting this insane war. Thea did too. Still, I couldn't stand by and do nothing."

"Like you could anyway. I'm sure all men of certain ages have to fight."

"I assume it's the same here."

"Pretty much." Ruby stood. "The greens are clean if you want to make your salad. I'll get the tomatoes."

"Do you have vinegar?"

"It's the only thing that makes turnip salad fit to eat. Boiled dandelion greens too."

"Brown sugar?"

Ruby opened a cabinet. "Mama used it to make apple pie." She placed the box and the vinegar on the table. "Anything else?"

"Do you have a safe place for my letters from Thea? I'd like to keep those and her picture out of the building for now. I'll take them back with me if we haven't decided on a plan before your sister returns."

"I'll put them in the cedar chest at the foot of my bed." Ruby took the bag to her room. "At Mama's service, Mr. Austin from the restaurant said Ginny and I could take off as long as we needed."

Erich, slicing carrots, stopped. "I'm sure you need time. Losing a parent is difficult."

"We *both* need time from losing folks we love."

"You said your sister will be away the coming week, which gives us plenty of time." The knife clunked through a carrot. "Still, I think it best if I stay in the workshop the last night." Erich filled two bowls halfway with the dandelion greens and carrots. Ruby opened the canned tomatoes. He forked several of the larger chunks into a bowl and added several pinches of brown sugar, lightly poured vinegar, mixed everything, and tasted. "Not bad for dressing our salads. Do you have pliers and a hammer for the crabs?"

"Old newspapers too." Ruby retrieved everything, spread the paper on the table, and added a large bowl. "There. Now we can crack these crabs and put the meat in the bowl without making a mess."

Hammering shells, squeezing claws, and tasting succulent, somewhat-salty samples, Erich helped Ruby fill the bowl. He licked his fingertips, sore from the sharp edges on the shells. "We're ready for the pier. I don't imagine you have a bottle of white wine handy?"

Brushing bits of crabmeat from her apron, Ruby eyed him. "You don't need wine to get a kiss. Water's fine."

"To get a kiss or to drink with dinner?"

"Look, Mr. Merman, if you plan on becoming an O'cocker, it's called 'supper.' As far as kisses, we'll see. You're the one wanting to court me, remember?"

"After our revealing conversation on the pier, I feel halfway there."

Ruby kissed his cheek. "That's all you get until you're *all* the way there." She picked up the bowl of crabmeat. "Let's eat."

## Chapter 31

## Just

In the white-enameled clawfoot bathtub, Virginia slid down into the hot water. Nothing, absolutely nothing, compared to being fully immersed up to her neck, especially not bathing in the washtub at home. She could hardly get her bottom and legs in that at all.

Charlie knocked on the door. "Enjoying that tub?"

"I could get used to this." Virginia palmed her breasts. "You better not be looking through the keyhole."

"You can see more through these big keyholes than you think."

Virginia threw a washcloth at the doorknob, hanging it so it blocked the keyhole. "What do you see *now,* Mr. Peeping Tom?"

The washcloth fell to the floor, pushed off by a pencil extending from the keyhole. "What do *you* see now?"

Virginia threw a towel, hanging the doorknob again. No matter how much Charlie poked with the pencil, the towel stayed. "Think you're pretty smart, don't you?"

"I'm good at aiming a towel, is what I am."

"Did you know these doors don't lock?"

"The hook is latched."

"When I thought to ask you here, I unscrewed that eyebolt." The door shook. "Just a push should be all it—"

"We'll never get to that steak place if you keep aggravating me with your teenage boy hormones."

"I've seen all I need to see. Enjoy your bath."

Virginia slid up to wash her shoulders, tingling with the idea that Charlie might've seen her naked. How would it feel to have his hands on—

She shook her head. Lose those thoughts and enjoy this tub. Above all, make sure those thoughts don't hit at bedtime.

The soothing bath passed all too quickly. Virginia drained the tub and knelt under the faucet to wet, shampoo, and rinse her hair, then wrapped a towel around herself and squeezed the remaining water from her hair with another towel. It should be dry by the time Charlie bathed and shaved.

She unhooked the latch. "I'm coming out in nothing but a towel." She opened the door. "Think you can handle—" She snapped her eyes shut. "Why in the blue crab blazes are you naked?"

"Just trying to make our bet more interesting."

"You said it was about sleeping together. Not *sleeping* together."

"See anything you like?"

"Shut up and take a bath."

Charlie's laughter came from behind the closed bathroom door, followed by water splashing into the tub. Virginia tapped the door. "Laugh it up. I peeked through my fingers and could laugh too. I've seen marsh rabbits with bigger—"

"Must've been one huge marsh rabbit. Get ready so I can, okay?"

Virginia opened her suitcase. How could she go out with Charlie in denims and a work shirt?

"Virginia?"

"What?"

"Look in the closet."

"Why?"

"There's a naked man in there."

"You're as bad as Ruby."

"Just look, okay?"

Virginia opened the door. "Forget what I said about being like Ruby." She finished drying, slipped on panties and a bra, and took the dress from the hanger to hold it up to herself. The deep blue pleats fell perfectly at her knees. The square neck should reveal her starfish necklace perfectly as well. The dress included a matching belt. She stepped to the bathroom door. "I don't know how to thank you. This is one of the nicest things anyone has ever done for me."

"You'll have to thank Breenda. I ran downstairs while you were bathing and asked if she had anything that might fit you. She said her daughter left that dress here."

"Too bad she didn't leave shoes too."

"Look again. Breenda and I wouldn't let you down."

Virginia took a pair of black high heels from the closet floor. "What are these called? They have a strap around the ankle and little openings in the toes?"

"Breenda called them Mary Janes. Do they fit?"

"I've got to dry my hair better before I dress."

With most of the moisture toweled from her hair, Virginia slipped the dress over her head and shimmied it over her hips. The shoes were a tad loose, but she didn't care. Compared to the denims and shirt, the dress and shoes made her feel like a queen. She stepped to the bathroom door. "I love it, Charlie. I'll be ready after I brush my hair. How long—"

Charlie opened the door. "Bet you're glad I'm wearing a towel. Mind doing your hair on the balcony while I get dressed?"

"You ask that after letting me see you naked?"

Charlie dropped the towel.

Virginia grabbed her brush from the dresser and ran to the balcony. "You're taking this bet too doggone seriously."

"Ready for that steak?"

"Did you get extra blankets for the floor from Breenda?"

"It's pretty warm, sheets will do." Charlie's sock feet thudded across the wood floor. "I sleep naked anyway."

"I don't."

"You will—when we get married."

Virginia whirled around and threw the brush at Charlie, hitting his bare chest. *"If,* Mr. Smithson."

Charlie rubbed his chest, buttoned his white shirt, and tucked it into his tan slacks. "Nice arm." He joined her on the balcony. "Nice everything else too."

"Thanks, I think."

"Don't tell me I'm getting on your nerves as bad as Ruby?"

"I don't mind fun."

He offered his arm. "Let's go have some."

Downstairs, after Breenda remarked on how well the dress fit, and after Virginia thanked her for allowing her to wear it and the shoes, Charlie called a cab. Waiting on the porch swing, he gave the floor a nudge to get it going. "Nice place, huh?"

"I'm glad you asked me to come."

The chains squeaked when the swing reached its backward rise and started down. In the huge oak, a bird squawked, similar to a car horn. Virginia pointed. "What kind of bird is that? It's sort of a beige and blue. The blue's almost purple."

"I doubt you see those on Ocracoke. It's a blue jay."

Virginia couldn't see the plane, but one took off from the airfield. Its hushed growl grew to a loud roar as it approached the Neuse. She stepped to the porch's edge. Appearing far to the left, above the trees on the opposite creek bank, the plane gained altitude, circled back to fly over the house, and became a barely humming speck in the sky on its way west. She returned to the swing. "I'm surprised how quiet it is, even with the airfield nearby."

"That's one of things I like about it." Charlie's eyes focused below her chin. "New necklace?"

"It was Mama's, she had three. Ruby's wearing a sand dollar. We put the other on Mama."

"A starfish for Virginia Starr. Very fitting."

"It was Ruby's idea." Virginia elbowed Charlie's ribs. "She has good ones now and then."

Charlie faced the driveway, where gravel crunched beneath the tires of their cab. Walking out to meet it, he stopped while Virginia continued a few steps. "Mm, mm, mm," he said.

Virginia spun. "Stop ogling whatever you're ogling and get up here so I can hold your arm before I fall in these wobbly shoes."

"Needless to say, you're not used to walking in high heels."

"Then why say anything about it?"

"They still make you look like you have legs up to your neck." Charlie offered his arm, which she took.

"Sorry for being snappy. Being the typical man, you deserve it."

"Your intelligence stimulates me as much as your legs." Charlie opened the cab door. "Doesn't that count for something?"

"I suppose having a man who thinks I'm stimulating in whatever ways isn't all bad." Virginia got in the cab.

It turned onto main street, drove half a block, and parked in front of a restaurant. Virginia got out and read the sign. "Charlie's Place? You've *got* to be kidding."

"I've always thought of owning a restaurant." Charlie paid the cabby. "Yes, I'm kidding."

Virginia stepped onto the sidewalk, wincing as her ankle gave way beneath the wobbly high heel. "Durn it, I twisted my ankle."

Charlie grabbed her arm. "Want to eat in our room? I was hoping we could dance, but ..."

"Help me in. I'd still love a steak."

The greeter led them to a table. Virginia sat and rubbed her ankle. "It's not too bad."

"I'll rub it later. You might enjoy it as much as I will."

"As long you keep your rubs limited to my ankle." Virginia looked around the room. Round tables for two with white tablecloths were scattered about. A piano waited for a player in the far corner next to the bar, where a bartender wiped glasses. She faced Charlie. "They always seem to be wiping glasses in the mysteries I've read."

"It's slow tonight. Will I have to carry you up the stairs, Scarlett?"

Virginia stopped rubbing her ankle to tap his hand. "Ha, ha, ha, Mr. Attempting-to-be-funny man. Ruby loves that book."

"You mentioned Poe. What other—"

A shorter than average man—thin and wiry, wearing a white apron, a red bow tie, and carrying menus—stepped to the table. He wore his dark hair slicked back, graying at the temples, and a gray goatee. "Hello dere, Charlie. You come back for to see me, I see."

The man's voice sounded similar to a Cajun fellow who had visited Ocracoke, until his wife showed up and took him home, so the gossips had said. The man offered Virginia a menu.

"How in de worl' dis heah man talk you into a date, I never know." The man pronounced "I" as "Ah" and "never" as "nevah."

Virginia took the menu. "He's obviously a rogue. Do you know him well?"

"Ah know he 'bout eat a side o' beef a sittin'. What can I gets for you dis beautimus eve'nin'?"

"I'll let Charlie order—he's got to be good for something." Virginia winked at Charlie, who waved the menu away.

"Virginia, meet Just."

"*Just* what? Is there more?"

"Da's me, Ah just plain Just. Charlie, you like a bottle o' dat beautimus red you had de udder night?"

"Exactly what I had in mind. Salads to start. For our meal we'll share one of your huge porterhouse steaks cooked to medium. A baked potato a piece."

"Just beautimus, just beautimus. It be my las' one, doh, wid dis here war an' all." Just took the menu from Virginia. "Be right back."

"What a character," Virginia said.

"A character who can cook," Charlie said. "He plays the piano on quiet nights."

"What time is your class in the morning?"

"Seven. I'll set the alarm for six. I'll be back around lunch."

Just returned with the wine. "Thought you two might be thirsty." He poured two glasses half full. "Two salads comin' up."

Charlie sipped wine. "You can sell that ring tomorrow."

"I hate to ask but …" Virginia looked at her hands.

Charlie lifted her chin with his fingertips. "I don't mind."

"Reading my mind, Mr. Smithson?"

"You were going to ask to borrow money for the cab, right?" Charlie withdrew his hand. "Know this before you answer—what's mine is yours—that's how much I care about you."

"That's sweet, but—"

"Oh, he sweet all right." Just placed two bowls filled with lettuce, tomatoes, and bell peppers on the table. "Be right back wid de dressin'. Vinaigrette okay?"

*If the Sunrise Forgets Tomorrow*

"Perfect." Charlie faced Virginia. "Although it's nice you think I'm sweet—I think you're sweet too—I'm glad to help. Besides, your feet might smell when I rub your ankle."

"Whatever, Mr. Smithson."

Just brought the steak out on a sizzling platter, including two extra plates with the potatoes. Charlie cut the smaller section of steak from the porterhouse and placed it on Virginia's plate. She forked a bite and sniffed the juicy meat. It didn't get any beefier than this "beautimus" portion of steak. Potato split and steaming, including butter, salt, and pepper, she'd never envisioned—or tasted—such a delicious meal.

They ate and shared small talk concerning her and Ruby growing up on Ocracoke, and Charlie growing up in the Blue Ridge Mountains. Halfway into the meal, Just took a seat at the piano. "Y'all gots a request?"

"Play that tune you played the last time I was here," Charlie said.

"Ah, you like dat one, eh? Maybe Miss Virginia like it too. It remind me o' her, just plain beautimus."

Just warmed up with a somewhat hesitant scale. Virginia leaned over the table and whispered, "What's he going to play, chopsticks?"

Charlie eyes narrowed. "So, the starfish has spines. Never judge a Cajun by his red bow tie."

"I only meant—"

"I know what you meant. The next time you judge someone, let's hope you do a better job than with Just."

Virginia sat back in the chair. What did Ruby tell her concerning this subject? It was about some strange man who— That's right, a hobo showed up at the house one day, asking for work. Papa told Ruby to never judge a man by his outside, and she whispered that to Virginia in bed that night.

The notes now streamed from the piano, surpassing chopsticks by a huge margin. Virginia placed her hand on Charlie's. "You're right—not because of how beautifully Just is playing—but because I was wrong."

"I thought you might figure that out. Living on that sandy slice of island away from the outside world could affect how a person sees others." The notes ended. "You're going to love this."

Just began with the hint of a song—soft notes whispered into a lover's ear. Gradually the notes strengthened, blending bass, baritone, and tenor tones into a harmony that pounded the room with intensity. The pattern continued, waves on Ocracoke rising and crashing. It slowed to soft again—the wings of a moth caressing Virginia's cheek. The notes faded. She wiped tears and then clapped.

Just stood and bowed. "Tank you, tank you. Ah so happy you like my playing, Miss Virginia."

"It was wonderful, Just. What's the name of your song?"

"Ask Charlie while I find y'all a couple slices o' strawberry pie."

Virginia faced Charlie. "Well?"

"I told him about you the last time I was here and asked him to write a song to reflect my feelings. I haven't heard it until now."

"You mean...?"

"That's right, it's *Virginia's Song.*"

Virginia wiped tears again. "I won't have a napkin for the strawberry pie with if I keep this up." She returned the napkin to her lap. "What am I going to do with you? Every time I turn around, you surprise me."

Just returned as she swallowed the last delicious bite of the pie. "Just, your pie is as wonderful as the steak and the music. I can't tell you how much I've enjoyed myself."

"Ah's just happy you is happy, Miss Virginia. Charlie, you bring dis fine young lady back soon, you heah?"

At the bed and breakfast, Virginia took Charlie's arm for the short stroll to the front porch and up the steps, not only to favor her ankle, but to be close to this sweet man. He stopped at the door. "Want to sit on the swing?"

"Let's go to our room, Rhett."

"Fine by me, Scarlett. I can't see the stars for the clouds, we might get rain." He helped Virginia up the stairs. "Want to get ready for bed now or ...?"

"It's getting cool. Better get a blanket or two from Breenda. I'll brush my teeth and slip into my nightgown." She started to the bathroom and stopped. "Don't get any ideas about seeing through my gown. I brought a robe too."

By the time she finished, Charlie knocked, and she said to come in. At the dresser, he clicked a radio on. "You like blues?"

"Being from the mountains, I thought you'd like *blue*grass. Banjos, fiddles, that kind of stuff."

"I do, but blues is more ... I suppose sultry describes it. Kind of like you, dark one. As much as I love how your denims fit, you're stunning in a dress."

"That's not getting me out of my robe."

"You still look great. My turn in the bathroom." Charlie picked up one of the blankets he'd gotten from Breenda. "I'll need this for a robe."

Virginia stepped to the balcony doors. Rain drizzled down, pattering against the glass. A gust of wind shook the doors. Despite the warmth of the robe, she wrapped her arms around herself. A steak of lightning, its intensity wavering in jagged brilliance, found its mark far across the creek. Thunder followed several seconds later, low and booming, rattling the glass door.

Charlie's feet pattered from the bathroom. Virginia didn't face him. "Storm's coming."

"Not in here it's not. What do you think of my robe?"

Virginia turned around. Charlie dropped the blanket, but she covered her eyes before glimpsing skin. "You're as sweet as that strawberry pie, Charlie, but you're still such a man."

"Take a peek before passing judgment."

"How do I know I can trust you?"

"By peeking."

Virginia spread her fingers. Charlie wore white pajamas with vertical blue stripes. She lowered her hand. "What happened to sleeping naked?"

He sat on the bed. "I was teasing you."

Lightning brightened the room, followed by the harsh crack of thunder. It rolled off into the night, fading as if it were one of the torpedoed ships off of Ocracoke, explosions dying as it slipped beneath the waves. Static sizzled on the radio, replacing the subtle sounds of a trumpet, piano, drums, and bass.

Charlie clicked the radio off. "How's the ankle?"

Virginia sat on the bed and worked the joint. "Not bad."

"Care to dance?"

"No music."

"We can make our own." Charlie held out his hand.

Virginia slipped her fingers into his rough palm. He placed his other hand over her shoulder blades and pulled her close. She placed her other hand on his shoulder. "Can you sing?"

Charlie touched his forehead to hers. "Like a pelican."

"Then how—"

"Hush." His cheek pressed against her temple. Aftershave. Hair tonic. Breath warming her ear. The soft hum of the beginning of *Virginia's Song*.

"You're terrible," she said.

"Really?" He hummed again. "I thought my humming was pretty good."

"You're terrible because ..."

Charlie looked into her eyes. "Hmm, hmm ... hmm?"

"I never thought this would happen."

"Hmm?"

"Will you stop that?"

He kissed her forehead. "Should I stop that?" He kissed her nose. "Or that?" His lips lingered near hers, warm breath sweet with strawberries.

Virginia worked free of his arms and sat on the bed, wincing at the remaining soreness in her ankle. "You're still terrible."

He sat beside her. "Why's that?"

She lay her head on his shoulder. "Because."

"You've gotta do better than that, Virgeeeeeenia."

Virginia fingered a button on his pajamas. "You know about Walter. I liked him fine but not love. He was the standard O'cocker boy—grew up fishing, crabbing, trying to make a living off the sea. I wanted more than that. I was proud of him for learning how to fly, but that didn't make me love him."

"I don't see how all that makes *me* terrible."

"When the Navy started building the base, I wondered if a man might come along and show me what I was missing. You did exactly that."

"I still don't see how that makes me terrible."

"Will you be quiet and let me finish?"

"Consider me quiet. And?"

"I decided I'd rather not have feelings for a man during the war."

"I wouldn't expect a woman to marry me when the world's gone insane. Are you saying you have feelings for me beyond a kiss on the beach?" Charlie squeezed her waist. "Was it the dress or the steak?"

Virginia snapped her head off his shoulder and punched his arm. "Tarnation to Ocracoke and back—I've fallen in love with a male Ruby. That's why you're terrible"

"Wha-a-a-t?"

"Go ahead, call a cab and run away in your pajamas."

"Not at all. From the first time I saw you, breathless from riding Jimmy, dark hair scattered around your face, darker eyes blazing, I think I loved you even then."

Virginia lowered her head. "Which means we're in trouble because of the war."

"Let's worry about the sleeping arrangements instead of all that. Do I have to sleep—I mean sleep—on the cold floor?"

"You just lost our bet, Mr. Smithson."

"Not at all." Charlie opened the nightstand drawer for a pad and pencil. "When Breenda showed me the room, she told me the pad was here in case I wanted to write someone." He tore two pieces of paper from the pad, wrote on one, and folded it. "You're turn."

Virginia took the paper and pencil. "My turn for what?"

"Write what you wanted if you won the bet."

"Then?"

"We trade and read them."

"Why all the secrecy?"

"I'm curious to know if they match. Don't you think it'd be fun to find out at the same time?"

Virginia wrote and folded the paper. "Here you go."

Charlie gave her his folded paper. "On the count of three. One, two—"

"Shut up and read." Virginia opened the paper. "You're still terrible."

"Darn right. Should we read them together?"

"Whatever, Mr. Smithson."

"Marry me," they said, "but after the war."

Charlie laughed. "What do you know about that? Does your future husband get a kiss?"

"He most certainly does not. Don't you want your future wife to be a maiden on her honeymoon night?"

"Aren't *you* smart? Ready for bed?"

"If you point the other way so I can spoon you. I won't get a wink of sleep if you spoon me."

"Right, the future Mrs. Smithson." Charlie pulled the covers back. "Time to get out of that robe."

Virginia hung the robe over a chair and climbed under the covers. "Sleep by the clock. I might feel like sleeping in, future husband."

"I like the sound of that, future wife." Charlie set the alarm and clicked the light off. Except for the departing flashes of lightning, darkness filled the room. The covers rustled as he settled into bed. Virginia snuggled close to his warmth and slipped her arm around his waist. "I love you, Charlie."

"I love you too, dear heart."

"Papa and Mama used to call Ruby and me that."

"Do you mind?"

"I take it as a good omen."

Charlie kissed her palm. "I'm not fond of omens. The bad ones seem to have a way of showing up when we hope for the good ones most of all. I better get to sleep, goodnight."

Charlie's chest rose and fell beneath Virginia's hand with the ever so slow ... the ever so steady ... rhythm of dreams. If not for the possibility of him being sent anywhere in the world because of this damn war, she could get used to this. The question—would he stay on Ocracoke? —begged an answer. She wouldn't ask him about it. As the saying went, sometimes ignorance was bliss, and bliss described this moment perfectly. Still, when lightning had struck close enough for thunder to rattle the glass in the balcony doors, dread had gripped her guts with the bony fingers of warning, exactly like when Mama wouldn't eat and Doc Wills had to be fetched.

Virginia kissed Charlie's neck. He stirred, mumbled, and stilled.

She cursed that dread, cursed it to hell and away from her and Ruby. Life had been a series of more downs than ups for them both, and it was time the ups gained the upper hand.

The quiet calm of Charlie's breathing soothed her. Lightning flashed bright enough to show beneath closed eyelids. Seconds later, thunder boomed again, rattling the glass in the balcony door. The rumbles faded into the night, a series of distant groanings and grumblings.

Let the storm come and wash away the dread. She and Ruby had handled many a storm, and they would handle more when the time came.

## Chapter 31

## Storms

On the way to the pier behind a hurrying Erich, Ruby carried a tray that held two salads and two glasses of water. She also clasped a folded quilt under her arm. "Slow down, hungry merman. You can't be that hungry."

Carrying the bowl of crabmeat, two plates, and two forks, he looked over his shoulder. "This crab smells delicious. It would make a fine omelet."

"That's the second time you told me about an omelet. I'll be dead before I taste one."

Erich's shoes clomped on the pier's gray boards. "You and your silliness."

At the end of the pier, Ruby let the quilt fall from under her arm and set the tray on the boards. Erich did likewise with the bowl, plates, and forks, then helped her spread the threadbare quilt of blue, red, and white scraps of cloth.

Supper in place, they sat cross-legged on the quilt. He started to spoon crab onto his plate, but Ruby tapped his hand. "I'd like to say a blessing. If that Jerry finds out I'm hiding you in Papa's workshop, he'll shoot us both." She bowed her head. "Dear God, thank you for this day and this food. Thank you for all the fish and shellfish you provide for us O'Cockers. My girls in the henhouse too, can't forget them. Please end this war soon. Too many people all over the world are dying because of it. Also, God, please give us an idea that helps Erich live his life in peace with me. We might have to lie, but I'm sure you'll understand. And please tell Papa and Mama how much Ginny and me miss them. I dearly wish I could hug them one last time. Amen."

"An eloquent prayer, dear one. I'd do anything to hug my parents again as well."

Raising a forkful of dandelion greens to her mouth, Ruby stopped. "Anything except dying. I draw the line at that. For me too."

"I'd much prefer to wait until I'm old and gray." The slightest of smiles teased Erich's lips upward. "And have discovered all the delights your island has in store."

Ruby swallowed salad. "Your smile tells me I'm one of those delights. I love the idea of being a delight. Being a delight sounds delightful."

"Most definitely."

"What would you do first?"

"That's extremely dangerous territory." Erich pointed his fork at her. "And you know it."

"I'm tempted to pout, just one thing?" Ruby fluttered her eyelashes. "Please?"

"Incorrigible." Erich rose and circled behind her. "One thing. Then you'll see why it's dangerous."

"Phooey, I can—"

Erich pulled her hair away from her neck and tugged at the gold chain. The sand dollar rose and fell between her breasts, a metallic tickle against her skin. "Very nice," he murmured. "Reminds me of a mountain valley in Germany."

"You're obviously not talking about my sand dollar, naughty merman."

Erich's warm breath caressed her ear. "What I would do with my tongue to your peaks would make you shiver, my intensely sensual mermaid."

A heated tingle surged through Ruby. How she wanted him to do exactly what he suggested. She started to undo a button. He placed his hand upon hers. "No, dear one. One more taste of what's to come. Then we'll have our supper."

"But—"

"Trust me, do you trust me?"

Ruby's answer hitched in her throat, so she nodded.

"Correct answer, my sweetness." His lips touched the curve of her ear, then her ear lobe. What must be his tongue traced circles of wetness to the sensitive skin just below her ear, then dipped to where her neck joined her trembling shoulders. Those manly lips kissed, nibbled, teased. More circles with his tongue ...

"Erich, oh my stars, please ..."

He fingered the top button of her shirt. "Yes, dear one?"

Ruby whirled. Her water glass clattered across the pier. "I can't ... I can't ..."

"I know we can't, which is why I teased you so savagely."

She fanned herself. "Now I know how Scarlett felt when Rhett carried her up the stairs of Tara."

"*Gone with the Wind?*"

Ruby righted her glass. "Yes, I adore it."

"Shall I get you more water?"

"We can share yours."

Ruby took a bite of the somewhat salty crab and drank water. Erich did also, followed by a bite of greens. A slight breeze stirred the marsh grass. Ruby touched her forehead and pulled away wet fingers. "Oh, poo."

Erich looked overhead. "No gulls, but it's cloudy."

"Yes, silly, that means rain. I'd hate for our supper to be ruined. There's hardly a cloud behind us, so ..." She turned around. A roiling mass hung over the mainland, lightning flashing within its black belly. "That's on the way to Havelock, where Ginny is. Maybe it'll stay away until we finish."

"I hope so." Erich forked another white mound of crabmeat. "This is the best crab I've ever tasted."

The fork continued to his mouth as Ruby's did to hers. Thunder rumbled behind her. She stood with her nearly empty plate. "Let's get inside before lightning helps us hug our mamas and papas sooner than later."

Ruby stacked dishes by the basin. Erich placed the crabmeat in the icebox.

Lightning flared again, illuminating the room in pulsing flashes of brightness. Thunder rolled from the direction of the mainland. Loud at first, it gradually faded to lesser and lesser booming suggestions of sound.

Ruby picked up the pail. "Can you fill this so—"

*Blam!* Sparks flew outside. Tree limbs cracked and crashed from the direction of the path. Ruby ran to the door. Smoke rose from the tree the lightning had struck. A huge oak limb, its end smoking as well, blocked the path. "Goodness! Any closer, we'd be smoking too."

Erich came to the window. "I heard either you or your sister sawing wood one day. I can saw that limb so we can get it off the path."

"That and the dishes can wait until morning. I better light a couple of lamps before it gets too dark to see."

A gray curtain of huge raindrops rattled the porch's tin roof, then died to a soft patter. "Did you see that?" Ruby said. "It's like someone covered us with a shroud."

Erich went to the screen door. "After the lightning stops, I'll get a pail of water so we can wash and brush our teeth." He pointed at his grin. "No need to ignore them now."

*If the Sunrise Forgets Tomorrow*

Ruby lit two lamps, placed one on the cupboard and one on the table. "We don't have a parlor. Ginny and me usually sit at the table to read, or go to our rooms." She sat. Erich did also.

"It's a bit cool. Do you want me to add a stick or two of that wood on the porch to the stove? I'll be quick with that lightning. I've no desire to leave you anytime soon."

Ruby tilted her head to one side. "How exactly would you *leave* me?"

"I just meant—"

"I'd rather you say won't leave me any time ever, Mr. Fischer."

"Of course, dear one, of course. I've yet to sample your delights."

"Listen to you." She poked his chest. "And *I'm* incorrigible."

Erich brought wood in and prodded it into place with a poker. Ruby squatted beside him, rubbing her hands together near the open door, where the embers glowed with warmth. "That feels wonderful. We can leave the door open and have ourselves a pretend fireplace. I've got an idea, be right back."

Ruby went to her room for her pillow and the quilt they used on the pier, then fetched Mama's pillow and quilt. "We'll lie on one quilt and cover up with the other one. We'll be as cozy as two oysters in the same shell."

"Can that happen?" Erich asked.

Ruby stopped unfolding one of the quilts to look his way. "Can what happen?"

"Can two oysters live in the same shell?"

"How could it? They're—" Ruby shoved the quilt into his chest. "You and your jokes. You might not get any of this at all."

They spread one quilt and pulled the other one to their waists. The sticks of wood now flamed red and yellow, radiating more heat than earlier. Ruby backed up to Erich. "Isn't this nice?"

He slipped his arm around her waist. "Very."

The wood popped and sparked. One of the sticks settled into the embers. Erich entwined his fingers into hers. The storm, with its lightning that had so violently downed the tree limb, rumbled into the night.

Erich nuzzled Ruby's neck, and she elbowed him. "Stop that."

"You don't like it?"

"That's the problem."

"We don't have water yet. I could lick your neck clean."

"I'm dirty all over."

"I'd lick you all over."

"I was thinking about letting you sleep with me." She looked back at him. "Guess who's sleeping in Mama's bed?"

"You said you trusted me."

"That's before I started to unbutton my shirt. I don't trust you, or myself." She faced the fire. "Do you have an idea for keeping out of Papa's workshop?"

"My accent is a problem. Have you thought of anything?"

"Maybe."

"And?"

"It's farfetched. I might use it if push comes to shove."

Erich pushed his hips against her bottom. "Your turn to shove back."

Ruby smacked his behind. "Stop that. You're—you know—is poking me."

"I have no earthly idea what you mean." Erich nuzzled her neck again, and Ruby jumped from the quilt.

"The storms gone, go get water. You wash and brush while I change the sheets on Mama's bed. I'll wash when you're through."

Erich grabbed the pail's wire handle. "What if I slip into your bed during the night?"

Ruby pointed. "See that drawer over there? The biggest butcher knife I can find is going on my nightstand. Any more questions?"

Erich's shoulders shook with a silent chuckle. The pail's wire handle rattled.

"What's so all-fired funny, Erich Fischer?"

"I think the courting is done. Now we need to come up with an idea that will allow us to do it."

Ruby placed her hands on her hips. "We'll *do* no such thing until we're married. I want my children's father to be my husband."

"Getting married is *exactly* what I meant, dear one. You are the most intriguing bundle of mischief and beauty and intelligence I think I've ever known. In short, I love you, my sweetness." He opened his arms. "Do you love me too?"

Ruby could hardly believe Erich's words. She'd come to think she loved him from the first moment she'd asked to see his tail, when he'd stood in the door of Papa's workshop, looking for all the world like a wet, sandy puppy. To finally hear him return the sentiment she'd been hoping for thrilled her. She rushed into his arms. "Yes, I love you. I've been hoping you'd tell me. Still, sleeping with me can't happen."

"Meaning?"

"You're more likely to think I need an all over licking after I wash." Yawning, she slipped from his arms. "Go fetch that water, I'm tired."

## Chapter 32

## Gifts

*B*rrrrrriiiiiiiiiiiinggggggggg.
Virginia poked Charlie. "Charlie. Clock. I need my beauty sleep." The lamp illuminated the bed in a circle of light. The ringing ended.

"Wenn die Dame noch schöner wird, würde ich denken, ich starb und traf einen Engel."

Virginia jerked upright from her pillow. "What in hades is that?"

"German. One reason the Navy sent me to Ocracoke is in case any German seaman are captured from U-boats."

"How did you learn German?"

"From a German neighbor when I was as a kid. He took me trout fishing when Dad couldn't."

"What did you just say?" Virginia plopped to the pillow.

"If the lady gets any more beautiful, I'd think I died and met an angel." Charlie leaned in for a kiss, but she pushed him away.

"My breath probably smells like the socks you left in the bathroom."

"We sound like a crusty pair of mated crabs already." He pecked her cheek. "I'll leave enough cash on the dresser for a cab." His footsteps pattered toward the bathroom, stopped before the door closed. "How's your ankle?"

*If the Sunrise Forgets Tomorrow*

"I'll probably sell the ring and look for a dress for Ruby and nothing else. I won't walk much then."

"I'll be back in time for lunch. I'm sure Breenda will have something nice on the menu."

A bright morning shone through the white curtains over the balcony doors. Virginia stretched and checked the time. How glorious to sleep in this beautiful room and perfect location for nine hours. Better yet, imagine doing it all the time.

The aroma of some type of meat cooking—not bacon or salt-cured ham—drifted into the room. She dressed and sat on the bed to slip on her everyday shoes and rotate her ankle. Soreness gone, thank goodness. Coffee? Definitely.

She followed the delicious aromas and sizzling sounds down the stairs and along the hall to the kitchen. Breenda—wearing a blue housecoat and matching slippers, a scarf covering her hair—flipped sausage patties at a stove. "That's what I smelled," Virginia said. "I don't recall the last time I tasted sausage. Some folks have pigs at home but not us."

Breenda flipped a browning piece of bread in another pan. "I'm so glad I chose to cook it then." She sprinkled brown powder on the bread. "Have you ever tried french toast?"

"I smell cinnamon. What's the yellow on the bread?"

"Egg. Add a touch of maple syrup and *voilà*, perfection. Especially with sausage."

"And coffee. Mind if I pour a cup? Can I get you one too?"

"I'll plate our breakfast while you do. Cups are in the cabinet with the glass doors by the window. Do you take sugar and cream?"

"Black's fine." Filled cups in hand, Virginia sat at the table. Breenda brought the plates.

"Char-*lee* said you enjoyed reading. Would you like to dine in my library?"

"Charlie didn't mention a library."

Breenda took a tray from a stack by the stove, placed the plates and cups on it, and gave Virginia another tray. "If you will, knives and forks are in the top drawer to the left in the same cabinet. Syrup in the lower cabinet."

Virginia followed Breenda down a hall wallpapered in floral print. They passed two closed doors and entered a room lined with bookshelves built into the walls. The shelves reached from floor to ceiling, each filled end to end. "Goodness, Breenda. I've died and gone to literary Heaven."

"*Oui*, I understand completely." She placed the tray on a round table in the far-right corner, beside a window with yellow curtains trimmed in lace. "I have some extremely special editions among these shelves. I'll show you one after we dine."

At the table, Virginia sat across from Breenda. "I'd about fallen in love with your home before I saw this room. Now I have for certain."

"You're too kind, Virgeenia." Breenda poured syrup on her french toast.

Virginia took the offered syrup. "Charlie surprised me by bringing me here." She forked a bite into her mouth. "Oh, my, I'm glad he did." She licked cinnamon-sweetness from her lips. "This is scrumptious."

"Char-*lee* is full of surprises, *oui?*"

"He didn't make this breakfast. If he had, *oui.*"

Breenda's lips formed a pursing grin. "Did you know a man loves it if you speak French while you're making love? I should teach you a special phrase or two."

"Charlie and me aren't ... you know." Virginia took a bite of sausage. "Great sausage."

*If the Sunrise Forgets Tomorrow*

"*Merci*, it is my pa-pa's recipe. I make it in the fall and freeze it, when the farmers butcher pigs." She sipped coffee. "I believe in being prepared for what may come. What French phrase might you like to try?"

"Don't tell me Charlie speaks French too?"

"Not that I'm aware of. It will be a surprise, *oui*? Char-*lee* says you have horses on your island. Perhaps this one will do. '*Je vous en supplie, mon chéri, s'il vous plaît me monter comme un étalon sauvage.* You try."

"What's that mean?" Virginia forked a piece of french toast. "I want to eat this before it gets cold." She chewed the crunchy-sweet bite while Breenda waited.

Virginia swallowed. Breenda gave her a sly grin. "It will drive him wild, I assure you. 'I beg you my darling, please mount me like a wild stallion.'"

Virginia gabbed a napkin but managed to swallow the french toast rather than spit it out, then snorted laughter. "I can't tell him that, he'll ask what it means."

"Pardon, but he will have a hint if you make a noise like that."

"A noise like— You mean I sounded like a horse?"

"More like a mare with her tail held to the side, *oui*? Come, let us enjoy our breakfast before it gets cold. Then I shall show you that special edition."

Empty plates in the kitchen and coffee cups refilled, Virginia patted her full tummy. "I'll try french toast at home. Ruby and me are always talking about different ways to cook eggs. Scrambled and fried and boiled gets dull after a while."

"Have you attempted soft boiled?" Breenda said. "They are— What am I saying? I must make you an omelet in the morning. Add young spinach and chopped green onions from my garden, a sprinkle of *Gruyère* cheese and a dash or dozen of coarsely ground black pepper, they are" —Breenda kissed her fingertips— "*magnifique*. Come, time for that special edition."

Coffee in hand, Virginia followed Breenda. "Are there any more guests?"

"The war has slowed vacationers—perhaps it will be over soon. I'd like nothing better than for us to get our lives back in order."

In the library, Breenda waved manicured fingertips, red nails shining, toward the shelves. "Tell me if you see something intriguing."

"They *all* intrigue me." Virginia stepped to the closest shelf and ran her fingertips along the spines of several books. "What's this one about? *Sense and Sensibility,* by Jane Austen?"

"Although it isn't the one I spoke of, it's one of my favorites. From what Char-*lee* tells me about you and Ruby, you both remind me of the two eldest sisters in that book." Breenda set the book on the table. "Consider it a gift."

"Thank you, but—"

"Believe me, if I didn't have another copy on my nightstand, I would not have offered."

"Is it that good?"

"*Oui, magnifique.* Please make another attempt. I'm certain you will locate *your* special edition."

On the way to the next shelf, Virginia stopped. "You say 'your' like it's specifically for me."

"I'll say this and nothing more—it was Char-*lee's* idea." Breenda fluttered red nails. "You'll see it soon enough."

"Is it that obvious?"

"A hint if I may ... look with your heart."

Virginia tapped her lower lip with a fingertip, scanned the next shelf, the next, and smiled. At the last shelf, she read the heart-shaped tag hanging by a string from between the pages of a book.

*I hope you don't have this volume. I can always keep it for myself if you do.*
*Charlie.*

Beneath his signature, Charlie had drawn a smiling face. Reading the book's spine, *The Collected Works of Edgar Allen Poe*, Virginia wiped a tear.

"Ah," Breenda said, "you approve, *oui?*"

"Charlie can be aggravating in a boyish way, but his sweetness makes up for it. Well, for the most part."

"He is full of surprises, no? Has he said good morning to you in German yet?"

"You could say that."

Breenda gave her a sly grin. "Perhaps a bit more suggestive, I'm sure." She sipped coffee. "Would you like your coffee warmed?"

"I better start my day."

"To sell your ring?"

"Does Charlie tell you everything?"

"He loves talking about you. He mentioned it before he left this morning."

"How long have you known each other?" Virginia sat at the table and placed the Poe book on top of the Austin book.

Breenda joined her. "Long enough for him to tell me about his nose."

"You mean how it's a little crooked?"

"*Oui*. It happened in a fight with some man who apparently has large lips."

"He told me about the man, not the fight."

"The man broke his nose. It took Charlie a while to get over that girl, so he said. He told me he doubted he'd ever love another like her. I'm happy that he's been proven wrong."

"Me too. For a dingbatter, he's amazing."

Breenda covered a laugh. "He told me about that word also. May I see your ring? I'm always in the market for jewelry. I don't wear my rings in the morning. Cooking and washing dishes would take a toll on them quickly."

"I have no idea what it's worth." Virginia took the felt box from her pocket and placed it on the table.

Breenda opened it. *"Oui,* this is very nice. The emerald is small" —she held it to her eyes— "but with fine clarity."

"Papa gave Mama an emerald ring. He said he saved for three years to buy it."

"I love them myself. Would five-hundred dollars be a fair price?"

"I'm ... I have no idea." Virginia envisioned a new radio. A new wagon. A shopping trip for her and Ruby. A saddle for Jimmy.

"Perhaps a small amount more?"

"No, please, that's fine."

"Would you like a dress for your sister? You and I are close to the same size, although I'm a bit larger in the bust. I could look through my daughter's things again as well."

"Ruby's a bit larger than me in the bust too. Isn't that convenient?"

"Perfection. I have a few I was considering donating to the local church for the needy. I may even have a new one I bought on a whim and never wore—matching shoes that hurt my feet after an hour of wearing them also. Alas, the store would not take them back."

"I'd rather not go into town anyway. Charlie said he'd be back around lunchtime."

Breenda rose. "I shall get my purse and pay for the ring. Then we can find something nice for your sister. I may have other things I'm not using or never used. You know how we purchase things on whims. How we accumulate things we don't recall having."

Down the same hall as before, they took a left at the second door, which opened into a spacious room with a canopy bed similar to the one upstairs. Breenda, at the far side of the room, opened two swinging closet doors. Dresses, skirts, and blouses of every style and color hung from hangers. Hatboxes filled the overhead shelf on one side while shoes lined the other. "I should've cleaned my closet ages ago."

"You have lovely taste."

Breenda shoved a few racks aside, took out one, and held up the tag. "Just as I thought, brand new."

Virginia took the hangar and held the red low-cut dress with short sleeves to her shoulders. "Oh, Breenda, Ruby will love this."

"It's fitted too. See how the waist narrows and then widens at the hips?" Breenda stood on tiptoe for a box. "Black pumps." She opened the top. *"Oui,* this is the pair that scrunched my toes so terribly. Do you think they will fit Ruby?"

"Knowing my sister, she'll rub bacon grease on her feet to get them on if she has to." Virginia took the box. "I can't tell you how much I appreciate this."

"My husband always said I was sometimes too generous for my own good. I enjoy making people happy, especially those I feel a kinship with."

"How do you mean?"

"When my husband and I were first married in France, Pa-pa offered him a job picking grapes. It was difficult work, with long hours. Still, at the end of the week, when the workers were dumping their last loads into the wagon, Pa-pa jumped down and told him how pleased he was with his labor. My husband absolutely beamed with pride. Soon after, Pa-pa promoted him to work in the winery. He excelled at that as well."

"I'm not sure what you're saying?" Virginia said.

"Charlie mentioned how life is difficult for you and your sister on Ocracoke ... how you work hard for the necessities of life. I admire that in a person. It shows *magnifique* strength of character, *oui?*"

"Thank you for everything, Breenda. I'm so happy Charlie brought me here."

"You will come again, no? Oh, but I insist. You must bring Ruby also."

"I better get the dress and shoes upstairs. How I'll get them in my suitcase, I have no idea."

Breenda leaned over in the closet, shoved boxes around, and removed a large suitcase. *"Voilà,* something else I need to give away." Behind her, several bags fell. Breenda picked them up and peeked inside one. "Would you care for new panties also? My *derrière* isn't much larger than yours, and likely not Ruby's."

"On one condition." Virginia left the dress and shoes on the bed and held out her hands. "I get to pay you with a hug."

In her room, Virginia put the suitcase, shoes, and panties in the closet, then held Ruby's dress to her shoulders again. That child's gorgeous blonde hair against the scarlet—almost blood red—would turn many a man's head on Ocracoke.

Charlie opened the door. "Looks like someone got a great price for her ring."

Virginia glanced at the clock. "You're back early."

"Do I get to see your sexy self in that dress tonight?"

"Breenda gave me this for Ruby—shoes too, and undies for both of us. To use her word for something special, she's *magnifique.*"

"Well, doggone, I thought I was pretty *magnifique* myself."

Virginia grabbed his cheeks for a kiss. "Does that settle your male mind? Thank you for the book, I told Breenda how sweet you are. I didn't taste any wine in the coffee either."

*If the Sunrise Forgets Tomorrow*

Charlie pulled her close. "Are you, the future Mrs. Charlie Smithson, saying you'd have to be drunk to say I'm sweet?"

"What's your middle name?"

"What's yours?"

"Doesn't matter, you're not taking it."

"You won't be taking my middle name either."

"Too late for secrets." Virginia dug her fingers into his sides. "I know how your nose got broken."

Charlie let her go. "I distinctly remember telling Brenda to keep that to herself."

"Why should Breeeeenda—you forgot her name again—not tell me your secrets when you tell her mine?"

"Which one? I blab terribly."

"About the ring."

"Are you mad? You don't look mad. Please tell me you're not—"

"Cut that out, Mr. Male Ruby. How could I be mad after she bought the ring and gave Ruby and me nice clothes?"

"Exactly."

Virginia pointed at the suitcase in the floor of the closet. "She even gave me that suitcase for the trip back and a book that reminds her of me and Ruby. I can't wait to read it. "Like I said, she's *magnifique*." Virginia hung the dress in the closet. "You never said why you're back early."

Charlie's face, usually calm and emotionless, tightened. "I had to leave class to return a radio call from Jerry. I could hardly hear him for the static when I did. Maybe the storm did something to the two-way radio. Anyway, I caught a few words that sounded like 'U-boat and prisoners.'" Charlie ran his fingers through his hair. "I wish he'd handle his damn job instead of calling me."

"You don't think it's important?"

"Before the Navy sent me to Ocracoke, I asked my commanding officer what the odds were of any of our patrol vessels capturing prisoners. He said they'd likely fight to the death or scuttle the boat to hide any documents or decoding equipment." Sitting on the bed, Charlie fell to his back. "Jerry will call again, even if it isn't important. I left a message to have it forwarded here if he does."

Virginia sat beside Charlie. "I hope we don't have to leave early."

"Me neither." Charlie stood. "Let's go see what Brenda—excuse me, Breeeenda—has for lunch."

*If the Sunrise Forgets Tomorrow*

## Chapter 33

## Hard Work, Baths, and a U-boat

Beneath Erich's pillow, the alarm clock's muffled ringing woke him. He turned the alarm off. Not a yell nor a question from Ruby about why he'd set the clock for 4 a.m.

Shoes on, he crept through the kitchen, stopped as the wood floor creaked, and placed his ear to her door. Still quiet. He held his palm against the wood stove's black, cast iron surface. Still hot. The wood floor creaked again on his way to the front door. He stopped, then continued. Both the wooden and screen doors rewarded his stealth with the slightest of squeaks.

To the east, above the live oak crowns, a pale-yellow glow, giving way to dusty orange, shared enough light for his walk to the workshop.

A small bundle of furry brown hopped through the thicket beside the path. Erich marveled at how rabbits existed on Ocracoke. The bundle paused. Snubbish ears twisted and turned on the rounded head, possibly an adaptation that had taken place over millennia. He felt a certain kinship with this small creature. Perhaps time would allow him to adapt to a life of innocence and peace on Ocracoke as well.

In the workshop, he took his father-in-law's letter—the last remnant of his German heritage—and closed the door again. With it secure in his grasp, he picked his way back through the oaks. Better to burn it now instead of waiting.

Leave the wood stove's door open. Watch the letter smolder and flare and crisp into ash. Another stick of wood. Ease the door shut. Return to the warm bed.

And security.

The sunrise transformed the curtains into pink wisps, bringing back memories of Thea's cheeks as they flushed, her soft moans, thighs clasping, back arching, shuddering cry of fulfillment, blue eyes bright with life and love.

She had saved him in so many ways with her light, while her letter had gifted him his will to live, the will to believe in life, the will to love again. How many ways yet to come might she save him?

*Thank you, my darling. Although I long to see you once more, I'll do as you ask, by keeping our love alive in my memory. My sincerest hope—yours too, I'm certain—is to have the chance to do so.*

A draft hinted the curtains with movement. Its cold breath whispered across Erich's forehead, as if the icy touch of death itself beckoned him to join Thea.

No, indeed, his darling wouldn't want that—her letter explicitly denied it—not with him standing on the precipice of years of happiness with Ruby.

The curtains stilled. The draft's cool touch faded.

Rest now, for the day—and Ruby—waited.

★

Ruby dressed and went to the kitchen. After all the scrambled eggs she and Ginny had eaten lately, eggs over-easy and a few blackened slices of the last ham Papa had bought, including buttered biscuits along with plenty of hot coffee to wash everything down, would be a welcome change of taste.

She peeked at a lightly snoring Erich. What would he do if she jumped on him like she sometimes did Ginny? Ruby closed the door. He needed all the rest he could get for moving that tree limb out of the path.

She stoked the fire, fed and watered Jimmy, and filled the pail with water for the house. Ham sizzling, coffee percolating—both smelled heavenly—she opened the bedroom door and clapped her hands. "Time to get your lazy merman tail up and show me what kind of worker you are."

Blinking like a hoot owl blown from the mainland, Erich rolled over. "My first night in a bed in days and you're already after me to work." He sat up. "And I don't mind a bit."

"That's the spirit, merman. That tree limb is ready to be wrangled from the path. I need to work the garden too."

"Do I get breakfast first? I was planning on making omelets."

"Ham's in the pan, no time for fancy. You can do omelets in the morning. Swim yourself out of bed and get out of Papa's old pajamas while I finish cooking."

"You didn't close the door." Erich sat on the side of the bed and yawned.

Plating the ham, Ruby pointed a spatula. "Can't you see I'm busy?"

At the door, Erich stuck his tongue out. "I see you're not a morning person."

"Ginny trained me good. Looks like you need training too."

"I can't wait until I meet her. Between the both of us, we should be able to keep you in line." Erich closed the door.

"You can forget that, fish butt! Neither you nor Ginny stand a chance at taming me!"

"I wouldn't dream of it!"

Ruby set the ham on the table. "My pert merman's learning my ways already."

She cracked eggs in a bowl. Erich came in and snatched a slice of ham from the plate. "Scrambled eggs again?"

"Over-easy, whether you like it or not."

"Didn't you have to gather them?"

"The girls were generous yesterday."

"Can I help with anything?"

"Biscuits are in the oven. Take them out and butter them if they're browned. Butter's in the icebox."

Erich sat to butter the biscuits. "If you think I mind work, I don't. I'm happy to get out and sweat after being confined in the workshop. What can I do after I move that limb?"

At the stove, easing the eggs into the pan, Ruby glanced over her shoulder. "Might as well cut it up for the stove. Ginny and I have been talking for ages about trimming the limbs in the path to the main road. Think you can do that?" She flipped an egg.

"How long is the path?"

"About fifty steps, give or take. Ginny and me counted them enough growing up."

"Do you have a sharp saw?"

"Papa taught us how."

"Then I have a full day's work ahead of me."

Ruby placed everything on the table and sat. Erich took her hand. "My turn to say the blessing." He bowed his head. "Dear Father, thank You for supplying our every need. Please tell Thea and my mother and father I'm safe" —he squeezed Ruby's hand— "and well-loved. Also, Father, when the time comes to inform others as to how I arrived here, please forgive us for being untruthful. Amen."

Ruby opened her eyes. "Thank you for knowing you're well-loved."

"You're quite welcome. Let's—" Erich closed his eyes. "Father, please don't allow my presence to endanger anyone. Amen."

"Why think that?"

"I never thought anything would happen to Thea. My parents either."

"I know, but—"

"It was only a precaution. Let's enjoy your wonderful breakfast. Then it's time for work."

---

Having finished the job of sawing the tree limb into lengths for the stove, including stacking them beneath the shed beside Jimmy's stall, Erich wiped sweat from his forehead with his shirtsleeve as he strode to the garden, where Ruby hoed weeds. "I'm going for water. Can I bring you a glass?"

"I'm going in after these last two rows." Ruby straightened. "Still planning on trimming the path?"

"Your sister will have a nice surprise when she returns."

"She needs a good one now and then. Do you want lunch?"

"I'm quite full from your biscuits."

"*Three* biscuits. At least be a fit merman until you're old enough for me to not care about your belly."

"Imagine *your* belly when we have children. You'll waddle around like a duck."

"How will you like my 'valleys' then?"

"I'm sure I'll be quite pleased. I'm off to trim those limbs."

At the well, Erich pumped the handle until cold water flowed from the spout. He drank, paused, drank again. When his tight stomach could hold no more, he continued to the path.

The limbs succumbed to his efforts—mostly smaller but a few larger—as he fell into the rhythm of work. Saw, drop a limb. Saw, drop a limb. The heat of the day rose. Pause to wipe sweat from his forehead before it ran into his eyes. The slick feel of it beneath his underarms. A river of it streaming down his spine to pool in the small of his back. Only aware of these things, including the rasp of the blade, the musty sweet aroma of wood chips, and the thud of the limbs to the sand, he reached the main road before realizing it. To his right, a ship's horn signaled some unknown meaning, possibly leaving or arriving. The faint pounding of hammers seated nails, likely constructing buildings for the Naval base.

He stepped to the end of the path to check for vehicles. Nothing but the faint crash and thump of the waves beyond the dunes, the *scree* of gulls dotting the sky, and the warm breath of the Atlantic, salty and humid.

He sawed a few stragglers and dragged those to the shed. No Ruby in the garden—she must be inside. Jimmy softly nickered. "What do you think, Jimmy? Do Ruby and I make a good match?"

Long lashes over huge, brown eyes blinked. Erich scratched behind twisting ears. "Pardon me, Mr. Flirting Pony, but I'm taken."

Behind him, Ruby laughed. "He sure is, Jimmy. All we need is a blessing from Ginny and Mr. Fulcher. Then we can get to the important part. I won't ever have to take a bath again if my merman does it right."

Erich wrapped his arms around her and licked her neck. "How's that for a sample, my salty sweetness? Think you'll like it all over?"

She wrestled from his grasp. "Goodness gracious, you smell worse than Jimmy after Ginny's run him on the beach."

"Like you're as fresh as those bluebells on the other side of the shed."

"I'll be fresh after a bath." She took his hand and led him away from the snorting pony. "And that's exactly what we'll do after I help you drag the rest of those limbs to the shed."

Ruby placed towels, washcloths, and a bar of soap on the table, within reach of the hot tub of water. "Me first, I'm nowhere near as stinky as you."

In a chair removing his shoes, Erich stood. "I don't get clean water?"

"You wouldn't feel privileged to wash in my bathwater?"

"An excellent point. I'll undress on the porch so I don't get sawdust everywhere."

"Shake it out of your hair too. Oh, and no peeking in the window."

"I'll lie down while you bathe. I'll leave my underwear on so I don't tempt you."

"Not on the bed, you'll get it stinky."

"I'll sit on the porch. Any ideas for dinner?"

Ruby snatched a towel from the table and snapped it at Erich. "You sound like a husband already. I'll ride my bike to the restaurant and see what Mr. Austin has left over from last night."

"Make sure you stay away from that man you scared with the shotgun."

"I can handle that dingbatter. Shoo so I can wash."

★

Ruby squeezed water from her hair, fluffed it with a towel, then dressed and went out on the porch. "The water's not bad if you want to use it. Be back soon."

Passing the building where Charlie and Jerry worked, she noted the jeep. She also noted how Jerry stood beside it deep in discussion with two uniformed men. Jerry faced away, and Ruby was glad—she didn't care to see his beady eyes glaring at her concerning the shotgun incident.

At Silver Lake Harbor, a Navy patrol ship steamed through the entrance. Black smoke billowed from its single stack in the center. Uniformed men stood along the rail.

Ruby leaned the bike against the side of the restaurant. Mr. Austin, slicing potatoes at the counter, whirled toward the door. "Bless my barnacles, Ruby, I never expected to see you here so soon." He dropped the knife in the pile of potatoes. "You back to work?"

"Not quite yet."

"No need to rush a thing like losin' your mama." He wiped his hands on his apron and took two paper bags from the refrigerator. "Bet you could use a bite or three. Got fried pork chops from last night. One of the villagers killed a pig and I bought part. Plenty of taters 'n onions too." He set the bags on the counter. "You see all the hubbub when you come over?"

"I saw some men talking where Charlie and Jerry work. A Navy ship was leaving the harbor too, is that what you mean?"

"Doc Wills stopped by for lunch. Said the Navy sunk a U-boat north of Hatteras."

"Why'd the ship stop here?"

"Doc Wills didn't say. Maybe they'll get them blasted Germans out of our waters so we can see some peace and quiet from them explosions and smoke over the horizon, God bless those poor men's souls."

Ruby hefted the bags. "Thank you for the food." She stopped at the door. "I'm not sure when Ginny and me will work again."

"It's no problem, Ruby, no problem at all. I'll be here when you're ready."

Ruby stuffed the bags into the bike basket and pedaled home. She passed the building where the men were talking by the jeep earlier. They were gone, jeep included. Whatever was happening with the U-boat had them acting like excited ghost crabs, scurrying sideways on the beach in search of the dead or dying remains of some sea creature.

Was the U-boat Erich's? He would have friends who had died if so. Would he want to know? As much as he had been through, no, the future demanded he leave the past. Still, the future might ebb and flow like the tide until a plan revealed itself to get him out of the workshop. Regardless, any man who threatened Erich would find himself against the pier-piling spine of a rough and ready O'cocker gal, come hell or high water, hurricanes or nor'easters.

Passing the house, she could swear a trumpet blared from inside. She left the bike beneath the shed and ran back. The tub was gone. Mama's bedroom door was closed. Erich must've bathed and was getting dressed. She set the bags on the table and knocked. He opened the door, slipped his right hand around her waist, and took her right hand with his left. "Care to waltz, mermaid?"

Ruby joined his sway. "How in the world did you fix our broken radio?"

"Didn't you know mer-people possess magic powers? It works even better when we find a screwdriver and pliers in the drawer of the cupboard." He released her to peek in the bags. "Our supper?"

"Fried pork chops and potatoes with onions. I'll heat everything up as quick as you can whack off an oak limb."

Ruby took a pan from the cupboard. Erich brought wood from the porch. Prodding the sticks into place with the poker, he glanced over his shoulder. "Our last day together will arrive before we know it."

"I'd rather you say our last day before you have to hide in the workshop again. Your version sounds like one of Ginny's Poe novels, all full of tragedy."

Erich set the poker against the wall. "We need a story that will make me a welcome guest. The longer I hide the sooner your sister might find me. Wouldn't *that* be a tragedy?"

"Whatever we do—if that happens, I mean—I think we should stay calm. If she walked in right now, for instance, I think we'd need to act like it's the most natural thing in the world for you to be here. I doubt she'll act a fool. She'll just ask questions."

"You're correct, we'd be immediately suspicious if we got excited." Erich went to the bedroom, where the radio blared. The music, what sounded like big band, ended. "Let's save the batteries. Do you know how old they are?"

Ruby put the pork chops in a pan. "I think Mama bought them right before the radio stopped working. Papa said he could catch fish, rescue a drowning man, and tease Mama to no end, but he couldn't fix a radio."

"A wire was loose." Erich slipped his hands around Ruby's waist. "Will you make me sleep alone tonight, dear one?"

"Phooey. You'd grab at me like a crab with a dozen claws."

"I'm sure I would." Erich squeezed her tight. "But I wouldn't pinch." He took the pan. "On top of the stove or in the oven?"

"Oven. I'll heat the potatoes on top."

⁂

Supper eaten, dishes washed, dusk arriving, Ruby lit two lamps while Erich, at the table, thumbed through her copy of *Gone with the Wind*. He closed the book. "You'd make a fine Scarlett."

Ruby hung her apron on a peg by the door. Fluttering her eyelashes, she placed her fingertips to her throat. "Why, Mr. Fischer, do tell."

"Do tell what?"

*If the Sunrise Forgets Tomorrow*

Ruby skipped around behind him and tousled his hair. "That's how fine ladies in the old south talked back then." She kissed his cheek. "Would you carry me to bed if I asked?"

"What an intriguing question. Do I get to stay if I do?"

"Not at all, Mr. Grabby Crab."

"I prefer being a sea gull. Then I can swoop into that exceedingly voluptuous valley of yours."

Ruby sat opposite him and hefted her bosom. "Dream on, Mr. Gull, there'll be no swooping in here until we're married." She picked up the book. "I'm tired from all that work."

"I'm looking forward to another fine night's sleep out of the workshop. Are we working tomorrow?"

"I haven't given it much thought." Ruby covered a yawn. "I won't rush around like a madwoman in the morning."

Erich stood. "Perhaps I'll make omelets."

"Omelet, omelet, omelet—how many times have you told me about omelets? Whatever they are, they better be good."

"They will. Get ready for bed. I'll get more water."

✷

Bedroom doors closed and lamps out, except for the one flickering on the nightstand, Ruby opened *Gone with the Wind*. A few pages later, her eyes closed and opened, closed and opened. She placed the book on the nightstand and blew the lamp out. The aroma of smoke drifted in the air. She cuddled into her pillow.

It was the strangest thing, lying in bed while the man she loved did the same thing only one room away.

The moon shone in the window, spilling dingy light through the curtains. She crept to Erich's door and opened it. On his side, he opened his eyes. "Can't sleep?"

"I thought I could but ..."

He raised up on one elbow. "Don't tell me you've thought of more work for tomorrow."

She sat beside him. "Do you think we could do it?"

"Perhaps you should explain what you mean before I answer."

"Why does sleeping together need explaining?"

"Think about it."

Ruby pulled his nose. "And *I'm* incorrigible, Mr. Dirty-minded merman."

"You like that word, do you?"

"Slide over."

"Then what?"

"Then you're going to kiss me and we're going to sleep. Don't you think we can be good?"

Erich slid over. "I believe so."

She climbed in beside him, pulled the cover up, snuggled into the warmth of his shoulder. "This is what I really wanted."

Erich kissed the tip of her nose. "How about that?"

"Ugh, onion breath. Did you brush your teeth long enough?"

Erich dropped to the pillow. "I'll hold you and nothing else. Satisfied?"

"Very. I love you."

"I love you too, dear one."

✶

The next morning, Ruby placed the percolator on the stove. Erich came in and dropped a handful of dandelion greens on the table. "I'll see what your hens have laid. I'd like to have fresh eggs for our omelets."

"I got eggs while you were asleep."

"Aren't you the busy bee? Does the stove need wood?"

"Nope. Is leftover bacon good in omelets?"

"If you have some."

"Then you know what to do."

Erich took the bacon from the icebox and crumbled it into a pan on the stove. Ruby glanced his way. "I didn't think men liked cooking."

"I considered culinary school before the war. You should've seen my parent's faces when they tasted one of my experimental recipes."

"Thea too, I'm sure."

"She actually spit out my attempt at pickled herring. She said it tasted too much like vinegar."

"Irk. I wouldn't want fish that tasted like the huge dill pickles Papa used to bring home from the general store either." She gave Erich the spatula. "I'm going to my room and read while you work your magic."

On the bed, Ruby opened *Gone with the Wind*. Big band music—trumpets, saxophones, drums, and sultry singing by a female singer—played in the kitchen. Ruby tapped the book cover to the rhythm. Two perfect nights with three to go. Thank goodness Ginny wouldn't be home until Tuesday.

## Chapter 34

## Lies, Truths, and Accusations

Virginia picked up her suitcases. Charlie picked up his and took the largest one from her. "Doggone, this feels like Breenda threw in a few more books along with the clothes you packed."

"I can carry it."

"Can't have you slipping on that planking."

Virginia followed him off the bug-eye boat, taking care not to slip on the damp boards leading to the pier at Silver Lake Harbor. In the jeep, she faced Charlie. "Drop me off at the front porch so you can see what's wrong with Jerry."

"Yeah, I need to see what's got him so excited. U-boat this, U-boat that, the man's half-crazed about a U-boat. Sorry. You've heard all this already."

"I'm not happy about it either."

"He's so damned cryptic about it. You know how some people tell you just enough to make you ask? That's him to a T."

Virginia rubbed Charlie's shoulder. "I don't think I've ever seen you so worked up."

"That's because I was enjoying our time together." Charlie cranked the jeep. "Let me get you home."

At the security building, he pointed. "The jeep's there. If I can get Jerry settled quick enough, you won't have to unpack."

They slowed to enter the path toward home, and Virginia pointed. "Tarnation. Looks like Ruby was busy while we were gone. The path is as clean as I've seen it in years."

Charlie accelerated. A marsh rabbit darted into the path; the tire struck it with a sickening thump. "I know you didn't mean to, Charlie, but I hate seeing one of God's sweet creatures taken ahead of time."

"I shouldn't have been going so fast."

At the porch, Charlie stopped but left the engine running. "Sounds like Ruby's likes big band. Let me get your suitcases on the porch."

"All I need is a decent goodbye." Virginia gave him a quick kiss and lugged the suitcases from the jeep. He accelerated into the path, sand flying from the tires.

Suitcases in hand, she stopped at the screen door. At the table across from Ruby, who was eating, a blond-headed young man was eating also.

Leaving the suitcases on the porch, Virginia went in. They still didn't see her. She slipped around the wall toward mama's room. Ruffled bedsheets. Indentions of two heads on the pillow. She turned the radio off. "Think you got this music loud enough in—"

"How did you get in here?" A fork clattered to a plate. Ruby jumped up.

"You were enamored with your guest is how, along with that radio drowning out everything from one end of Ocracoke to the other."

"Why are you back so early?"

Virginia offered her hand to the young man. "You going to tell me who you are so I can ask you what the hell you're doing in my house?"

Ruby ran around the table and grabbed her arm. "Sit a minute, want an omelet? Erich made them, there's another you can have. You look hungry, aren't you hungry? I bet you're hungry."

The man didn't take Virginia's hand. She lowered hers. "Erich, is it? Crab got your tongue, Erich."

"He's ... he's mute, that's what he is, he can't talk."

"I know what mute is." Virginia dropped into a chair. "I'll take an omelet—coffee too, if that's what I smell. I bet this story will take an entire meal to hear." Ruby flurried away. Virginia eyed Erich. "How does he tell you anything?"

"He—" Ruby stopped pouring coffee. "He writes it—that's what he does, he writes it."

"Sounds like you're trying to convince yourself more than you are me, *Rube*. How did you fix the radio?"

Ruby brought the omelet and coffee. "Erich fixed it. He said—wrote—it had a loose wire. I'm not trying to convince anyone about anything, Ginny, I'm flustered because you came home early. Can't I be—"

"*Flustered?* Obviously." Virginia faced Erich, whose eyes darted back and forth between her and Ruby. She faced Ruby again. "Those ruffled sheets tell me the hired hand is sleeping in Mama's bed. By the damned dents in the pillows—the *two* damned dents in the pillows—this story gets better by the minute." She faced Erich again. "And I haven't heard a single word of it yet."

Erich pointed at the omelet.

"You want me to taste your omelet?"

"What do you think he wants you to do, ride Jimmy naked?" Ruby snatched a fork from the table and cut Virginia's omelet. "Stick that in yer yap. It's the best way to cook eggs I ever tasted."

Virginia forked the omelet and examined it. "It's different, I'll give you that." She took a nibble. "What's the green in it?"

*If the Sunrise Forgets Tomorrow*

"Dandelion greens. Erich made a salad with them one day too."

Virginia chewed and swallowed. "I saw the red but didn't think to ask. Tomatoes?"

"Some Mama canned. You eat while I talk. Erich showed up one day and—"

Erich placed his hand on Ruby's. "I can't let you lie for me, Ruby." He offered his hand to Virginia. "My name is Erich Fischer. Ruby's afraid you won't believe why I'm here."

"So, she makes up some fool story about you being mute. I can see that, she gets in a tangle now and then. Put your hand down and eat. By your accent I'd say you're not—" Virginia dropped her fork and eyed Ruby. "You've been hiding your hired hand in the workshop. I knew you were up to something, with all your running back and forth." She sipped coffee. "No need in ruining this fine meal now. You're in love with him too, right?" Ruby's mouth worked like a gigged flounder's, and Virginia pointed the fork at her. "You forget I have eighteen years of experience dealing with you—I know you better than you know yourself."

"I know you, too, *Virgil* Starr. How long did it take Charlie to bed you in Havelock?"

"How long did it take you to bed the hired help, *Rube?*"

Erich held up his hands. "Ladies, ladies, please don't fight."

"Better get used to it." Virginia picked up her fork. "That's what you'll hear if you marry into *this* family."

"That's the truth if I ever heard the truth." Ruby sipped coffee. "Now, sweetheart, please tell your story."

Virginia eyed Ruby. "Sweetheart?"

"Yes, I love him. Now shove another bite of that delicious omelet in yer yap and listen."

"I'm from Britain," Erich said. "You're correct about my accent not being from nearby. I was engaged to marry Thea, a lovely girl. We described it as being engaged since we were sixteen, I'm seventeen now. Of course, you know about the war. Our parents were attempting to come to America to escape the bombing. I worked in an arms factory. Labor was scarce, so they took younger men than normal. While I was away, our neighborhood was bombed. I returned to find Thea and our families dead."

Acquainted with the recent deaths of Papa, Mama, and Walter, Virginia felt sincerely sorry for young Erich. Thank goodness no one else she knew was about to die soon. "I'm sorry to hear that, but how did you get here?"

"We all booked passage to come here. I was the most miserable wretch you could ever imagine—no home, no family, no love. I decided to come ahead and start my life over. You see why I had no reason to stay."

"The closest major port, I believe, is Norfolk. How did you get to Ocracoke?"

"When I left the ship, I was overwhelmed. I started walking around the docks and hired on to a fishing boat. The two men were quite scruffy, but offered honest pay for honest labor. I climbed aboard their vessel and—"

"Don't tell me," Ruby said. "They fished down the coast and kicked you off here when you asked for your pay to come ashore."

"If I didn't know any better, *Rube,* I'd say you hadn't heard a word of Erich's story."

"I'm just hurrying him along before our food gets cold. I don't want our food to get cold. Do you want your food to get—"

Erich chuckled. "Your sister is quite incorrigible."

"Excellent word, Mr. Fischer. If what she said is how it happened, how did you get in my papa's workshop?"

"I was looking for work at the village and overheard people talking about someone hiring on to fishing boats in Hatteras. I asked where that was and started walking."

"Did you know you would've had to swim Hatteras Inlet?"

"I recall those men who kicked me off the boat mentioning it. I competed in swimming in high school."

"You didn't compete against tide and current in an inlet. What then?" Virginia forked another bite of omelet.

"I walked by your path and smelled food. I thought I might work for a meal."

"That doesn't explain the time you spent in the—"

*Wham!*

Virginia glared at Ruby. "Why're you smacking the table?"

"Because I'm tired of how you're treating Erich. Remember when I asked Doc Wills for aspirin? Erich stepped on a sandspur on the way to the house. He said it hurt so bad it made him sick. That's why he went to the workshop instead of coming here. Would you care to go to a stranger's house to ask for work if you'd just gotten sick?"

"What about after?"

"He got a fever from the sandspur. That's why I asked for the aspirin. You should know how I feel about fevers."

"Because of Mama. Then that time you got sick from a sandspur."

"About time you started acting like you have a lick of sense, Virgil."

"What about this falling in love thing?" Virginia said.

"Did Charlie drop you off? I suppose I didn't hear the jeep for the music."

"What's that got to do with—"

"Hush." Ruby said. "My turn to ask the same question."

"What same question?"

"About you falling in love with Charlie."

"What are you getting at?"

"You just spent two nights with Mr. Rogue himself. How'd that happen if you didn't love him?"

"Just when I think I've got you corralled, you jump the fence. I love him more than I ever thought possible."

"Then stop asking questions and eat. I think Erich should cook for a fancy restaurant on the mainland. Maybe in Havelock."

"Now we have another way to cook eggs." Virginia faced Erich. "Radios, cooking, and tree work—what else can you do?"

"Don't you think that's sufficient in light of how I manage to not turn Ruby over my knee in the mornings? She is certainly not a morning person."

Virginia clinked her coffer cup to his. "Ha! He's figured you out, Rube. I think I like your young hired hand." She sipped coffee. "When's the wedding?"

"When's yours to Charlie?" Ruby said, poking Virginia's arm.

"We're thinking after the war." Virginia nodded toward the door. "My suitcases are on the porch. The lady who owns the bed and breakfast where Charlie and I stayed is as sweet as can be. She offered me a dress for you and a dress for me—shoes too. I couldn't say no. She even bought Walter's ring,"

"Are you and Charlie going back? You can thank—" Ruby's furrowed forehead formed a washboard of wrinkles. "That's right, you're back early."

"Jerry's been aggravating Charlie about a U-boat. We might go back once he sees why Jerry's so stirred up."

"He wouldn't say over the radio?"

"Charlie said he acted like it was a big secret."

Ruby went to her room, returned with a piece of paper, and gave it to Erich. "I was wondering if you'd like to show Ginny Thea's picture?"

The young man, not much more than a boy, took the picture. He stared at it for a moment, then fingered tears from his eyes. "I ... I'm ... I apologize." He offered the picture to Virginia.

"Don't be sorry for loving to the point of tears." Virginia returned the picture. "Your Thea is beautiful. The way she's smiling, I think I know who's holding the camera."

Erich swallowed while slipping the picture into his shirt pocket. Virginia sipped coffee, wanting to give him time to compose himself for another question. "Why does Ruby have the picture in her room?"

Ruby's fork clattered to her plate. "More questions. You know as well as I do how damp it is in the workshop. He asked me to keep it inside, *Virgil*. Does that meet your approval?"

Erich placed his hand on Ruby's. "Don't chastise your sister for asking questions. Wouldn't you do the same in her place?"

"Don't bother, Erich, I'm used to her pertness." Virginia took her plate to the basin. "Thanks for the fine meal. What do you have planned for—"

The whine of a jeep engine came from the path, and Virginia went to the screened door. "Charlie said he might come back before I unpacked my suitcases." She opened the door as he topped the steps. "Come on in and meet our new hired hand before we leave."

"I suppose this fellow helped with the tree limbs."

Erich started to rise from the chair. Charlie waved him back down. "Keep your seat, Mr. ..."

"His name's Erich Fischer," Virginia said. "He came here from Britain after losing his family and fiancé in the bombing. He's also Ruby's new beau."

The muscles in Charlie's neck twitched. "What's the chance I could hear Mr. Fischer's story?" His hand fell to the pistol holster at his side, which hadn't been there when he had left earlier.

Another jeep engine whined from the path, sliding to a stop at the porch. Charlie whirled to the door. "That damned hothead Jerry, I told him I'd handle this. Charlie shoved through the screened door.

Ruby jumped from the table and went to the cupboard for a butcher knife.

"Good idea," Virginia said. "I did that very thing the last time Artknot came here. Stick it in the back of your pants in case he acts a fool."

Ruby stuck the knife in her pants. "Don't forget the shotgun."

"I doubt it'll come to that."

Virginia looked out the screen door. By the jeeps, Charlie gripped Jerry's arm. She couldn't understand their words, low and hard as oak. She faced Erich. "I apologize for all the excitement. Jerry Artknot's been nothing but trouble since Ruby and me met him. He's—"

Footsteps thudded up the wooden steps. The two men stomped inside. Erich joined Ruby at the cupboard. Charlie stepped beside Virginia. Artknot, red-faced and glaring at Erich, stayed by the door. He raised his hand to the pistol at his belt, index finger curling and uncurling against the leather holster.

Virginia cut her eyes from Artknot to Charlie. "Hell of a way to enter our home. Calls for a hell of an explanation, I'd say."

Charlie's brown eyes met hers. "I have reason to believe Mr. Fischer—Seaman Fischer I should say—came from a U-boat."

"You mean a *German* U-boat. What makes—"

"Lies," Ruby hissed. "Lies made up by that beady-eyed rat of a man Artknot. Because he ..."

"Because he what?" Virginia said.

"I didn't want to cause trouble. I handled it and thought that'd be the end of it."

"What did he do?"

"He showed up the night I worked at the restaurant—made comments I'd rather not hear. I thought I'd made it plain and simple that I wanted nothing more to do with him. Instead, he sneaks into the path to jump out and grab my bike."

Artknot pointed a rigid finger straight at Ruby's face. "That's what you get for acting like you're willin' when you're not. You have this here German tucked away then? Look at you standing cozy. Bet I know what you was runnin' back to give him."

"You can go straight to hell, looking at me with them damned beady eyes that night and telling me how you wanted to see me naked."

"Charlie," Virginia said. "Seems like you've got more of a problem on your hands than a made-up U-boat seaman. Even if Erich *were* German, I'd prefer him over that excuse of a man you've allowed into my home."

"We'll have a serious talk when this is over. As far as my claim that Erich is German, I—"

"Tell 'em." A vein bulged in Artknot's neck. "They can't deny what—"

"Didn't I tell you I'd handle this?" Charlie took a single step toward Artknot. "Keep your damned mouth shut before someone gets hurt."

"You cain't let this murderin' Nazi get away with killin' my kin."

"Stop riding that excuse for bad behavior."

"Then do—"

"Shut your damned mouth."

Silence filled the room. Artknot's fingernail scraped the leather holster.

*Scratch ... scratch ... scratch.*

Charlie Faced Virginia. "A villager told Jerry how he saw a set of footprints leading from the surf to the dunes one day. The villager also found a single shoe that matches nothing seen around here. A set of—"

"You come here over a shoe?" Ruby's chin trembled. Virginia had seen this sign of rage in her sister on rare occasions. Seeing it now was serious, especially with the knife hidden behind her. Time to calm this situation—if possible.

"I have to agree with my sister. Footprints and a shoe are all you have?"

"I was about to add more," Charlie said. "The villager went down the beach and came back by the main road. About where the footprints came out of the dunes, the same set went toward the village. They turned in near your path."

"I don't know anything about what some villager supposedly said. Did you talk to whoever it was?"

"All this was told to Jerry while I was away the first time. He dropped the shoe in his desk drawer and forgot about it, until that U-boat was sunk off Hatteras."

Ruby slipped her hand behind her back. "He's lying to make trouble for not having his way with me."

"I agree again," Virginia said. "What proof do you have of—"

"I questioned the villager after I dropped you off a minute ago. He or she—I'm not saying who—showed me where the footprints entered near your path."

"So the hell what?" Ruby slid a foot forward. "You didn't see them yourself."

"Shut your mouth," Artknot said. "Things is about to be wrapped up nice 'n tidy."

"I agree with Ruby again," Virginia said to Charlie. "You've got to come up with more than that."

"I saw what was left of the prints myself. They lead straight to your father's workshop."

"Lies and more lies." Ruby's throat worked with a hard swallow. "The storm would've washed them away."

"There were places it did exactly that, but not under the thickest of the live oak branches."

"None of that proves Erich's German." Ruby eased another foot forward.

"Get on with it," Artknot said. "We need to get him in shackles and call that ship back." He unsnapped the cover over his pistol. "Unless you want me to shoot him where he stands."

"Damn it all, Charlie," Virginia said. "Finish what you came to say and take him or not. I don't want anyone hurt."

"Ginny ..." Ruby's eyes pleaded while Erich stood transfixed—exactly like a man waiting for the death sentence to be read.

"Trust me, Ruby. Mama said to watch out for each other and that's what I'm doing. Finish your story and be damned, Charlie Smithson."

"Three Germans were captured before the U-boat sank. The Navy ship brought them here for me to interrogate. When I didn't come right away, the captain decided to take them to Norfolk. He told Jerry they had another man there who could speak German."

"I assume you have more than what you've said."

"Jerry went aboard the ship and asked if he could see the prisoners. He wanted to see if the shoe the villager found matched the prisoner's shoes. One spoke a bit of broken English." Charlie faced Jerry. "What was his name?"

"Hans—drag it out why don't you. This Hans was twitchy. I could tell he wanted to know something. All I wanted was to see the faces of three Nazi bastards that killed my kin. I was almost out the door when this Hans asked if we'd found a body lately. I laughed and asked him what this body's name was so I could scratch it on a rock for his tombstone." Artknot sneered a crooked grin, pulled the pistol from the holster, and waved it toward Erich. "These traitoring bitches gave you away as soon as they told Charlie your name and he told it to me, Mr. Erich Fischer."

"*No,*" Ruby wailed, "you can't take him, I love him!"

"Didn't I tell you to trust me?" Virginia said. "This man's a German and I can't abide a liar. For all I know he fired the torpedo that killed Walter." She stepped to the door for the shotgun and returned to Charlie's side. "Remember how I told you about the hobo?"

"What?"

"Doesn't matter." She leveled the shotgun at Erich. Seconds ticked off on the cuckoo clock. Chests heaved and fell. She pointed the shotgun at Artknot's back. "Get *this* out of my house."

Artknot's gun hand shook. "Do ... do something, Charlie. I'll cover the German."

The *snap* of Charlie's pistol cover was the loudest thing in the room, even louder to Virginia than the inhales and exhales of the four people on the verge of living or dying. She raised the shotgun to her shoulder, aimed the gold bead dead center of Artknot's head.

And what had to be the cold barrel of Charlie's pistol touched the back of her neck.

"I need you to lower that shotgun, Virginia. I'm trying hard as I know how to keep everyone in this room safe."

"Then leave and take Artknot with you. I've broken bread with Erich and seen his girl's picture. I'm sure Ruby thinks he's as sweet as that marsh rabbit we hit. I don't want another of God's sweet creatures to die because—"

"I can't let you do this."

"Do I have to tell you again to get Artknot out of my house?"

"Virginia, please. You don't want his life on your conscious."

*If the Sunrise Forgets Tomorrow*

The gold bead on the end of the shotgun's barrel wavered on the back of Artknot's sandy crew-cut. One quick squeeze of the trigger, buckshot would splatter his brains all over Mama's kitchen. Her and Ruby would scrub and scrub, but the memory of killing a man would haunt her forever. She lowered the shotgun.

Charlie raised the pistol to prod Artknot's back. "Holster that damned pistol—*now!*"

Instead of lowering the pistol, Artknot aimed it.

Ruby whipped the knife from behind her back and lunged.

Erich jumped in front of Ruby; twin gunshots exploded.

Smoke rose from Charlie's pistol. Artknot's smoking pistol clattered to the floor. He doubled over, stumbled to the screen door, and fell out onto the porch.

Erich groaned and crumpled to the floor at Ruby's feet. She dropped to her knees beside him. *"No!* Oh, God, *no!"*

Charlie dropped to his knees also. "Let me see how bad it is, Ruby."

Ruby didn't move. Virginia pulled her up by the shoulders. "Charlie's got medical training, let him look."

Ruby sat up. Blood stained her hands. Tears streamed down her cheeks. "Please help him, Charlie."

Charlie placed his hand on Erich's chest.

And shook his head.

"He's—" Ruby covered her face, sobbing pitifully. "He's with Thea now. They're finally ... they're finally togeth—" Hands on her chest, she collapsed in Virginia's arms. "Ginny? Ginny, I can't ..."

Virginia pulled Ruby's hands from her chest. "She's been shot!"

"Jerry's bullet must've passed through Erich and hit her." Charlie ripped Ruby's shirt open. A spot of blood stained an area below her right breast.

Ruby raised her bloody hand to Virginia's cheek. "Love … love you, Gin—"

## Chapter 35

## Decisions

An icy wave of blue and green tumbled Ruby over and over. Blonde hair swirled into her eyes and mouth. She scrabbled for a handhold and her fingertips scraped sand, which rose from the sea floor to surround her in a creamy cloud of white. The wave pummeled her on all sides as if it were a wall of liquid fists, somersaulting her in a spinning struggling mass of naked elbows, knees, feet, and hands. The pull and draw of another wave sucked her down, rolled her again, beat her into the sand, attempted to scour her soul from her chest and back. Claw and kick. Lungs aching, burning, the need to expel the heat for a cool, fresh breath. The undertow of another wave sucked her down further. Darkness then blackness, a squid's inky jet engulfing her.

"Ruuubyyyy! Time for supperrr! Bring Ginny and your papa too!"

The darkness hazed to misty gray, similar to morning fog after a summer night's storm. Live oak limbs hid within the haze, along with the tombstones of the village cemetery, where Ruby stood barefooted in the sand.

Slick and wet against her face, arms, and legs, sea water dripped from her hair, wet her lips with salt, drizzled down her breasts, stomach, and legs.

Like the gray backs of whales rising from the Atlantic, three tombstones rose from the sand, each made of graying oak planks with rounded tops. Lichen clung in muddy browns, reddish greens, and orangish yellows, edges snowflaking to white. The fog shifted again. A woman kneeling. Hooded. Crying softly. Dark tendrils of hair, tinged gray, curled from beneath the hood.

Ruby's feet left the sand, floated to the woman, sank into the sand again. A violent sob shook the woman's shoulders.

Wisps of fog hid the names on the tombstones. A breeze wiped the clinging wisps away, similar to white eels slithering, dissipating, and Ruby shivered at the sight.

On the left:     Augustus Lee Starr
                 1900-1940
                 Beloved Husband
                 Beloved Father

Beside Papa:     Elizabeth Light Starr
                 1904-1942
                 Beloved Wife
                 Beloved Mother

Beside Mama:     Ruby Virginia Starr
                 1924-1942
                 Beloved Daughter
                 Beloved Sister
                 Ride the Tide

Despite the obvious—Jerry's bullet had somehow taken two lives—Ruby smiled at Papa's joke of giving her and Virginia each other's first names as middle names.

The woman—Ginny—stood.

And walked straight through Ruby.

Her tears clung to Ruby's spirit face like morning dew on a wilting rose.

"Did you hear me, Ruby? Come on now, it's time for supper! And tell Ginny and Papa too!"

The gray lightened to brightness. Perfectly dry, blonde curls, unsettled by a sultry summer breeze, wavered in ringlets around Ruby's cheeks. Still barefooted, wearing a brilliant white gown, she stood in the sand beside the first curled and cracking boards of the pier at home. On the end, Ginny and Papa tentatively took iridescent blue crabs, claws and legs waving, from a pot and dropped them into a bucket.

Though their mouths moved as they smiled and spoke, their words failed to reach Ruby's ears. Though the marsh grass shifted in the breeze, no warm breath caressed her cheek. Though a red-winged blackbird bobbed on a cattail head, yellow beak opening and closing, its raucous call ended before it began. The bird left the cattail head. Wings blurring in flight, it faded to a dot in the bluest of skies. Tobacco smoke swirled from the pipe in Papa's gap-toothed grin, but the aroma could only be imagined. It was as if Ruby were trapped within a butterfly's cocoon. The year she and Virginia had turned thirteen, a butterfly's cocoon had hung on the railing on the front porch. It was waiting to be reborn, waiting like she and Ginny at that age—when Mama, just before she died—had said she and Ginny were ready to ride the tide of life.

Ruby tried to face the house. *"Mama?"* Her mouth refused to open. Her head refused to turn.

"Oh, God," she prayed, *"please make it—"*

A wrenching sensation tugged at her. Muscle and tendon stretched. Joints popped. Yet she felt no pain.

*"—stop?"*

Her bare feet touched the damp planks of a pier at Silver Lake Harbor. A ship—similar to the same four-masted schooner that she and Ginny had seen on the day of Mama's funeral—rounded the point from the direction of the ocean. It entered the Pamlico with dazzling white sails billowing, continued past the squat, white lighthouse, and entered the harbor, to sail toward the pier where Ruby stood. Like the day of the funeral, no men were visible. A strange roiling fog engulfed the deck, swirling and twisting with the unfelt wind.

The sails rolled until they met the spars. As if braids of sea grass wriggling in midair, ropes wrapped around the sails and tied themselves. The ship drifted to the dock and settled perfectly at the end. The huge anchor splashed silently into the gray depths.

Ruby had no time to think, to question, to marvel. The fog shifted. Wisps and tendrils flowed and teased apart, revealing a woman. The fog remained about her face, caressing her cheeks with silken secrets. She wore a plain cotton shift. At her throat hung a necklace, with two large and two small seahorses. The fog over her face feathered away.

Ruby fell to her knees. The hard planks *thunked* but she felt no pain. "Mama? Is it" —her throat hitched— "is it really you?" Words and time and love and sadness echoed between her and the ship. Mama took a single step forward, completely clearing the swirling, shifting haze.

"Who else would come to see you on your journey, dear heart?"

"Journey?" Ruby stood. "Are we going to Heaven?"

Another figure emerged from the fog, a pipe clenched within his gap-toothed grin. Papa removed the pipe. "Tarnation, Ruby, look how you've bloomed."

Tears streamed down Ruby's cheeks. "Why can't I come aboard, Papa? Why won't the ship come closer? Aren't I going to Heaven with you and Mama?"

"That remains to be seen, dear heart."

*If the Sunrise Forgets Tomorrow*

"Can't I hug you and Mama?" Ruby stood on trembling legs. "It's been so long, Papa. I've missed you so."

"Do we need to tell you how much we've missed you too?" He stole a single glance at his wife. "I think it best you tell her, love of my life."

"Tell me what?" Ruby's knees sagged. "Tell me now—tell me so I can do whatever it is I need to do to come aboard and hug you. I want to feel you in my arms, is that a crime?"

Mama's blonde hair swirled about her shoulders. "The crime is to leave life before it's done. Your papa and me believe you have more to do, dear heart."

"Erich's dead and Ginny has Charlie. What good will it do me to go back?"

"Isn't your love for Erich the sweetest thing to ever fill your young heart? Love always finds a way, if we allow it."

"But—"

"No backtalk this time, dear heart. I remember you and Ginny whispering into the wee hours as young girls. Your papa and me knew your dreams and wanted the world for you."

"Which includes love," Papa said.

"But I don't have anyone to love, Papa."

"No buts, dear heart. Love has a way of finding those willing to love."

Mama glanced at Papa. "And as we well know, love is a miracle. Don't you think love is a miracle, Ruby?"

"I don't know anything about miracles. God took you both and now He's taken Erich. Why have I lost everyone I love if love is a miracle?"

Papa chuckled. His pipe waggled in his gap-toothed grin. "The folly of youth and their unbelief. Love is about others, not self. Love is a gift to be given. When given full of heart, miracles can and do happen." He took a single step backward, melting into the fog. "You have a choice to make, Ruby ... believe in love and miracles or not. Live your life free as the wind off the waves or not. Regardless, you'll have all the hugs you can stand." The fog surrounded him.

Ruby stretched out her hands. "Mama, please—please don't go. All I want is to hug you one more time."

"Didn't you hear a word your papa just said?"

"It's all twistygibbet. It's all nonsensical. It's harder to understand than when Papa drowned trying to save someone from drowning."

"You must return to understand, dear heart. To us O'cockers, Ocracoke is more than an island where we scratch a living from the sand and the sea. The cattail stalks are our bones. The salt water is our blood. The pulsing jellyfish are our lungs, filled with gusts off the Atlantic and the Pamlico. We're creatures born to it. We welcome the struggle. We don't let anyone tell us we can't survive here because we've proven them wrong for hundreds of years. Even those dingbatters who come here and stay understand these things in hardly no time at all. Even those O'cockers who leave can't be happy unless they're near water of some kind—like a lake, a river, a stream—or even a blackwater creek."

"But Mama, all that's as twistygibbet as anything Papa said."

"Don't you love Ocracoke, O'cocker gal?"

"I do and I don't."

"Hardly a day passed when I didn't see you sitting on the pier at dusk. When the world hushed. When the rowboat bumped against the pier. When the last breath of the day lapped tiny wavelets in the marsh grass. There's no prettier picture nor sound in the world than a sunset over the Pamlico. Nor one that can settle the soul at days end."

"I still don't see—"

"Hush and listen. Can't you stay for Papa and me? And Ginny too?"

*If the Sunrise Forgets Tomorrow*

"I shouldn't have said I didn't have anyone left to love. Even if Ginny marries Charlie, she'll want me to live with them."

"I'm happy you trust your papa and me, dear heart." Mama unclasped the seahorse necklace. "A gift for when you go back."

Cold as a nor'easter's blast, the necklace joined the sand dollar at Ruby's throat. She held the seahorse family so she could see it. "Thank you, Mama. Tell Papa—"

She raised her head.

The ship was gone.

## Chapter 36

## To the Land of Sand and Salt

Morning light tinged with creamy orange streamed through the open window. Air crisp with the dawn softly fluttered the curtains like two spirits at peace. From the direction of the pier, a red-winged blackbird cried its shrill, warbling call: *kree-kreeeee, kree-kreeeee.*

Ruby started to rise from bed, but a dull pain below her right breast took her breath away. She dropped to the pillow. "Ginny? Are you there, Ginny?"

Wearing the red-checked apron, Ginny came in. "Look who's back to the land of sand and salt." She creaked into a ladderback chair beside the bed. "For a while I thought I was doomed to feed you eggs and milk and clean your behind for the rest of your life."

"How long have I been here?"

"A week, give or take. Do you remember anything?"

"All I remember is guns blasting and me telling you I love you." She swallowed. "That happened after Erich …"

Ginny pulled a tissue from the apron pocket and wiped Ruby's eyes. "Stop all that before we run out of tissues. There's no telling how many I soaked while I sat in this chair."

Ruby raised her hand to the top button on the nightgown, and Ginny said, "I buttoned you up because we had a cold snap last night. Feel like breakfast?"

"I suppose." Ruby pressed the gown at the base of her neck. The seahorse necklace rested in the hollow of her throat.

### If the Sunrise Forgets Tomorrow

"You feel that necklace I bought you? It matches Mama's perfectly. Thought we could use a bit of luck. Milk too?"

"You left me here by myself?"

"Not important. Milk too?"

"But ..."

"Milk too. Be right back." Ginny left the room.

The radio came on.

Dishes clattered in the kitchen.

Ruby cupped her hands around her mouth. "You should've had it cooked already!" She closed her eyes and shook her head. "Mm, mm, mm. I'm away for two weeks and this place goes to—"

"Breakfast was already cooked, dear one."

Ruby opened her eyes. Erich stood in the doorway, plate and glass in hand.

"Erich, but ... but how ...?"

"Virginia and I will tell you." Plate and glass on the nightstand, he caressed her cheek. "May I hold you?"

"You better."

"No squeezing. I'm still sore from being shot." Erich took her into his arms and whispered, "Do you know how much I missed you?"

"Not as much as I missed you." She eased him away. "I think it's time—past time—for a kiss."

"And get you in a lather like Jimmy? No, ma'am, we'd best save our passion for our honeymoon." Erich sat, sliced omelet, and forked a bite to Ruby's lips. "Good?"

Ruby swallowed. "Is it ever. Milk, please."

Ginny came in and sat on the other side of the bed. "Do you want us to tell you everything now or wait until after you eat?"

Ruby sipped and gave Erich the glass. "Have I been acting like I was dreaming?"

"You did that almost from the start. You'd mumble and squirm and stop. It got worse around sunrise, why?"

"No reason." Ruby fingered the necklace at her throat. "No reason at all. Did you stay in here *every* night?"

"Sure did." Virginia stretched. "I've got an aching back to prove it. I assume you know Jerry shot Erich. The bullet went through his lower lung and out to hit you. It did little damage to Erich's lung. That's why he's up and around before you. Your wound got infected, Doc Wills said. He expected you to come around, and here you are."

"I thought I heard two shots."

"You had all your attention on Erich, I'm sure. Charlie shot Jerry right after Jerry shot Erich. As much as it pains me to admit, Jerry's another casualty of this damned war. Who knows the man he might have been if he hadn't lost those closest to him in Pearl Harbor?"

"How do you know that?"

"Charlie told me first. Then, when Jerry apologized to me for how he acted the night I went to ask Charlie to supper, he told me too."

Attempting a sigh, Ruby cringed at the soreness in her chest. "It's a shame people have to die, not only in war but here too. Charlie didn't take Erich, what happened?"

"He told Doc Wills Jerry assaulted you. And—"

"I call grabbing my bicycle in the path and scaring me half to death assaulting me. That and talking about seeing me naked."

"Can't argue that. Charlie told Doc Wills he brought Jerry here to get the truth out of him. Then—"

"That's correct," Erich said. "He told the doctor that Jerry shot me out of jealousy before anyone could stop him."

"Imagine how I felt when Charlie put his gun to my neck," Virginia said. "When he said 'I can't let you do this,' he had come to the conclusion that Jerry was so angry, the only way to keep him from shooting anyone was to shoot him first. Charlie didn't want me to have taking a life on my conscious."

"He was mad all right," Ruby said. "The way his veins were bulging, I thought they were gonna geyser all over the doggone kitchen. Now I know he was mad because of losing his relatives at Pearl Harbor. What about the villager who saw Erich's tracks?"

"All that villager knows is he or she saw tracks and found a shoe. Neither Charlie nor Jerry said anything to him or her about anyone from a U-boat. No need in causing a stir."

Ruby slipped her hand into Erich's. "Ginny, are you sure you don't mind Erich being German?"

"It was hard to get used to at first—a U-boat sinking Walter's ship didn't help. War is the enemy, not good men like Erich and Charlie."

"Ruby mentioned your friend's ship," Erich said to Virginia. "I'm happy to say my vessel had nothing to do with it."

"Let's not worry about that," Virginia said. "Let's leave the past in the past and concentrate on the future. So, Rube, I was wondering if you heard me ask Charlie if he remembered the hobo?"

"I'm still fuzzy yet."

"We had dinner in Havelock at a restaurant where the owner played piano. I'm ashamed to admit it, but I judged his playing by his scruffy appearance and how he talked."

"Like how you got all bug-eyed at the hobo."

"Exactly. I asked Charlie if he remembered the hobo because I had learned my lesson about judging others before I get to know them. I hoped that would make him understand why I was going to take Erich's side over his."

"What did Charlie tell Doc Wills about Erich?"

"The same story Erich told me about being British. Doc Wills said since he came here to escape the tragedy of losing his wife, he didn't fault Erich for coming here to escape the tragedy of losing his loved ones either." Virginia patted Erich's shoulder. "We've been getting to know one another. He told me all about Thea, and let me read her last letter to him. How can I call a man my enemy when he possesses a love like that in his heart?"

"He's amazing, isn't he?"

"Amazing enough to teach me how to make the omelet you're eating."

Erich forked another bite toward Ruby. "It's better warm."

She chewed, sipped milk, and swallowed. "When can I see Charlie? I'd like to thank him for everything."

Virginia's lips barely parted. "I …"

"What's wrong, Ginny?"

"Give her a moment," Erich said. "It was a shock when she heard it."

Ginny's chest rose and fell, as if her breath were a long, slow tide sifting through the marsh grass.

"The Navy sent Charlie to the Pacific a week ago. I don't know when—or if—I'll ever see him again."

## Chapter 37

## An Offer and a Sunrise

*Three years later, May, 1945*

Virginia climbed the steps to the general store. Behind the counter, the recent new owner, Sam Evans, who also served as the post office clerk, waved an envelope. "Got mail for you, Ginny. Was sorting it just now." Virginia took the envelope, and Sam leaned his elbows on the counter. "By the look of those hang-dog eyes of yours, I'd say you're hoping it's from Charlie."

"Did I tell you I haven't heard from him in three months?"

"Yesterday. Day before yesterday. Day before day before yesterday."

"I'm sorry."

"Not at all, Ginny. Everyone on Ocracoke is worried 'bout their loved ones." Sam placed a letter in a slot. "That's an interestin' name on the return address. Ain't Brenda usually spelled with one E 'stead of two?"

"Not this one, she's special. See you tomorrow." Beside her bike, she ripped the envelope open and unfolded the letter.

*Dear Virginia and family,*
*I hope to find you flourishing on your island home. I am well in Havelock, but I assuredly miss company, especially you, Virginia, as well as Charlie. We correspond by letter, but I haven't heard from him recently, so I was hoping you had.*

*Be that as it may, I'm writing to invite all of you to my home for the upcoming weekend. We shall eat, visit, and perhaps there will be a surprise. I'm terrible at keeping secrets, so I'll tell you I've purchased an ice cream maker, and I'm dying to try several recipes.*

*As far as transportation, I've a fisherman friend who seeks his catch near Ocracoke. He never told me his real name, but the first time I met him at the seafood market in Havelock, he said to call him Red. His boat is called the Sunrise. He shall be at Silver Lake Harbor Friday morning at ten and can also return you Monday.*

*Please come if at all possible. I'd so enjoy your company.*

*Love,*

*Breenda*

Virginia folded the letter, shoved it in her pocket, and pedaled home, chain rattling, calves and thighs burning, wind blowing her hair about her shoulders. A visit with Breenda would set a grin on everybody's faces, fill their stomachs too. At the porch, she braked so hard that the back tire skidded in the sand. Sitting on the steps, James, her blond-headed, two-year-old nephew yelled, "Au Gin! You wreck!"

Virginia ran up the steps and knelt beside him. "Is your mama and papa inside? I need to tell them something."

Nodding, James stuck a finger in his mouth.

Virginia adored her twin nephews, born exactly like she and Ruby, one dark and one light, except Daniel's hair had lightened to a medium brown. They couldn't say "aunt" yet, so they said what they could manage, either "Au Gin" or "Gin."

James took the finger from his mouth. "Papa, he—he makin' saw-dirt."

"You mean sawdust. Hasn't he finished adding that window in you and your brother's room yet?"

"Papa, him make—him make face."

"Did he hit his finger with a hammer again? What kind of face did he make? Did he say that funny word again too?"

James bared his teeth and nodded.

"That's the face he made? Goodness! What about the word? Was it *verdammt?*"

"Was *it*, Au Gin."

"I'll have a *word* with him myself." She scooped James into her arms. "Let's find your mama."

Inside, kneeling by Daniel, Ruby wiped his face. "I have a hard time believing we stayed as dirty as these two."

Daniel ran to Virginia. "Me up, Gin!"

James shook his head. "No, Dan-Dan, James' turn."

Virginia set James beside Dan and hugged them both. Baby soft hair against her cheeks. The unmistakable aroma of milk and cookie breath. "Mm-mmm, I love you both." She stood. "No fighting now, run to your room and check on Papa while I talk to Mama." The two pairs of feet pattered away. "Tarnation, Ruby, did you have any idea having children could be such a joy?"

Ruby wiped her hands on her apron, a present from Erich, with red hearts. "I love them as much as forever, trial that they are at times. Hear anything from Charlie?"

Virginia gave Ruby the letter. "The next best thing."

Ruby read the letter. "Glad to see it, Virgil. Brenda inviting us to her place for the weekend is exactly what we need to get you out of your mood."

"Breeeenda, remember? As far as my mood, leave it be."

"Can't do that." Ruby returned the letter. "I'm tired of you moping at the end of the pier."

"What do you expect me to do?"

"I understand. Not hearing from Charlie for three months has got to be the trial of all trials." Ruby slipped her arm around

Virginia's shoulders. "Charlie won't leave you, he loves you too much."

"You're right about my mood. Other than James and Daniel, if there's anyone who can cheer me up, it's Breenda."

"Well fry me a flounder." Ruby crossed her arms. "What about me?"

"Isn't that a given? Let me see how Erich's doing with the boy's new room." Virginia started to leave but stopped. "Tell your husband to watch those German swear words. You know how children pick up anything."

"I'll mention it."

Virginia followed her nephew's chatter, the aroma of sawdust, and Erich's laughter. The room, adjoining Ruby and Erich's room, shared beams, walls, and the roof from Papa's workshop. Virginia stopped in the doorway. Erich held a plank while James tried cutting it with a handsaw. James stopped and frowned. Erich held out his hand for the saw. "Time to let your brother have a turn."

Daniel attempted a single stroke, then threw the saw to the floor. "*Verdammt*, Papa."

Virginia joined them. "Tell me, Mr. Brother-in-law, what will you do when someone asks you or Ruby why your sons know German curse words?"

"I haven't considered that." Erich stood. "If Charlie had sent mail, you'd have told me by now."

"Remember when I told you and Ruby about Breenda? She's asked us to visit this weekend. Do you think Mr. Austin can spare you from the restaurant?"

"He should. I've made enough money for him with my cooking. Who would have guessed O'cockers liked omelets so much?"

"Or oysters Rockefeller with dandelion greens. Maybe you can teach Breenda."

⭐

Friday afternoon, after a choppy ride across the Pamlico Sound, the water calmed as the *Sunrise* entered the Neuse. It smoothed even more when it slipped into the still, black waters of Slocum Creek. Virginia and family stepped onto Breenda's pier, where she met them with open arms. "Oh, my darlings, look at you all." She tousled James' hair and tickled Daniel beneath his chin. "Such fine sons you have, Ruby and Erich. Please, everyone, follow me inside to your rooms."

Inside the back door, the aroma of coffee greeted Virginia, including the fresh-baked cinnamon aroma of a cake of some kind. Breenda led them down the hall to the stairs. "After you're settled, the adults will have coffee and apple-nut cake. I have milk for the two growing boys."

"Your fisherman surprised me," Virginia said. "With a name like Red, I had no idea he'd resemble Blackbeard."

"Edward Teach you mean. I've been reading about that scoundrel of a pirate who frequented Ocracoke." Upstairs, Breenda opened the door to a room on the left. "This is for you four, Ruby and Erich. There's a large bathroom behind that door to the right."

Ruby flipped a light switch. "My goodness, electric lights. Do I dare ask if there's hot and cold running water too?"

"Of course, of course—a huge tub to soak in after a day of running after your two boys as well." Breenda winked. "For a bit of privacy with your handsome Erich, there's also two single beds in the adjoining room for the boys."

"Must we leave on Monday?" Erich said "I'd like to stay here forever, especially with the separate room for the boys already finished."

Ruby brushed by him. "I can't wait to try that tub. No more hauling and heating water for nothing but a wet behind."

Breenda closed the door. "Come, Virgeenia." In the same room with the canopy bed where she and Charlie had slept, Virginia set her suitcase on the floor by the nightstand. She ran her fingertips along Charlie's pillow.

"I know you are worried about Char-*lee*," Breenda said. "I was also but no more. I feel in my heart that he is safe and will return to you soon. This war ... there are so many ways to describe it, yet none compare to the pain it brings us." She stepped to the door. "Take all the time you need."

Virginia dropped to the bed. So much had happened in the last few years—so much happiness, so much death. Tempted to bury her head in the pillow and cry, she shuffled to the bathroom and filled the tub instead. A hot soak might do miracles for her mood.

She undressed. Twenty-one now, a girl no more. No time for young girl dreams of young girl things.

At the mirror over the sink, she touched the slight crow's feet at the corners of her eyes. O'cocker eyes—aged with sun and salt—perhaps a hint of wisdom. No lipstick colored her full lips. No rouge tinted her tanned cheeks.

*Where are you, Charlie? Dead? Alive? Wounded and unconscious?*

She should've given herself to him. Then, if she had become pregnant, she could treasure his child if he were killed. No. The two years without Papa had been some of the hardest of her and Ruby's lives, even more for Mama. Despite Breenda's assurance that Charlie would return, a certain O'cocker gal needed to set her hat for life without him. He hadn't even told her his hometown or had given her his parent's address, so she might never know what happened to him.

Yes, time to learn to live without Charlie.

*If the Sunrise Forgets Tomorrow*

Virginia settled into the steaming water. Eyes closed, she attempted to erase the thoughts of what Charlie might be experiencing—or had experienced and died—from her mind.

The Navy had requested he train as a corpsman, so his letters had said, and he took pride in saving lives in the field. When Erich and Ruby were shot, he stopped the bleeding with rags almost immediately. Doc Wills mentioned how well he'd done with so little training.

The names of the islands where Charlie attended the wounded came and went so quickly, they ran together. The final location he'd described in his last letter—Iwo Jima—stuck in Virginia's mind because of the news reports on the repaired radio, to the point of forcing her to her bedroom and closing the door when either Ruby or Erich turned it on.

A door squeaked open. Footsteps crossed the creaking wood floor. Likely Ruby, Erich, and the boys going downstairs.

The cooling water forced Virginia from the tub. Toweling her hair, she opened the bathroom door to let the humid air out.

And dropped the towel.

Lying on the bed, Charlie smiled. "My goodness, Miss Starr, this is quite the welcome home surprise for your fiancé."

"You ... you ..."

"It's me, yes, it is."

"But ... but ..."

"I've been dreaming of you naked ever since I left. Might want to wrap up before we start the honeymoon before the wedding."

Virginia snatched the towel around her. "But ..."

"Charlie winced as he sat up. "But how, right?" He raised his shirt. "I'll put it this way, I have a scar to match the one on Erich's chest and some more to go along with it. Come sit but don't jostle. There's another on my left leg and hip."

Virginia sat. "Do you know how badly I want to hug you? *And* kill you for not writing me?"

"That's hard to do when you're in a hospital bed in the Pacific after a grenade blew you up." Charlie tapped a fingertip to his lips. "Nothing wrong with these."

"You've been wounded since February?"

"Since the last of March. I was glad I got to stay that long. While I was being carried to a transport—did you know the beach on Iwo Jima has black sand?—I got to see our flag raised over Mount Suribachi. That's a sight I'll never forget."

Virginia slipped her arm beneath his. "I'm terrible, aren't I? *You* were wounded and bedridden—and *I* complain about you not writing."

"I'll forgive you for a kiss." Charlie leaned in. Virginia leaned away.

"Not so fast, how long have you been here?"

"Been where?"

"*Here,* Charlie Smithson. Did you and Brenda set this up?"

"Breeeenda, remember? Would you expect otherwise from the man you called a male Ruby?"

"I might expect it from you."

"Would you believe it was Breenda's idea?"

Virginia rose from the bed. "I don't know what to believe."

"You'd believe she wanted to do something nice for us, right?"

"I'm more likely to believe you hoodwinked her into something."

"No, ma'am, and there's more to it." Charlie eased up from the bed. "Whew, that hurts. Let's sit on the balcony while I tell you."

Virginia sat. "I'm glad you're back, Charlie, but I've about reached my limit for shenanigans. Go ahead."

"Unfortunately, some of it's not good. Breenda lost her grandson in Germany."

"I didn't— I'm sorry to hear that. I was going to say I didn't realize her son was old enough to have a son in the military."

Breenda doesn't look it, but she turned sixty her last birthday. Her father died a few years ago. Her mother's on the way from France. She and Breenda are going to stay with Breenda's son in New Orleans. He and his wife are having a tough time."

"I thought Breenda was sort of ... I guess subdued is a good word." Virginia could imagine what Breenda was going through. Losing a friend like Walter was hard enough. Losing a grandson must be as bad as losing Mama and Papa. "I'm surprised she feels like having company."

"I think the joy she gets from doing for others helps," Charlie said. "Now that I've told you the sad part, it's time for the good part."

"Will she come back from New Orleans? I'd like see her again."

"That's part of the good part. She'll be back and I won't even charge her."

"You're not making any sense, you dingbatter. How much wine did you drink while you were waiting for me to get here?"

"A glass with lunch. Any idea where we can find a cook?"

"A who?" Virginia started to raise one eyebrow at Charlie, but he'd probably think it was sexy.

"Come on, Virginia, work with me here. I need someone to run the book store in the library too. Anyone in mind?" Charlie leaned back in the chair and grinned. "Don't answer yet. I also need someone to tidy up after the guests leave."

"Are you trying to tell me Breenda has sold you this place?"

"Not yet. I wouldn't dream of denying you the privilege of having your name on the mortgage. That means we have to get married too."

"As simple as that? What about all those people you need to hire?"

"I understand your brother-in-law is quite the cook. I also recall someone saying she'd like to own a bookstore one day. I'll ask Ruby about housekeeping."

"She might not like that."

"Everyone will help. I was watching from the window when you got off the *Sunrise*. James and Daniel can handle a whisk broom and a dustpan."

"Got it all figured out, don't you, Charlie Smithson?"

"Can you think of anything better to do with the rest of your life?"

"I'd like to keep our house on Ocracoke for visits. It's a hard place to live but I'll always love it."

"Where else will I teach our boy how to surf fish and our daughter how to drive a jeep on the beach?"

"What about Jimmy and our hens?"

"There's enough land here for a fence and a stall—a henhouse too."

"You *do* have it all figured out."

"That's because I'm smarter than the average bear."

"Why a bear?"

"That's what we say in the Blue Ridge Mountains when someone makes a good deal or marries a fine woman. Don't you think I fit that description?"

Virginia got up and eased into Charlie's lap.

"I'll decide that after a kiss."

*If the Sunrise Forgets Tomorrow*

Virginia awoke and stepped to the balcony. A concentration of light, crimson and shimmering behind wisps of clouds, shone beyond the treetops on the far bank of Slocum Creek.

Last night had been perfect.

At dinner, Charlie took the chance to broach the subject of them all living and working in the house. Ruby mentioned taking a hot bath in the huge tub in her bathroom, vowing to never leave after doing so. Erich, after seeing Breenda's huge kitchen overlooking the pier, said the view of the Pamlico was better, but he could be happy cooking with a view of Slocum Creek. He also said he could teach James and Daniel how to catch crabs off the pier.

Two hours later, after Erich and Charlie took turns cranking the ice cream freezer, with James and Daniel taking turns adding ice and rock salt, everyone gorged on the unimaginable treat of banana ice cream.

Not wanting to set a bad example for James and Daniel, Charlie waited downstairs when everyone went to bed. Footsteps creaked across floors. Bedroom doors softly closed. Lights dimmed or darkened. He slipped into Virginia's room, where they had slept blissfully through the night in each other's arms.

The sun peeked above the tree line. Virginia went to kiss Charlie's cheek. "Wake up, sleepyhead, you need to see this."

Charlie fingered the top button of Virginia's nightgown. "I'm already seeing something I need to see."

She pulled his arm. "You're not hurt here, get up."

At the balcony railing, Charlie slipped his hand around her waist. "Looks like it didn't forget."

Virginia snuggled into his warmth, a contrast to the cool morning air. "You're talking about our first night on the pier back home, aren't you? When you said the sun might forget to rise if the people in the world couldn't figure out how to get along."

The tendons in Charlie's neck tightened. What had he seen in the Pacific? What had he seen while tending the wounded in the hell of battle? The tendons in his neck relaxed.

"Right before you pointed your shotgun at Jerry—when you asked if I remembered the hobo—I didn't remember. It was only when I stopped Ruby's bleeding and started working on Erich that I did. I also remembered how you thought Just was going to play chopsticks that night at his restaurant. And then, how he completely floored you with what he likes to call his 'finger dancin' on the old ivories.'"

"He certainly did. And your point?"

"The one it sometimes takes people a while—if ever— to learn. Good can be found in those you least expect it." Charlie brushed a lock of hair away from Virginia's eyes. "Ruby found good in someone who was supposed to be my enemy. Someone who, had I been on the battlefield in Europe, I would've killed and thought nothing of it."

"He would've done the same to you."

Charlie kissed Virginia's forehead. "My roundabout way of making my point is this: There's good. There's evil. There are people. People—except those who are pure evil—basically want the same things, like to live and love and earn their way. Then they can take care of their families like Erich wanted to do for Thea. I'm happy he found a new life here with Ruby. After everything he's been through, he deserves it."

From across the creek, in a blinding burst of golden light, the sun rose above the horizon.

Virginia slipped her arms around Charlie. "I know what you mean." She pointed toward the brilliant glow flooding her face with warmth. "And the sunrise didn't forget tomorrow."

# Book Club Questions

1. What did you like best about this book?

2. What did you like least about this book?

3. What other books did this one remind you of?

4. Which characters did you like best?

5. Which characters did you like least?

6. If this book were a movie, who would you choose to play the characters?

7. What other books by this author have you read? How did they compare to this book?

8. What feelings did this book evoke in you?

9. If you got the chance to ask the author of this book one question, what would it be?

10. Which character in the book would you most like to meet?

11. What do you think of the book's title? How does it relate to the book's contents? What other title might you choose?

12. What do you think the author's purpose was in writing this book? What ideas was he or she trying to get across?

13. How original and unique was this book?

14. Did this book seem realistic?

15. How well do you think the author built the world in the book?

16. Did the characters seem believable to you? Did they remind you of anyone?

17. What did you already know about this book's subject before you read this book?

18. What new things did you learn?

19. What questions do you still have?

20. Were you happy with the ending?

Please enjoy the first chapter from the third book in the Outer Banks Series, *Love, Jake.*

It doesn't take much for a person to question their sanity, and sometimes it's completely justified.

I got married yesterday to a woman I love more than I ever thought possible. For our honeymoon, Andy and I drove to South Nag's Head, North Carolina. The sand and the shells, the salt air, the October sun glistening on the surf, the gulls crying and wheeling overhead—absolutely nothing compares for us.

We unpacked at our oceanfront rental, went out for seafood, and came back to make love late into the night. To start the next morning, I planned to make breakfast while she slept.

Instead, I woke to an empty bed, threw on shorts and a T-shirt, and went all over the house calling her name. Giving that up, in case she was on the beach looking at the sunrise, I went to the living room window facing the Atlantic, and that's how I ended up where I am now.

On the slight rise above the dying waves, where they transform to foam and hiss their final breaths, I'm sitting in the sand, soaking wet and shivering. My elbows are on my knees. My forehead rests in my hands. Vomit drips from my chin.

Yes, I'm justified in questioning my sanity. Look away, look at something else. Anything else.

On the eastern horizon, all crimson and shimmering and gorgeous above the ocean's aquamarine swells, the sun frees itself from the grip of the Atlantic.

Now—now I can look again.

Beside me, wearing a one-piece swimsuit in cobalt blue, Andy lies in the sand. Wet hair hangs in slitted eyes. Sand coats red-painted toenails. One hand lies limp at her side, the skin as pale as a nearby seashell.

No, I can't— This can't— Is this real? Did this really happen?

The surf rises and falls, whispers and calms, similar to the white lace on her nightgown last night, delicate and feminine, a deep V diving to her heart.

Yes, it happened. It really did just happen.

I carried her from the surf and tried mouth-to-mouth resuscitation and chest compressions. I tried turning her over to drain the water from her lungs. I tried everything I could think of until I pulled her into my lap and cried myself sick.

What was she thinking? It's the second week of October, too cold to swim during the day, much less at sunrise. At least I saw her blonde hair before the suck and pull of the undertow took her away.

Footsteps shuffle sand beside me. "My Lord," a gravelly voice says. Walking a golden retriever, the elderly gentleman stops and takes a phone from his pocket to call 911. His voice breaks, he says to hurry. The retriever whines. Its nose, wet and cold, nudges my arm. Catching a whiff of wet dog smell, I look into brown eyes filled with canine empathy. The dog whines again, long and high at first, ending soft and low in his throat.

Sunrise beachcombers gather around us in a fragmented circle. "Is she dead? What happened, did she drown? He must be her husband, did he get sick? Yes, he's her husband, I talked to them on the beach yesterday. They just got married and came here for their honeymoon." A woman quietly weeps. A blinking man shakes his head mournfully. Someone covers my shoulders with a towel.

A siren's scream halts the murmurs. A vehicle engine rumbles near, a door slams, and a different voice speaks to me. I only know the words are questions because of the upward lilt of the inquiring tone at the end of each sentence. Another siren comes, whooping and dying. Paramedics administer CPR, check blood pressure, place a stethoscope into the hollow between Andy's breasts. Electricity from defibrillator paddles arch her upward. Water seeps from the corner of her mouth. The stethoscope returns, then the paddles. She arches upward again and again. Water gushes. Blue eyes half-open, unfocused and dull, will never see me again. The stethoscope returns. The paramedic listens, listens, listens. "I'm sorry, sir, she's gone." I roll to my knees and heave and cry again, until I'm out of both tears and bile.

They load her onto a gurney. Take her away. Someone lifts me by the arm and leads me to a vehicle. My vision blurs. My hearing fades until only heartbeats thud within my brain. Grief has driven a wedge into my senses; the world around me is awash with loss.

What does it mean to love so much? "Soulmate" doesn't do my emotions justice. White lace and kisses and caresses and *I love you, Jake,* are all gone forever, including the intimate promise of a future with the one person who knew me better than I know myself, cut fresh and bloody from my heart.

This is going to kill me. I know it is. I *know* it is.

I smell vanilla. My sight clears. My heartbeat abandons me.

The vehicle door opens. I drop to the rear seat. Someone reaches around me to click my seatbelt. A brunette ponytail withdraws from the door and it slams. Another door slams. Air from a vent, stale and warm, blows into my face. We bounce over vehicle tracks left in the sand. Tires sing on pavement.

To my amazement, I find more tears.

*Not* to my amazement, I want to join Andy.

## ABOUT THE AUTHOR

J. Willis Sanders lives in southern Virginia, with his wife and several stringed musical instruments.

With several novels published and more on the way, he enjoys crafting intriguing characters with equally intriguing conflicts to overcome. He also loves the natural world and, more often than not, his stories include those settings. Most also utilize intense love relationships and layered themes.

His first novel (not this one, but he plans to publish it) is a ghostly World War II era historical that takes place mostly in the midwestern United States, which utilizes some little-known facts about German POW camps there at that time. It's the first of a three-book series, in which characters from the first book continue their lives.

Although he loves history, he has written several contemporary novels as well, and some include interesting paranormal twists, both with and without religious themes.

He also loves the Outer Banks of North Carolina, and has published three novels within different time frames based on the area, what he calls his Outer Banks of North Carolina Series.

Another genre he enjoys is thriller novels, so he has launched a series with a main female character named Reid Stone.

Other hobbies include reading (of course), vegetable gardening, playing music with friends, and songwriting, some of which are in a few of his novels.

To follow the author's work, please visit any of the following:

https://jwillissanders.wixsite.com/writer

https://www.facebook.com/J-Willis-Sanders-874367072622901

https://www.amazon.com/J-Willis-Sanders/e/B092RZG6MC?ref_=dbs_p_ebk_r00_abau_000000


Readers: to help those considering a purchase, please consider leaving a review on Amazon.com, Goodreads.com, or wherever you purchased this book.
Thank you.

Made in the USA
Middletown, DE
01 March 2025